ZINNIA SHERWOOD

Maladaptive

A novel

First published by Spirality Publishing 2026

First edition

ISBN: 978-0-9940407-2-5

Prologue

When I think back on everything that happened, the memory I come back to the most is this one, even though technically it isn't a memory, it's just how I imagine it must have gone.

* * *

The little house was still. Its vibrant walls and boldly patterned furnishings remained, looking impersonal as ever despite their attention-seeking appearance. The silence gave everything a strange, stage-set feeling, like the actors had left mid-scene. The only remaining sign of the house's previous inhabitants was a single object on the fireplace mantle. A small, deliberately placed snow globe.

Styles Chilton peered through the window and squinted as he narrowed his focus through the kitchen to the living room at the back of the house in the distance. He leaned his face close to the glass, but his baseball hat brim hit the windowpane, prompting him to remove it before leaning in again and cupping his hands on either side of his head to shield his view from the sun's bright glare.

He had already tried the door at the front of the house, looking up and down the quiet street beforehand to make sure there was no one around. The kitchen window wouldn't budge. Because breaking into houses that aren't yours is generally perceived as uncool, especially when you're internet famous, he was trying to avoid calling attention to himself, hence the ball cap, sunglasses, and his intrepid demeanor as he skulked around the house. Deciding the coast was clear, he climbed up the wooden fence gate at the back of the house and hopped over it, gaining access to the backyard.

He stood in the yard for a moment and looked around wistfully. The sound of a neighbor's barking dog startled him, and nudged him to make one final attempt to get into the house. He tugged on the sliding patio door, and to his surprise, it moved. Pushing it as quietly as he could, as if to not disturb any ghosts, he slipped through the door into the living room and went to the fireplace. He looked at himself in the mirror above it. He looked older, smaller, disheveled, not at all like how he saw himself through the lens of his perceived persona. 'What am I doing here?' he thought.

A feeling had brought him back to this house in search of an intangible "something" that might give him the answer he was seeking. He took the snow globe from its place on the mantle. His initial surprise at finding it still there was quickly overtaken by a contemplative loneliness and the realization that he probably shouldn't have been surprised at all. He tipped it gently and watched the snow fall over the little world inside, safely contained in its protective dome. Then he shook the snow globe again, this time with more force. "Look what I just did," he mused. "I made it blizzard in Los Angeles."

Then Styles slipped back out of the house as carefully as he went in, with the snow globe in his jacket pocket.

* * *

Or maybe the landlord gave him the key. That's also plausible.

Chapter 1

When the flight attendant handed me the champagne flute filled with pale yellow deliciousness, I did my best to maintain my composure to avoid flailing in a way that would lead to smashing it into tiny shards. Which, knowing me, was entirely possible.

Graceful is not a word many would use to describe me. My mother used to say she should have sent me to charm school, but I always insisted that my clumsiness was part of my charm. The bruises on my elbows and knees can tell that story better than I can. But on that day, they were covered by jeans and a hoodie sweatshirt, to insulate me from the plane's air circulation system.

I also tend to overthink things, like, a lot, and in that moment I was overthinking the hell out of everything from the tiny champagne bubbles tickling my nose to the fact that the flight attendant had just called me "ma'am" with what sounded like actual respect.

"Can you believe this?" my husband Griffin whispered, luxuriating in the seat beside me with a grin that made his whole adorable, freckled face crinkle up. He held up his own champagne flute like he was toasting the universe. "First class, Cara. We finally made it."

I clinked my glass against his, careful not to use too much force. "To being contest winners."

"To you, who said entering was a waste of time."

"To you, for knowing when to not listen to me."

Griffin chuckled with that easy laugh that made me fall in love with him a bajillion years ago. "That's why we work so well."

A gorgeous flight attendant appeared at my side. "Can I get you anything else, Mrs. Becker?"

Mrs. Becker. Not "Oh, you again," in the slightly annoyed tone I usually got when asking for extra pretzels on economy flights. This was a whole different world.

"I'm good, thank you." I managed to keep my voice steady, trying to sound like I believed I had every right to be in first class. Inside I was doing that thing where my brain starts cataloging everything for later analysis. The way the flight attendant smiled. The fact that she remembered my name. The shocking reality that Griffin and I were sitting in seats we would never splash out on ourselves.

"Mr. Becker?"

"I'll take another one of these," Griffin said, waggling his empty champagne flute. "You know, when in Rome and all that."

She whisked away his glass. I watched her go, then turned my attention back to Griffin, who was fiddling with all the buttons on his seat like a kid with a new toy.

"Griff," I said, relaxing into the spacious airplane seat, "remember that time we flew first class to LA to go see country superstar River Deane?"

Griffin's face lit up and he chuckled. "Remember that time... as in what's happening right now?"

"What was the contest again?"

"River Deane's thirtieth anniversary tour contest. Essay question: 'What docs River Deane's music mean to you?' Five hundred words or less." He pulled out his phone and started scrolling. "I wrote about how I had him in my MySpace Top 8 back when that meant something. Remember how interactive he was with fans on there? And we had those conversations about whether pineapple belongs on pizza?"

"Oh God, not the pizza conversations."

"He's team pineapple! We bonded over that. And he asked what I do for a living, and when I told him I'm a massage therapist, he asked me what to do about his *guitar shoulder*."

"I love that you gave River Deane shoulder pain advice through MySpace messages."

"Hey, I know we weren't exactly *friends*," he explained, punctuating the operative word with quotation marks, "but it did seem like he enjoyed those conversations as much as I did. At least, he didn't seem to mind."

"I'm honestly surprised that's what won the contest."

"Well, I did also mention how *Whispered by the Wind* was playing when I first kissed you and became our wedding song."

I nearly groaned out loud. "You wrote about our first kiss?"

"It worked, didn't it? All-expenses-paid trip to LA, first-class plane tickets, orchestra seats to the concert, and..." He paused dramatically. "A meet-and-greet backstage."

My stomach fluttered with the butterflies of near-overwhelm. But it was Griffin who was really reeling. "I still can't believe he's going to be an actual person we talk to. Like, in person."

"Oh, come on, Griff. He's just a guy who makes music."

"He's not just a guy. He's River Deane. Don't forget you had that poster of him shirtless in your dorm room when we first met."

"That poster was very tasteful."

"Debatable, but it *was* what made me come in and say hi to you."

There really is something special about champagne at thirty thousand feet in the air, it turns out. This wasn't my first time drinking actual good champagne, but it was my first time drinking the good stuff at this altitude, and that only increased the buzz.

"You know what's funny?" I said, watching the bubbles rise in my glass. "Yesterday I was writing instructions for a G-spot vibrator."

Griffin looked at me with peak curiosity and a tiny hint of annoyance.

"You tested it without me?"

"It was disappointing."

"That's because I wasn't involved."

"I'll remember that the next time the manufacturer insists I have to write a disclaimer to tactfully explain that if the device doesn't produce the desired result, it's not the device's fault."

Griffin laughed into his fresh glass of champagne. I took another sip and let the bubbles go to my head. "Do you ever think about what your life would look like if you weren't you? Like, if you were someone who belonged in first class?"

Griffin turned to look at me, the pupils of his eyes expanding to take in every detail he already knew about me. "Car, we do belong here. I worked hard to win that contest."

"We won because you have a non-sexual man-crush on a guy who peaked in the late 90s."

"That's not fair, his latest album is brilliant."

"No shade, but it sounds like every other country album that came out in the last decade."

"You're just jealous because he's prettier than you."

I gasped in mock offense. "I take back my *non-sexual* comment. And he's prettier than both of us."

"True. I stand corrected," Griffin conceded.

The flight attendant returned with a small plate of impressive looking snacks instead of the peanuts or pretzels I was used to. "Complimentary appetizers," she said, setting the plate down. "We have smoked salmon canapés, prosciutto-wrapped asparagus, and artisanal crackers with brie."

I stared at the plate. "This is free?"

"Of course," she said, pleasantly, but the look in her eyes said "Nothing is free. Someone paid for this, just not you." She was on to me. Probably because I asked if it was free.

After she left, I picked up one of the canapés and examined it like the morsel of edible art that it was. I ate the canapé in one bite and closed my eyes to savor the moment. First class wasn't just about gourmet food, bigger seats or free champagne. It was about being treated like you mattered.

"You know what this reminds me of?" I said, reaching for another canapé.

"What?"

"Those episodes of *The Lifestyles of the Rich and Famous* my mom used to watch. What was that catchphrase that the host used to say?"

"Please tell me you're not about to start talking in that accent."

"I wasn't, but now that you mention it..." I cleared my throat and attempted my best Robin Leach impression.

"'Tonight, we take you inside the luxurious world of...'"

"Oh my God, stop."

"'...where the champagne flows like water and the canapés are topped with edible gold!'"

Griffin snort-laughed, which made me cackle, which made the posh lady sitting in the adjacent seat look over at us with a furrowed expression which clearly telegraphed that she was wondering how we'd snuck past security.

"We're those people," I whispered to Griffin. "The ones who get too excited about free food."

"Good. I like being those people."

The captain's voice came over the intercom, all smooth and confident, informing us of some potential turbulence. I gripped Griffin's hand. He loved being up in the air, but I've always been a nervous flyer. Now that familiar anxiety bubbled back up despite the champagne's best efforts to keep me chillaxed.

"Hey," Griffin said, squeezing my fingers. "You okay?"

"Yeah, just... you know. Flying." Griffin put his champagne down and took my hand in his, massaging it with the exact amount of pressure needed to relax me. That thing where he would pull on my fingers gently but firmly... that'll do it. Being married to a registered massage therapist definitely had its perks.

"Want me to distract you?" he asked.

"How?"

"Tell me about the vibrator."

I laughed a little too loud. "People can hear us."

"If it keeps you from thinking about crashing in a fiery ball of death, I'll allow it."

"Well, when you put it like that..." I wasn't ashamed of

my job, but I already felt like I had been visibly and audibly *too much* for everyone else on the plane. I kept my voice low. "So, it's called the Arousal Arc 7X G-Spot Stimulator. It's Bluetooth enabled, so you can connect it to music streaming apps and the vibration patterns will sync to the rhythm of your playlist."

"And how did that go?"

"Let's just say I wrote a step about choosing your playlist *before* you insert the device."

"But then where's the thrill of the surprise?"

"Hey, I'm a technical writer, not a romance novelist."

* * *

For the record, I could totally be a romance novelist and I've no aversion to pornography. An unintended side-effect of my job writing user manuals for personal pleasure devices is that I'm basically a product tester.

Companies send me the products and give me a basic explanation of how they are supposed to work. But sometimes what they give me makes no sense, or is just wrong, or they don't give me anything at all. And then I need to figure out all the ins and outs of how the damn thing works.

As you can imagine, I have amassed an extensive collection of sex toys from my various work projects. Speaking of one's vocation benefiting their spouse, I'm pretty sure Griffin would say that he loved my job. Especially that time I had to write instructions for the Prostate Pulse Pro 3000.

* * *

How to Use the Prostate Pulse Pro 3000

1. Get horny. This part is essential. No one's getting anywhere with a tepid level of curiosity. You need to achieve at least a Level 1 arousal to begin.
2. Choose your position. You may need to try all the positions until you find one that provides comfortable access to your butthole. Consider these options: A) Lay face down and spread your butt cheeks. B) Lay on your back and bring your knees up, no spreading required. C) Lay on your side and spread 'em. D) Get on all fours, you dog.
3. Apply a generous amount of lube to the Pulse Pro 3000. You can't use too much.
4. Not that much, that's too much.
5. After the Pulse Pro 3000 slips out of your hands, flies across the room, rolls across the carpet and gets covered in cat hair, wash it off with soapy water and start over from Step 1.
6. Gently insert the Pulse Pro 3000 into the anus, about 3-4 inches deep, and tilt it toward the bellybutton.
7. Gradually increase the vibrations and experiment with different vibration patterns.
8. Moan and writhe with the combined pleasure of anal and prostate stimulation.
9. Try not to fart.
10. Fart.
11. Run after the Pulse Pro 3000 and wash it off again.
12. Try it out on your partner, even if she's a lady.
13. Repeat Steps 1-12. You'll get the hang of it eventually.

* * *

The plane bounced over the air bumps. You know that feeling of being in a rapidly dropping elevator? Not my favorite sensation while suspended in a metal tube thirty thousand feet above the ground. I started having visions of plummeting to Earth while the oxygen masks dangled uselessly above my head, and then took a deep breath.

"Can I tell you something?" I said, looking through the window at the clouds below. Griffin responded with a sleepy grunt, and I glanced over to find him with his eyes closed, resting peacefully, completely unfazed by the turbulence.

Instead of rousing him for another round of "What's Cara catastrophizing about now?" I decided to let him have his nap, which gave me the opportunity to lull myself into the soothing mental void where a multi-layered, interconnected, constantly evolving world that only I knew about existed. My daydream world.

In this episode, I tried to anticipate what we were in for over the next few days.

* * *

The LA sunlight made everything look like a music video and even made the haze look kind of romantic. There was something about the light that just hit me different than it did back home in Niagara Falls. My skin looked smoother, like the city had a soft-focus filter built into the atmosphere. I looked... glowy. My body was leaner, longer and more lithe, like somehow every time I caught a glimpse of myself passing a window, my reflection showed the version of me from the good mirror at home.

Griffin and I spent the day wandering around in a loose, unstructured way, like you do when you feel like you belong somewhere. He was his relaxed, funny self, touching my back the way he does when he's slightly turned on.

We were walking through a neighborhood full of fancy boutiques and overpriced juice stands when a woman stopped us. She was wearing oversized sunglasses and a hat that suggested she might be famous, or at least trying to be.

"I'm sorry," she said, studying me, "but are you someone?"

That caught me off guard. Griffin smirked beside me while I recovered my composure.

"Not yet," I said, and to my eternal credit, I said it with just enough humility and belief to make it work.

She beamed. "Well, you have something." And then she asked for a selfie. I pursed my lips and tilted my head, the sheen of my bright pink headscarf illuminating against the blue sky and palm tree background. For the record, I have literally never worn a headscarf in my life, except for in my daydreams about walking around in LA, looking like I could be someone.

Griffin teased me about it for the rest of the day, calling me "Ms. Not-Yet" and insisting I should start preparing for my viral influencer debut. But he looked at me differently, too, like he was starting to believe the version of me I sometimes imagined for myself.

Back at the impeccably stylish and opulent hotel, we engaged in a little bomp-chicka-wah-wah with the windows open and the city stretching out beneath us.

The curtains moved with the breeze, and from somewhere below we could hear people laughing, car doors slamming, a distant speaker playing something with too much bass. It made everything feel alive, like the whole city might be listening. Like maybe someone could hear us, if we got loud enough.

That idea turned me on more than I expected.

Griffin kissed me slow, one hand gently cradling the back of my head, the other slipping through the front of the hotel robe that hung open in the front. He smelled like sunscreen and sex, and the way he touched me with an intense curiosity and attention, it reminded me of our first time.

His mouth moved down my body like he was discovering it again for the first time, and when he landed between my legs, he pulled back for a second and squinted up at me.

"You taste like pineapple."

I moaned and looked down my body at him. "What?"

He grinned. "Fruity. Definitely pineapplish."

I laughed as I groaned. "Oh my God. It's the pineapple whip. From the fruit stand."

He licked his lips and nodded thoughtfully. "Note to self: Buy pineapples when we get home."

As he continued devouring my pineapplishness, I let my head fall against the cool hotel pillow and moaned uninhibitedly, hoping someone outside would catch a hint of it. There was something deeply titillating about the idea that we were contributing something by sending ripples of pleasure out into the greater Los Angeles soundscape.

Chapter 2

The chime of the *it's now cool to remove your seatbelt* alert pulled me from my reverie, along with a symphony of seatbelt freedom clicks. Griffin was still asleep, his mouth slightly agape. If only I could switch off like that myself.

But all I could do was wrap myself up in the first-class airplane blanket and let myself drift back up into my head, to try and pick up where I left off. I wanted to get to the part of the sex scene where LA is so magical that we manage to miraculously both climax at the same time. Unfortunately, an intrusive thought kicked me out of my daydream and sucked me through a wormhole in my mind to a recent memory instead. I hate it when that happens.

* * *

This was my last therapy session, and the room smelled a little mustardy. A mustard-scented candle was certainly an odd choice, I thought. Or maybe that was just my armpits. Anxiety perspiration dampening my tee shirt. Yep, that mustard smell was all me.

If my therapist, Paige, had a smell, it would be cucumber, as in "cool as a." I loved her chill vibe, to the point where I was super envious of it. Her moments of silence often sent my mind a-wandering to fill the space.

"Where did you go just now?" she asked in her buttery soft voice.

"Oh, nowhere. Still here!" I declared.

"We were talking about what you dreamed of doing when you were a kid."

I laughed, but it came out a little hollow. "You'll think it's stupid."

"Try me."

"I used to think I was going to be... somebody. Like, actually somebody. I wanted to make cartoons. I used to write my own episodes of my favorite cartoon shows and draw pictures to go with them. I had this whole fantasy about working on those shows and seeing my name in the credits. Then in high school, the fantasy shifted to being a pop star. I love to sing. I'm pretty alright at it, too. I had these fantasies about being on stage, you know? Having thousands of people sing along to songs I wrote, feeling that connection, that... recognition. By the time I became an adult, the fantasies evolved to being a celebrated published writer."

Paige's eyebrow raised and her expression was warm. "That's not stupid."

"It kind of is. I mean, look at me. I'm in my forties and I write user guides for sex toys. Not even for fun, for a living. The closest I've gotten to getting my writing out to the world is explaining how to properly clean an electric dildo after use."

I interpreted Paige's silence as a cue to keep talking. I guess that was the point.

"It's okay. I made my peace with it. Ambitions are for people who take risks, and I'm not a risk-taker. I'm a person who chooses

steady paychecks over artistic fulfillment. And you know what? That's fine. We have a good life. We pay our bills. We take our cats on camping vacations."

But even as I said it, my chest ached with a heavy feeling. The one that showed up whenever I thought about the stories I'd written only to hide away, the characters whose adventures were confined to stacks of printer paper, the dreams I'd filed away in the filing cabinet in my home office where I kept my college poetry and my half-finished screenplays and novels.

"Do you still have those fantasies?"

"That's the thing. The fantasies have gotten more... vivid. I'll be out for a walk and suddenly I'm on a talk show, discussing my bestselling novel. Or stuck in traffic, accepting a Grammy."

"How often does that happen?"

"Too often." I dropped my voice. "Whole afternoons vanish. It's like... I'm addicted to it. Griffin comes home and asks how my day was, and I can't tell him that I tranced out while working and almost missed my deadline because I was too busy imagining this other, brave version of me."

"Brave?"

"In the daydreams, I'm fearless. In real life, I'm terrified that I'll fail, or even worse, that I'll be seen or worse still, be successful. It's like I want to be famous and anonymous at the same time."

"Fear of success and failure often overlap." She made a note. "Can you describe what it feels like when you're in one of those scenarios?"

"It's not just imagining. It's like I'm there. I can feel the lights, the crowd, what I'm wearing, hear how my voice sounds. Sometimes it's more emotionally satisfying than actual good things in my life. I've spent a lot of time living entire other lives in my head."

Paige leaned forward. "That sounds like maladaptive daydreaming. It's common, especially for neurodivergent people. Daydreaming can regulate stimulation. Your brain's creating a world that gives you what your real one doesn't."

I let that sink in. "It feels like I'm defective."

"You're not defective. Just someone whose brain needs different kinds of nourishment." She looked at me kindly. "The daydreaming itself isn't the problem. It's that it's getting in the way of you living your real life."

She wasn't really telling me anything I didn't already know, but she saw me in a way that was comforting instead of scary.

"What if we reframed this?" she said. "Instead of seeing your fantasies as escape, what if they're your creative mind showing you what you really want? They're blueprints."

"Okay, but in the meantime, I'm stuck writing about prostate massagers." I gestured vaguely at the ceiling. "How do I get from here to there?"

"You don't need the whole map today. Just one small step toward aligning your inner world with your outer one."

But what could that step even be?

* * *

I sighed loudly without realizing it. Griffin, who had awakened and looked rested, noticed my mood shift. "Hey," he said, reaching over to brush a strand of hair out of my face. "You good?"

"I'm just thinking about how when I was a kid... I thought I'd go to LA to, like, *make it*, you know? Not just as an NPC, but a main character. But we didn't earn this trip, we lucked into it. And that feels shitty all of a sudden."

"You want to know what I think?"

"What?"

"We didn't win this trip with luck, it's fate."

"Griff, you know I don't believe in fate."

"I know. But check us out. We're on our way to a place you've always wanted to go to because I entered a contest on a whim. If that's not the universe telling us to take more chances, I don't know what is. We're supposed to be here."

I looked around the cabin again, at the comfortable seats and the attentive flight attendants and the other passengers who all seemed so confident in their right to be there. Maybe Griffin had a point. Not fate, necessarily, but a gentle nudge to shake things up. The idea excited me.

Standing up suddenly, I declared, "I need to use the bathroom."

"Alrighty."

I tilted my head and mouthed the words "come with me."

Griffin's eyes widened. "Car, we're on a plane," he whispered.

"You just said we should take more chances."

"There are a lot of people here. And I'm pretty sure it's illegal."

I tilted my head to the other side in that *come hither* manner once more. Griffin looked around the cabin nervously, but I could see the exact moment on his face when his reservations turned into intrigue.

"What are they going to do, kick us off the plane?"

My mind suddenly flashed to our pilot taking the plane down for an emergency landing where Griffin and I would be arrested by the Mile-High Club Police (if that isn't a band name, it totally should be). Then I promptly kicked the image out of my head. This was me living my life, instead of thinking about living my life. It was all very urgent.

"Okay," he whispered, "let's do this."

We made our way to the first-class bathroom, trying to look casual. The flight attendant was busy in the galley, and most of the other passengers were either sleeping or watching an in-flight movie.

"This is crazy," Griffin whispered as I opened the bathroom door.

"Good crazy or bad crazy?"

"To be determined."

The first-class bathroom was slightly larger than the standard facilities in coach, but it was still an airplane bathroom. Which meant that as soon as we both squeezed inside and I locked the door, we were pressed together with not a lot of room to maneuver.

I put my arms around Griffin's neck and he leaned down to kiss me, and for a moment it was actually working. We were making out in an airplane bathroom like romcom characters, and I was thrilled with the spontaneity of it all.

Then the plane suddenly hit turbulence again. The jolt knocked me sideways into the wall, and Griffin grabbed for the sink to steady himself, accidentally hitting the faucet handle with his elbow, turning the water on.

"Shit," he hissed, turning the water off while trying to maintain his balance.

"Are you okay?" I whispered.

"I think I bruised my hip on the door handle."

Another bump of turbulence sent us both lurching in different directions. I fell forward and nearly went headfirst into the toilet, losing my hair scrunchie in the bowl, which Griffin accidentally flushed while he tried to steady himself.

"This is not going how I pictured it," I said, pulling my hair out of my face while trying to avoid stepping on Griffin's feet.

"Really? Because this had possible concussion written all over it from the minute we got in here."

The plane bucked again, harder this time, and Griffin's head connected with the ceiling.

"Mission accomplished," I joked.

"Ow. Fuck. Okay, new plan."

"What's the new plan?"

"The new plan is we get out of here before we both actually get concussions, and we wake up handcuffed to our hospital beds."

I couldn't help myself, giggling uncontrollably. "So much for being spontaneous."

"Hey, we tried. That counts for something."

The captain's voice came over the intercom. "Ladies and gentlemen, we're experiencing some moderate turbulence. Please return to your seats and fasten your seatbelts."

"I think that's our cue," Griffin said, reaching for the door handle.

"Wait." I grabbed his arm. "Kiss me one more time."

He cupped the back of my head in his hands and kissed me, slow and sweet, while the plane shook around us and I held onto him for dear life.

"There," he said when we broke apart. "We're officially in the Mile-High First Base Club."

We slipped out of the bathroom one at a time, trying to look innocent. The flight attendant was strapping herself into her seat and didn't seem to notice our guilty expressions or disheveled appearances.

* * *

Back in our seats, buckled in and holding hands while the plane bounced through the turbulence, I felt something I hadn't experienced in a long time. I think it was exhilaration. So what if our attempted mile-high romp only got to first base? For just a few minutes, I'd become the kind of person who took a risk and lived in the moment instead of only fantasizing about it.

"So," Griffin said, rubbing my knee as the air-bumps eased, "what's next on the spontaneity agenda?"

I wanted to say something fun, but as I looked out the window at the endless blue sky stretching ahead of us, toward Los Angeles and River Deane and whatever adventures waited for us in a city where anything seemed possible, the crash from my spontaneity-induced buzz was suddenly too much. Noticing I was lightheaded and holding my breath, I exhaled slowly and let Griffin's question hang between us as I spaced out until we landed in LA.

Chapter 3

River Deane was past his arena years, and had clearly settled into mid-size concert hall territory. The venue was big enough to boast about the sold-out show, but just small enough to feel intimate, at least from our vantage point. We had good seats. Not front-row-spit-zone good, but close enough that River Deane looked like an actual human being instead of a country music ant performing for a colony of screaming insects.

Griffin was vibrating with excitement. He almost looked twenty again, as if looking forward to something nostalgic had paradoxically rejuvenated him. That or the overpriced beer in his hand had been distilled from the fountain of youth (or maybe I was just ogling him through my own vodka cooler goggles). He was taking shaky phone videos of literally everything: the stage, the crowd, us clinking drink cans, and me looking mildly embarrassed and also slightly turned on by his enthusiasm.

"Can you believe we're here?" he asked me for the gazillionth time as the lights dimmed. "Can you actually believe this is happening?"

"I can believe it," I said, though honestly, the buzz from our flight had worn off and been replaced by my default setting of low-grade anxiety about being in public spaces with too many people. "The real question is whether you're going to survive it without having a fanboy stroke."

"I'm not going to have a stroke."

"Your hands are literally shaking."

Griffin looked down at the beer can trembling in his hand. "That's excitement-shaking, not medical-emergency-shaking."

The opening act was some indie band whose name I forget now, but in the moment, I was all like *oh, that's pretty good, I should check out their stuff* (I never did). Griffin tolerated them politely.

When River Deane's light show started, the crowd erupted in an ear-splitting soundwall of anticipatory adulation. The venue went completely dark, and then a single spotlight hit the stage, and there he was... River Deane in all his lanky, corduroy-suited, cowboy-hatted glory.

Griffin and I had bonded over our River Deane fandom back in our college days, so I was well familiar with the man and his many good works. I really did have that *tastefully shirtless* poster of him in my dorm room that Griffin still brought up whenever he wanted to win an argument. But I wasn't prepared for how seeing him in person all these years later was going to make me feel.

It wasn't just that he was conventionally gorgeous. There was something about the way he moved, the way he held his guitar like it was part of his body... no, wait, his *being*, and the way his voice traveled through your ears straight to your soul and the part of you that still believes in magic.

"Holy shit, there he is," Griffin breathed beside me, and I gasped along with him.

River launched into *Break of Dawn*, one of his earlier hits, and the crowd sang along so loudly I could barely hear his voice. Griffin was singing too, his eyes closed, like the song was a bookmark that took him back to relive whatever memory was associated with it.

I tried to sing along, but I kept getting distracted by the logistics of it all. How did he not get nervous with thousands of people staring at him? How did he make it look so effortless? I practically got stage fright just by ordering coffee from an unfamiliar barista.

Three songs in, I caught myself analyzing his stage presence instead of enjoying it, which was a very "me" thing to do, separating myself from the experience instead of letting myself get carried away by it. That's what happens when you spend most of your life caught between desperately wanting to be seen, and hoping the fuck that no one ever sees you. You develop this weird distance from your own emotions at the exact moment when feeling them should be all that matters.

"You good?" Griffin shouted to me over the music, probably noticing my glazed expression.

"Yeah," I shouted back. "Just trying to be present."

"Don't you feel that?" Griffin swooned.

I closed my eyes for just a moment, to block out the spectacle and focus on the music, and the ensuing goosebumps were a good sign. I had managed to find my way back to that part of me that felt things more deeply than I like to admit.

When I opened my eyes, River Deane was looking right into them. Like, into my soul. Granted, we were only a few rows back, but I swear it was like he was making eye contact with everyone in the place, even in the furthest reaches of the venue. It sounds kind of creepy when I say it like that, but it wasn't. It was comforting, as if he was singing directly to every one of us about our specific heartbreak or joy or whatever emotional baggage we'd brought to the concert.

* * *

About an hour into the show, River's band left the stage, and he settled onto a stool with just his acoustic guitar and a single spotlight. The crowd quieted. We all knew this was the sacred part of the evening.

"This next part," River said into the microphone, his voice all gravelly and intimate, "is for the folks who've been with me since the beginning." Griffin grabbed my hand and squeezed gently. This was his moment. The part of the show designed specifically for obsessive fans like him who hung out on discords and message boards and praised the "deep cuts" that never achieved mainstream success.

River started with *Midnight Train (To the End of the World)*, a song I vaguely recognized from one of his earlier albums. Then *Kentucky Moon*, which was never my favorite, but prompted a large group hug among the people in front of us.

The acoustic versions were different. They were more raw, more honest, stripped of their radio-friendly polish. It was like seeing someone without makeup, their true beauty on display.

And then he started playing *Whispered by the Wind.*

Our song. It had soundtracked some very specific moments in my life. Like the time that Griffin and I broke up for a while, right after college. The heartbreak, the late-night driving, the crying-in-the-shower moments when Griffin was having his quarter-life crisis and I thought I was going to die alone and no one would know until it was too late and I would be found having been half-eaten by my cat. The song that got me through those dark times and the song that would eventually become the one we danced to at our wedding. The song that won us this contest and was the whole reason we were here. *That song.*

River's voice on the album version was beautiful, but live, acoustic, with just him and his guitar and that spotlight, it was something else entirely. It was like he'd reached into my chest and was playing my heartstrings like a fucking harp.

He closed his eyes as he sang, as if the music was coming from somewhere sacred inside him. I felt something flutter in my chest as his voice cracked slightly on the high notes. And there it was. That weird twingey internal pulling feeling I get when I'm moved by art (and sometimes, the person who made the art). The best I can do is describe it as a *uteral* experience.

I snuck a glance at Griffin, who was completely absorbed, mouthing along to every word. Safe in his oblivious fanboy bubble, thankfully unaware that I was having a lady boner over his musical hero.

The song ended with River holding that final note for what felt like a hundred hours, his voice climbing into this heart-shattering falsetto that could make every ovary in the venue simultaneously explode. I was practically floating off the ground. The crowd went bazonkers, and I was clapping so hard my palms actually stung.

Griffin looked at me with wide eyes and his mouth slightly agape, an expression that said he was reeling from his own transcendent experience. It was like we were both floating back down to the ground together with our eyes locked on each other's.

River transitioned into his final song of the acoustic set. It was something newer that I didn't recognize, and it gave me the chance to get my hormones back under control. I blinked and suddenly he was just a man with a guitar again. Still hot, obviously, but, just a man, nevertheless. It was just *that song* that had made me come all undone. A perfectly normal reaction to art that I would 100% be keeping to myself.

* * *

The lights came back up for the rest of the set, the band returned to the stage, and River launched into his biggest hits, the songs that had made him famous, the ones that got played in supermarkets and at graduation ceremonies and in those movie montages where the protagonist finally gets their life together.

The energy was different now, more *we're all in this together* celebration than intimate confession, and I found myself tuning into Griffin's joy. This was his night, his moment, his reward for years of unwavering fandom.

Raise the Roof was the closer, naturally. The big, anthemic sing-along that sent everyone home happy and hoarse. By the end of it, I was genuinely having fun instead of psychoanalyzing my emotional responses, which was a relief and gave me something I could actually talk about when people back home inevitably asked us how the concert was.

* * *

When the encore finished and the band left the stage, we made our way to the backstage area to cash in our meet-and-greet pass. The crown jewel of Griffin's contest prize package. It was originally scheduled to happen before the concert, but River had been delayed unexpectedly. Instead of canceling, the meet-and-greet was rescheduled to happen after the show.

Truth be told, I'm not a huge fan of being a fan. It's sort of embarrassing. I don't want to meet my heroes. I want to appreciate them from afar. Far far afar. But this meant a lot to Griffin, and I hoped his excitement would carry me through the experience.

The backstage area wasn't exactly magical. Just concrete floors, a non-descript headachy smell, and fluorescent lighting that gave even the most genetically blessed the complexion of the undead. River was situated in a staged living room area in front of a background depicting his latest album cover. We joined a line of other contest winners and VIP package purchasers, all clutching vinyl records and posters like pilgrims with holy relics.

"I'm so nervous," Griffin whispered, bouncing slightly on his toes. "What should I say to him? Do you think he'll remember me from MySpace?"

"Maybe just play it cool," I suggested, though I had no idea what playing it cool looked like in this situation. My own experience with running into famous people in person was limited to that time I dove under the table and hid when Keanu Reeves came into the Flying Saucer during a brunch with my bestie, Hannah.

The line moved kind of like a conveyor belt. Smile, sign, photo, next. Each interaction lasted roughly ninety seconds, just long enough for everyone to pretend they were having a meaningful moment before being gently ushered along by an intimidating woman with a clipboard who looked like she could bench press a small car.

When our turn came, River Deane looked exactly like someone who'd just performed for two hours and wanted nothing more than to go back to his hotel room and order room service. A tired dude who was using the last bit of his energy to do this thing, for us. There was a glazed quality to his smile that suggested his soul had left his body somewhere around the gazillionth identical interaction.

"Hey there," he said, extending his hand to Griffin. "Thanks for coming out tonight."

"Hi!" Griffin practically squeaked. "I'm Griffin, and this is my wife Cara. I won the contest? I wrote about how *Whispered by the Wind* is our song, and... I don't know if you remember me, but we used to chat on MySpace, you know, back in the day..."

"That's awesome, man," River interrupted with a smile that flickered in his eyes quickly before dissipating. "I really appreciate fans like you who've been there from the beginning."

He signed Griffin's vinyl copy of his debut album with an impressively reflexive flick of his wrist, and then we took our obligatory photo. River stretched his arm across our backs and smiled along with us as if we were old friends instead of strangers participating in an awkward idol worship ritual.

And then it was over. "That was incredible," Griffin said as we were efficiently herded toward the exit by the clipboard lady. "Did you see how he perked up when I mentioned MySpace?" I made a noncommittal sound that could have been agreement, not wanting to point out that River had given the same patient nod to everyone.

Don't get me wrong. River wasn't rude or dismissive. He was perfectly professional, exactly what you'd expect from someone who'd mastered the art of making hundreds of strangers feel special while preserving his own sanity. But there's a difference between meeting someone and actually connecting with them, and this felt more like getting your passport stamped than having a genuine human interaction.

* * *

As we emerged into the arid Los Angeles evening, I felt oddly deflated. Not because River had failed to live up to some impossible standard, but because the whole experience had felt so transactional. So removed from the pure emotion of his music and the vulnerability he'd shown on stage during those acoustic songs.

"So," Griffin said, checking his phone, "what now? Back to the hotel? There's that bottle of wine in the room, and it should be nice and cool in there by now."

I looked around at the crowd dispersing into the neon-lit night. It was chilly back home when we'd boarded our flight. But the dry, hot LA air made the night feel young and full of possibilities. We were only going to be there for a couple of days. When would we ever be back? When would I ever again have the chance to be the version of myself that gets to do LA things?

"Actually," I said, surprising myself and Griffin and possibly the universe, "what if we didn't go back yet? What if we found somewhere to hang out for a bit? Burn off some of this energy?"

Griffin looked at me like I'd just suggested we bone in an airplane bathroom and then remembered we almost had. *Who the hell was I and what had I done with Cara?*

"What did you have in mind?" he asked, cautiously.

"I don't know. Let's walk and see what we find. Be spontaneous."

"Two spontaneous gestures in one day? Are you sure you're feeling okay? Should I check you for a fever?"

He placed his palm, slightly clammy from all the excitement, on my forehead.

"I'm feeling like we're in Los Angeles and we don't travel much and maybe we should make the most of it before I return to my natural state of overthinking everything and wanting to hide in our hotel room with room service and weird local TV."

Griffin grinned. "Cara, I love that version of you, always. But I have to admit, I kind of have a crush on this version of you."

"Wait, are you cheating on me with... me?" I teased.

"I mean... am I?" He hugged me playfully from behind as we walked away from the concert venue.

"That's kind of hot," we said in unison before breaking out in hysterical laughter.

Chapter 4

We walked with no particular plan in mind, just following the flow of post-concert energy with the hope for something authentic, if not magical.

What we found, after about fifteen minutes of wandering through side streets lined with dive bars and late-night taco stands, was a karaoke bar. Or rather, a regular bar having its weekly karaoke night, which was infinitely better than some glitzy karaoke palace designed for tourists. *Friggin' tourists.*

Griffin had some reservations. "Really? Karaoke? Like we do on Saturday nights at home? After we just saw an actual legendary musician perform?"

"Griff, you know how much I love karaoke. Karaoke people are good people. It's the one activity in the world where you can completely suck and still get wholehearted applause from strangers who are just happy you tried."

The place looked like most karaoke bars I'd been to, which is to say it looked like someone had decorated it using the clearance section of a dive bar supply catalog. String lights hung from low-ceiling beams, and the wood-paneled walls were adorned with neon beer signs and old local photos in dollar store frames.

A slightly raised stage (it was generous to call it a *stage*, it was really just a platform big enough for one or two people to stand on without falling off it into someone's nachos) was situated at one corner of the room. The bar itself was layered with photos, each layer documenting different eras of the establishment's evidently long and storied existence.

We squeezed through the crowd to get our beers, and while we waited, I examined the photographic history tacked to the walls around and behind the bar. Photos of people who looked like they'd been coming here since time began. Local celebrities, bachelor and bachelorette parties, and a light smattering of what appeared to be actual famous people.

"Whoa, isn't that..." Griffin began, pointing to one particular photo that seemed to glow with its own special energy.

"Jack Black!" we exclaimed in unison, along with the enthusiastic bartender who'd obviously had this exact conversation roughly eight thousand times but still seemed excited about it.

"Jack tends to hog the mic when he comes in," the bartender said with fond exasperation, like he was talking about a beloved relative, "but we love him, of course. Haven't seen him in a while, but you never know!"

Griffin and I grinned at each other with the stupid happiness of *friggin' tourists* who'd stumbled into the authenticity we'd been hoping for. Maybe Jack would show up tonight. Maybe this was where the real LA magic happened, not at post-concert meet-and-greets, but in dive bars where celebrities could be human beings who got drunk and sang badly like the rest of us.

We found a table in the back corner, a cozy little nook that was far enough from the stage to provide a good vantage point of the whole bar. The place was about half full, with most of the serious karaoke regulars claiming the front tables.

I immediately scanned the QR code for "The Book." You know, the sacred song catalog. I opened the app with reverence and began searching for songs like I was on a mission from Gloria Gaynor.

I checked for anything that might be on my personal song list. Yes, I have a carefully curated collection of go-to karaoke songs for different occasions. There are the crowd-pleasers that everyone can sing along to (a guaranteed dopamine hit), the less obvious songs that are like a secret handshake with that one other person in the place who gets it, and of course, the safe choices for those less confident times. It all just depends on the vibe.

Despite my sudden spontaneous leanings, I found myself craving something safe, and settled on an upbeat River Deane song. That one massive crossover comeback hit he had around 2010 that sounds nothing like the rest of his music. Having just come from his show, it felt right.

I filled out my slip of paper, made my way to the DJ booth, manned by a guy who looked like he was born to run karaoke nights, and submitted my song request with a cortisol-induced flurry of pre-performance jitters.

Back at our table, I sipped my beer and watched a slight man in acid-washed jeans on the stage bounce his way through *It's My Life* by Bon Jovi with uninhibited joy. His vocals were off-key and unpredictable, punctuated by occasional exuberant shouts that had no relationship to the actual melody, but the spectators were eating it up like he was headlining the Hollywood Bowl.

When he finished, he got a genuine round of applause and high-fives from his friends, and I felt a warm glow of recognition on his behalf. This was exactly what I'd been hoping for. Real karaoke culture, where enthusiasm matters more than talent and everyone's rooting for everyone else to succeed.

"Can we get Cara to the stage, please. Give it up for Cara!"

I jumped up, along with my nerves. Griffin gave me an encouraging whoop as I made my way to the stage, and I realized that despite years of karaoke experience, I still got that weird mix of terror and excitement every single time.

The microphone was warm and slightly damp from the previous singer. A delightful reminder that I was about to put my mouth near something that had been in close contact with a stranger's saliva and sweat. I wiped it on my jeans because hygiene, and cleared my throat.

"Hi," I said into the mic, my voice sounding smaller and more uncertain than I'd intended. As the first verse began, I immediately realized something was wrong. The lyrics on the screen didn't match the lyrics I knew by heart. They weren't completely different, but off enough that I couldn't rely on them.

I knew this song well enough to sing it from memory, but suddenly being forced to ignore the screen meant I was actually looking out at the audience instead of my eyes clinging to the monitor as my security blanket. This wasn't karaoke anymore. This was performing.

Panic set in as I stumbled through the first verse. I wasn't prepared for how exposed I felt without the familiar safety net of timed lyrics. For a moment, I seriously considered just stopping, making some excuse about the wrong version, and slinking back to my table to hide behind my beer for the rest of the evening.

Instead, I took a breath and decided to watch the on-screen visuals while ignoring the incorrect words, and pushed through. Once I found my place again, I was able to relax into the song and actually enjoy it.

Because I was focused on the screen for most of the performance, trying to navigate the lyrical minefield of incorrect words, I didn't notice that the bar had gotten significantly busier since I'd taken the stage. When I finished and looked back up, I had to search for Griffin's face through a crowd that had roughly doubled in size.

The applause was warm and enthusiastic. I basked in a glow of relieved accomplishment mixed with slight disappointment that it hadn't gone as planned. Regardless, people were calling out compliments as I made my way off the stage. I was mostly focused on getting back to Griffin and processing what had just happened.

"That was great, babe!" Griffin said as I approached our table, but he was wearing a slightly stunned expression, and was distracted by something that wasn't me.

"Thanks. That was weird with the lyrics being wrong, but I think I recovered okay..."

"Cara." His eyes were fixed on a point that was back near the bar.

"What?"

"Don't look now, but I think River Deane is here."

I tried to casually glance around the room without being obvious about it, which is to say, as subtle as a helicopter search light scanning for its target. But the place had gotten crowded enough that I couldn't immediately spot anyone who looked like a country music star. Maybe Griffin was seeing things. Maybe the combination of beer, post-concert adrenaline, and wishful thinking was making him hallucinate a celebrity mirage.

"Are you sure it's River Deane?" I whispered, in case it really was him, and he had superhuman hearing and would somehow overhear us talking about him across a crowded, noisy bar.

"Pretty sure. He's over by the bar, talking to some people. Same cowboy hat. Unless LA is full of River Deane impersonators, which is entirely possible."

Suddenly, the thought that River Deane might actually be in the bar triggered me to want to run and hide. Nature wasn't calling, but I embarked on a journey to the bathroom for cover.

The crowd had definitely thickened since my performance, and I had to navigate through clusters of people engaged in animated conversations. I was focused on weaving my way through, when I walked directly into someone's chest.

A tall someone's chest. A cowboy-hat-and-signature-corduroy-jacket-wearing someone's chest.

"Oh God, I'm so sorry," I said, looking up into River Deane's amused dark brown eyes.

"That's alright," he said with a chuckle that bypassed my ears and went straight to the lump in my throat. "I should be the one to apologize."

Holy fucking shit. This was surreal. An hour ago, Griffin and I had been standing in line waiting to get ninety seconds of his attention at the meet-and-greet. Now here I was, colliding with him in a dive bar like that was totally normal.

"It's really busy in here," I said, stating the obvious with my brilliant conversational skills, tilting my chin upward so as not to speak directly into his chest. I tried to find a way around him, but the place was packed and there was nowhere to go. I started to feel a little faint, and very much wanted to find an exit to get some fresh air, but I was stuck.

"Typical LA traffic," he replied, and despite the awkwardness, I laughed.

"We saw your show tonight. My husband's one of your biggest fans."

"Your husband is, but not you?" River smirked.

"Well yeah, you know... me too, but him... more."

His turn to laugh. "Fair enough. You know, I actually came over here on purpose," he said. "I wanted to tell you I loved what you did with my song up there."

I was trying to find my words. You know, like *thank you*, or something equally appropriate. But my consciousness went to a place where all rational thought ceased to function and was replaced by a high-pitched whirring sound like a computer trying to process too much information at once.

He'd heard me sing *his song*? He'd been watching *my performance*? The one where I'd stumbled through the first verse and had to recover from what was essentially a mild panic attack?

"The lyrics were wrong," I managed to say, because when faced with a compliment, my instinct is to immediately point out everything that went badly.

"I didn't notice," River said with another one of those devastating chuckles. "You have a really sweet voice. Made it sound kind of... ironic, but earnest. It was a trip."

It wouldn't have surprised me if smoke had started to pour out of my ears. I tried to perform a *Ctrl-Alt-Delete* reset on my brain, but instead of resuming normal function, my gray matter conjured the proverbial blue screen of death. Just as my knees were beginning to buckle, Griffin suddenly appeared, slamming up against me from behind, becoming the other piece of bread in an awkward human sandwich.

"River! I can't believe you're here!" Griffin's voice was pure, undiluted excitement, muffled by the din of the wall-to-wall packed bar. "Dude, you kicked ass tonight! It's me, Griffin! We just met you backstage? The MySpace guy?"

River looked momentarily confused, as if he was trying to remember where he left his car keys, and then his eyes lit up with recognition like he'd found them. He extended his beer-holding hand toward Griffin for an over-my-head clink while I remained the unwilling filling in this human hoagie situation.

"Oh, right! Yeah, good to see you again, man. Thanks again for coming out tonight."

I decided I needed to turn around to face Griffin so I could at least breathe properly while he reminisced at River about their past internet chat history. The maneuver was complicated by the ever-thickening crowd, the beer glasses, and the fact that I was essentially trying to rotate in place without bumping into anyone's sensitive areas.

"I need to pee," I announced, now truthfully.

"Sure," Griffin said, tilting his body to let me pass while keeping his attention laser-focused on River. I was relieved to finally be moving, and even more relieved when I reached the relative safety of the ladies' room lineup, where I could process what had just happened.

Chapter 5

The line for the bathroom was long enough to give me time to think, and by think, I mean zone the fuck out. By now, you've probably figured out that I have what my parents and teachers always called an *active imagination.* They likely assumed it was just a cute thing I did as a kid, and that I'd grow out of it. Instead, it became so much more than that. Like, basically a whole alternate reality dominated by a nearly endless stream of fantasies.

Waiting my turn for something? Zoned out. Enduring a boring work meeting? Head in the clouds. Stressed the fuck out? Space Cadet Cara reporting for duty. Perfectly at peace? Mental vacation time.

I've spent A LOT of time in this realm. Probably more time than I've spent in actual reality, if I'm being honest. It's like having a private movie theater in my brain, except I'm the writer, director, and star of every film, and I've won every imaginary award you can think of. *And the Oscar for Best (Un)Original Daydream goes to...*

As I stood waiting in the ladies' bathroom line, I flipped through the mental catalog of daydream scenarios I've created over the years, not unlike a metaphysical jukebox. It only took a minute to find the one I was looking for.

* * *

I'm on stage, wearing an opulent and alluring costume. So many sparkles. My powerful voice blasts through the skulls of my fans, rewiring the circuits in their brains and bodies, lifting them off the ground, making them high on nothing but the sound of the supernatural notes I'm hitting.

My body is a perfect composition of strength and beauty, carrying me across the stage with the grace of a ballerina. I am an idol, a goddess, a force of nature with a microphone. When I finish the verse, I hold my microphone out toward the audience so they can give me the chorus with the same collective intensity that I give to them, and the sound is like the ocean roaring my melody back to me.

* * *

The line moved forward, bringing me back to reality just long enough to shuffle a few feet closer to an actual bathroom stall before I went back into that exact place in the story inside my head.

But how did I get to that place? I needed to take a step back, map out how this version of me could have achieved that level of acclaim. This would be a new scene, something I had to create from scratch, and River Deane had just given me exactly what I needed to make it believable.

Instead of inhabiting my alter-ego's body this time, I watched from above like a voyeuristic security camera.

* * *

River Deane's band entered through the door at the far end of the recording studio. The room was lit by colorful glass vintage lamps and decorated in a bohemian shabby-chic style.

Pouf chairs and a large, patterned kilim rug dominated the floor space, while intricately woven tapestries covered the walls and windows. A small gaggle of microphones on stands stood in a semi-circle in the open space, looking like a choir holding their sheet music.

As the band unpacked their gear, I entered the room wearing a 70s-inspired outfit that matched the room's vibe perfectly. Lustrous fabrics flowed down my body, wisping through the air as I moved. River followed close behind me, dressed in his typical understated fashion of blue jeans, plaid shirt and his corduroy jacket.

* * *

At the front of the bathroom line, my body present but my mind in another dimension, the door of the middle stall flew open and a tipsy lady staggered out of it, taking up a lot of space for such a fragile-looking figure. I dodged her jaunty movements and entered the stall. Unfortunately, the door's locking mechanism was busted, so I had to hold it shut with my hand. By this time, I really had to pee, so I quickly unpeeled my jeans from my body and sat down.

Now, where was I?

* * *

River and I greeted our band... because in this fantasy, they were somehow our band, a collective that had formed through the magical power of shared artistic vision. He pulled wrinkled sheets of lined paper from his shoulder bag, scrawled with deep thoughts and artistic notes in careful handwriting, and handed them to me and the band members.

We sat down on the poufs and began to rehearse the songs, layering delicate harmonies over his deep drawl. This was magic, and everyone could feel it like creative electricity buzzing in the air. This would be the beginning of something big, something that would change everything.

* * *

Then suddenly, the bathroom stall door opened with a force greater than my hand's ability to hold it shut. And standing before me was none other than River Deane.

"What the..." I started to say, but he put his arm around my back and bent down to kiss my lips as I sat on the toilet. My head was spinning. What was even happening? I stood up from the toilet, and River wrapped both his arms around me, rubbing my back while he kissed my neck. Despite all the voices inside my head screaming at me that this was not freaking okay and that I should really be pushing him away and slapping him across the face, some other voice, far stronger than all of the others, silenced them all with emphatic consent and let nature take its course.

"We should be fast," I whispered, trying to be mindful of the other occupants of the bathroom. I did wonder how he managed to infiltrate without causing a commotion. Surely my stall neighbors were aware that something out of the ordinary was happening. But no one said boo, so the shenanigans continued.

River spun me around, and I could hear the hasty unbuckling of his belt and the sound of his pants zipper. The ceramic tiles on the bathroom wall felt cool on my palms. The butterflies in my stomach decided to spill out into the rest of my body, and flutter out up my esophagus, causing an effervescent burp to emerge. I started to say "Excuse me..." but I couldn't finish the sentence because all of a sudden, there it was. The push deep inside and the pressure that follows, that indescribably pleasant discomfort of that initial thrust, and then the easing of that sensation as the rhythm is established.

The difference in our height and the intensity of River's thrusting was enough to knock me a little off-balance, so I tried to steady myself by repositioning my hands on the wall, but they slipped. I tried to catch myself from falling, and my hands landed on the toilet seat. Unfortunately, gravity took hold of my glasses and pulled them into the toilet bowl.

River continued pounding me as I reached into the toilet water to retrieve my glasses (they're prescription, I need them), but River's next plunge into me hit particularly hard and knocked me off-balance again, and my hand hit the flush handle. I watched in horror as my glasses were sucked down into a hellish oblivion.

"Oh my God!" I exclaimed with dismay about my lost spectacles. River echoed the words, but I suspect with a different sentiment. And that's when I heard a familiar voice. "Cara? Are you still in here?"

Still facing the wall with River inside me, I couldn't see what was happening, but I heard the sound of the stall door being flung open in dramatic fashion and the shock in Griffin's voice as he yelled "What the fuck?!"

I held back a dry heave, when suddenly...

* * *

The stall door had indeed flung open, and a woman appeared in the doorway, startling me back to reality. That is, just me, sitting on a toilet in a dive bar bathroom, slightly embarrassed about where my mind had just taken me.

"Oh! I'm sorry!" the woman shouted as she retreated from the stall, probably wondering why I was sitting there looking like I'd just been caught doing something inappropriate when I was literally just using the bathroom.

"No worries," I assured her, though I was pretty sure my face bore the visible remnants of being yanked from a vividly detailed and totally inappropriate fantasy.

I pulled up my pants, flushed the toilet, and exited the stall at record speed. As I approached the sink to wash my hands, I caught sight of myself in the mirror and realized I looked exactly like someone who'd been having some kind of "episode" in a bar bathroom. I was flushed, paranoid-looking, and my glasses were slightly askew on my face.

I fixed what I could, dried my hands, and hurried out of the bathroom to hopefully find that River had retreated and Griffin had returned to our table, and that the horror of having an unplanned interaction with a famous person was over.

Instead, I arrived back at the cozy corner table to find Griffin and River now sitting together, still engrossed in deep conversation. Or rather, Griffin talking animatedly while River listened with polite interest. As I approached, I caught the tail end of whatever story Griffin was telling.

"...it turns out that my grandmother's secret family recipe was just a can of evaporated milk," Griffin admitted.

River was incredulous. "In everything?" His eyes caught mine as I approached our table, and I quickly averted his gaze.

"There she is!" Griffin stood up as I sat down, his face

glowing with happiness. "Long line?"

"Uh, pretty long, yeah," I replied meekly.

"Bathroom lines are like being trapped in some kind of space-time vacuum," River hypothesized. *You have no idea*, I thought.

"Glad you made it back safely," he said. I managed a small, embarrassed smile and looked down, taking a sip of my beer.

Griffin grinned at me. "River was just telling me about his new project."

"Oh?" I said, trying to act like I had regular conversations with country music stars all the time instead of the fact that most of my social interactions involved explaining to my cats *again* why they shouldn't be on the counter.

"It sounded like you were telling him about your grandmother's secret ingredient."

"Before that," Griffin explained.

River turned his eyes to me, and I felt that same electric current I'd experienced during the acoustic set. "I was telling your boy Griffin here that I'm working on some new material. Different direction from the last album. More acoustic, more personal. Like what you heard tonight during the solo set."

"That was amazing," I said, and immediately felt stupid for such a generic compliment, like telling Michelangelo that the Sistine Chapel was "nice."

"Thanks. But the thing of it is... I keep feeling like something's missing. Like there's a piece I can't quite find, you know?" He paused and took a sip of his beer. "When I heard your voice tonight, I thought, 'Maybe that's it.'"

I almost choked on my saliva. Griffin made a sound that was somewhere between a gasp and a cheer, like he'd just witnessed his favorite team score the winning goal. I felt like I was about to pass out, or throw up, or possibly both simultaneously.

"I mean," River continued, apparently oblivious to the fact that he'd just caused my entire nervous system to short-circuit for the thousandth time that day, "if you'd be interested. I'm talking about recording some duets, maybe putting together an EP. Nothing huge, just seeing what happens when we blend your voice with mine."

The rational part of my brain was screaming about how this was insane, how I wasn't a professional singer, how this kind of thing didn't happen to people like me. How I was just a chick who'd stumbled through his song at a dive bar karaoke night, not someone who belonged in a recording studio with an actual musician.

But there was another part, the part that lived in my daydreams and private fantasies, that was switched all the way on, electrically speaking. The part that had just spent twenty minutes in a bathroom stall imagining exactly this scenario, except with better lighting and more flowing sleeves.

"I..." I started, then stopped, then started again like the sputtering gasps of a failing car engine. "I don't know what to say."

"Say yes!" Griffin practically shouted, probably disturbing every conversation within a three-table radius. "Car, you have to. This is a once in a lifetime opportunity! You love to sing. And you told me once that you wanted to be in a band. Isn't this everything you've always dreamed of?"

"Well... not *everything*..." I interjected.

River laughed warmly, but with a slight edge that seemed dangerous. "I don't want to pressure you. It's just an idea. But I'm going to be booking some studio time soon, and if you wanted to come out and see what happens..." He shrugged, making it sound casual, like inviting random karaoke singers to record with him was a super normal thing to do.

"Can I think about it?" I asked, which was probably the most sensible thing I'd said all night and also probably the one that scared me the most.

"Actually," River said, leaning back in his chair with casual confidence, "what are you guys doing tomorrow? I'm having some people over for a pool party at my place. Nothing fancy, just hanging out, barbecue, playing some music. It could be a good chance to talk more about this whole thing."

Now it was Griffin's turn to choke, this time on his beer. I watched his face cycle through approximately a quadrillion different emotions in the span of three seconds... surprise, excitement, disbelief, and finally what looked like certainty that he had just made a new best friend.

"A pool party?" I managed to say, because apparently when faced with life-changing invitations, my conversational skills revert to those of a confused parrot. *Squawk. Polly want a pool noodle.*

"Yeah, at my house. My wife Naomi loves entertaining, and we've got a nice setup in the backyard. Pool, fire pit, good vibes."

I looked at Griffin, who was nodding so enthusiastically I was concerned he might hurt himself. This was *his* dream scenario. Not just meeting his musical hero, but being invited into his actual life, his actual home, like they were actual friends.

Alarm bells clanged in my head. "That sounds... like a thing," I said, because what else do you say when a famous person invites you to their house? That you have other plans?

I had to give him a chance to back out. "Are you sure? I mean, we don't want to impose, and we're just..."

"You're not imposing," River interrupted with a smile that could win the Nobel Peace Prize. "I wouldn't have asked if I didn't mean it. Besides, something about tonight feels... I don't know, serendipitous? Like maybe we were supposed to meet each other."

He thought our meeting was serendipitous. I filed that word away to obsess over later, probably while lying awake at 3 AM replaying this entire conversation in my head and cringing at my every word and reaction.

"We'll be there," Griffin said, decisively. "What time? What should we bring? Do we need to..."

"Just bring yourselves," River said, standing up and putting on his cowboy hat with a gesture that should have looked ridiculous but instead made him look iconic. "I'll send a car for you. Let's say around four? That'll give everyone time to recover from tonight's adventures."

He pulled out his phone. "What's your number?"

I recited my digits like I was under hypnosis, watching him type them into his contacts with his talented guitar-playing fingers. *Celebrities, they're just like us.*

"Alright," River said, sliding his phone back into his pocket. "I'll send you the details in the morning." He looked at me again with eyes that seemed to see right through all my neuroses and insecurities to some version of myself I didn't even know existed. "I'm really glad I ran into y'all tonight. I have a feeling this could be the beginning of something cool."

After River left, Griffin and I sat in stunned silence for approximately five seconds before he exploded with excitement. I legit looked around at our immediate surroundings to make sure pieces of his brain hadn't landed everywhere.

"CARA. What just happened? Did I imagine that? Seriously, pinch me."

Did Griffin imagine it? Ha. "Nothing's decided," I said, not wanting to go there.

"Nothing's decided? Are you insane? Don't you want this?"

And there it was, the problem I couldn't articulate to Griffin. Wanting something but being so afraid of what could happen. Failure? Oof. Success? Even worse. What would I do with that? Because the person in my daydreams who gets discovered and becomes a star wasn't really me. She was confident, talented, ready for anything. She was everything I wasn't.

How could I possibly live up to the version of myself that lived in my head?

"Let's get out of here," I said, craving air and space to process the events of the evening privately. My buzz had receded into a headache. What's more, I was starting to feel somewhat annoyed and, if I'm honest, a teensy bit resentful toward Griffin's commitment to a path that I wasn't sure I really wanted to take. I really just wanted to go see the Griffith Observatory and maybe take a movie studio tour, like normal tourists.

As we walked back to our hotel through the warm LA night, Griffin chattered excitedly about contracts and recording studios and how this was going to change everything. Meanwhile, I felt like I was floating somewhere outside my own body, watching my life unfold like a movie I hadn't auditioned to be in. It was 98 degrees, but I felt cold inside.

Chapter 6

A blast of arctic-like air nearly knocked us both out cold when Griffin opened the door to our hotel room. He had cranked the A/C up so high I'm pretty sure there was ice on the unit. Instead of relief from the heat, it was just going from one extreme to the other. And it definitely matched the chilly vibe that had breathed into the space between us since leaving the karaoke bar.

We crawled into the king-size bed silently from each side, trying to rub some warmth into our bodies with our hands. Earlier in the day, we had luxuriated in the cushiness of it all, making the most of the ample playground for sexy-time shenanigans. But that night, I found myself fighting the compulsion to maintain king-size distance between us against the need for the warmth of Griffin's body.

The cold beat me into submission and I allowed myself to let him wrap his body around me, making sure he felt the iciness of my feet between his thighs. He gasped a little but didn't really seem to mind. Then, he kissed the top of my head which thawed me enough to relax. I hated being mad at him.

Even after the easiest, quietest of days, falling asleep required locking into a scenario (a bedtime story, I guess, but ugh, that sounds so juvenile) and hopefully not getting too engaged with it. Exploring new pathways in the scenario could easily lead to being too mentally active to relax. The trick was finding that sweet spot of mind submersion that would allow me to drift off into glorious sleep. My mind was tired and I hoped sleep would find me quickly without any unpredictable mental detours.

* * *

The circle of chairs in the cozy room surrounded by packed bookshelves looked like we were about to discuss the latest read. But this was no book club. This was group therapy, my least favorite kind. It's supposed to help you feel like you're not alone in your weirdness, or even like you're not weird at all, and yet, my experiences were somehow so subjective that no one in the group ever seemed to get it. But maybe they all felt that way.

The therapist leading the group, Sasha, radiated therapeutic patience. I liked Sasha, but sometimes I felt like this was more than a job to her. Like we were her energy source, and she was feeding off our experiences to survive. Like she had an insatiable craving for new and interesting flavors of batshit crazy.

"Rory, would you like to share how your week went?"

Rory, a mid-thirties guy with a perpetual five o'clock shadow, ran his hands through his unwashed hair. "My wife caught me acting out my daydream again. It was the lottery one. Two hundred million this time."

"Did you buy the Scottish castle again?" inquired one of the other group members.

"No, this one went in a different direction. I bought a yacht. And my wife came upstairs to tell me something and found me

standing on our bed, casting an imaginary fishing line into the pile of dirty laundry, mumbling about how money can't buy happiness, but it sure can buy a hell of a fishing boat." He winced like he was reliving physical pain and buried his face in his hands.

"She asked if I'd been drinking and startled me so much I fell off the bed. Honestly, I wish I had been. At least that would explain why I was reeling in tube socks and calling them prize-winning trout."

A murmuring chorus of "ouches" and "oofs" and other grunts of understanding helped to ease Rory's discomfort. I could have sworn Sasha licked her lips. "Anyone else like to share?" she asked.

"I just freeze," mumbled Marnie from across the circle, her voice barely audible. "Sometimes for hours. My roommate found me standing in the kitchen yesterday, staring at absolutely nothing and just silently mouthing words. I'd been there for three hours living this whole other life where I'm a marine biologist discovering new coral species in the Maldives."

Dustin nodded knowingly. "I run. Like, literally sprint through my neighborhood while I'm mentally headlining at Coachella. My neighbors think I'm training for a marathon. At least they don't know I'm just trying to keep up with my fantasy DJ alter ego."

Sasha's eyes found mine with laser precision. "Cara?"

Ugh.

"Before I started working freelance from home, I got fired from, like, so many jobs," I said, picking at my sleeve. "Turns out spending all day in the bathroom at work instead of, you know, working, leads to a less-than-stellar performance review. The daydreams just... stage a hostile takeover of my brain, and I have to go find a place to be alone with them until the compulsion

passes. If I try to ignore it and focus on my work, I turn into this flickering ball of anxiety.

Sasha nodded sympathetically. "It certainly can feed itself in a vicious cycle..."

Suddenly Rory's body started to morph from his three-dimensional form into a two-dimensional cartoon, eyes going midnight black, then glowing red, and when he spoke, his voice was a growling whisper from out of a horror movie. "But what if none of us are real? What if this is just another daydream, and we're all characters Cara created because she's so pathetic she has to invent people who understand her desperate need to escape her meaningless existence?"

The other participants in the circle began transforming into cartoons in the same style as Rory, their eyes all glowing red. Surprisingly, Sasha was the last one to join the 2D world.

"What if you never wake up, Cara?" Cartoon Rory hissed, his voice echoing from everywhere and nowhere. "What if you're just dreaming that you're daydreaming, trapped forever in your own pathetic imagination? What happens to us?!"

* * *

I bolted upright in bed, heart hammering, sheets soaked with sweat. The hotel clock said 4:28 AM. Had I really been asleep that long?

Griffin stirred beside me. "Bad dream?" he mumbled.

I stared at the ceiling, wondering if I was really awake, or just inside another layer of the infinite Russian doll of my subconscious.

Chapter 7

We woke up to bright sunlight glaring through the cracks between the curtains the next morning. The pull was tantalizing. California sunshine. Forget sunbathing, inject it directly into my veins, please. Griffin was already awake but still in bed, doing that thing where he stretches every part of his body individually.

Considering how our plans for the day had now changed, I was faced with the reality of my packing choices. Based on our itinerary and planned activities, I had been of the disposition that packing swimwear would be a waste of suitcase real estate. Yes, on a trip to California. What can I say, I was never much of a swimmer. Conversely, I'm pretty sure that swim trunks were the first item Griffin packed in his suitcase.

"I may have made a tiny strategic error in my packing choices."

Griffin propped himself up on his elbows, sensing his vision of how our day was going to unfold might not match reality. "What kind of strategic error?"

"The kind where I brought three different cardigans instead of a single swimsuit."

"Car, we're going to a pool party."

"I know that *now.*"

"At River Deane's house."

"Yes, I'm aware of the venue."

"Where there will be a pool."

"Hence why it's called a 'pool party', yes, I know."

"Well, the party's not until four. We could go shopping," he suggested, kicking off the covers and then stretching his arms up and pointing his feet. I caught myself admiring the little tufts of golden hair in his armpits and the way the morning light caught the sparse hairs on his big toes. "I wouldn't mind watching your little butt trying on swimsuits as an appetizer."

The last thing I wanted to do was go shopping. "Hear me out... I have this." I held up a cute sundress and a light cardigan to keep the sun off my shoulders.

Griffin sat up fully, rubbing the back of his neck with one hand the way he does when he's a little bit 'over it', but knows he's not going to win the swimwear argument.

"You're going to be the only person at a pool party who refuses to get within ten feet of the pool."

"I'll be the mysterious one. The enigma. They'll be all, 'who is that fascinating prim looking woman lurking in the shadows?'"

"You'll be the weirdo in the cardigan."

"It's a *strategic* cardigan."

"Strategic how?"

"Strategic in that it allows me to attend a pool party without having to display my body in tiny strips of stretchy fabric in front of people who probably all have personal trainers and nutritionists and stylists, and those weird red light face masks that cost eight hundred dollars."

Griffin reached over and pulled me down to the bed so I was lying next to him, his face suddenly serious. "Car, you know you're beautiful, right?"

"I know I'm beautiful to you. There's a difference."

"Not really."

"Griff, honey, I love you for saying that, but let's be realistic here. We're about to go to a party with fancy LA people who look like they were carved out of marble by Renaissance masters. Meanwhile, I look like a walking vitamin deficiency."

"You're being ridiculous."

"Am I? Because last time I checked, my idea of contouring is making sure I don't have toothpaste on my face before leaving the house."

Griffin was quiet for a moment, gently pulling my tank top straps down and rubbing my bare shoulders. "Don't be scared. I'll be with you." I felt some of the tension drift away as he massaged. I moaned a little with the release.

Then, just as I was about to collapse in readiness for a full body treatment, he stopped and jumped out of bed. "You'll destroy in that cardigan. You'll be the chic, mysterious woman who's too sophisticated for water-based activities. I love it."

* * *

A few hours later, we were sitting in the back of a sleek black car with leather seats that had surely charioted far more illustrious bums than mine, and a driver who looked like he moonlighted as that actor from that movie. You know that movie where the guy does the thing and then the other thing happens and there's a big explosion and he walks away from the explosion in slow motion? You know the one I mean, it's a classic. Most likely a Robert Rodriguez flick.

"This is insane," I whispered to Griffin, trying not to leave fingerprints on anything in the interior that looked expensive, which was basically everything.

"I could get used to this," he whispered back, running his hands over the seats like he was a cartoon supervillain petting his beloved cat.

As the driver expertly navigated through the traffic, I tried to settle back into the exquisite leather seats and enjoy the sights through my window, but sitting in transit obviously meant my brain was going to wander.

* * *

Paige's office was carefully curated with calm colors and objects. I wondered if she had gotten them from an IKEA for therapists. I considered asking her, while she waited for me to respond to her question, but decided against it.

"I... I forgot what I was going to say, sorry," I admitted, picking at a loop of thread on my jeans, an unnecessary alteration made with love by my cat Clover.

"I've been thinking about what you said," she redirected. "How you often project a different version of yourself instead of who you really are."

"Doesn't everyone do that?" I said, now trying not to pick the skin around my fingernails, and failing. "Like, adapting to the situation? I mean, I don't act the same at work as I do with friends."

"That's normal. Adjusting your behavior for context is something we all do. But what you're describing is filtering yourself even in casual situations. It sounds more like masking."

"Masking?"

"When people suppress their natural traits to fit in. It's common with neurodivergent people. The brain learns to hide the parts that might seem 'too much.'"

Something clicked. "So, when I spend the whole time at a party monitoring my volume, my face, what I talk about... you mean, that's all masking."

"Yes. And the exhaustion you feel afterward is the cost."

I hesitated. "What's the alternative? Be myself and hope people don't run screaming?" I gestured with my hands and promptly sat on them after noticing how picked over they looked.

"What would happen if you tried?"

"They'd find me annoying."

"Would they?"

"Yes. I know from experience. Before I figured out how to tone myself down, I got left out of everything."

"That must've hurt."

I was quiet for a long time. The urge to fidget was super distracting. I bounced my knee.

"What would it look like," she asked gently, "to show up as your real, unedited self?"

"Terrifying."

"Anything else?"

"Lonely. What if the real me isn't lovable?"

"What if she is?"

I sat in the silence, sweaty and unsure.

Paige changed the subject. "Have you thought more about taking medication for your ADHD?" she asked.

"I'm not a kid. I'm not hyper. I'm practically catatonic half the time."

"Inattentive type is the most common presentation in women.

It just means you're hyperactive on the inside instead of on the outside where it's visible."

"I mean, I've made it this far in life without medication. I think I'm doing fine."

"You've achieved a comfortable life, yes. But not without significant struggle."

"Everyone struggles."

"Sure they do. But there are ways to lessen that struggle."

I felt my jaw tighten. "I need to struggle. Otherwise, how can I call myself an artist?" I was half-joking, but I guess Paige missed my sarcasm. Or maybe she didn't.

"Are you an artist?"

The question hit like a slap. In that moment, I wanted to overturn her stupid desk with the stupid zen garden on it and storm out. How dare she question whether I was an artist? But... was I really? So many things I wanted to make only existed in my head. When I did create something, I hid it from the world like a dirty secret.

It was a valid question.

***

As we cruised toward River's house, Griffin was peering through his window like a kid at a zoo, ogling the habitats of the rich and famous and hoping for a glimpse of one of the glorious creatures in captivity. Honestly, it kind of felt a little creepy, watching him point out houses that looked like fancy hotels and luxury cars that glistened in the sun like jewels.

"Look at that one," he said, gesturing at a mansion perched on a hillside. "That's someone's actual home."

"That's the guest house," the driver corrected, in his most

Animal Planet documentary narrator sounding voice. "The main house is behind those trees."

I stared at the roofline visible through the carefully manicured foliage and felt my nerves tingle. This was a world where people had guest houses that were bigger than regular houses, where sending cars for dinner guests was normal, and where being myself might be a luxury I couldn't afford.

But Paige's voice echoed in my head. *What would it look like to show up as yourself?*

Showing up as myself, empty-handed, even at River's insistence, suddenly seemed not just like a terrible faux pas, but a plot point in a horror movie where guests who don't bring a gift become a sacrificial offering to some monstrous folk deity. I gulped that thought down inside me like a freakin' cartoon.

We pulled through high security gates and then up a hillside driveway that curved through lush landscaping, and I tried to anticipate what was to come.

* * *

How to Catastrophize a Simple Social Interaction That Hasn't Happened Yet

1. Receive a social invitation. It could even be as vague as "We should hang out sometime." That's it. That's the whole trigger. Let the spiraling commence.
2. Try on seven outfits. Cry in three of them. Choose the first one but with slightly different accessories. Now start over because what if they think you're trying too hard?

3. Envision the entire event from start to finish. Visualize showing up, saying something weird, and being politely tolerated until the hosts suddenly remember there was something else they were supposed to be doing.
4. Rehearse your lines like it's opening night. Practice saying "The finish on this wine is magnificent" in several different intonations.
5. Imagine accidentally revealing something deeply personal. Like your weird rash or your fantasy about running away and starting a new life as a ribbon dancer.
6. Read their minds. You know exactly what everyone is thinking, and it's somehow everything you're thinking about yourself.
7. Pre-emptively cancel in your head with a text like "So bummed to miss it!!!" while bracing for no reply.
8. Have a decent time while behaving totally normal. When you get home, replay every moment in your mind to scan for all the ways you probably embarrassed yourself.

Note: This process works best when applied to interactions with zero actual consequences.

Chapter 8

To call River Deane's residence "a house" would be like calling the ocean a puddle. It spread out in front of us like the entrance to a sprawling luxurious resort. River was already waiting at the front entrance with his wife Naomi, both of them looking so astonishingly put-together I immediately wanted to go back in time to earlier that day and change my outfit. Go shopping after all. Maybe get a full face and body transplant, too.

River greeted us with a smile that went all the way up into his eyes. He looked rested and refreshed. "Cara, Griffin! So glad you're here."

Then Naomi stepped forward with a smile that was so warm it could have raised sea-level by several meters. "I'm Naomi," she said, extending her hand. "It's so great to meet you!"

To know River was to know Naomi. Their love story predated his fame, when he was still a struggling indie musician and she was a volunteer giving him orange juice after giving blood at a charity blood drive. He wrote her a song on the spot, a cappella, while all loopy and lightheaded from his donation. It was called *No Pulp Natalie.* She didn't have the heart to correct him until their second date.

While she always looked lovely in photos, her in-person

radiance was on a whole other level, and I hoped it wasn't obvious how instantly, how stupidly, and how damn *much* I wanted her to like me and be my friend. I was feeling a little loopy and lightheaded myself. Maybe she just had that effect on people.

"Thank you so much for having us," I gushed.

Naomi's effervescent sincerity put me right at ease. "Are you kidding? River's been talking about you two non-stop since last night." Naomi linked her arm through mine like I was the new kid in school and she was my designated recess companion. "Come on, let me show you around."

She led us around the side of the house to their so-called backyard, which looked like something you might see at a posh vacation destination. The pool was an intense blue, surrounded by lush landscaping that must have had its own staff to care for it. Multiple seating areas, a full outdoor kitchen, outdoor bathrooms, and what appeared to be a small greenhouse in the distance made the yard feel like an epic oasis of tasteful opulence.

"Holy shit," Griffin exclaimed, apparently having decided on leaving the last crumbs of any pretense behind in the back seat of the fancy car that brought us there.

"I know, right?" Naomi laughed. "It's ridiculous. River let me go a little overboard when we bought the place, but we do a lot of entertaining back here."

Three dogs suddenly came bounding up to us. A cocker spaniel, what looked like a border collie mix, and something small and undefined but super fluffy. They immediately surrounded us in an enthusiastic tongues-out, wag-happy welcome wagon formation.

"Meet our kids. Well, the canine ones, anyway," River said.

"That's Bogey, that's Star, and the little one trying to climb up your leg is Crumpet."

I knelt down to pet them, instantly feeling even more at ease. Dogs don't care if you're wearing the right outfit or saying the right things. They just care if you're willing to scratch behind their ears and tell them they're good babies.

"I love you," I said, crouching down to rub my face on Bogey's soft golden forehead, while Crumpet attempted to make my squatting lap his nap spot.

"They're rescues," Naomi offered. "Through Willow. You'll meet her today. She runs an animal rescue operation out of her house. We adopted Bogey and Star through her, and Crumpet just... well, Willow needed fosters and we tried but... you can guess how that went."

"Foster failures are the best kind of failures," I said. "We adopted our cats, Daisy and Clover, from a rescue. Went to look at one, came home with two because they were bonded and couldn't be separated."

"You'll have to tell Willow all about them, she loves rescue stories," Naomi beamed.

As if on cue, the sound of loud music suddenly stopping, and car doors slamming came from the front of the house, followed by the unmistakable chaos of multiple dogs greeting each other.

"That'll be them," River said. "Brace yourself."

Two more dogs rounded the corner, followed by another couple exuding enough charisma to make the cast of *Ocean's Eleven* step back for them (for all I knew, Clooney and Pitt were also on the guest list). Quinn "Styles" Chilton was a pretty-faced dude with impeccably coiffed, silver-streaked hair, glittering eyes and a pair of dimples that could knock you on your ass (if you're into dimples).

He had a wry smile and a vibe that suggested he knew exactly how charming he was and wasn't sorry about it. Think *Ferris Bueller* has returned from his stint working at a fast food joint on Venus followed by a long headlining lip-syncing tour across the galaxy to finally make a name for himself on the internet here on Earth. I recognized him immediately from his podcast, *Making It: Conversations about the Spark.*

But it was the woman beside him who immediately reminded me that I was from a completely different world. A retired model (but not *too retired*, if you know what I mean), Willow's ethereal, classic beauty was the epitome of Hollywood glam. She looked like she had just walked out of a magazine photoshoot for a pool party at a mansion, her hair a gleaming masterpiece of sunlight-catching wondrousness, her outfit both effortlessly casual and obviously designer.

Her very existence made me shake in my proverbial boots (which were actually huarache sandals). Here was my moment of truth. Masked Cara or Real Cara?

"You must be Cara and Griffin," Willow said, extending her hand with a kind smile. "We've heard all about you."

"Only good things, I hope," Griffin replied, summoning his own brand of good-old-boy charm.

"Well," Styles said with a grin that suggested he was about to say something either witty or slightly inappropriate, "River did mention that you won the contest with an essay about your first kiss." He gave a crooked smile. "Romantic, sentimental and expertly manipulative. Very well played, sir."

Before I could make a conscious decision to pretend not to care or deflect with self-deprecating humor, the real me just kind of... fell out.

"Definitely romantic," I said, making the leap. "Though I have to admit, Griff embellished a little for dramatic effect. The song wasn't actually playing when he kissed me. It came on about thirty seconds after, so... I guess he technically committed contest fraud?"

Griffin looked at me in surprise. We'd never discussed this particular detail, mostly because I'd never felt the need to correct his memory. Until then, anyway.

"There are a lot of ways to tell the truth," Styles said. "A little creative editing can make the truth even more..."

"Truthier," I finished his sentence, slightly embarrassed at having made up a new word in his impeccably articulate presence.

"Exactly," he agreed. "Journalistic accuracy is important, but it's nothing without a little *emotional* truth."

Of course, Griffin and I knew exactly how Styles and River knew each other, because we had consumed every piece of River Deane content available on the internet, including the legendary podcast episode from five years ago that had basically launched Styles from "guy with a microphone in his living room" to "guy with a microphone and millions of subscribers hanging on his every word."

"I have to confess something," I said, buoyed by how well the unmasked version of me was holding it together. "I've been a fan of your podcast since that episode River was on."

"You and everyone else, L-O-L," Styles said, pronouncing each letter like he was a human text message, which should have been annoying but somehow came across as endearingly self-aware. "That episode changed my life. It took me years just to get to a couple hundred subscribers, and then bam! A following and a viable career. And I owe it all to River."

River laughed, shaking his head with fond exasperation, having heard and told this story a quadrillion times already. "I still can't believe you were nervous about that interview. You made me think about songwriting in ways I hadn't considered before."

"Nervous?" Styles snickered. "I was terrified. This was back when I was doing the show out of my house with a setup of old gear I pieced together from garage sales and refurbished electronics stores. I'd been interviewing local artists for two years. Painters who sold their work at farmers markets, musicians who played coffee shops to scant, disinterested audiences, writers who'd self-published supernatural romantasy novels, you know, basically the entire starving artist cadre."

"Supernatural romantasy, you say. Tell me more," I said, because my brain immediately started workshopping plot points for a story about a realm where Orgasmia, the goddess of sex dreams, falls for her mortal human insomniac subject Dormian but they can only be together when he's in REM sleep.

"Don't encourage him," Willow said, rolling her eyes and teasing him with pretend boredom. "He'll start talking about the werewolf day trader series next."

I gasped. "Werewolves of Wall Street!"

"Anyway," Styles continued, undeterred, "River was playing this surprise intimate concert at a tiny venue in Highland Park, and I managed to convince myself to approach him with my tragic little recording setup. I felt like a pathetic fanboy."

"Hey man, I loved it. You just walked up to me after the show with that old banged up laptop and asked if I wanted to talk about the intersection of vulnerability and artistic expression,“ River said. “Most people ask for selfies. You asked for my thoughts on what it means to be authentic in creativity.”

“I was trying to sound professional. I’d practiced that line in my car for twenty minutes.” Styles looked slightly embarrassed, which just added to his likeability scale. “I figured you’d either say yes or have security escort me back to whatever sad corner of the internet I’d crawled out of.”

“But he said yes,” I said, wanting to hear the rest of the story even though I knew how it ended up. I was living vicariously through Styles’ courageous experience.

“He said yes, and then sat with me for hours talking about using your own experiences as inspiration and what it’s like when your most personal songs become bookmarks in people’s lives.” Griffin and I looked at each other knowingly. Styles looked at River with gratitude.

“The episode went live and suddenly I had listeners who weren’t my immediate family and friends. Real people were leaving real comments. I even had other artists reach out asking to be guests.”

A pang of envy mixed with the desire for recognition reverberated through me. It happened whenever I heard stories about people who’d taken a chance and discovered the universe was more generous than they’d expected. Styles started out daydreaming just like me, but instead of being paralyzed by it, he had taken a necessary brave step and stumbled into the life he envisioned for himself.

“Now look at you,” I said. “Internet famous and everything.”

“Internet famous is generous,” Styles said with a laugh that didn’t quite hide his ambition. “I’m more like internet-adjacent-to-famous. People recognize me at coffee shops, mostly because I go there every day and the baristas know my order."

I saw something in his eyes, a hunger for something bigger, a restless dissatisfaction. It was inspiring to actually meet someone who had accidentally started living his dreams by refusing to accept that they were supposed to stay safely locked up in his head.

"My favorite interview," I admitted, "besides the one with River, is the one you did with that painter who only works in shades of blue. That episode got me through some devastatingly boring workdays."

Styles' face lit up with visible pleasure. "Seamus Croft? Oh man, that guy was fascinating. Did you catch the part where he talked about synesthesia making blue taste like his lonely childhood?"

"I actually had a flashback to that during a zoom call with a client who was describing the color options for the device I was writing about. Imagine having to explain why I was having an emotional breakdown over the word *azure*."

Willow gracefully slid into one of the patio chairs nearby, striking a Pulitzer-winning pose through the simple act of sitting down. "What do you do that is devastatingly boring?" she asked, curiously, without a trace of malice. I suspected she had never once been bored in her life.

I was dreading this moment. I mean, I knew that at some point during the party I'd probably be asked what I do for a living. That, in and of itself, wasn't really the issue. In fact, telling people I write user manuals for sex toys usually gets an interesting reaction out of people, sometimes even a hilarious reaction. But talking to these particular people who lived the kind of lives I could only daydream about made me feel extremely inadequate.

"I write instruction manuals," I said. "In the beginning it was everyday appliances and electronics, but somehow I ended up working on more... specialized products. Recently I had to write instructions for a cock ring with fifteen different vibration patterns. Got a lot of use out of my thesaurus for that one."

There was a moment of silence that felt like it lasted approximately three years, and I immediately regretted everything. This was exactly why Masked Cara existed, to prevent moments like this where I said too much and made everyone uncomfortable and proved that I was fundamentally unsuited for polite society.

Then, laughter. Styles' reaction was especially joyful, but there was nothing about his laughter that seemed like he was laughing *at me*. Have you ever met a person that made you feel like you were special to them somehow, even after knowing them for all of five minutes? He was like that.

"Amazing. Do you get to keep the uh... devices?"

"She does," Griffin said with a devilish grin, "and let me tell you, my wife takes her job very seriously, and I'm happy to be of service for her field-testing and research."

"Cool job," Willow said, unironically, with a tone of respect. "Someone has to make sure people know how to use their toys safely. That's basically a public service."

"That doesn't sound devastatingly boring to me," said River. It was a good point.

"There are definitely things I love about my job. But having to sit through project meetings is not one of them. My mind tends to wander," I put it mildly.

A chorus of nods and agreements rang out.

"I hear that. The business side of things was never my forte either," River agreed. "I just want to make music."

He raised his glass to mine, and then a mass clinking of beverages ensued, and I realized I was having actual fun. These gorgeous, successful people who had previously inspired intimidation and envy in me were suddenly inspiring a different sort of feeling.

As Naomi refilled my wine glass and little puppy Crumpet flopped onto my feet like a tiny warm blanket with a heartbeat, I heard Paige's voice in my head. *What if the real you is lovable?*

Chapter 9

The gathering grew into a perfect California evening where the light had turned everything golden and it basically felt like being inside a postcard. More guests, mainly friends and colleagues of the non-famous variety (no Clooney or Pitt, which was probably for the best), had arrived while the six of us were getting acquainted. River and Naomi's twin teenaged daughters, Rowan and Gemma, had joined and were taking selfies together by the pool. It was a low-key hang that felt refreshingly normal, if you could call anything about this situation normal.

The increasing number of guests meant that it was time for me to transform into the resident wallflower, as is my usual style. If it's not clear by now, large groups kind of irk me. That's when I fade like Homer Simpson into the bushes, preferring to observe the interactions unfolding around me.

Enjoying the crisp rosé wine, I took in the stunning scenery and made sure to snorgle the four-legged fluffy guests whenever they approached. I considered for a moment whether "professional pet cuddler at parties" could be a job, then quickly filed that idea under "not if that means I have to go to parties every day, even if there are pets."

I'd positioned myself in what I considered the optimal

party location. Close enough to the conversation clusters to listen, yet far enough from the pool to maintain my carefully constructed dry-land mystique.

Griffin, meanwhile, had fully assimilated into one of the beer-and-banter clusters near the grill, laughing with a group of people I'd been introduced to briefly. They all seemed to be operating on a natural California wavelength that I felt blocked out of. He held a bottle of some local craft suds, and looked completely in his element. I envied it, which also made it mildly annoying.

Over by the pool, Styles was in the middle of telling an amusing story to a small group about a podcast guest who'd insisted on conducting the entire interview while juggling. To demonstrate the chaos, Styles was juggling his own set of invisible balls with dramatic hand gestures that were getting progressively more animated as he got to the good parts. I remembered the guest he was talking about and decided to float over to listen in.

That's when Styles, reaching the climactic moment of his juggling story, threw his arms wide. His hand connected with my face, specifically my prescription sunglasses, and I stumbled backward, crashing into the pool with a loud splash that alerted everyone to my folly.

This. This is why I stay away from pools. To be fair, I can picture exactly what it must have looked like and I'm quite sure it would have been hilarious if it were happening to someone else in a movie instead of to me in real life.

The water was thankfully warm, *so I got that going for me, which is nice,* I thought, as I sank toward the bottom of the deep end. Once the initial shock wore off, I started kicking my way toward the surface, only to be met with the unexpected sensation of being hooked with an arm. Someone had jumped in after me and was pulling me to the pool's edge, which was very chivalrous but completely unnecessary. I'm not a fan of swimming, but my childhood swimming lessons had sufficiently armed me with the ability to get myself out of this embarrassing, but not life-threatening situation.

That someone turned out to be Styles, who promptly let go of me and then surfaced next to me with a concerned expression and my glasses in his hand.

"Are you okay?" he asked, treading water next to me.

"I'm fine," I managed, taking my glasses from him and trying to put them on despite the fact that my hands were shaking from adrenaline and the embarrassment of being rescued like a damsel in distress when I was perfectly capable of rescuing myself, thank you very much. "Thank you for the rescue, but I actually can swim."

Styles smiled apologetically as he found his own sunglasses floating in the pool and reapplied them to his face, his normally voluminous hair all drenched to his head. "I didn't want to assume. You're not wearing a swimsuit, so I figured, better safe than sorry."

"I appreciate the gesture," I said, swimming toward the edge of the pool, realizing that it was his dramatic arm gesture that had gotten me into this mess. I swam to the ladder to get out, but then changed my mind when I saw that my white sundress was now transparent and clinging to me, probably revealing more than anyone at this party had bargained for.

That's when I heard Griffin's voice, cutting through the general party chatter with an edge that suggested he was not entirely pleased with the current situation and was about to make that everyone else's problem.

"Dude. She can swim."

I looked up to where Griffin was standing, and through my water-spotted glasses I could see that on a scale between concern and annoyance, his expression had blown past annoyance and landed somewhere firmly in the pissed-off zone. Add to that a side of territorial masculinity that was uncharacteristic for him. He glowered at Styles.

"Griff..." I started, but Styles was already responding with diplomatic bewilderment at Griffin's thinly veiled hostility at his heroic impulses.

"Sorry, man, I didn't know she could swim. It's my fault she fell in, and jumping in to help just seemed like the right thing to do."

"You didn't do anything wrong," I said firmly. "You were trying to help. Thank you."

But Griffin was not swayed by my fineness with the situation. "I'm just saying, maybe jumping in after her was a little presumptuous."

The word "presumptuous" hung in the air like an awkward party guest who'd overstayed their welcome and was now making everyone else uncomfortable. I could feel the other party guests trying very hard to pretend they weren't witnessing this spectacle.

Styles, to his credit, was clearly trying to de-escalate. "You're right. I should have assessed the situation better before jumping in. I was just reacting on instinct."

"Yeah, well, your instincts were wrong."

"Oh my God, Griffin, stop," I said as I finally climbed the ladder out of the pool. "Can you please just chill and grab me a towel? You're making this into a thing. It doesn't need to be a thing."

Griffin looked stricken, as if he was suddenly worried about what all his new fancy friends would think about him being "that guy" at the party. His tone shifted toward apologetic, even if his words didn't quite get there. "I'm not... making it a thing." Griffin tossed me a towel, his head lowered with self-awareness that maybe he was, in fact, making it into a thing. I reached for it but it flew over my head and landed in the pool.

Fuck it. I climbed out of the pool, very aware that I was regaling a group of people I'd just met with everything they never wanted to see, dripping wet and looking like I'd shown up to a wet tee shirt contest in a dress, my braless 34Bs on display. My strategic cardigan was heavy and sliding down my arms like it didn't want to be seen with me.

Naomi, bless her socially competent heart, appeared at my side with a dry towel. "Come on," she said, swiftly wrapping the towel around me. "Let's get you into some dry clothes." She guided me toward the patio doors. Behind us, I could hear what sounded like the beginning of a meek reconciliation between Griffin and Styles, but Naomi had whisked me inside before I could be sure.

"I'm so sorry," I said, following Naomi into the house while trying not to drip too much on her extremely polished and slippery looking floor. "I can't say this is not how I imagined this would go, but I definitely hoped for better."

"Are you kidding? That was barely even a thing." Naomi's kindness was like a salve for my soul. As we made our way through the halls of the massive, impeccably styled, unstuffy art gallery of a house, I imagined her opening a bedroom drawer and offering me a soft dry tee shirt and some cozy sweatpants, and happily pulling them onto my body for some much-needed comfort and a respite from trying to be prim and proper.

Chapter 10

I emerged from Naomi's infinity-sized dressing room looking as if I had been styled by Hollywood's most in-demand fashionista. "Oh, that's CUTE on you! I haven't even had a chance to wear that dress yet." Apparently, Naomi's definition of 'cute' was pretty much my definition of 'glamorous'. I didn't want to imagine what she thought of the outfit I arrived in, or worse, what I had been hoping she'd offer me.

"Are you sure this is okay? I'm seriously fine in a tee and shorts," I said, terrified that I would drip barbecue sauce on the chic fabric.

"You look divine. Now get back out there." She flashed a gleaming grin at me that felt like being smiled at by the sun.

By the time Naomi and I returned to the party, a mild tension from the Great Pool Rescue Controversy was still in the air, even though the incident was now over. The other guests had resumed their conversations about real estate prices and the optimal brewing time for cold brew coffee, while Griffin awkwardly sipped on his beer, looking for a conversation to join. Styles had stripped down to his swim trunks and was wringing out his clothes by the pool. But things were calm, and I hoped an 18th century style duel had been avoided.

I glanced at River, who hadn't given any indication that the mishap was something he should get involved in or worked up about. He continued working at the grill as if nothing had even transpired.

"Is River always so... even?" I asked Naomi.

"You have no idea," she gushed. "He's a mountain in a hurricane, that one."

"Sounds like a song he'd write."

"Funny you should say that. I know it looks like he's oblivious, but he soaks up everything. Little dramas like that do find their way into his songs from time to time."

I was about to ask which of his songs might have started out as real life kerfuffles, when Willow, who by this time had shed her outer layer of pool party attire to reveal a jaw-dropping bikini adorning her smokeshow body, came to sit on one of the comfy chaise lounges near where Naomi and I were standing. She winced as she stretched her neck from side to side and rolled her shoulders.

"Ugh," she said, catching me looking. "My neck and shoulders have been killing me. I feel like I'm turning into Quasimodo." As if she could, ever.

"Have you tried massage?" I asked, then immediately realized that asking a model living in LA if she'd tried massage therapy was probably like asking if she'd tried breathing or drinking salmon sperm smoothies. Of course she'd tried massage.

"Oh God, yes. I've tried everything. Swedish massage, deep tissue, hot stone, cupping, acupuncture, that weird thing where they tap a tuning fork on a Himalayan salt crystal and *ohm* the pain away. I even tried one of those massage guns that is basically like a mini jackhammer. Nothing sticks.

The pain goes away for a day and then comes back with a vengeance."

Griffin drifted over then, summoned by the mention of his vocation. This was his chance to be remembered for something other than being the "don't rescue my wife" guy. It was practically handed to him on a silver platter.

"What type of pain is it?" he asked, sliding smoothly into his massage therapist persona. "Sharp, dull, radiating? Does it get worse when you move your head in certain directions?"

Willow looked at him a little sus and said nothing. "I'm an RMT," Griffin explained, and her eyes lit up. "Oh, it's like a constant ache right here," she said, gesturing to the space between her neck and shoulder, "and it gets worse when I'm stressed or when I sleep wrong or basically whenever my body feels like reminding me that I'm not twenty-five anymore."

"That sounds like classic upper trap tension," Griffin said, slipping into full diagnostic mode. "Probably some levator scapulae involvement too. It's usually not just one muscle, more of a pattern that gets worse with stress or posture. Most people just chase the pain instead of treating the underlying mechanics."

I watched him explain the biomechanics of shoulder tension with... I guess you could call it passion. And honestly, I was proud of him. It was cool to see him get so excited about helping people, even if it meant he was showing off a little. He was good at what he did, and I didn't begrudge him that.

"The problem," Griffin continued, "is that it's very easy to just focus on the most obvious knots. But if you don't address the whole kinetic chain, the tension just comes back. You've got to release the scalenes first, then work down through the upper traps, and finish with some focused work on the insertion points."

Now he was showing off *a lot*, and Willow was listening with rapt attention. "Sounds like you really know your stuff," she said. "How do I even ask my massage therapist for that?"

Willow had just given Griffin the opportunity to demonstrate his therapeutic magic, which would have been the normal, helpful thing to do. Instead, he glanced over at Styles with pointed intention and said, "Well, I could show Styles the technique. That way he can help you out when this flares up."

Oh. OH. I saw exactly what was happening. This was Griffin's version of an olive branch wrapped in a thinly veiled message of "I don't touch other men's wives outside of a professional clinic setting, unlike others who perform unnecessary pool rescues for hero points." It was passive-aggressive peacemaking disguised as therapeutic assistance, and I had to admit it was kind of brilliant in its petty sophistication.

I could tell from Styles' slightly furrowed eyebrows that he was also picking up on what Griffin was throwing down. He seemed to consider Griffin's offer for an intense moment, and then, knowing full well this could be a trap but not wanting to deny Willow something that could help her, he played his chess piece.

"Well, sure," he said cautiously. "I've tried to help before, but I admit I don't really know what I'm doing."

"Right, well, technique matters," Griffin said, returning to his magnanimous state. "Here, I'll demonstrate on you first so you can feel what it's supposed to feel like."

Not my husband giving an impromptu massage lesson to the man he'd been practically growling at twenty minutes earlier, am I right? Things had certainly taken a weirdly unexpected turn, and I wasn't sure whether to be concerned or aroused. Honestly, it was a little of column A, a little of column B.

Griffin stepped behind Styles and began the demonstration while he explained the technique in a calm, teacherly voice. "Okay, so you want to start here, right at the base of the skull, and use your thumbs to apply pressure along the suboccipital ridge..."

Styles closed his eyes as Griffin worked his magic on him. "Wow," he said, his voice slightly muffled because Griffin had him positioned with his head tilted forward. "That's... wow. That's incredible. I didn't realize how much tension I was carrying up there."

"Stress and desk work," Griffin said, continuing his work. "Plus, you probably sleep on your stomach, which can wreak havoc on your spine."

"I do sleep on my stomach. How did you know that?"

"Twenty-five years doing this job. I can diagnose sleeping positions from across the room just by looking at someone's posture."

I fought the urge to clap. Griffin was putting on a pretty good show, and while I knew it wasn't completely altruistic, it was a relief to see him in helper mode, which was one of the qualities I admired most about him.

"Okay," Griffin said, stepping back as Styles rolled his shoulders. "How does that feel?"

"Miraculous," Styles said, rotating his head from side to side with wonder. "I'm impressed. Thank you."

"Now try it on Willow," Griffin said, positioning himself where he could observe and correct Styles' technique.

"Remember, start at the suboccipitals, work systematically down through the upper traps, and don't forget to check the scalenes."

Willow adjusted herself in her chair with eager anticipation, and Styles moved behind her and began applying what he'd just learned.

"Like this?" he asked, placing his thumbs at the base of Willow's skull.

"You got it. Now remember, you're not trying to dig through the muscle, you're trying to encourage it to release. Think of it as a conversation, not a wrestling match."

I watched Styles work through the technique Griffin had just demonstrated on him, his movements becoming more confident as Willow's shoulders began to visibly relax.

"Oh my God," Willow breathed, her voice suddenly sounding slightly drugged. "This is... this is actually working. I can feel the tension just melting away."

"That's the levator scapulae releasing," Griffin said with the pride of a teacher whose student was exceeding expectations. "Keep working along that line, but remember to check in with her about pressure."

"Perfect pressure," Willow murmured. "Don't stop. Ever. I'm serious, I might never let you stop doing this."

I looked around at the other party guests, some of whom were politely pretending not to watch this impromptu massage therapy session while others were clearly fascinated by the whole thing.

"This is so cool," Styles said, working through the technique with growing confidence. "I can feel the knots releasing under my hands."

"That means you're doing it right," Griffin said, like he

was proud of his protégé. "Most people think massage is just about applying pressure, but it's really about listening to what the tissue is telling you and responding appropriately."

Willow made a sound that was somewhere between a sigh and a moan of relief. "I think you just fixed three months of chronic pain in about ten minutes. So much better than that Swedish massage therapist who charged me two hundred dollars to basically handle me like Salt Bae slapping a steak."

"I wish Bernard was here to see this," said one of the other party guests, a woman wearing a flowy dress I'd been introduced to earlier whose name I'd forgotten in the chaos of trying to remember everyone else's names. "He just pokes random spots and asks if that's better."

As Styles finished the massage and Willow sat up looking blissfully pain-free, I noticed something had shifted in the group dynamic. The tension had released not only from Willow's shoulders, but from the spaces between people that had previously been infused with drama.

"You," Willow said, pointing at Griffin with the fervor of a recent convert to a new religion, "are officially my favorite person at this party. Possibly my favorite person in all of Los Angeles."

Griffin beamed. "Happy to help," he said, but I could tell he was pleased by the praise and feeling much better about things now that he'd covertly one-upped Styles in the most gentlemanly way possible. A duel had, in fact, taken place. Dominance asserted, balance restored.

And as I watched Styles thank Griffin for it while Willow relaxed into her chair wearing a contented grin, I too was feeling a little better about the way this side adventure was unfolding.

Chapter 11

"Hey Willow," said the woman in the boho flowy dress whose name I suddenly remembered (Magda, it was Magda), "how's Henry doing? He's at UCLA, right?"

Willow smiled. "Yeah, second year. He's nailing it. Way too busy to text me back, which I'm told is a sign of healthy independence."

"Mine just discovered you can't microwave tinfoil," Magda said. "College is wild."

Styles, now seated again and visibly looser in the mood region thanks to Griffin's magic hands, chimed in. "Delphine is opting out of the college track entirely. She's currently pursuing a career in becoming famous for... being extremely online."

River, who had watched the massage part of the evening unfold from a bemused distance as he manned the barbecue grill, almost choked on his beer as he stifled a laugh. "Apple doesn't fall too far from the tree."

Styles cast River a look that could almost have been read as *watch it,* but quickly softened. He added dryly, "Which, to be fair, is also how I make a living. Thanks, River. But I like to think mine involves a tad more critical thinking."

River rolled his eyes. "Influencer is a valid career choice

nowadays."

"It's certainly a choice," Styles replied. "Her boyfriend's the real star, though. He's got sponsorships, a brand deal with some kind of mushroom coffee company, and a skincare line. I can't keep up. I just hope she'll be able to jump off his coattails into her own thing."

Willow reached over and nudged him gently as if to say *be kind to her even when she's impossible.*

"Is she still in LA?" Magda asked.

"She is, but... I don't see her much anymore," Styles said, and there was a flicker of something in his expression. It looked like a combination of wistful affection and disappointment, with a long finish of unwilling estrangement.

"They're figuring things out," Willow said gently. "It's complicated."

"That's actually how Willow and I met," Styles redirected, turning toward me like he suddenly realized I didn't know this story. "Through Delphine's boyfriend."

"Timo," nudged Willow, as if to say, *he has a name.*

Styles continued. "He's very active as an influencer."

"And has a very persistent PR team," Willow added.

"Timo," Styles explained, miming air quotes around his daughter's boyfriend's name, "was throwing an event to promote his new merch drop. This was a few years ago, obviously. Delph begged me to go. I think she promised him I'd live-post the whole thing, which, spoiler alert, did not happen. But I did notice this exquisite lady ogling me the whole evening," he smirked and tilted his head toward Willow.

"I was not ogling. If I remember correctly, it was the other way around," Willow said, smiling. "And I was only there because Timo's PR team booked me to appear. I was trying to leave. When I tried to maneuver around Quinn's eyeballs popping out of his head, I unfortunately spilled red wine on his brand new, white, designer sneakers. Total disaster."

It shouldn't have shocked me to hear Willow refer to her husband by his given name, but it did anyway.

"Those were expensive sneakers, but I didn't mind, much," Styles said, grinning. "It was the best accident that's ever happened to me."

Willow rolled her eyes but looked pleased. "The shoes didn't survive. But the rest is history." Willow then stood up, stretched languidly, and announced she was going to refresh her wine.

"Anyone else need anything from the kitchen?" she asked, but her eyes hung on Styles like she was sending him messages telepathically.

Styles, clearly fluent in her telepathic language, shook his head. "I'm good."

Willow headed toward the house, but not before flashing Styles a *come hither* look with a heavy intensity. If there was one word in the English language for *we need to talk right now*, the look in Willow's eyes would be next to it in the dictionary.

Styles waited approximately thirty seconds, long enough to not be obvious, but not long enough to fool anyone who was paying attention, before excusing himself to "check on something in the kitchen."

Griffin had trapped River in a conversation about rotator cuff injuries in musicians, so he didn't notice the domestic intrigue unfolding. But I had a perfect view through the kitchen window, and what I saw was definitely not a contented couple casually refreshing their beverages.

Willow was talking animatedly, her hands moving like she was trying to convince him of something important. Styles, meanwhile, had assumed a posture that said *I'm listening, but I don't like where this conversation is going.* His arms were crossed, and he was leaning slightly back, yet deeply focused on her.

The conversation seemed to escalate quickly. Willow's gestures became more emphatic, and I could see her pointing toward the backyard through the window. Styles uncrossed his arms only to run his hands through his hair. Whatever this argument was about, he was not winning.

Through the window, alone with his wife, he suddenly seemed like a completely different person. The charming, confident guy who knew how to work a room now seemed insecure, reserved, and conflicted. He never took his eyes away from her, and the look on his face was loving, but hurt.

After a few minutes, they returned to the backyard together. Willow looked like she'd just won her argument through sheer persistence, while Styles looked defeated.

The sun had officially disappeared below the horizon and the sky was beginning to darken when thousands of string lights flicked on all around us, adding an indescribable magic to the atmosphere. Willow held her wine glass to her chest as if she was relishing the moment.

"That could not have been more perfect if I had planned it myself," Willow said, sipping her wine and savoring it while entranced by the new mood lighting, before turning her attention to Griffin and me. "Actually, Quinn and I were wondering if we could ask you guys something."

She looked directly at us with an eager and curious expression. I had no idea what had just transpired between her and

Styles, and I had even less of an idea what she wanted to talk to us about, but I had an icky feeling that the pool incident wasn't going to be the only drama of the evening.

"Sure," Griffin said, because he had evidently not eavesdropped on their private conversation. But wait, is it really eavesdropping if you don't actively try to hear what's being said and just watch through a patio window that is in full view of everyone and infer from expressions and body language and make all kinds of assumptions?

"We should go inside for this," Willow suggested, glancing around at River, Naomi and the other guests. "More private."

Well, there it was. Nothing good ever came from conversations that required privacy at dinner parties. This was how people ended up involved in pyramid schemes or being asked to participate in an art project that involved nudity and interpretive dance. Something was definitely afoot. And yet, with Griffin's hand pulling mine, I found myself following them inside.

Despite the huge size of the space, River's lavishly decorated living room felt much more intimate than the expansive backyard. The perfect environment for a surprise intimate conversation.

"So," Willow began, taking a seat on one of the white leather sectional sofas that rimmed an elegant mid-century style conversation pit like two Cs facing each other. She patted the cushion next to her for Styles, who perched there tentatively. We sat adjacently, so that no one would have to yell across the pit. "Quinn and I have been together for a few years now..."

"Best few years of my life," Styles interjected, with the

fervor of someone who needed everyone in the room to understand exactly how much his wife meant to him.

"...and we have a great relationship," Willow continued, smiling at him affectionately. "But we've been talking about... exploring. You know? Trying new things. Adding some excitement."

Griffin, bless his oblivious heart, was nodding along like this was perfectly normal living room conversation between people who barely knew each other. "For sure. It's important to keep things fresh. We tried to bone on the airplane on the way here! Not sure I recommend that, though."

Oh, Griffin.

"Yeah, well, whatever works!" Willow said enthusiastically, gaining momentum. "So, we've been thinking about... well, we've been thinking about maybe trying... swapping."

The word landed in the middle of the four of us like a grenade with the pin pulled out. I felt my brain do that thing where it stops processing information and just starts buzzing with static while trying to figure out if I'd heard correctly.

Swapping? As in swinging? I understood the definition, I just didn't understand how it could be something that Willow was suggesting to Griffin and me, two people she'd met approximately two hours ago, in the living room of a country music star while I was still wearing his wife's borrowed dress because I'd fallen into a pool like a sitcom character.

"Oh," I said, which was the most coherent response my brain could manage under the circumstances.

Griffin, meanwhile, had perked up with a hopeful glimmer in his eyes. "For real?"

FOR REAL? That was his response to being propositioned? *For real?* Like someone had just offered him free sportsball tickets at Whothefuckcares Stadium?

"Yes, for real," Willow confirmed, and I could see Styles looking like he wanted to sink through the sofa and disappear into another dimension. "I mean, we've never done anything like this before, but we've talked about it, and we think it could be... fun."

Fun. She thought swapping spouses with virtual strangers could be *fun*, like miniature golf or karaoke or any other recreational activity that didn't automatically involve nudity and the potential destruction of more than one marriage.

Nude mini golf though...

"The thing is," Willow continued, yanking me out of my imagined nude mini golf excursion, "it can't be with people we know well. That would make it too complicated. And it can't be with random strangers because that's just... risky. But you two meet the criteria. You're not from here, so there's no risk of things getting messy locally. You're both attractive and seem like good people. And..." She looked directly at me. "I think Quinn is fond of you."

I looked at Styles, who had gone approximately the color of a ripe tomato and was now staring so intently at a spot on the floor I thought he might burn a hole in it. I didn't like seeing him like this. For someone who was used to being on camera all the time and leading conversations with all kinds of people, he sat there looking like a teenager whose teacher had just outed his crush to the entire class. I hated that for him.

"I mean..." he started, then gave up and just gestured vaguely in my direction while continuing to study the floor. And I guess I was staring at him or something because then Willow said, triumphantly, "See? Chemistry!"

In that moment, all I could hear was the blood whooshing in my ears in time with my elevated heartbeat. I had imagined approximately eleventy-billion ways this evening could have gone. This was not one of them. In fact, this was not how I'd imagined any evening going, ever, in any possible situation or universe. I had no prior preparation for this.

And so, before I could formulate a response that was more coherent than another "Oh," the part of my brain that needs to protect me from threats like answering the phone or deciding which ice cream flavor to try slipped into a semi-conscious state, abandoning the present to explore at least one scenario to help me process what I was hearing.

* * *

I was in the same living room, but now Styles and I were the only ones there. The lights were dimmed, there was music playing softly from somewhere, and we were sitting on the curved sofa with several cushions between us, looking at each other like two kids who escaped their parents' soirée to show each other their ding-dong and woo-woo but were now not so sure about it.

"So," Styles said, running his hand through his hair, "this is happening?"

"I guess," I replied, acutely aware that somewhere else in the house, Griffin and Willow were presumably... doing their part, while we sat here fully clothed and awkward.

"We don't have to," Styles said quickly. "I mean, we could just... talk. Pretend we went through with it."

"Ironically, that feels like cheating," I said. "You know what I mean? If they go for it and we don't, we're cheating them, and ourselves, aren't we?"

"What do you want to do?"

I thought about it. "Honestly? I want to go home and pretend this never happened. But since that's not an option, I guess I want to understand why we're here. Like, what is it about this situation that's supposed to be appealing?"

A fascinating conversation ensued. Styles talked about feeling like he was constantly trying to prove he was worthy of Willow, like he'd won some cosmic lottery when she agreed to marry him and he was worried that if he didn't go along with the idea, she might go have adventures on her own, and that would be even worse.

I told him I was exhausted from spending too many years trying to be easy to love. How I'd gotten so good at adjusting, smoothing out the ragged edges, that even I wasn't sure where the act ended and the real me began. I admitted I had this constant fear of being too much and not enough, simultaneously. That I spent a lot of time pre-rejecting myself before anyone else could.

"That's rough," he said, validating my entire existence with two simple words and zero resistance.

"Why does everything always have to be so complicated?" I griped, as if no one on the planet had ever made that observation before.

"I know," he sighed quietly. "It's moments like this I try to draw on my faith for strength."

"Your faith?" I inquired, tentatively. "I would never have guessed you were religious."

"Well yeah, if you count my unwavering belief in Our Lord and Savior Kermit the Frog."

I laughed. "You set me up."

He chuckled back. "Yeah, I guess I did."

"But I have to agree with you on that," I admitted. "Everything

I know in life I learned from Sesame Street."

"Amen to that," Styles declared, raising his wine glass for a clink of like-minded fellowship.

And somehow, that conversation sparked something. Not just common ground, but an actual connection. I don't know if I would call it chemistry, necessarily. It was more like recognition of each other's vulnerabilities. And suddenly, going along with the swap plan didn't feel like crossing a line, it felt like a compulsion.

So, when we closed the distance between us on the sofa and kissed, it didn't feel impulsive or wrong, it felt inevitable. Because once you've bared your soul to an attractive human being who is under these specific circumstances, it seems rude to not go with it.

The kissing led to more than kissing, and before I knew it, our clothes began to be peeled away. The sofa felt ridiculously soft against my skin, and I hesitated.

"This is a lot of very expensive leather," I observed.

"It would be a shame to mess it up," Styles agreed.

We looked at each other, then at the sofa, then back at each other.

Fuck it.

Still, as the intimate relations got underway, it became apparent that this furniture was designed more for looking impressive than for gettin' it on. As our bodies warmed, the leather stuck to our skin, which resulted in some very unappealing and yet hilarious sound effects every time we moved and tried to peel ourselves away from the sofa.

"The gross sound effects are a real turn-on," Styles observed.

"Did you just fart?" I joked.

"That was the sofa!" he insisted.

"I'll believe you this time."

It turns out, peeling yourself off sticky leather while maneuver-

ing another person's body is a lot of sweaty, drippy work. Styles was positioned above me, which meant gravity was working against both of us, and when a drop of his sweat hit my eye, it felt like someone had squeezed lemon juice directly onto my cornea.

"Ow, shit!" I yelped, blinking rapidly while trying not to completely derail our momentum.

"Oh God, what happened?" he asked, immediately stopping.

"Your sweat is burning my eyeball, did you exfoliate with ghost pepper seeds this morning?" I yowled, tears streaming down my face.

"Oh! It's probably the sunblock," he said, looking apologetic. "I put on SPF 50 earlier because I burn like a vampire in direct sunlight. I'm so sorry, this wasn't exactly on my radar for today's activities."

"Sunblock is supposed to prevent burns, not cause them!"

"Should I get you a towel? Ice pack? New cornea?"

"Just maybe... different angle?" Despite the sting in my eyes, the actual sex part was too enjoyable to stop.

We shifted, laughing a little as we rearranged ourselves so that Styles was behind me, and any sweat drippage would land on my back. His hands found my hips again, he thrust himself into me, and we both leaned into each other's bodies.

There was more kissing, and a moan from him that hit me right in that spot deep inside me. You know the one, the same place that River's falsetto had hit during the concert, but this time it came with the physical sensation of Styles' pelvis rhythmically pounding against me from behind.

He felt incredible, but I wanted to look at his face. I was about to suggest he lay on his back so I could go cowgirl on him, but he began to pound faster and he was hitting me in just the right spot... when a powerful queef threatened to ruin the whole shebang.

I gasped. "That was the..."

"That was NOT the sofa. I felt that."

"Oh God, I'm sorry!"

"Don't apologize," he said breathily, clearly as close to cumming as I was. "Best. Queef. Ever."

He said those last three words in time with his final three thrusts, which reverberated through my whole body. We fell together on the sofa on our sides, facing each other, slick with sweat, which made the cushions feel slippery under our bodies.

"That was..." he whispered, still catching his breath.

"Yeah," I agreed, because sometimes "Yeah" is all you can say.

"Are we okay? I mean, emotionally?" he asked. "Do you need to flush your eye with water?"

I thought about it. "Emotionally, I think we're good. Ocularly, I might need some eye drops."

"There must be some around here somewhere," Styles said with theatrical urgency, immediately leaping up and yanking open the drawer of the nearest table in the conversation pit like he was handling a medical emergency. He rummaged through remote controls and coasters for about ten seconds before closing it and moving to the next one.

"You know there's no eye drops in River's entertainment center, right?" I said, watching him perform this ridiculous naked cabinet-searching routine.

"You never know," he said solemnly, opening another drawer full of charging cables. "Super famous people keep all kinds of things in weird places. Could be eye drops. Could be Grammys. Could be diamonds."

I started laughing so hard my knees came up to my chest, leaving a gross pool of moisture on the sofa. "Come here, you adorable weirdo."

He abandoned his fake search mission and dove back onto the sofa and hovered over me, which produced another drop of sweat that was about to release from his forehead. I wiped it away and pulled him down for a finishing kiss.

Chapter 12

The sound of someone clearing their throat yanked me back to reality, and I was flooded with the realization that just yesterday I was fantasizing about River Deane in a bathroom stall, complete with nearly flushed glasses. And now here I was, less than twenty-four hours later, mentally choreographing a sexual encounter with his friend (and someone whose work I admired) on River's sofa.

What was happening to my brain? Had the California air done something to my dissociation habits? Was I just going to work my way through every attractive man I met like I was collecting sexual daydream Pokémon cards?

"Cara?"

I don't recall who said my name. As I came to, I realized I was staring at Styles with what was likely a very strange expression on my face, while Willow waited for some kind of response to her swapping proposition. On top of that, my brain was trying to process the fact that I'd just mentally cheated on my husband with two different men in the span of two days.

What the fuck, me. Get it together.

"Sorry," I said, blinking rapidly to dispel the lingering images of my fantasy scenario. "I was just... thinking."

"It's a lot to think about," Styles said, and he sounded relieved that someone was acknowledging the magnitude of what had just been suggested. He also looked completely oblivious to the fact that I'd just mentally ravaged him on his friend's sofa, thank fuck. I blushed, which he seemed to interpret as discomfort with the situation, rather than an admission of what had just occurred in my head.

Griffin, meanwhile, was looking between Willow and me like he'd already made up his mind and was waiting for everyone else to catch up. "I think it sounds neat."

Neat. My husband thought spouse-swapping with people we'd just met sounded *neat*, like it was a movie he'd heard good things about or a restaurant with positive reviews.

"Griffin," I said, using both syllables and a tone that implied *we need to have a private conversation before you commit us to anything life-altering*, but he was apparently too excited by the possibility of a new sexual adventure to pick up on my subtle communication cues.

"What? Come on, Car. When are we ever going to get another opportunity like this? We're in LA, we're with cool people, we're being spontaneous now, right? Why not go a little further?"

Why not go a little further. As if swapping spouses was just the next logical step in our vacation itinerary, right after seeing the Hollywood sign and trying that trendy restaurant everyone was talking about.

"An hour ago, you were practically beating your chest like a gorilla because Styles had the audacity to pull me up from the bottom of the pool. But you're okay with... this?" I gestured wildly and made sure to sound as incredulous as possible.

"This is completely different," Griffin replied.

"No shit."

"This is 100% four-way mutual agreement. We all get something out of it."

Griffin's rationale sent me into an internal rampage. *Oh, this is about consent? Are you serious? As in Styles didn't have your consent to rescue me? Like he should have said, "Hey man, you okay if I jump in after your wife, or do you want to be the hero?" Is that it?*

I looked at Styles, who unnervingly looked back at me like he had somehow tuned into my internal monologue. He seemed to be hoping I would be the voice of reason that would save him from having to disappoint his wife by saying no. Then I looked at Willow, who was watching me with wide doe eyes and a hopeful smile, biting her bottom lip slightly, like she'd just asked for a pony for her birthday. Finally, I looked at Griffin, who was practically vibrating with excitement at the prospect of riding Willow's birthday pony.

"I..." I started, then stopped, because I dared not say all the things I was thinking. How do you politely decline an invitation to swap spouses without sounding rude and judgmental?

"Actually," Styles interrupted, and I was saved, again, in a manner of speaking. We all turned to look at him. "I don't think this is a good idea." He followed his statement with a huff of air that sounded like he was blowing the idea away from him.

The relief that flooded through me was so intense I actually felt dizzy.

"Wait, what?" Willow turned to stare at her husband, looking surprised. "But we talked about this. You said you were open to it."

"I said I was open to the concept in theory," Styles said carefully, and I could see him struggling between not wanting to disappoint her and not wanting to do something that made him uncomfortable. "But in reality, right now, with these people we just met... I think maybe we should get to know each other better first."

"How much better do we need to know them? The whole point is that it's not complicated by friendship."

It was like watching a car accident. This was not the first time they'd had this argument, and it was obviously not going to be the last.

I was trying to think of something to say to break the increasingly uncomfortable tension. Preferably something along the lines of *we should go now*, when the sliding door to the backyard opened and River appeared, holding a large barbecue spatula, looking like he'd beaten fire and smoke into submission. He cracked a cute grin, showing a side to him that only his family and friends usually got to see. Oddly, it felt like Griffin and I had invaded his privacy by witnessing it.

"Sorry to interrupt," he said, wiping his hands on a professional-looking barbecue apron, "but dinner's ready. I think I've achieved the perfect char on these steaks, and if we don't eat them soon, well, let's just say the dogs will be eating better than us tonight."

Holy fucking relief. River had basically just thrown a life preserver to the four of us, drowning in an ocean of awkwardness.

"Perfect timing," Willow said, bouncing up from the couch with forced enthusiasm. I got the impression that she was absolutely not done with this conversation but was trying to maintain a cool exterior. "I'm starving."

River looked around at our little group, and I wondered if he could sense the weird tension that had been building in his living room while he'd been outside preparing our meal. If he did, he was too polite to mention it.

"Naomi's already got the sides set up outside," he said. "And I may have gone a little overboard on the wine selection, so hopefully everyone's prepared to make some questionable decisions about their booze limits."

"I think we've already covered the questionable decisions portion of the evening," I muttered under my breath, but apparently not quietly enough because Styles snorted with a nervous chuckle.

"What's that?" River asked.

"Nothing," I said quickly. "Coming!"

As we filed out of the living room toward River and Naomi's exquisite outdoor culinary table setting, I couldn't help but quietly muse to myself that this dinner party already was way more eventful than I'd bargained for. And the main course had only just begun.

Chapter 13

After everything that had happened at this weird-ass party, dinner was, thankfully, normal. It was your standard barbecue fare: steaks, burgers, sausages, and impeccably grilled vegetables. As I filled my plate, my mind drifted to an imagined but probably accurate vision of mama Naomi making boxed macaroni and cheese, the expensive one from Erewhon, for their girls in her opulent kitchen. High end box meal or not, the secret ingredient in boxed mac and cheese is always love.

River did a spectacular job at the grill, which shouldn't have surprised me because he was sort of turning out to be one of those people who's just naturally good at everything. Imagine being able to sing and play the guitar like that, *and* write songs that make people cry, *and* char meat to perfection at your Beverly Hills mansion? Who do you have to please in a past life to make that your reality? (And who did I piss off?)

"Damn this is good," Griffin said, taking a bite of delicious steak. "I know I saw you grilling, but are you sure you didn't secretly order this from a Michelin star steakhouse?"

"Thanks," River chuckled, looking pleased. "I've been practicing. When you're on the road for months at a time eating on the run, you develop a real appreciation for being able to cook something decent when you're home."

Styles started asking River about life on his latest tour, and River sat back in his chair with his wine, regaling us all with tales from the tour bus.

"On tour," River said, "I have to constantly remind myself to be grateful. All that time being in between places, hotel rooms that all look exactly the same, eating the same chain restaurant and room service food. It all blurs together."

"I remember that time you did a show in Paris and you asked the audience what country you were in. They did not like that," Naomi interjected. I recalled the show she was talking about. Phone videos from that concert went viral. So much booing *en français*.

"No, they did not," River laughed. "And I don't mean to sound like it's all bad, because it isn't. I get to see amazing places and play for people who love my music. But the worst part of it is missing stuff at home."

"Like what?" Naomi asked, already knowing the answer but wanting to hear it again. The way she listened to him tell these stories for probably the quadrillionth time, you'd think it was still all brand new to her.

"Just the regular, day-to-day normal stuff, like watching Rowan and Gemma grow up through video calls," River said. "Missing birthdays and Christmases because the tour schedule didn't line up with real life."

Weirdly, I was able to relate to what River was saying. I mean, obviously, my life was nothing like River's. I had not been *on tour*. But the idea of living two lives, simultaneously. The real one, and the *other* one in my head. Except in my case, I would sometimes find myself missing out on stuff in reality while I spent too much time in my imagination, pretending to live another more exciting reality.

"Do you ever think about quitting?" I asked. "Like, just walking away from the whole thing and doing something completely different?"

"Oh, sure. Especially after I've been away from home for months and I can't remember what it feels like to sleep in my own bed," he paused. "But then I remember that I get to make music for a living. I get to connect with people who want to give me money to hear me sing my songs in person. That's a unique blessing and not something you walk away from lightly."

"Plus," Naomi said, "I've seen what he's like when he's not making music. Nobody needs that energy in their life."

Everyone laughed, but my heart ached a little at what I was *really* missing. Living my life through creative expression, turning all the strange, secret stories in my head into something other people could relate to and be entertained by. If only I was brave enough to release them into the world.

* * *

As dinner wound down, we relocated to the fire pit which was already magically burning as if some invisible force had been kindling it and tending it in readiness for our arrival. The sparks floating up from the fire looked like fireflies against the darkening landscape. Evening turned into night and the fire pit chatter lulled into flame-based hypnosis. Gradually, the other party guests began drifting away, heading back to their own perfectly imperfect lives.

That left just the six of us. I wondered if that was our cue to retreat back to our hotel. It had been an eventful day (to say the least, holy shit), but the fire was nice, and I didn't want to be a party pooper. I just knew that Griffin wouldn't be ready until someone was physically dragging us back to the driveway and throwing us into a car.

"What about you, Cara?" Styles asked, turning my question to River around to me. "Do you ever think about doing something totally different?"

The question surprised me, because I had already been thinking about it since asking River the same thing. Why ask *me* that? I thought back to earlier, when it seemed like Styles had mentally tuned into my stream of consciousness for a moment.

"All the time," I said. I took a sip of wine, trying to decide how much truth I was prepared to share. "I mean, yes, I've always wanted to make things. As a kid I made my own comic strips. In high school I wanted to be in a band, and I confess I still have a mild but lingering longing for that. But when I finally grew up, I really wanted to be a writer."

"But you are a writer, Car. It's in your job title," Griffin reminded me.

"That's true, but *that* writing isn't for me. I do write for me, sometimes. But it never goes anywhere. I have this file drawer at home that's basically a graveyard of abandoned writing projects. Every now and then I stumble across them when I'm looking for tax documents or something, and I get all excited and think, 'Oh, I like these, I should do something with them.' Then I'll quickly close the drawer before the shame can fully set in."

"Like what?" Willow asked with sincere curiosity.

"Well, there's the screenplay I wrote about an Elvis Presley fanatic and journalist named Lucy who finds out he's still alive. Immortal actually, the result of a supernatural deal that ended up taking his voice away. And now he's DJing in a seedy bar in the middle of nowhere, and Lucy reports the story to bring him back into the mainstream, and all these tabloid-style events start happening in real life, like aliens and gangsters and whatnot. I called it *Lu's News*, which should have been my first clue that it wasn't exactly groundbreaking material."

"That sounds pretty funny," Naomi giggled.

"Then, there's my abstract expressionist 'graphic novel' about a girl from the landlocked north who runs away from home with her cat to Hawaii and they become a famous surfing duo."

River chuckled. "An abstract expressionist graphic novel?"

"It's exactly what you think. The art is all shapes and colors and all the components are symbolic of elements from the story. There's even an 'art language' glossary in the back."

"That's not at all like what I was thinking, but it sounds cool," River admitted.

"These ideas are so fun. What else?" Styles asked, leaning forward across the fire with interest.

"Well, there's the screenplay about a girl with sound-to-color synesthesia who becomes an artist's muse. I have a weird-ass story about a group of spirits in the afterlife going crazy watching their incarnated soulmate humans fuck up their lives in this plane of existence. Oh, and my children's TV series about a daycare for pets called *That Animal Show* where the kids leave their pets for the day and then the pets, who can talk when their humans aren't around, go on these wild adventures.

"Then there's my comic strip about the boy who turned

into a clown. I had like fifty strips drawn and plotted out an entire mythology about how clowns are made. Some put on makeup and act the fool, but some don't have a choice in the matter."

A muted but satisfying chorus of acknowledgments harmonized around the fire. I was on a roll now, like a beat poet who'd found my rhythm.

"And the big one. My full-length dystopian novel about a time in the not-too-distant future when teenagers who have only been exposed to AI-generated music controlled by corporations, and have never heard, seen or played real musical instruments before, start hearing echoes of music from the 1960s in their heads. They basically start a music-based revolution with their grandparents who are all part of a secret organized 'basement network' hiding troves of old music on analog formats from the government in secret basement hideaways. I called it *Sixty-Six.*"

"I love your ideas. Why didn't you try to get any of them made or published?" Styles asked, like he was puzzled by the psychology of my creative self-sabotage.

"Because they're unpublishable?" I said, though even as I said it, I wasn't entirely sure that was true. "I mean, *Sixty-Six* has a ton of copyright problems, and I'm not sure the story can really be told without the song lyrics and other pop culture references."

"You'd be surprised," River said. "There are ways around problems like that. I've seen stranger concepts become successful. There are a million ways to execute a solid idea."

"Easy for you to say. You're not the one who spent three months trying to write a query letter, then chickened out because what if they said no? Or worse, what if they said yes? What if *Sixty-Six* ended up in bookstores and everyone realized I was a fraud who'd somehow convinced the world that people even care what music kids are listening to in the future?"

"So, you chose to reject yourself before anyone else could," Willow observed. Her tone was gentle but blunt.

"Well, it's much more efficient. Why wait for the inevitable rejection letter when you can crush your own dreams in real time from the comfort of your home office?"

Crickets. My roll was over, but the silence that followed wasn't cold. It wasn't that they didn't get the joke, but that it wasn't a joke at all. It was silent recognition, like I'd just described something they'd all experienced.

"You know what's funny?" Styles said finally. "I started my podcast for exactly the same reason. I wanted to be the artist being interviewed, not the person doing the interviewing. But I was too scared to put my own work out there, so I figured I'd talk to other people about theirs instead."

"So now you're successful at something you never planned to do," I said.

"Yeah. Which makes me wonder what would have happened if I'd been brave enough to try what I actually wanted to do instead of what felt safer."

River leaned forward, poking at the fire with a stick, taking over the invisible fire-tending entity's job. "Here's what I think," he opined. "Most people spend their lives waiting for permission to be the person they want to be. Permission from other people, permission from the universe, permission from some imaginary authority figure who's going to tell them it's okay to want what they want."

"And?" I asked.

"And the permission never comes. You just have to decide you're going to be that person anyway, even if you're terrified and even if you're probably going to fail a bunch for a while."

I felt something spark inside me. It was not quite inspiration, but maybe the ingredients of inspiration. "But what if *Sixty-Six* really is a terrible idea? What if I open that filing cabinet and discover that my writing is actually just word vomit I tried to disguise as art?"

"Then you'll know," River said simply. "And knowing is better than wondering for the rest of your life."

The fire popped, sending sparks up into the California night sky, and I felt something crystallize in my mind. Not a decision exactly, but an inkling that maybe it wasn't too late to stop being afraid of the stories in my filing cabinet, or the ones in my head that had yet to be written.

Maybe it was time to find out what could happen if I finally had the courage to unlock that drawer. Or not. Whatever.

Chapter 14

Talking about my graveyard of abandoned projects made me feel exposed but also, unexpectedly, kind of relaxed at the same time. At that point in the evening, I could have put it down to any number of things, like the wine, or the firelight, wearing Naomi's dress, or even the audacity of others to bring up far more scandalous subject matter.

Or maybe it was just the relief of unburdening myself to people who could understand. Even if we never met these passing acquaintances again, someone in the world now knew my life's work wasn't only about preventing people from calling 911 to find out how to remove a sex toy stuck in their hoo-ha.

Griffin had been steadily working his way through River's selection of top shelf boozes and was now inebriated to the point where he'd become introspective and sentimental, punctuated by bursts of silliness. He wasn't usually one to get sloppy drunk, but I was just glad that he had moved through that weird edgy phase and morphed back into my sweetheart.

After all, things had landed on a good note, and I was starting to think that meant it was time to head back to the hotel, as a way of preserving the good vibe and making this party a happy memory instead of a wholly uncomfortable one.

We did have a flight home the next day.

But Griffin was just so darn rapt with the whole situation that it didn't feel right to pull him out just yet. He was basically living his dream, hanging out with his musical hero, while I ruminated on my own dreams.

And then River dashed over to one of the other outdoor lounging areas and came back with a scruffy looking acoustic guitar that looked like it had seen its share of times both good and bad, visibly scarred from all kinds of shenanigans. The guitar that launched his whole career.

He sat back in his chair and started tuning the guitar reverently. Or maybe that was just me projecting onto him. All I knew was that we definitely couldn't leave yet. We were about to witness River's soul in person one more time, but this time, in his backyard instead of on a stage in front of thousands.

He ran through a few dreamy test chords before launching into a slowed-down, acoustic version of the anthemic, highly produced song I had sung at karaoke the night before. But hearing it isolated to just his voice and guitar transformed it completely.

Everyone fell silent to listen. River sang with an intimate timbre to his voice, quivering and vulnerable, almost like he was singing to himself under a tented blanket, alone in his bedroom. What was always a catchy, radio-friendly tune about boozing with your friends became a melancholic retrospective about good times that you can never get back.

I glanced quickly over at Styles, to find him looking positively gobsmacked. His restless energy had become focused on his friend, and I wondered if he was discovering a side of River that he hadn't fully appreciated before.

When River finished the song, it kind of seemed like no one knew what to say or do. I wanted to clap, but that seemed weird for such an intimate environment. Then Naomi started to clap, and everyone else joined in, and I started just as they finished, because winner, right here.

"Wow," Willow said. "I've heard that song a thousand times, but never like that."

"Changing the arrangement completely transformed the meaning," Styles added.

River looked pleased but also slightly nervous. "Thanks. Credit where it's due, the way Cara sang it with that delicate voice of hers at the karaoke bar last night inspired me. It's exactly like some of the new stuff I've been working on," he said. "Just trying to figure out what direction I want to go next."

"I'd love to hear more," Styles encouraged him.

River's expression shifted to uncertainty. "I have some ideas but... they're pretty rough. Not really ready for a public reveal."

"We're not the public," Griffin said with a huge goofy grin and an abundance of misplaced confidence. "We're friends."

But I couldn't deny that somehow, over the course of that super strange day, it felt like it might be a little bit true. I marveled at how we got to this point. How a polite invite from a virtual stranger led to an inordinate number of absurd kerfuffles, and finally a feeling that if we needed to call any of these people at two in the morning to help us cover up a crime, they might actually show up.

It reminded me of an overseas backpacking trip I'd taken after college during the temporary break with Griffin. When you know you only have a limited amount of time to spend with new friends, the bond manages to form faster and deeper than if you knew you had all the time in the world. At least, until you friended them on social media after coming home and found out all the things you wish you hadn't.

River took a deep breath and started playing again. This time, the melody was more subdued and complex than his usual style, less immediately catchy but more emotionally bare. The lyrics were about stepping into uncharted waters to feel something new, but not being able to see the dangers hidden beneath the waves, getting carried away and pulled under, not knowing which way is up or down. And what at first sounded like an unintentional wrong note turned into an intermittent pattern that became part of the story.

It was haunting and sad and completely different from anything I'd heard from him before. When River finished, the silence stretched a little longer this time. Finally, Styles shook his head slowly.

"Damn," he said quietly. "That's different, man. Like, *really* different."

"Yeah?" River asked, and I could hear a note of trepidation in his voice. Imagine selling millions of albums and performing for massive crowds of people all over the world, but feeling nervous that friends, some of them close, might not like your new song. Did the need for external validation from others ever go away?

"I mean, it's not what I'm usually into," Styles admitted. "The discordant notes threw me, some. But by the end it clicked. It was really moving. I like where you're going with it."

River's face lit up with relief. It was really kind of sweet, watching their friendship navigate this moment. And then

I envied them, and found myself yearning for a similar kind of interaction, having someone in my life to act as a trusted soundboard to develop ideas and make something with.

Well, there I was in that moment with the opportunity to maybe get a taste of what that was like, and before I could hold myself back for fear of saying something stupid, I chimed in. "I love it, too. It feels like there is a story you're trying to tell, not just trying to make a nice sounding, entertaining ditty."

"That's exactly it," River said, getting excited now. "I've gotten away from what's real. But what's real to me now is different from what was real to me twenty... thirty years ago. I'm tired of writing commercial sounding songs that could be about anyone. I want to write songs that could only be about me, even if that makes them harder to relate to."

"Not necessarily," I said. "I think it's still relatable, just maybe to not as many people."

Styles agreed, "It does run the risk of alienating some of your audience," he warned. River considered that angle.

"I know, but you know what? Fuck that. This isn't for my record company."

That sudden tension was alarming to me, and I felt like I needed to ease it.

"But you said you liked it, didn't you, Styles?" He nodded, looking sorry he'd upset River.

I continued. "Think of it like this. There are people that maybe River hasn't reached yet."

Then I directed my attention to River. "Not that you need my permission, but I think you should go ahead and get weird with it. Maybe it's too subjective for some, but there are people out there who will connect to it and feel less alone in their own specific weirdness."

"See, that's what I mean," River said. "That's why I was drawn to your voice at the karaoke bar last night. You're so... not generic. Unpolished. But in a good way. I can hear it really working on these new songs."

Oh. Right. I had forgotten about the recording offer he had made the previous night. It was looking like it wasn't just a casual suggestion made in the moment. It was a real, serious invitation, and he had orchestrated this entire evening around it. We should have left when I first had the inkling. I suddenly felt like I might throw up and looked around for a potted plant that would accept my offering.

Griffin didn't just let it slide. "Holy shit. My baby featured on a River Deane record. I knew this all felt like fate from the moment I saw the contest ad."

River clocked what Griffin was saying.

"I don't know about fate, but, yeah. That song I just played? I keep hearing another voice in my head when I sing it. Not harmony, exactly, but conversation. Two people working through the same feelings from clashing perspectives. And for the life of me, I could not think of an established artist who had the right... thing."

"But that's just it. I'm not a professional singer," I said reflexively.

"Neither was I when I started," River replied. "Professional just means someone pays you to do it. And I'm offering to pay you to do it."

The words hung in the air like a dare. And all I could think about was how this kind of thing didn't happen to me, and if it did, there must be some cruel fate attached to it. Maybe Griffin was right about the fate thing, in a way that was much more sinister than he thought.

"I still need to think about it," I said, needing time to process this through a voluminous series of detailed scenarios that would, more than likely, ultimately lead to me deciding that the real reward would be the delicious satisfaction of letting this once-in-a-lifetime chance pass me by, in living up to the self-perceived evidence of my own ineptitude.

"Of course," River said. "But while you're thinking about it, let me play you one more thing."

With a flicker of manipulative genius, he launched into *With a Little Help from My Friends* by the Beatles. A particularly persuasive choice, given where the conversation had turned. Within a few bars, everyone was singing along, because it's actually impossible to hear that song without participating.

But then something magical happened. River caught my eye and nodded, inviting me to join him for the next verse, just the two of us. And without thinking about it, without analyzing it to death, without worrying about whether I was good enough or professional enough or *whatever* enough, I started singing.

Our voices blended together in a way that shouldn't have worked but did anyway. River's gravelly, whiskey-soaked warmth and my softer, airier, more tentative tone created something that was better than either of us could have managed alone.

When we finished the song, I felt something inside that I hadn't felt in a really long time. It was a word that I'd like to coin as *glee-bliss-joy* that can only be described as that warm sunshiny feeling in the chest that threatens to burst you right open if you try to contain it. If *glee-bliss-joy* doesn't work for you, call it whatever you want.

"Okay," I said, looking at River while my heart was still

racing from the adrenaline of what I had just experienced. "I'm in," I announced, without any other thoughts in my head, which was weird for me.

"Yeah?" River beamed like I'd just agreed to go on an adventure to explore a new, undiscovered part of the world with him, which I guess I had.

"Yeah. But I have no idea what I'm doing, so you're going to have to be patient with me while I figure out how to be this person."

"To be expected," River said. "And for what it's worth, I think you're going to be a lot better at this than you think you are."

I glanced around the circle, catching a quick flash of something on Styles' face. It flickered too fast to really identify. Not quite disapproval, not quite surprise. Could it be jealousy? I didn't know him well enough to tell the difference.

As the fire's flames had given way to embers, and the evening was finally winding down toward its natural conclusion, it hit me that I'd impulsively agreed to something I'd only ever daydreamed about. How was I going to go from performing for my cats in the living room with a broom for a microphone to... this? *What the fuck did I just do?*

We started gathering our things to head back to the hotel. Griffin, who had watched this all unfold with awe and wonder, rubbed my back reassuringly, as if he was reading my mind.

"I'm proud of you," he whispered to my ear. "You got this." The hug that followed closed the fleeting gap that threatened to form earlier that day, and I couldn't wait to be alone with him again and burrow into his arms all night.

Chapter 15

Finally, inevitably, it was time to go. As we moved into the "thanks for everything, we had an amazing time" part of the evening, I remembered that my clothes were likely finished tumble-drying in Naomi's laundry room. The borrowed outfit had served its purpose. I'd like to think it carried me through some of the day's more distressing moments and misadventures with more grace than my not-so-mysterious-when-wet sundress and cardigan could have.

Yes, I'm giving Naomi's spectacular taste in clothes all the credit, even if the dress looked strange on me to my own eyes. But now I was ready to get back into my own skin.

I waited in Naomi's dressing room while she retrieved my clothes, still warm from the dryer, and I changed back into my original dinner party attire as if I was returning to my natural state from an extended period of camouflage. Looking back on it, I'm glad that I wasn't wearing my own clothes when the dreaded *swapping* conversation took place. How could I wear that dress ever again with that ordeal attached to it?

Naomi escorted me out toward their magnificent doorway where the good-bye chatter awaited me. "We'll be in touch about the recording?" River asked.

I experienced a brief moment of panic. "For sure," I heard

myself say, from outside of my body, before I managed to pull myself back together. "There is the teensiest problem of the fact that I live thousands of miles away," I added, and noted to myself the potential for a way out of this plan.

"Minor issue. We'll make it work," River insisted. "If you can't get back to LA, I could even book something out your way and come to you." *Of course he could.*

The hugs and handshakes contagiously made their way around our small group, when Griffin suddenly seemed to experience a delayed-onset attack of social awareness. My guess is that the combination of sobering up slightly and realizing we were about to leave triggered a need for him to be remembered fondly.

Willow seemed to have come down with the same affliction, and when their turn to bid adieu came around, instead of a hug, they remained at arm's length from each other and awkwardly outstretched a hand toward each other, resulting in a tentative fist bump.

And then Griffin turned to Styles and offered his hand. "Hey man," he said with audible regret, "I'm sorry about earlier. The whole pool thing. I was being a douchebag about it. I'm glad there are people like you who jump in to help. The world needs more of that, not less."

Styles shook Griffin's hand and promptly waved off the apology with a vague dismissal that I had trouble interpreting. Maybe it was really a simple "No worries, it happens," or maybe it was his way of politely deflecting Griffin's admitted douchebaggery about the whole thing. Given Griffin's earlier enthusiasm about the potential of having a consequence-free shot at Styles' wife, I suspected it might have been the latter, though Styles was too diplomatically inclined to let it show.

"No one got hurt," Styles replied casually, with a weak smile that didn't quite make it to his eyes. The quick look he gave me over Griffin's shoulder intimated that maybe that wasn't completely true. But that was a conversation for another time, possibly never, and definitely not while we were saying goodbye to our hosts after what had already been the most dramatically eventful dinner party of my entire adult life.

* * *

As our driver helped us into the fancy car for the return trip to our hotel, the first thought I had was how we may not have gone shopping on this trip, and yet I felt like I was bringing back a lot more stuff with me than I brought. How on Earth was I going to fit River's offer into my suitcase? And how was I going to unpack it?

People back home were inevitably going to ask us how the trip went. Mental rehearsals for how to reply began immediately. I started with the truth, just to see how that might land.

"How was the trip?"

"Oh you know, the concert was great, the meet and greet was meh, we went out for karaoke after and River Deane showed up and hung out with us, invited us to his house, and asked me to sing on his next record."

"You went to LA for a concert and came back with a recording deal?"

"Well... not a deal, exactly. More of a 'we'll see how it goes' kind of thing. There was no ink or handshake, just a group singalong and a verbal agreement."

"With River Deane?"

"Yes, and I know how impressive that sounds, but I promise you he's just a super nice dude and is probably trying to think of a way to get out of it without letting me down too hard."

Yeah, right. No way anyone would believe me. Even with photographic evidence in the form of selfies and phone videos from the party, they'd say I was embellishing, or misinterpreting, or flat out making it up. But it *had* happened. I'd been there, I'd sung, he'd offered and I'd said yes. Griffin would back me up, but they'd probably accuse him of over-romanticizing our vacation to distract from the mundanity of our normal lives.

* * *

How to Raise Your Cortisol Levels by Living in the Future

Materials needed: Chronic anxiety and an overactive imagination.

1. Receive an invitation to make one of your most deeply coveted dreams come true, unexpectedly, through virtually no effort on your part.
2. Notice a dramatic influx of adrenaline coursing through your entire nervous system.
3. Immediately imagine every possible outcome, ranging from accepting your future Grammy to humiliating self-reckoning in the bathtub after a bottle of wine.
4. Draft fake conversations in your head where you try to explain the unbelievable situation to skeptical people in

your life.

5. When Step 4 generates enough paralyzing self-doubt, begin obsessively rehearsing a version of events in which you back out before any damage can be done.
6. Smile politely and say "The show was brilliant!" when someone asks how your trip went.
7. Lie awake in bed all night looping on the above. Never sleep again.

Note: These steps are most effective when there is no threat to your personal safety, like being attacked by a ferocious wild animal. If a bear attack is imminent, redirect your attention to that, as it's more important and a more appropriate use of your adrenal system.

* * *

I stared out the window at the cacophony of traffic lights, wondering whether it wouldn't just be best to wake up tomorrow and pretend none of it happened. The alternative was definitely going to lead to my mother showing up to take me straight to the nearest psych hospital and her telling everyone that I was *going through something.*

Chapter 16

It's a weird sensation, flying home from a potentially life-changing experience. One minute, you're in main character mode with all this momentum and action. Then you board a plane and suddenly you return to non-player character mode, sitting in stasis, confined to a small space with hours of uninterrupted in-flight airtime ahead of you. You're going somewhere, but you can't go anywhere. All you can do is replay the highlights of your brief stint in MC mode, and obsess over what's going to happen next.

I was sitting next to Griffin in economy (because apparently contest winners only get the first-class treatment in one direction), staring out the window at the cottony clouds, when the full magnitude of my situation hit me. Agreeing to record music with River Deane felt akin to agreeing to perform brain surgery because I'd successfully removed a splinter once.

And of course, my fidget was acting up. I'd been clicking the pen in my bag so compulsively that the man in the seat in front of me kept turning around and glaring at me over the back of his seat like I was deliberately trying to ruin his flight. I'd already flipped through the in-flight magazine, adjusted my seatbelt a bunch, and made a mental inventory of every item in my carry-on. I tried reading. I tried deep breathing.

But mostly I just fidgeted, sighed dramatically, and ground my teeth so hard that a cracked molar was likely in my future.

"You're being weird," Griffin observed, noticing I was practically vibrating in my seat.

"I'm calibrating."

"You're so funny. Anyone else in your situation would be celebrating. Want me to order us a couple glasses of champagne? I think they're only..." he perused the limited alcoholic beverage menu. "Uh, nevermind." I appreciated his attempt to lighten me up, but unfortunately, it didn't really land.

"What if I suck?" I asked, swallowing the anxiety rising in my chest.

"River doesn't think you suck," Griffin reminded me.

"But what if he's wrong, and I do suck?"

"Well then, you'll suck."

Wow. Thanks.

"And the world will keep spinning, and you'll keep breathing, and you will have lost nothing, except maybe the desire to sing any more River Deane songs at karaoke."

This was supposed to be comforting, and I knew he was right, but it was like he didn't understand at all that my oldest and most cherished recurring daydream, the one I'd been having since I was twelve years old, about being a famous pop star singing on stage to legions of adoring fans, depended upon me not actually knowing the answer to the question "What if I suck?"

I needed to think about something else. Normal things, like work. It was an oddly comforting thought.

I imagined myself nestled into my cozy work chair in my home office, sipping a mug of hot coffee, wrapped in a blanket, and starting on the next user manual. So calm. So peaceful. So suddenly aware of my filing cabinet graveyard of creative writing projects, taunting me from the other side of the room.

Should I open it? After all that talk around the fire at River's, the idea was compelling. Everyone liked my ideas. Styles had been especially encouraging. I thought about him and his own creative trepidation, and how one small step forward changed everything for him. But... that dreaded question popped back into my head again like an invasive weed. What if I suck?

A sudden dropping sensation caused my hand to flail and my mug of hot coffee to spill over my hand onto my fleecy blanket.

The feeling of hitting a bump jolted me back to the reality of flying 30,000 feet above the ground. Turbulence.

* * *

The plane started shaking. This wasn't the gentle turbulence that makes nervous flyers like me grip the armrest while feeling a little bit queasy. This was completely different. The plane shook violently, with a mechanical shuddering that signaled that something was very wrong.

Oxygen masks dropped from the overhead compartments. Then came the sound of the pilot's soothing voice over the intercom, lying by omission about what was about to come.

"Ladies and gentlemen, we're experiencing some technical difficulties. Please remain calm and follow the flight attendants' instructions."

I knew that what he'd left out was "We're going down and

there's nothing anyone can do about it, but let's all pretend everything is fine until we crash into whatever unforgiving landscape happens to be beneath us."

The plane lurched forcefully to the left, and as I turned to look at Griffin, I found myself looking at another familiar face instead.

"Styles? What the..."

He was sitting across the aisle, gripping his armrests with the same white-knuckled intensity that I was applying to my own. He turned to face me, and I recognized in his eyes the same fear that I was experiencing.

I wanted to ask him what he was doing on this flight, but before I could get the words out, the plane dropped sickeningly downward. The last thing I remembered before impact was thinking that this was not how I'd imagined my life ending. Walking out into traffic absentmindedly during a daydreaming episode, sure. But not this. Not in a fiery ball of twisted metal somewhere in the American desert.

And... black out.

When I came to, I was hanging upside down in my seat, held by a seatbelt that had miraculously managed to keep me attached to an intact chunk of airplane. My head was pounding and there was a gross taste in my mouth, but a cursory examination of my visible body parts showed no detectable sign of injury.

"Hey," came a voice from somewhere nearby. "Hey, are you alive?"

I turned my head toward the voice to see Styles carefully extricating himself from his own tangled predicament.

"I think so," I replied, tentatively, as I unlocked my seatbelt and wriggled out of my seat and up to my feet. "Are you?"

"Jury's still out," he said, dropping to the ground with a grunt that hinted at some minor pain. "But I can move, which is more

than I expected considering we just fell out of the sky."

We seemed to be in the middle of nowhere, with desert stretching in all directions, punctuated by scrubby vegetation, red rock formations, and a hazy blue ridge of mountains way off in the distance. The plane's wreckage was scattered across a wide area, pieces distributed like a morbid puzzle in progress.

"Where's everyone else?" I asked. The silence that surrounded us was almost more terrifying than the crash.

Styles squinted his eyes and scanned the debris field with his jaw slightly agape, assessing the scene without really comprehending what he was looking at. I know because I was doing the same thing. "I don't think there is anyone else," he said quietly. "I think we might be it."

Even though I was standing on solid ground, my stomach dropped as if the plane was nosediving all over again. It was enough to knock me on my ass. I thought about Griffin and felt a sob begin to rise in my throat, but then, with a flick of my mind, I put him on a different flight. An airline representative at the gate had asked if anyone was willing to give up their seat for a passenger who needed to get home to see a sick relative. Griffin volunteered, and said he'd meet me at home. He would make it there safely.

That meant it was only Styles and I, alone in the desert, possibly hundreds of miles from civilization, with no roads visible from where we stood.

"Okay," I said, from where I sat on the ground, because someone had to take charge and I was super hoping it was going to be Styles. The look on his face said otherwise, however. "What do we know about survival?"

"Everything I know about survival I learned from movies, TV and books. Basically fiction," Styles offered.

"Me too. Didn't you do Boy Scouts as a kid?" I asked.

"Only long enough to get my Wedgie Badge," he joked. "But I can start a fire, as long as I have a lighter or matches, so there's that."

"What about that podcast episode you did with the performance artist who climbed Everest? Learn anything from him?"

"Just how to insult someone in Nepali."

"Mūrkha," I remembered.

"Hey now, be nice. It's just you and me until we get out of this mess."

It was good to laugh for a moment, even if our new reality was the opposite of funny.

"So, we're definitely going to die," I said matter-of-factly.

"If I had to guess, our odds of surviving are statistically disappointing," he agreed. "But maybe we can die in an impressive way."

"Well, if we're going to construct a 'henge' of sorts from the plane wreckage, we better get started before we succumb to dehydration," I recommended.

"You just gave me an idea. Come on." Styles reached his hand out to me and pulled me up off the ground.

The first order of business was figuring out what was salvageable from the wreckage that might be of use. Styles had managed to locate a partially intact emergency kit, while I'd found several bottles of water and some unfortunate passenger's trail mix in a battered tote bag, which felt a bit like winning the lottery.

"The good news," Styles declared, examining our meager supplies, "is that we have enough water for maybe three days if we're very careful about rationing."

"And the bad news?"

"The bad news is that, last time I checked, we're still in the

desert with no phone reception, no idea which way to go, and nightfall is coming."

I turned myself in a 360-degree circle to once again survey the endless expanse of sand and scrub brush. Weirdly, instead of the expected overwhelmed feeling, I felt comforted. Even though I was pretty sure I had the survival skills of a kitten on a highway, channeling my scattered energy into the singular purpose of surviving was actually kind of liberating. And I'd be lying if I didn't admit that Styles' charming and adorably bedimpled presence made it feel more like an adventure than an emergency.

Maybe this disaster was exactly what I needed. It was a chance to stop overthinking and panicking about non-life-threatening events and simply act in the interest of basic survival.

"Let's walk," I said, surprising myself with how decisive I sounded. "Pick a direction and just walk until we find something that isn't desert."

"Leave the crash site? What if someone comes to rescue us?"

"You want to wait and see?"

Styles stared off into the distance for a moment, considering our options. He exhaled a gust of breath after a moment with his decision. "I guess we walk."

Thus began our trek across the desert. Who would have thought that two people who met at a dinner party twenty-four hours ago would now be bound together by the unlikely shared trauma of falling out of the sky.

The walking was harder than it looked in movies. The desert was vindictively and unrelentingly hot, like the sun was watching us try to walk away from it and was like "Oh yeah? Fuck the both of you." The sand clearly had a vendetta against us too, as it worked its way into everything, including our shoes, our clothes, and our consciousness. Exfoliation quickly gave way to chafing and blisters. Fucking everywhere.

"Tell me something," Styles said after we'd been walking for all of eternity. "Did you really want to do the music thing with River? Maybe I was imagining it, but Griffin seemed more keen on it than you were."

I thought about how to answer. "Honestly... I think I'd rather be stranded in the desert."

Styles laughed.

"My turn to ask you an uncomfortable question. What would you have done if I said yes to Willow's indecent proposal?" My heart was beating so fast I thought it might pound right through my chest.

"You wouldn't have," he replied quickly, totally side-stepping my question.

We walked in companionable silence for a while. The setting sun painted the desert in shades of orange and pink that would have been breathtaking if we weren't actively focused on not having our breath taken from us. Eventually, our plan to keep walking until we came upon something that was not sand, stone or scrub paid off.

"Is that...?" Styles squinted ahead.

"That's a road," I finished. "An actual road with actual tire tracks and everything."

We ran toward it, and for a moment I felt like a "Looney Tunes" character running toward a mirage of a desert oasis and considered that this might be a version of that. But the road was really there. It was narrow and unpaved, and did not promise a high volume of traffic, but its existence was a good sign. Following the sun, we trudged forward.

* * *

"Cara!"

Griffin's voice cut through my desert survival fantasy like he was cutting through a movie screen with a machete. I was momentarily disoriented by the transition from my daydream back to the airplane cabin. I had no idea how long I was out for.

"Hmm?" I said, pretending like I was having normal airplane thoughts.

"I've been talking to you for like five minutes," Griffin said. "You were completely gone. I was getting worried. You didn't hear me at all?"

"Sorry," I said, ashamed for scaring him, and also for... well... you know. "Just thinking about stuff."

"Are you okay?" he asked.

"Yeah," I said, wistfully. We were about to begin our descent, which meant that reality (whatever that meant now) wasn't far off.

"You know what I just realized?" I asked.

"What's that?"

"We forgot to buy a souvenir."

Griffin chuckled. "What, like some tacky knickknack that the cats will just knock off the mantle?"

"Yeah, for the cats."

"Well, your LA adventure isn't really over yet. You can get one when you go back to record with River."

The plane landed safely, and as we disembarked and made our way home, I imagined a protective dome forming around the city of Niagara Falls, sealing us safely inside an impenetrable barrier that would shield us from promises made in an uninhibited state.

Chapter 17

You know what I love about normal life? It gives zero fucks. Even if you find yourself in the ridiculously unlikely and surreal position of having agreed to become a recording artist while you were out of town, normal life doesn't give a shit. Normal life wants... no, *needs* you to wake up at your usual time, feed the cats, clean your house, check your email, and go back to your fucking job.

You don't have to be grateful about it. Normal life doesn't care. It is not interested in your artistic awakening or whatever insane thing happened on your vacation. Normal life gives you permission to decorate its structure with the photos you took and then blinds you to them with routine. Fuck yeah, normal life.

I was sitting at my desk in my home office, reading an email from my most reliable client, basking in the serenity of it all. This is what I really wanted, wasn't it? The comfortable predictability of a job I was good at, minus my intermittent tendency toward dissociative breaks.

The email was from Gunnar at Senseros Technologies, the company that had been so thrilled with my Prostate Pulse Pro 3000 manual that they were offering me something more substantial than my usual project-by-project arrangement.

Cara,

We were so impressed with your work on the PPP 3000 manual that we'd like to offer you a more formalized contract for an exclusive arrangement with us.

We've got a new product line launching next quarter. It's called the Cachet Series, and it's going to need comprehensive user documentation. Think of it as the BMW of personal pleasure devices. High end stuff.

Let me know if you want to set up a call to discuss details.

Best, Gunnar

I re-read the email a bunch of times to make sure I wasn't missing anything. I loved these types of longer-term contracts. They meant steady income and room to breathe. And as much as I have complained about having to practically hang onto my desk for dear life to avoid floating into space during virtual meetings, I liked working with Gunnar. He was a good dude with a fun accent.

This was exactly what I needed. A safe, practical choice to keep me grounded and continue living a normal life.

I emailed him back immediately.

Gunnar,

Yes, I'm definitely interested. Let's set up a call to discuss terms. I'm available anytime this week.

Thanks for thinking of me for this opportunity.

Regards, Cara

I hit send without second-guessing myself, and was immediately flooded with endorphins of relief. This was what I was good at. This was what I knew how to do. This was me.

Sure, from time to time I daydreamed about myself living in an alternate reality where I'm a celebrated artist and a star. But doesn't everyone? I didn't actually *want* that life, did I?

My phone buzzed with a text message, and for one heart-stopping moment I thought it might be River following up on recording plans. But it was Griffin, letting me know he'd be home a little later than usual due to a late walk-in at the clinic.

And so, riding the gentle wave of normal life, I went back to work on a project with an open-ended deadline that I'd been neglecting. It was an update to a user guide for a new version of a device I'd written about previously. Someone over at Anytime Delight Personal Devices Inc. thought it would be a cool idea to add smart home features to their existing basic pleasure model, in case people wanted to start their coffee brewing or answer their doorbell intercom while they were in the thicc of it (or while the thicc of it was in them, take your pick).

I'd been working with intense focus for about twenty minutes when my phone rang. This time, River Deane's name appeared on the caller ID, and holy shit, you'd think I was being chased by an axe murderer, the way I practically left my body in a panic trying to figure out if I should answer it.

I didn't. It went to voicemail, which meant I now had to deal with *that.* I have kind of a thing about notifications. The whole reason I started therapy with Paige was because I'd let my voicemail and email notifications reach such an unnatural number that I felt like I couldn't even brush my teeth, let alone get dressed or start work until I'd attended to all eleventy-gazillion of them. Thankfully, she taught me about inbox hygiene, which means I still can't brush my teeth, get dressed or start work until I've attended to my notifications, but at least there are only a few of them.

The point is, if I didn't make myself listen to the message, Griffin would come home and ask me how my day was and I'd have to tell him I had phone call paralysis again, but there's burnt turkey burgers, if he's hungry.

The message went thusly:

"Hey Cara, it's River. Hope you had a good flight home. Just following up on our chat. I've been thinking about those songs we talked about, and I'm really excited about the direction we could take them. I was hoping we could set up that studio time we talked about."

There was a weird pause with some muffled mumbling before River continued, his voice sounding slightly more edged than seconds before.

"Oh yeah, and those writing projects you mentioned. Styles won't stop talking about them. He wants to take a peek, if you're up for it. Maybe bring some samples when you come out? Anyway, give me a call when you get a chance."

I played the message again. Then again. Then I put the phone down and stared at it like it might explode or catch fire.

This was real. River had meant everything he said. And now Styles was interested in my writing? How was it that these guys were so serious about me as an artist after knowing me for five minutes, when I could never take myself seriously after knowing me for my whole life?

This is what I got for practicing good voicemail hygiene. It was all Paige's fault, obviously. But at least I was invigorated with the energy of a thousand burning questions, like "What the hell do I do now? and "How do I make this not a thing?" to the point of being motivated enough to make dinner.

* * *

Paige was on speaker as I flitted around the kitchen, my phone wedged between a bottle of olive oil and a bag of wilted arugula. If only turkey burgers would bubble up like pancakes to tell you when they were ready to be flipped. But no, you're supposed to follow the instructions, and I had already thrown the box out.

"What if I told you that something big kind of happened in LA? I don't want to say what it is specifically, but it's... an opportunity."

"I'd say congratulations! Are you ready for a big change?" Paige's excited voice was exactly the same as her deeply empathetic and concerned voice.

"That's just it," I said, "The *opportunity* called me to follow up and..." I went silent. I knew she knew what it meant.

"You didn't call them back," she said in her usual non-judgmental, therapist-y tone.

"I could just not call him back, like as a choice." I tried to flip a burger, but it had fused with the pan.

"Remember when we had that conversation about how much being ghosted by your last therapist hurt you?" Paige replied.

"Wow, way to remind me of that. Wait, is that a threat? Are you leaving me?"

There was a pause, which was a little unnerving.

"Of course I'm not. I didn't mean it to sound that way. I just mean, whatever this opportunity is, there is a person attached to it. Maybe they're counting on you."

Turkey burger juices spat onto my bare arm, which hurt almost as much as the shame I was feeling for considering ghosting River.

"I know. You're right. But..." I turned off the stove and pushed the pan to the back, turning my attention to tossing the wilted side salad, "if I do this and I'm terrible at it, then I'll know I'm terrible at it. If I don't do it, I get to keep imagining that I might be brilliant. I get to hold onto the fantasy. Stay in Schrödinger's box of simultaneous self-loathing and self-aggrandizement."

"I must admit I'm not seeing the appeal."

"It's kind of addictive," I admitted.

I leaned against the counter and stared at the wall, chewing the inside of my cheek. "I don't know how to be someone who *does* the thing. I only know how to *imagine* doing the thing. The fantasy version of me is fearless. Real me is... just this." I gestured around the room as if she could see me standing amid the apocalypse called dinner scattered across the kitchen.

"You don't have to do anything you don't want to, Cara. But I've learned to sense when our next session is going to be about regret."

I hated how much I loved when she said things like that. It made me feel exposed and seen and slightly pissed off.

"It's too big, it's too much," I whined.

"Then take smaller bites," Paige said gently. "You don't have to plan out the rest of your life right now. Just focus on what's immediately in front of you."

She paused, but I didn't feel like filling the silence. I just wanted to listen. She was good at knowing that, and she continued. "Starting a new career is definitely a big deal and takes a lot of energy. You know what takes a lot less energy? A phone call."

When my session with Paige was finished, I hung up and stared at my reflection in the cupboard glass, where my eyes always looked more tired for some reason.

The smart choice was obvious. I had steady work lined up with Senseros. I could call River back and explain that I'd gotten carried away by the moment, that I was honored he felt I could contribute, but that he should find someone who had earned an opportunity like this. I could just say *no.*

Instead, I trudged to the living room and scanned my record collection for the perfect album to become the soundtrack to thinking about literally anything else, but when it didn't reveal itself to me, I let myself fall bonelessly onto the couch in defeat, where I was quickly joined by Daisy, my cuddliest cat.

* * *

How to Successfully Avoid Doing a Thing

1. Identify a task that requires immediate attention and has genuine consequences if delayed. It could be something as simple as a phone call.
2. Go on your phone and check all of your socials in cyclical fashion. Google questions like "Why am I like this?" and "Has anyone ever peeled off all of their skin in one pull like an orange?" Doomscroll to the bottom of the internet.
3. Sign up for free self-help newsletters and workshops that will absolutely make you able to do the thing you're avoiding doing just by subscribing.
4. Imagine doing the thing and what you would ideally be

wearing when you're doing it. Realize you don't have those clothes. Commence online shopping for the right *doing the thing* outfit.

5. Realize with horror that you forgot to respond with LOL to a friend's text earlier in the day. LOL that shit immediately.
6. When guilt reaches critical levels, put the phone down and try to muster up the energy to mobilize yourself to action. An hour and a half later when you regain consciousness and wonder what it was you were doing, start over at Step 1.

Congratulations! You have successfully turned a five-minute phone call into a multi-day anxiety spiral.

* * *

Styles and I continued to follow the desert road until after the sun had set. It was dark now, with only a sliver of moonlight to guide the way. It was also cold, and there was nothing around to build a shelter out of. All we had was each other. I pondered for a moment whether we'd make it through the night huddled together for warmth. The lack of protection from the elements and creatures of a scorpion nature made me realize that this scenario had reached its narrative limit, and I decided to transport us someplace a little more forgiving, with more plot options.

Like a switch had been flipped (because it had), we were suddenly no longer trudging down a lonely desert road at night, but through a jungle on a tropical island in daylight. I mean, it was still high stakes with plenty of ways to die. But at least now we had palm trees and a sandy beach. If maladaptive daydreaming had a motto, it would be "By all means, continue suffering, but make it prettier."

We found a waterfall within minutes. What can I say? We needed a win. The pool at the bottom was clear and fresh, and looked like it was from an ad for a secluded eco-resort getaway. Styles cupped some of the water in his hands and drank like he didn't give a damn about waterborne tropical diseases. But if it was good enough for him, it was good enough for me, so I did the same.

Besides fresh water, the island also had an abundance of shade. We decided to set up camp in the palm grove where the jungle ended and the beach began. We built a palm-leaf shade structure between two trees, layering the fronds on the ground for comfort. It wasn't exactly hurricane-proof, but it was a place to call home until rescue came.

Now all we needed was to find a reliable source of food. The island was overrun with coconuts, which at first seemed like a blessing. Unfortunately, getting into them without a machete was a problem. But Styles was determined to not let such an obvious food source go to waste. Thus began his vendetta against the coconuts.

"This is ridiculous," he said, panting as another one skittered off the rock unscathed. "How did anyone ever figure out these had food inside?"

"They had tools," I offered, knotting another palm leaf strip. "Or rage issues. Probably both."

"Do rocks count as tools?"

"Possibly, but only with enough rage."

"Give it a minute," he warned, and I was curious what his particular brand of rage might look like. He balanced the coconut on the rock slab, then inhaled and exhaled quickly, as he raised

another heavy jagged rock over his head and brought it down forcefully onto the coconut with a loud yell.

The coconut cracked open, and we celebrated by prying it into two halves and exclaiming "Cheers!" while clinking the halves together before sipping the unspilled coconut water, and making a meal out of the firm, white flesh.

It's crazy how accomplishing something as basic as building shelter and finding food and water can feel like a reward.

Chapter 18

If you've never experienced it, I don't know if I can adequately describe to you what it's like to not be able to make yourself do something you want, no, *need* to do. Maybe you've been there, and you already know what I'm talking about. But if this is a foreign concept to you, then think of it like quicksand. You know that meme about how movies and TV made it seem like there would be a lot more quicksand to contend with in our daily lives?

Well, guess what? I have spent an inordinate amount of time mired in abyssal pools of metaphorical quicksand in my life. Looking back on it, the time I spent stuck in it while ruminating about calling River back and trying to get any work done was probably one of the stuckest times I've ever lived through up to that point.

Gunnar had sent over the Cachet Series specs, along with the complete range of devices for functional testing. There were several, and they looked as upscale as he had described.

The testing part should have been the easy part. It was normally one of my favorite aspects of the job, obviously, but the sheer amount of effort it took to proverbially rise to the occasion was a sign that I had ceded all power over to my avoidant state. Not me lubing up, switching the vibrator on and applying it to my body, only for my mind to go someplace else entirely.

* * *

We were hiking through the jungle interior of the island, carrying our handwoven palm frond tote bags as we foraged for edible berries, mushrooms, and insects. Styles rolled a fallen log from its place on the ground to reveal a thriving city of, fortunately or unfortunately depending on your take, protein-filled grubs and bugs.

"Jackpot!" he exclaimed.

"I guess..." I agreed, slightly.

As we immobilized the crawly critters and scooped them into our tote using a coconut half shell, Styles seemed to become distracted by something. He stopped what he was doing and stood up, looking around like a prairie dog who had picked up what was going down.

"Do you hear that?" he asked me quizzically as I continued to collect our dinner from the log's bounty.

"Hear what?" I asked.

"That sound. It's like a buzzing sound."

"The bugs."

"No, it's like a mechanical sound," he paused, and then chuckled. "If I didn't know any better, I'd say it sounds like a vib..."

* * *

It was even worse when it came to actually trying to write the manual. Having finally explored the full capacity of the

Cachet Series VibeLux Vibrator, I sat at my desk with the specs open on my laptop, my fingers positioned over the keyboard, waiting for the words to flow from my head through my fingers onto the page, only for absolutely nothing to happen.

It wasn't writer's block, because I knew what I needed to write. It wasn't a lack of motivation, because I really wanted to get the work done and pay my bills and be a functional adult. It was just a heaping pile of nothing but a blank page, with a side serving of paralyzing guilt seasoned with potent frustration. *I should be working. I want to be working. Why can't I just fucking work?*

* * *

Enough time had passed on the island to allow Styles and I to settle into a daily routine:

1. *Wake up with the sun.*
2. *Relieve ourselves in the designated location and dispose of solid matter in the no man's land known as Poop Gorge.*
3. *Obtain and consume water.*
4. *Check the coconut traps and throw tantrums while trying to get the fresh ones open.*
5. *Forage for non-poisonous berries, fungus, and insects.*
6. *Occasionally, get dive-bombed by territorial birds.*
7. *Secure our shelter from any damage from the elements.*
8. *Attempt fishing in the ocean. Fail as usual.*
9. *Bathe in the waterfall (as needed).*
10. *Build our fire and sit down to dinner and tell stories about the various ways that nature had tried and failed to kill us that day.*

"That mosquito better not have had Zika," I said, swatting at the offending insect and missing my target.

Styles nodded solemnly. "I think the fruit from that tree we found made me hallucinate. I spent half the afternoon trying to call home with a turtle."

"Oh yeah, turtlephone. I saw that," I said. "It looked intense."

He poked at the fire with a stick. "No reception," he laughed.

"We could've had that turtle for dinner," I pointed out.

"I can't eat a turtle whose belly I've spoken to."

"Fair enough."

"Hey, at least we're still healthy. Nothing broken, no major infections. That's got to be some kind of miracle."

"And yet you still won't try the fungus that smells like rotten fish," I teased him. "I promise you it tastes better than it smells."

"I'm saving that for a special occasion."

We fell into a comfortable silence while staring into the flames. Every night, the things we left unsaid, like opinions about whether or not we'd ever get home, billowed up in smoke to the sky. They couldn't stay unsaid forever.

"They're not going to find us," I said after a while. "Everyone probably thinks we're dead. We were the only survivors. I doubt they're looking for us. Actually, they don't even know we're here."

Styles looked at me, confused. "What do you mean?"

I hesitated. "Well... after the plane crash, I did move us from the desert to this island. You know, for aesthetic reasons."

He peered at me curiously. "What?"

"Nothing."

He looked off into the distance and seemed to be trying to do logic or math or something in his head.

"I mean, technically you weren't even actually on the plane," I continued.

"Wait, what? Did you eat that hallucinogenic fruit, too?"

I shrugged. "It's not important."

Styles opened his mouth, then closed it. The sound of the fire crackling did the talking. It was both comforting and a little bit ominous.

"They're looking for us. I know they are," Styles insisted.

He gazed out at the horizon as if our rescue vessel would be arriving imminently. But as the evening passed into night, we eventually moved to our shelter and cuddled up next to each other, more for security than warmth. My side of the shelter still creaked in the wind, and Styles' foot stuck out from under the palm-frond wall like bait for curious wildlife, but it was fine. We hadn't died yet, and that counted for something.

And we were planning to try making fishing spears in the morning.

* * *

Days blurred together. Gunnar from Senseros Technologies called a bunch. I let it go to voicemail. The deadline for the first Cachet Series product guide came and went while I stared at my cursor flashing on the blank page. It was a bit like being buried alive by my own disembodied consciousness with alarming shovels full of dread. This was certainly one way to control the outcome. It wasn't going to be good, but at least I had that certainty. There were bigger things at stake.

* * *

The spears were a surprising success. It took a full afternoon of trial and error (mostly error) but eventually we figured out the right angle and timing, and that shouting profanity at the water did not entice fish to the surface but did provide much-needed stress relief.

Styles was the first victor of our inaugural spear fishing excursion. It wasn't gigantic, but he held it up like he had won a prize, and shouted "Dinner!"

We feasted pretty much immediately. And by "feasted," I mean we crouched by the fire eating roasted fish off sticks, making exaggerated moaning sounds of satisfaction to celebrate the miracle of non-insect protein. It could have used some garlic, but hey, who's complaining?

* * *

My phone kept hassling me. Gunnar, calling about the Cachet Series. The project manager from Anytime Delight wanting to check progress on the smart dildo. Griffin asking if he should bring home dinner after work. River wondering if I had gotten his voicemail. My best friend Hannah wondering if I was still alive. I ignored them all, completely absorbed in an imaginary world where the only thing that mattered was basic survival, not finding the courage to get back to anyone.

* * *

And then, just when we thought the day couldn't get any better, the ocean gave us a gift. A backpack washed up on shore, bloated and sun-faded but intact. We opened it with overblown hope, like it might contain a popup tent or at least some beef jerky. It didn't. But if you'll allow me to go a little Wes Anderson for a minute, it did contain:

- *One toothbrush (bristles slightly squished, but clean in appearance),*
- *A travel-sized bar of soap,*
- *Dental floss (minty),*
- *Nail clippers,*
- *A multi-tool with a mini blade and tiny scissors,*
- *A hairbrush with the owner's hair laced through the bristles,*
- *And a towel that was thin and ragged from years of use. It was breathtaking.*

We were so excited, unpacking the backpack felt like we were making an unboxing video. Once the items were inventoried, we immediately began incorporating them into our daily routine.

We shared the personal hygiene items equally. Yes, even the toothbrush. Before you gag or judge, let me just say that grossness is a scale and where things land on it is a matter of circumstance. That shared toothbrush was a goddamn blessing.

There was no razor, and Styles' beard was reaching "island sage" territory. He looked handsome with facial hair, but I was sad to see his irresistible dimples disappear behind the brush. As for me, I was growing hair back in all the places I had fought so hard to keep hairless for decades. I couldn't decide if growing it back meant I had lost or won that battle, but I did my best to only scratch the relentless itching of the regrowth in private.

* * *

I was losing track of time. Weeks went by as I languished in a quasi-paralytic state, unable to accomplish much of anything. I sank deeper and deeper into the mental quicksand, feeling utterly powerless to pull myself out. Until I opened an email from Gunnar that zapped me back to reality.

Cara,

I've been trying to reach you for weeks. The Cachet Series launch date is firm so there can be no extensions. Regrettably, I have no choice but to terminate your contract and move forward with another technical writer who can meet the deadline.

I'm disappointed because your work on the PPP 3000 was excellent, but we can't work with someone who's unreliable.

Best of luck with your future projects.

Gunnar

The email bore with it the realization that I had managed to torpedo not only a good project, but a great working relationship. It made my throat and eyes burn, but I only had myself to blame. Heavy-hearted, I closed my laptop. But instead of panic, I felt relief, kind of. I know, so stupid. My lack of action had the effect of reducing my options, for better or for worse. I can't really say I did it on purpose (and for the record, I do not endorse this behavior). But something suddenly clicked in my brain, like I had urgently shifted into a new gear.

I looked at my phone, where River's calls and voicemails were still awaiting my reply.

* * *

The towel was a hot commodity. It was technically designated a shared resource, but in reality, we both wanted full custody. Ever seen "The Gods Must Be Crazy"? We were heading into similar territory, except instead of a Coke bottle, it was a ripped, stained towel with very little absorbency power left in it. After a brief but intense negotiation, we hammered out what Styles proudly called The Towel Agreement. Morning use would alternate daily, and at night, it served as either a blanket or a privacy screen, depending on the need. Towel tensions were high, but we weren't going to let it tear us apart.

Surviving overall was getting a little easier. If you squinted and ignored the scary looking bug bites, you could almost believe we were having a good time. At night, as we lay under our palm-frond roof, we spread the towel across both of us. It was barely enough to cover our torsos, but it felt kind of luxurious.

"You know, I have a dance playlist downloaded to my phone. We're just a solar battery charger and a rechargeable Bluetooth speaker away from opening a resort," I said, turning onto my side to face him.

He did the same. "Packages could include coconut-opening workshops and complimentary existential crises."

Chapter 19

When you've lived with someone for so many years, they eventually notice when you've sort of faded into the background.

Before Gunnar let me go for being a professional ghost, I'd perfected the art of looking busy while spacing out into the island survival scenario.

I'd position myself at my desk or on the couch with my laptop open, staring into space while I was "composing".

I'd go out to the store but come home empty-handed after forgetting my shopping list and pushing the cart through the aisles in a zombie-like daze.

I'd go outside to do yard work only to wonder how long I'd been standing with the rake in my hands as the neighbor waved at me from their driveway.

I'd sit in front of the record shelf to pick something to put on, and finish a whole scene on the island without choosing anything.

All while Griffin moved through our house like a man living in fast-forward, comparatively speaking.

He'd wake up, shower, make coffee, kiss me, go to work, come home, cook dinner sometimes, clean up, play with the cats, watch TV, and go to bed, while I haunted our house and our neighborhood like a phantom who desperately wished she could move objects or communicate, but couldn't, despite her best efforts.

So when Griffin arrived home one day to find me in the process of hanging all the art that was leaning against various walls for roughly the entire time we'd been living in our house, I'm pretty sure he had to redirect his planned conversation from "Why are you so spacey lately" to "How much caffeine have you had today?"

This was my invitation to tell him the truth about everything. That I'd been dithering on calling River back. That I'd procrastinated my way out of a job and sabotaged my good will with Gunnar for future work. And that I was now unemployed and mentally preoccupied by an imaginary island survival scenario instead of dealing with reality.

I couldn't say all that, obviously, but I did have a morsel of good news to share. "I called River back. About booking the studio."

Griffin's face lit up. "For real?! I was starting to doubt that you wanted to."

"Yeah, I mean, I left him a voicemail, so I don't have the details yet. But I'm doing it!" I exclaimed, a ball of nervous energy standing on the couch with a drill in my hands. I turned back to the wall and finished attaching the hook and setting the painting onto it.

It was like an energy block had been magically cleared. I was so energized, in fact, that after I finished hanging all the art, I deep cleaned and reorganized the entire kitchen and then took to the treadmill at a speed I had not previously run.

* * *

"So let me understand," Paige said, consulting her notes with a semi-concerned expression. "You got fired because you were avoiding the big opportunity, and now you're pursuing the big opportunity because you got fired?"

"Isn't it poetic?" I asked, knowing the answer, and also knowing she was not going to dignify my question by telling it to me.

"Are you ever going to tell me what this opportunity is?"

"It's classified," I said, attempting to look mysterious instead of just evasive. "Like, top secret. Griffin knows, but I've sworn him to secrecy. I haven't told my mom, or even Hannah, and she's been telling me for years something like this was in my natal chart."

Paige raised an eyebrow curiously. "Classified from your therapist?"

"Believe me, you wouldn't believe me anyway."

She gave me that look that I'm pretty sure all therapists learn in therapist school. You know, the one that says *I'm professionally obligated to remain non-judgmental, but I can't help you if you won't tell me what's going on* with just the right amount of concerned eyebrow action.

"Whatever it is," Paige said finally, "and however you made this decision, I want you to know that you have my full support. You can do hard things."

"Thanks," I said, needing her encouragement, but also afraid to accept it. "I'm going to need your support when I inevitably fail."

"Cara," she said gently, "what you think is failing is actually just a step in the right direction. Actual failing is not trying at all."

"I just don't know what I'm doing," I pouted, looking down

at my nail-bitten hands.

"New things are definitely scary. But you don't have to be 100% prepared to participate in your own life. It's okay to start something before you feel completely qualified to do it."

I hated how much sense that made.

* * *

It only took River a day to return my call, but the time between me leaving him the message and my phone ringing with his name on the display felt like an agonizing trillion years. With waves of cortisol crashing through my body, I answered, expecting him to sound annoyed, disappointed, or totally confused about who I was and why I was calling him. Instead, he sounded excited to hear from me.

"I was starting to think you decided I was crazy," he said with a comforting laugh that made me remember why I'd agreed to this terrifying venture in the first place.

"It just took me a while to convince myself I wasn't the crazy one."

* * *

And that's how I ended up back in LA. I was on my own this time, now that it was *business*. Griffin very enviously tried to get more time off work to tag along, but the clinic got busy and he very responsibly heeded his calling.

The first recording session was surprisingly not a disaster. River had booked time at Burntree, a small studio that looked more like a high-tech living room than what I imagined a professional recording studio must look like, which immediately put me at ease because I could pretend we were just hanging out.

We spent the first hour just talking through the songs, with River playing acoustic versions while I tried to find where my voice fit without completely overthinking every note. I tried to channel how I felt that night around his fire pit, but I was easily distracted by the fancy sound equipment that I had no knowledge of, which just reminded me how out of my element I was.

Then something clicked. We started with a new version of one of his more well-known songs, but now instead of River's solo vocals, it was a duet. I honestly don't know how this happened, but my voice wove itself into the melody in an uncomplicated way that felt good, like it worked. For a whole three minutes and forty-seven seconds, I forgot to be afraid and just sang.

"Holy shit," I said when we finished, then immediately clapped my hand over my mouth. "Sorry, I probably shouldn't swear in a professional studio."

"It's not that kind of professional," River grinned. "And yeah, holy shit is right. That was exactly what I was hoping for."

By the end of the day, we'd recorded rough versions of three songs, and even though hearing my own recorded voice took some getting used to, I had to admit, there was something there. I mean, River carried most of the load, but the combination worked.

That's when Styles showed up with coffee and a metric fuck-ton of curiosity. He had been texting River throughout the session.

"How'd it go?" he asked, clearly dying to hear the recordings.

"Play him the last one," River said to his producer, Darian. And before I could object or flee to the bathroom to have a panic attack, my voice was filling the studio speakers, harmonizing with River's on the song he had first demoed to us by the fire at his pool party, the one called *Riptide*.

Styles listened attentively, and when it was finished, he looked at me with a glimmer in his eyes.

"You nailed it," he said, smiling broadly.

"She did, didn't she," River agreed. He looked like he was about to say more, but his intentions seemed to hit an impenetrable wall and clink to the floor as Styles turned his attention to me.

"So, Cara," he said, "did you bring those writing samples by any chance? I haven't been able to stop thinking about *Sixty-Six* since you told us about it at the party."

An urgent but unidentifiable tingle shot through my entire body. It wasn't fear or anxiety, I knew those feelings too well. Nerves, maybe? A little. But wasn't that... excitement? Desire even? But not that kind of desire. More like a desire to impress. A desire to please. Even a desire for recognition. For me to feel that way about something that was actually happening in real life instead of my imagination, well I'd say that meant that something about this felt... right. Like there was reason to hope.

"I haven't even looked at it to remind myself what shape it's in," I said, handing over the folder with my hand shaking from excitement.

Styles accepted the folder with a light in his eyes that delivered a pretty major dopamine hit directly to my *desire to please* target. He took it to the far corner of the studio and began flipping through the pages while River and I resumed a discussion about microphone placement, which I suddenly did not care about, like at all. Trying to be stealthy, I kept Styles in my periphery to catch a whiff of any potential reaction he might have while simultaneously trying to focus on what River was saying, but let's be real, River's microphone placement opinions didn't stand a chance.

After an excruciating wait and absolutely no memory of what River had been saying to me, Styles finally closed the folder, stood up, and started walking toward us. It took everything I had in me to pretend I barely noticed, opting for a nonchalant turn of my head from my seated position as he arrived.

"*This...*" he held up my dystopian teenage music revolution manuscript and waggled it from on high, "this is exactly the kind of project I want to develop. It's brilliant and weird and completely original. And Cara, the writing is so *good.*"

It was exactly what I wanted to hear, so of course, doubt took over. I stared at him in wonderment, whilst also wondering if the studio had some kind of gas leak that was making everyone a little loopy. "You want to help me publish a novel inspired by music nerds who hang out on discord servers and message boards, weeping and clutching their pearls about the doomed future of popular music?" As if I wasn't one of them.

"I want to develop it with you," he corrected. "Whatever final shape it might take. Working together. We brainstorm, you write, I produce. We figure out together how to make it, and then we make it."

I looked at River, who had gone slightly tense. There was something in his expression that suggested he wasn't entirely thrilled about Styles crashing this party.

"Well, that's cool," River said, with just a hint of territorial edge, "I'm glad you found your project. Maybe when Cara and I are finished ours then you can talk about yours."

Styles' eyes widened. "When you're finished? How long is that going to take? I know how you work, your last album took a year to finish."

"What's your rush?" River asked in a polite-but-slightly-annoyed tone.

"Inspiration doesn't just sit around and wait," Styles said, leaning forward with determined fervor. "Cara, what if... now just hear me out... what if instead of flying back and forth to record with River whenever the mood strikes him, what if... you moved to LA?"

My eyes must have popped out of my head, because he didn't give me a chance to object. "I don't mean permanently," he added quickly, seeing my expression. "Unless you want to, that's up to you. But you know, just for a little while. Try it out. See what we can come up with."

River's neutral expression belied the look in his eyes. "That's... a big ask."

"Maybe it is," Styles shot back. "But... Cara, if you're up for it, this just seems like it could work out for all of us."

"Look," River said, his tone becoming more pointed, "I appreciate your passion, Styles, but Cara and I already have set this in motion. We have momentum now. She's going to be busy," he ruled, looking right at Styles.

And then River turned to me, "And I'm more than happy to take care of the travel arrangements. Don't feel like you need to uproot your entire life on someone else's whim."

The air in the recording studio felt charged, and while I

couldn't pinpoint a specific thing that I might have done to cause the negative shift, it felt like it was all my fault. I never meant to come between the two of them.

I realized I was clenching my jaw and grinding my teeth, watching them argue about how I should spend my time. What was initially flattering now felt deeply uncomfortable, and I started to feel a little perturbed.

"Okay, STOP. This is nuts. I'm not sure what this is, but I'm pretty sure it's not what I signed up for."

They both had the grace to look embarrassed.

"You're right," River said. "I'm sorry. I just... I don't want to see you get pulled in different directions," he explained, tugging metaphorically on one arm.

Styles tugged on the other. "Different directions?" he echoed. "There is no reason we can't all find a way to make this work." He turned to face me. "No pressure," he said, softer now. "Just think about it."

River exhaled, offering a faint smile and a forgiving glance at Styles before turning back toward the mixing board.

"Okay," I said, nodding in agreement to something I had definitely not processed yet, trying not to leave my body while I did the math on how many appointments I could miss before irreversibly disappointing everyone.

Somehow, I managed to pull myself back down to the ground and respond with a definite maybe. "I'll... think about it."

Chapter 20

By now, I'm sure you can imagine what my journey home to Griffin was like to share how my first recording session with River went. But somehow, none of the eleventeen-thousand scenarios I'd imagined and scripts I'd composed and mentally rehearsed had prepared me for having the actual conversation. Funny, that.

My flight had been delayed and had landed late into the night, so when I finally claimed my suitcase and made my way out to the airport pickup zone, Griffin was looking happy to see me, but also tired, like a dutiful husband who'd stayed up well past our regular bedtime to shuttle me home on a stormy night when his wake-up alarm was only a few hours away.

It occurred to me that the *normal life* I had been so eager to get back to after the first LA trip had finally caught up with him, and that for him, it was now nothing more than a pleasant memory, a little vacation bubble isolated from reality, and that he might have been sad about it while I was off having my dream adventure.

We had a long drive ahead of us, and while of course he was going to want to hear all about it, I wasn't sure whether the long drive home in gross weather and darkness was the right time to tell him *the news.*

"So," he said with a yawn, struggling to keep his eyes open, "how was it? Did you and River finish the songs?"

Finish the songs should have been the first clue that he was coming down the other side of all this dream-chasing stuff, and that as thrilled as he was that I got to temporarily take a break from my own *normal life*, he was ready to relegate it to "remember that time when..."

But he asked, so...

"We made progress, for sure. And Styles read my manuscript and he loved it! He wants to..."

I paused, thinking carefully about my next words. Tell him the story in a plodding, linear narrative, or get to the point.

"Wants to what?" Griffin asked, wearily.

"They, River and Styles, want me... *you and me*, to move to LA."

Griffin braked a little as he flashed a quick glance toward me and then back to the road. "Move to LA? Like, pack up our lives and permanently relocate to California?"

"Not permanently, unless we want to. But just for however long we need to, while I'm working on these projects with them. I know it sounds crazy, but honey, I feel like I've got this momentum all of a sudden and I don't want to lose it. I think I'd like to see if I can actually do this thing I've been dreaming about doing for my whole life."

"But what about that new contract with Gunnar?" Griffin asked the dreaded question, and now I had to come clean.

"I never got back to him," I admitted, which was accurate when you look at it from anyone else's perspective other than mine, but didn't capture the full-color, deliciously agonizing director's-cut montage of mental world-building I went through to reach the point of not getting back to him. How could I explain to anyone, let alone Griffin, that all that time I was not getting back to Gunnar, I was trapped in an imaginary realm on an island without internet or cell service?

Griffin stared straight ahead at the road and cleared his throat. He seemed a little more awake now, or maybe it was a bit of anger bubbling up.

"Are you serious? You didn't get back to him? Cara, that was a solid gig. He might as well have giftwrapped it with a little card that said 'Here, take this hefty stack of cash in exchange for telling people how to insert fancy doo-dads into their hoo-has.'"

That hit me pretty hard in the guilt-spot. "I mean... you're right. I could have handled that better."

Griffin adjusted his grip on the steering wheel to a more relaxed position and started to fiddle with various dashboard settings like the radio volume and the heat, as if he was looking for the *positivity button*, somewhere in front of him. I was afraid that he wouldn't find it.

He sighed. "I know when you get onto something that you're excited about, it's practically impossible to shake you out of it. And I love it when you get excited about stuff, it's *you*, in your purest form."

I gasped. "So, we're doing it?"

We. That word seemed to land on Griffin like a ton of bricks. "What about my job? My friends? Hockey? I have a life here, too." He was right, and my guilt spiraled into shame as I realized how selfish I was being.

We drove in silence for a little while, watching the windshield wipers rhythmically glide back and forth across the glass in front of us, wiping the raindrops away only so they could instantly reappear. Enough time had passed that I figured we'd reached the end of the conversation, at least for the time being. And then Griffin laughed.

"It hardly ever rains in LA," he mused, which immediately filled me with renewed hope and gave me the crack in the door I needed to try and convince him.

"We have friends there who can help us both get set up," I said urgently. "I'm sure Willow would love to be your client." I seriously almost immediately regretted that suggestion but didn't take it back. To his credit, Griffin let it pass.

"I'm not going without you. I can't. It's just temporary. Can we please?" I paused for a moment to see if he'd answer. When he didn't, I continued. "This could be like part two of our adventure together."

I watched Griffin's expression change from skeptical to thoughtful to just a flicker of excitement. "We could be like those couples who sell everything and buy an RV, except instead of driving around the country vlogging about visiting weird folk monuments, we get to be California people for a little while."

"Midlife Crisis: Sleet to Sun Edition!" I exclaimed.

"It's been done before," he said.

"Maybe not original," I agreed, "but if somebody else has done it, so can we."

Griffin sat up in his seat, suddenly very alert. "When you put it that way..." he paused briefly. "Before I call the clinic and ask for a leave of absence, are you absolutely sure?"

"Am I ever sure of anything?"

He chuckled. "You weren't even sure you turned forty-eight on your last birthday."

"I'm still not sure about that. But this kind of feels like the wheels are already in motion and stopping it could be the biggest mistake I ever make." At that point I realized my mind had basically already packed up the house and the cats and was heading down the highway in the opposite direction. Still, there was always a chance my mind might do a U-turn if I didn't commit right this second.

Griffin smiled and cast a quick glance over to me. "Well then, okay."

"For real?"

"Yeah, let's do it. Let's move to California, baby!"

I just about hugged his arm from across the car but stopped myself to avoid jerking the wheel. I did a little dance in my seat instead. Griffin laughed. "I haven't seen you bust a move like that since you drank too many of those Redbull vodka drinks at Trevor's wedding."

"It's your brother's fault for having Redbull vodka drinks at his wedding, they weren't going to drink themselves."

"Okay," Griffin said, his laughter fading, "now how exactly do we tell people we're moving to California?"

I didn't have an answer for that yet, and the question made me shiver a little. This was sure to send shockwaves of disappointment and disdain through the people in my life known as my biological familial units. The people who never got it, could never understand. The idea of them knowing I was actively chasing something bigger than they believed was possible for me? Mortifying. No one must know what was really happening.

"With spoonfuls of lies sprinkled with stevia," I answered.

* * *

As expected, telling my family about the move was akin to trying to describe a vivid dream that only makes sense in the context of its own surreal logic, and only to you.

"I'm trying to understand," my mother said to me over video chat, notably exasperated. "Griffin made friends with some random people in Los Angeles, and now you're both moving there so he can expand his massage practice?"

"That's the basic idea," I said, squinting my eyes and tilting my head to bring into focus the parts of the lie that had a kernel of truth to them.

"And what are *you* going to do there?"

"Oh, you know. I work from home. I can do my job from anywhere."

I heard my father's vague mumbling in the background.

"Your dad's right here, he doesn't want to talk to you. But he's saying your uncle Keith needs someone at the warehouse to do... what did he call it... he needs a documentation and compliance specialist, I think? More respectable than writing about... you know."

The most boring job I could possibly fathom. Uncle Keith had asked me to work for him so many times. At every family gathering. To the point where I basically had a Pavlovian yawn response the moment he walked into the room.

"Sex toys aren't going to cease to exist just because I'm writing standard operating procedures for Uncle Keith from nine to five every day," I defended my career choice, for the millionth time. We both knew where this argument would end up. Thankfully, she decided to move on, this time.

"Well anyway, mighty big of you to uproot your life to indulge Griffin's whims. It just doesn't seem like him."

"Well, you know, once a place like LA gets into your veins,

it changes your DNA."

"Just be careful, they have natural disasters out there."

"Yes, only there." The smarm slipped out before I could check it. She replied with an elegant, judgmental mother-shaped silence, my dad grumbled something about hucksters and shysters, and the world continued to make sense.

* * *

It was also time to finally reach out to Hannah, who, despite the fact that I was always the worst at keeping in touch, still managed to remain besties with me for reasons I could never understand.

I was nervous about telling her about the move for entirely different reasons. Hannah had... abilities. Maybe she was really psychic, or was super in tune with The Universe (capitalized, for her), or maybe she just had an impeccably calibrated bullshit detector built into her physical being that defied scientific explanation. Any of those could be possible.

She'd been telling me for millennia that my astrological destiny was screaming to be fulfilled and my commitment to fighting my true purpose was a direct violation of The Universe's decree, as if I was personally responsible for Mercury in retrograde being a thing, or something.

And so, spilling the tea to Hannah was a different story. No way I'd get away with blaming this all on Griffin. I had to be more real with her.

She answered before the first ring could even start, because of course she did.

"Oh my God, Cara, I was just pulling cards about you," she said without the standard phone call greetings, because this was how conversations with Hannah always started. "All major arcana, which is fucking wild. The Chariot, The Tower, and The Star. Big life changes, new paths emerging, with buckets of inspiration at the helm. What's happening?"

No beating around the bush here. "Griffin and I are moving to California."

The silence on the other end of the line lasted exactly long enough for me to wonder if we'd been disconnected, then Hannah made a sound that contained a metric fuckload of emotions, none of them identifiable.

"Finally! But why?"

"Just... exploring some creative opportunities."

I could hear her eyes rolling over the phone. After decades of watching me hoard unfinished drafts like they were secret government documents, Hannah had developed an instinct for when I was withholding.

"You don't even let me read your stuff, and I've believed in you since you had braces and a crush on Joey McIntyre."

"I let you read my *Jem and the Holograms* fan fiction in seventh grade. You said it was *unrealistic*."

"Cara, oh my God. I'm sorry, but Rio would never have hooked up with Stormer."

You know that one minor diss from your childhood that seemed insignificant at the time but then went on to cripple your ambitions well into adulthood? That was mine. But I'd never tell Hannah that.

"All I'm saying is, there is more to this than you're telling me."

"You're right. I'm sorry about being cryptic, it's just... I want this to work out. I need to see where it goes."

"Okay, look, I've seen you obsess about stuff before. Remember your rock tumbling phase? And that period when you were collecting original pressings of every album released in 1966?"

"The most iconic year for music."

"Some might say 1967 wins that title."

"Hush now."

"My point is, this is different. This is cross-country-for-vague-purposes different."

There was no good way to explain it without explaining all of it. And I wasn't ready for that.

"I don't think this is like those things. I think this is maybe who I really am, who I've been too scared to be until now."

Hannah was quiet for a moment. Then:

"Cara Nicole Becker," she said in her most serious witchy voice, "I have been burning manifestation candles and charging rose quartz and pulling cards about your destiny for YEARS and watching you let messages from The Universe pile up like collection notices. Whatever this is, or whatever it turns out to be, I'm glad you're finally answering the call."

Relief. I could handle judgment from my mother. But I needed Hannah's brand of enlightened new age encouragement to power me through, even if I needed to take it with a grain of salt. I also knew she could sense the undercurrent of terror zapping through me.

"Babe. Have you been doing those breathing exercises I taught you? The ones where you inhale the light and exhale the darkness?"

"If you count hyperventilating, yes, so many breathing exercises."

She laughed, but then stopped quickly with an unsettling gasp.

"Just... be careful, okay?"

A warning from my mother was par for the course. A warning from Hannah was something to take more seriously.

Her voice dropped. "This whole thing has Big Disruption Energy. There's a reason I pulled the Tower card. There might even be a Saturn return."

I had no idea what that meant. "I hated that car," I muttered.

"Not the car, babe. The cosmic reckoning."

"Meaning...?"

"The Universe keeps track of your major life transitions, and you are definitely due for one. But seriously. Your third house is lighting up like one of those old-school operator switchboards. Major voice and expression vibes. And probably some chaos. But like... good chaos? I think?"

"As long as it's the good kind," I said.

"Anyway. You're right, you have to do this. But keep those grounding crystals I gave you handy and your guard up. This is supposed to happen, but only you can decide how it unfolds."

Chapter 21

Ahh, teleportation. Absolutely the most superior method of relocating from one place to another. Even better than first-class air travel. All you need to do is mentally tag the people and items you want to bring with you and then *think* them over to the new location! Poof! So efficient and satisfying! And you can even edit or redo it as many times as you like until you achieve the perfect moving experience. 10/10, totally recommend.

Unfortunately, teleportation had yet to be invented (someone's working on this, though, right?) and so Griffin and I were forced to move the old-fashioned struggle-bus way, with boxes, wheels, and the ennui-fueled anguish of logistical planning.

Thankfully, we had a little help from our friends on *the other side.* River had apparently acquiesced to Styles' insistence that me relocating to LA would be good for all of us, and they had started working together to help me and Griffin get set up.

He connected Griffin with a new wellness clinic that needed experienced massage therapists and was willing to help him navigate the licensing requirements for practicing in California.

Styles sent links to apartments in neighborhoods near his studio. I knew LA was expensive, but we were definitely going to have to adjust our grocery shopping and dining out habits. Having to sacrifice avocados in the place where adding avocados to things makes them "California" was a hardship we were just going to have to endure.

"Look at this place," Griffin said, showing me a listing for a two-bedroom house in Silver Lake with a small backyard. "It's twice what we pay here, but River says the wellness client base there will more than make up for it."

I grunted my approval, while suppressing an acidic burp.

"And Styles says he knows the landlord and can put in a good word for us," he continued.

"Fingers crossed."

Griffin looked at me over his laptop screen. "You're being weird about this. I thought this is what you wanted?"

"I do. I'm just..."

...mentally concocting a crash-and-burn scenario to establish a baseline of imaginary inevitable failure so that I can survive the real thing when it happens...

"...cushioning myself with low expectations. It's comforting to me, you know? It's just how I'm wired."

Griffin closed the laptop and looked at me seriously. "I get it. But promise me something?"

"Okay," I agreed, tentatively.

"No matter what happens. No matter how this turns out. Let California do a little rewiring up there."

That stung a little, but he wasn't wrong. If this was going to work, forging some new neural pathways was going to be necessary. Breakthroughs don't always come with an earth-shaking tremor. Sometimes they're more subtle. After all the therapy I had been doing, I didn't expect Griffin's rewiring suggestion to shake me up so gently. A minor, fraction of a shift that triggered a light bulb to flicker on and off again in a place in my brain that had not yet been lit.

* * *

The drive to California took a week. It was a scenic road trip with no major kerfuffles. That is, if you exclude a brief but intense existential crisis after Griffin missed an exit somewhere in Nebraska. Cue me trying to be navigational while managing our road trip playlist at the same time.

Pausing the music to be able to think was my intention, but unfortunately resulted in me accidentally skipping to *Life is a Highway*, which was entirely the most jarring song for that moment.

The frustration made me drop my phone into that abhorred gap between the left side of the passenger seat and the compartment thingy, forcing Griffin to find a place to stop so I could dig it out, leading to a roadside fight about whether or not we were past the point of no return and were we bad cat parents for making them endure this road trip with us.

By the time we pulled into the driveway of our new house, we were pretty exhausted. Our new abode was a charming furnished bungalow with a mild demeanor on the outside, and a wild streak on the inside. I didn't remember it looking so... *expressive?* in the listing's photos, but in person, the combination of high-quality furnishings and psychedelic color palette gave me the impression that its decorator had been trained in the Vegas-hotel-room-in-the-1960s style of interior design.

Look, I'm not saying that's a bad thing. It's just that my own personal aesthetic has always tended more towards comfortable rustic, so I hoped the bold colors and patterns wouldn't induce a twitch.

"I'm going to need to rewire my brain immediately to make *this* work for me," I said, gesturing wildly at everything in the house.

I opened the cat crate to let Daisy and Clover out to explore, and they both slunk low, bellies to the floor, before immediately slithering underneath the couches, presumably to hide from the screaming wall color. "See, the cats agree with me."

"It'll be okay. We packed all the plaid blankets and throw pillows, you have your comfort items."

"Buffalo checks in this space?" I imagined trying to mesh my relaxed style with the wild palette and decor of our new home. The clash was severe. I felt the urge to put my head between my knees and apply Hannah's breathing technique, when there was a knock on the front door.

We were barely there an hour when Styles and Willow arrived with a lavishly curated welcome basket. "Welcome to LA!" Willow announced, enveloping me in a hug with warm and pure vibes. "How was the drive? Are you exhausted? Do you need anything? We brought snacks."

Styles presented me with a small, hopeful looking areca palm that immediately filled me with concern for its future under my care. "It's supposed to be good for creativity," he said. "Something about the oxygen production helping with mental clarity."

"Do you have one of these?" I asked.

"He did, but dare I say it was not living its best life in his office." Willow answered for him. "Don't worry, it's safe for cats. I have it in the cat room now and everyone's happy."

Moments later, River and Naomi arrived with even more gifts. River handed Griffin a bottle of some small-batch whiskey. "From a distillery in Kentucky. Figured you might need something to take the edge off the moving stress."

Once the snacks were sampled and the conversation turned to moving horror stories, the energy in the room began to mellow.

"Oh River, remember that time the movers dropped your granddad's old piano down a flight of stairs?" Naomi said, holding a delicate seed cracker topped with walnuts in Manuka honey. "I'll never forget that sound."

River laughed. "How could I forget. That poor piano. Murdered."

"Thank goodness for insurance," sang Naomi, clinking glasses with her husband. "Not that it makes up for it," she clarified.

"Remember what happened to our friends in Echo Park?" Styles added. "They accidentally left their dog in the old place and didn't realize it until they were halfway to Pasadena."

There was laughter, some mock horror, and then eventually a lull in the conversation signaling that it was time to wrap up.

"Well," Willow said, standing and smoothing her dress, "we should let you get settled."

"So glad you're here," Styles added warmly, giving Griffin a quick shoulder pat and aiming a smile in my direction.

As we all began moving toward the door for thanks and see-you-soons, Willow caught my eye and motioned for me to follow her toward the kitchen.

"Hey," she said softly, glancing back to make sure we weren't being overheard. "Can I just... say something really quick?"

"Sure," I said, bracing for something outlandish given her track record with private conversations.

"I just wanted to apologize. For what happened at River and Naomi's. My idea. It was... a mistake. And I'm truly sorry." She looked down at her feet, then back up at me. "If I could have seen the future and known you and Griffin were going to be more than passing acquaintances in our lives, I never would have suggested it."

I empathized with her. "I mean, how could you have known?"

"And now that you and Griffin are here," she continued, "I really hope there's no awkwardness between us. I want us all to be friends. I totally get it if you're still weirded out. But I hope we can get past it."

Her humble apology felt like a whoosh of fresh air through the room. The window might have also been open, but I was willing to give her the credit. Just because we had gotten off on the wrong foot, it didn't mean we had to keep standing on it.

That said, it was a good thing she couldn't see inside my mind. She'd likely take it all back if she knew about a certain plane crash survival fantasy.

"I appreciate that," I said, and I meant it. "And yeah, no worries, we're cool." She exhaled, visibly relieved, and gave me a quick, grateful hug before we rejoined the others.

While our welcome wagon didn't stay long, it was just enough time to make sure we had everything we needed and to make plans for the next few days. Their visit helped soften the house's loud vibes enough to feel like we might actually get comfy there.

"They're really going out of their way to make us feel welcome," Griffin observed after they left, chilling on the retro floral-patterned fuchsia couch with his welcome whiskey. He surveyed our new ambitiously decorated living room.

"They are," I agreed, but wasn't it all a little too much? No one had ever rolled out a red carpet for me like this before, I thought as I scrunched my toes into the fibers of the lush scarlet area rug that somehow really pulled the room together.

Chapter 22

"How are you settling in?" Styles asked as I arrived for my first official day at his office-slash-studio, which turned out to be a converted warehouse in a commercial-industrial neighborhood. He moved a pile of books and papers from one chair onto another chair already occupied with stuff, so that I had a place to sit.

His office was uncomfortably cozy, if that makes any sense. I appreciated his penchant for soft cushy seating and places to put your feet up, but his particular brand of clutter felt chaotic to me (my own clutter, I can handle).

A week had passed since Griffin and I had moved, and on one hand, it was pretty much what you would expect. Unpacking, getting the lay of the land, identifying the best grocery store in the area, getting used to driving in a new, very trafficky city, just your standard, run-of-the-mill, getting acquainted kind of stuff. Boring.

Our new neighborhood wasn't exactly glam. Instead, it was oddly familiar, like it was the LA equivalent of our NF community, except, you know, sunnier. And yet, I kept getting the weird sensation of having infiltrated a dimension that we weren't supposed to be in, and if we weren't careful, we'd run into different versions of ourselves and the multiverse would collapse on us.

I say *we*, but I guess I really just mean *me*. Griffin had no trouble adapting. In no time at all, he'd figured out the best route to his new clinic, identified the nearest gym, and struck up conversations with our neighbors like they were old friends. He never once complained about the bright orange accent wall in the kitchen. Whereas every time I walked past it, I almost tripped and spilled my coffee. Who can trip over a wall? This girl.

But I digress...

"It's great," I said, politely. "I don't know what I expected, but it's like, everything is the same as at home, but also different." I didn't tell him how it felt like I had slipped sideways through a crack in reality and landed in one of my own daydreams.

"Different good or different bad?"

"Different... weird."

Styles nodded like this was a perfectly reasonable response.

I hesitated, then asked, "Speaking of weird, can I ask you something?"

"Sure," Styles said, leaning back in his chair.

"How do you deal with being seen? Like, actually seen. Not just... noticed, but recognized for your work. I mean... I know I'm not there... but..."

"Not there *yet*." He tilted his head, considering my question. "I can't speak for others, but in my case, I guess I just always wanted it. Craved it, maybe. But sometimes it still freaks me out. Like someone's going to tap me on the shoulder and say, 'You? Really? You don't belong here.'"

I exhaled, relieved that he knew what I meant. "Yes. That. I want to be part of this world. I want people to know me for what I make. And then I think about how I would feel if that actually happened, and I panic. Like I would be exposed as a fraud."

Styles smiled plainly. "Welcome to imposter syndrome. Everyone here has it. Well, the ones who aren't narcissistic sociopaths, anyway. Some people are just better at hiding it."

"You think River has it?"

"Totally. It's what makes him not an asshole. Most of the time."

I laughed. That seemed to please him.

"You do belong here," he insisted. "It takes a while to find your rhythm in a new city. Especially this city. LA has a way of making you question everything you thought you knew about yourself."

Styles was right about the whole "finding my rhythm" thing. I'd never worked with someone creatively before. I was used to working in near-isolation, whether it was my own secret writing efforts or for work. As someone who always had trouble following instructions, writing them did have its own special kind of satisfaction for me.

But now, I was sharing my ideas with someone who knew how to turn those ideas into momentum, and the feeling was both disorienting and electrifying. Styles wasn't just invested in the outcome, he was legit excited by the process.

He turned to me. "I loved all the samples you let me read, but the one I'm still freaking out about is *Sixty-Six*. A dystopian epic about teenagers in the future starting a musical rebellion with their grandparents against the corporate establishment? I can't stop thinking about it. Honestly, that's why you're here right now."

"I mean, it's probably the most ambitious of anything I've ever written. I didn't even know I had a 90,000-odd word novel in me."

"It's one of those stories that feels like it's about the future but is really about right now. And it's got a built-in generational appeal. Trust me, it has legs. Where did it come from?"

He couldn't help himself. I felt like one of his interview subjects, and before I even opened my mouth to respond, I could almost feel him feeding off the energy of an inspiration story about to be told like it was the fuel he survived on.

"Um, well... actually... I didn't even *want* to write it. When the idea came to me, I remember thinking I loved it but that there had to be someone else out there who would do a better job. I even talked out loud to the idea, like, told it to find a better writer who could do it justice and get it out there. But it just wouldn't leave me alone."

I felt like I had been rambling on forever, so I paused to see if Styles was satisfied, but he continued looking at me like he knew there was more, so I kept going.

"So I thought, okay, I'll do the bare minimum to let it out. I'll just write an outline. A plot summary. But before I knew it, all of these characters seemed to blast their way out onto the page just fully formed. I know it sounds insane. But I almost felt like I had nothing to do with it, like they were forcing my hands on the keyboard."

That did it. Styles was on his feet, pacing in a small circle and rubbing a chill out of his arms like he had just heard the voice of the Greek muse Calliope herself speaking through me.

"Literal goosebumps," he said, pushing his long sleeve up and showing me his forearm. I didn't actually see any goosebumps, just a moderate amount of hair and a prominent vein, but his reaction was so pure I believed him.

"But it was wasted on me," I continued. "I tried to tell them, the characters, but they didn't listen. And for what? To end up trapped on those pages and hiding in my closet for years."

"Don't you see? That idea picked you for a reason. It knew its time would come. And here you are."

I was struck by how he got exactly what I was saying. Like, he knew what I was talking about, and I didn't have to try and explain it and end up sounding like a child who invented her own magical realm where it's cool to talk out loud to an idea (or end up sounding like an unhinged adult who requires immediate psychiatric intervention, take your pick).

"Okay, now I have goosebumps. You really think so?"

"Yes. It's timely. It's visual. It's 'out there' in all the right ways. I think it could work as an animated web series."

"Wait, not a novel?"

"I'm seeing it more visually than in text form," he said, as if he was channeling a vision from the same source that the idea came from in the first place. "Is that alright? Only if you agree."

I nodded slowly, kind of in awe of what was happening.

"Yes," he said, like he was transmuting my awe-inspired nod into something he could work with. "What do you think? Are you ready to give those characters the life they were always destined to have? Make something that people will finally see?"

I froze. This was exactly the kind of question I'd been avoiding for most of my adult life. Was I ready for that? Was I prepared for the possibility that people might love it, or hate it, or have opinions about it that I couldn't control?

"I am," I said, unable to contain a wide smile and surprising myself with how much I meant it. The energy in the room was so intense that I swear we could have willed the thing into existence just by concentrating on it hard enough.

That is, of course, if our focus hadn't been interrupted. My phone buzzed. It was a text from River.

"Hey. Now that you're settled in, I thought we could get back in the studio? I've got Burntree booked for tomorrow. Let me know."

I stared at my phone silently.

"Everything okay?" Styles asked, catching the change in my expression.

"Yeah. Just... River checking in about studio time."

Styles gave a small nod, but didn't push. I appreciated that about him.

"I can do both," I added, as much to myself as to him.

"I know you can," he said, his voice steady. "Just remember that only one of them is really yours."

* * *

Meanwhile, Griffin was settling into the dream version of his own career, giving therapeutic massages to actors, models, stunt people, executives, and pretty much anyone with money to throw at regular bodywork as a basic life necessity.

That evening, we tried not to bump into each other as we made dinner together in our small kitchen, me prepping the salad while Griffin cooked the chicken.

"River was right. You should see my client list," he said.

"Who knew working in Hollywood was so bad for your back?"

"Anyone I'd recognize?"

"Oh yeah, but I signed confidentiality agreements. Let's just say that several people you've definitely seen on TV will be much more limber the next time you see them on TV."

He paused. "Willow booked a session next week. I guess she got tired of asking Styles to work my technique on her and him never getting it quite right."

That made me feel a little weird. I couldn't say I was really surprised that she'd asked, or that he had agreed. He was a professional. And Willow and I were cool now. It was all good. Everyone was getting what they wanted.

"Are you happy?" I asked him.

"Yeah, actually. I really am. Are you?" He turned his head to face me, beaming with a cute smile.

Was I happy? I was definitely something. Challenged, stimulated, frequently anxious, occasionally exhilarated, perpetually uncertain about whether I was living my dream or just getting in way over my head.

"I think so," I said. "It's hard to tell the difference between happy and scared shitless when they both keep me up at night."

"We made the right choice, Car. Everything about this feels right, don't you think? Even if it takes a little longer for you to find your feet, I got you. We're in this together. I don't want to jinx it, but doesn't this already kind of feel like home?"

He had a point. I wasn't really missing much about my *old life*, except for Hannah, and I knew distance was no match for our bond and her ability to astral project herself into my consciousness whenever she wanted to chat.

That night, lying in bed in our California house, still getting used to the neighborhood sounds, I listened to Griffin breathing beside me. And I realized that for the first time in years, I actually was more excited about tomorrow than I was afraid of it.

I had trouble falling asleep as usual, but this time it wasn't because I was looping on some imaginary scenario, but because the proverbial wheels of inspiration were turning. A real idea, one that Styles and I had been brainstorming, spinning itself into a concept with shape and motion. I itched to get out of bed and start writing, but settled for tapping out a few notes in my phone, hoping they'd make sense in the morning.

Then, the oddest sensation reverberated right through me. I glanced at Griffin, still sleeping soundly. Daisy stretched while Clover purred softly, so either they didn't feel it, or they did but they just didn't care. It was over as quickly as it started, like a ripple through the house. Was that in my head? Some kind of stress-induced vertigo?

Was that... an earthquake?

Chapter 23

I was sitting in River's home studio, which was so incredibly outfitted that I wondered why he even bothered with commercial studios. It was well-organized and tidy, with an impressive collection of vintage instruments adorning the space that almost made it feel like a museum. It was actually a little intimidating.

River was holding a pair of headphones to one ear, listening to the playback of what we had recorded weeks ago, before the move. Something felt a little off about the vibe in the room, but it's entirely possible I was just projecting my own self-disappointment onto him.

"Sorry I didn't make it to the Burntree studio appointment the other day. I guess I got... distracted."

River looked up at me, still holding the headphones.

"No worries. I remember what it was like when I moved out here. It's a lot at first." He sounded alright. Not angry, not even really annoyed, which actually kind of made me feel worse.

"Thanks for understanding," I said, secretly sinking into a pit of guilt for missing the appointment to work on *Sixty-Six* with Styles instead. Then, without me asking, he answered the question that was on my mind.

"Every studio has a different kind of sound to it," River explained. "There's something really warm about Burntree, and I dig the guy who owns it so I do what I can to support his business. Anything we record here today won't match what we did there, but that doesn't mean we can't make some progress until I get another block of time."

Annnnnd spiral. I sipped my water to try and swallow the massive shame capsule in my throat.

"I've been thinking about the arrangements," River said as he sat in the chair next to mine. "I want to strip back the production even more. Really focus on the vocal interplay."

I nodded like I understood what he meant by "vocal interplay" which totally might have been different from what I thought it meant. "I love that," I said, which was my go-to response when I wanted to contribute but couldn't back it up with knowledge or experience.

River picked up his guitar and started playing a slowed-down version of one of his newer songs. It was called *Broken Key*, and it was about the feeling of being locked out of something that belongs to you, like your house or your car or your... heart, I guess.

"I keep hearing a female perspective on this," River said, pausing between verses. "Like, what would it sound like if someone was responding to these lyrics instead of just harmonizing with them?"

"You mean like a conversation?"

"Exactly. Like you're the voice of the person on the other side of the door."

I closed my eyes and listened to him play through the verse again, letting the melody wash over me while I tried to imagine what I would say to someone who was singing about locking someone out of something they shared. What would I want to hear?

"What if," I said slowly, "instead of blaming, the other voice was feeling just as locked out? Like, what if she was saying 'maybe the problem isn't that all of this is your fault', maybe it's like she's saying 'it's the only way you can move on without me?'"

River stopped playing and looked at me like I'd just solved an ancient mystery. "That's... that's really good. That changes the whole emotional arc of the song."

"It does?"

"Yeah. Instead of being about who did what to whom, it becomes about letting someone go to save them. That's way more interesting."

I was suddenly bathed in the warm glow of validation. I barely had enough time to bask in it before River was on his feet, adjusting his guitar. "Should we try it?" he asked.

For the next hour, we worked through the song, with me improvising responses to his lyrics while he calibrated the melody to accommodate my vocal range. It wasn't exactly what I would call physical exertion, but tell that to my drenched armpits.

By the end of the session, we had something that sounded like it could be a thing, and I had an underboob sweat situation going on that thankfully only I was aware of. River played the rough recording back, and it was still a shock to hear my own voice on the speaker like that, but I liked how it sounded. I actually felt what might have been the onset of a *thrill*.

"We make a great team," he said with a pleased look on his face, and raised his hand to give me a high-five. I didn't mean to leave him hanging, but my phone buzzed with a text from

Styles.

"How's the recording going? Want to grab a coffee later and talk about the *Sixty-Six* outline?"

As I checked my phone, River's high-five hand dropped, and I realized his buzz had been killed.

"All good?" he asked, but his tone suggested he knew exactly who was texting me and wasn't feeling all that thrilled about it.

"Just Styles wanting to meet about the writing project," I said, which somehow felt like I was confessing to something illicit.

"Right." River started packing up his guitar with movements that seemed just a little too brisk. "How's that going?"

"Amazing, actually. We're developing it into a web series."

"That's cool," River said, and he sounded like he meant it, but I was sure I detected a note of disappointment underneath. "You guys'll knock it out of the park." He looked up at me earnestly and with a slight smile.

You know that feeling when an unintentionally reckless gesture ends up taking out a fragile object and you wish you could just hit the proverbial redo button and edit the offending incident from the timeline? If I could have gone back in time and high-fived River, I would have. Instead, all I could do was try to salvage the quickly deflating energy.

"So, what else did you want to work on?" I asked, hopefully, but it was too late.

"We should probably wrap up for today."

"Of course," I said, bummed that I had killed our momentum. "Same time next week?"

"You know it."

I offered him a new high-five as a show of good faith, and

he hit it with a chuckle. But as I gathered my things, I couldn't shake the feeling that we were not the same people we were just a few minutes ago.

* * *

Coffee with Styles turned out to be at a trendy cafe where the baristas looked like they'd all been hired straight from a commercial about the place. Ordering a plain black coffee seemed to offend the entire cast... I mean... staff, as well as the regulars behind me in line.

"Before we get into work stuff," Styles said, sliding into his chair coolly, "I got you something."

He reached into his messenger bag and pulled out a small paper sack from one of those tourist shops that sold postcards and "I ❤ LA" tee shirts. "It's not fancy or anything. Just saw it and thought of you."

I opened the bag to find a snow globe containing a miniature Hollywood sign on the hills with tiny palm trees lining the street below. It was kitschy and ridiculous, and when I turned it over, the *Made in China* sticker cemented it as my new favorite tchotchke.

"It's awesome," I said, and I meant it. There was something so charming and honest about its artificiality. Fake snow falling on fake Hollywood and fake palm trees above a fake street leading toward a fake reality.

"I figured you could put it on your desk while you're writing," Styles said. "Like a little reminder that you're here, living your dream."

I shook the globe and watched the snow swirl around the Hollywood sign like a tiny blizzard in the most unlikely of places. "You know what snow globes make me think about?"

"What?"

"When you buy one on vacation, it represents everything you experienced there. You bring it home, and inside it is that little slice of life you lived for a short time. It's completely separate from the real world, and you get on with the rest of your life. But it's like that moment in time lives on inside that little dome. It's so cool to me to imagine that what's happening right now is going to end up inside this thing, like a little version of me, captured in a moment, destined to relive it, over and over again."

Styles was looking at me with that famous gleam in his eyes. "I mean, that's like literally the definition of a souvenir, but I have to admit, I never thought that deeply about it before."

"I guess that's pretty lame."

"I think it's pretty cool. I like the way you think."

"Well anyway, I freakin' love it. Thank you."

"You're welcome."

I set the snow globe carefully on the table between us, where it caught the afternoon light.

"So," Styles said, pulling out his laptop, "how'd the recording session go?"

"Honestly, it's hard. River's so patient with me, and sometimes I'm amazed at what we accomplish, but it's kind of exhausting on, like, a physical level."

"Well, I'm sure you'll hit your stride," Styles said. I could tell he was trying to be encouraging in a neutral sort of way, but it seemed like there was something more to his detached interest in the matter.

"Anyway, I've been thinking about the pilot episode structure," he said, changing gears. That fiery flash of light appeared in his eyes again, whenever he became *switched on*. "I really loved your idea of opening with each protagonist's experience of suddenly hearing this ephemeral, magical music in their heads during some kind of altered state, like a fever, or a laughing fit..."

"Or a head injury," I blurted. "Like the audio version of getting those little stars around your head in cartoons."

"Yes!" he exclaimed. "We could even show a ring of dizzy stars when each character fades in, it would be a great way to establish the animated world."

"1960s-Beatles-*Yellow-Submarine*-style animated world," I declared.

"Totally!" He threw a wild high-five hand in my direction and, this time, I immediately responded the way you're supposed to. Our hands missed on the first attempt, but we nailed it on the retry.

Fumbled high-fives aside, we had fallen into a friendly simpatico almost instantly. He was so easy to be around. And the way he was able to make my ideas come to life without sacrificing the subjective weirdness that made them mine... I guess they call that *vision*.

River had vision too, but it was quieter, harder to read, and less prone to bursts of excitement. The dynamic was definitely different. It was like what Styles had said. With River, I was there to help him with his ideas, while Styles was there to help me with mine.

"Can I ask you something?" Styles said, typing away on his keyboard and then stopping to glance at me over the monitor.

"Go for it."

"Is this project with River something you really want to do? Or do you just feel like you're supposed to. Like you don't want to say no?"

A chill rippled through me along with the sensation that he had somehow tapped into my stream of consciousness and caught an echo of the version of him in my fantasy scenario that had asked me that exact question not that long ago.

"I don't know," I said slowly. "River's such an awesome guy, I don't want to disappoint him."

"He's pretty hard to say no to," Styles agreed.

"I love the idea of it. Art and music have always been... a thing for me. An obsession, I guess."

"I can relate," he said, pointing with both index fingers toward the *Sparks* tour tee shirt he was wearing.

"Sometimes I get carried away. My therapist calls it hyper-focus."

I cut myself off, mortified about mentioning Paige and *my... condition...* out loud. Styles' reaction was to close his laptop, lean forward on his elbows and lock in with full eye-contact. Award-winning listener.

"I do love singing, when there's no pressure to be good at it." I took a sip of my coffee, momentarily breaking my eyes away from the intensity of his attention.

Styles nodded, thoughtful. "But writing is different, right?" he asked.

"I mean, writing started out as a hobby too, but somewhere inside me, it felt closer to who I actually am. I guess that's how I ended up doing freelance technical writing. I get to do what I'm good at, while hiding behind the façade of another company's identity, without worrying about having to take the credit, or the blame. But as far as being an *author*, or *screenwriter*, even... I never thought I'd be taken seriously. Or even try to be."

"Well," he said, with that dimpled smile. "Too late for that now."

I smiled too, feeling a little uncomfortable about maybe having said too much. He didn't say anything else about it. Didn't imply that I *shouldn't* work with River, or ask me to choose. But the fact that he'd asked the question I was already asking myself gave me the sensation that we were tuned into the same frequency.

We sat in silence for a moment, and my mind drifted back into my daydream from that time at River's house after Willow's infamous proposal. Styles had looked so good naked in my imagination, and his kiss was intoxicating. I must've blushed because...

"Is it warm in here?" Styles asked, fanning himself with his hand a little. It was a valid question, given that it was 90 degrees and the A/C in the coffee shop seemed to have cut out.

I felt exposed as I jolted back into the present moment. My impure thoughts were suddenly replaced with waves of guilt and embarrassment, then thoughts of Griffin, followed by confusion about what my thoughts meant, followed by more guilt about the confusion. Fleeting fantasies about *whoever* didn't usually leave me feeling like I'd done something wrong.

"So, what's next?" I asked, clearing my throat and trying to redirect my attention to our project instead of the complicated feelings that were swirling around inside me.

"Next, we set up a meeting with some development people, they ask questions about our vision for the series, and hopefully they decide they want to give us money to make it."

"And if they don't?"

"Then we figure out how to make it ourselves."

"You make it sound so simple. Have you ever done this

before?"

Styles paused and tilted his head thoughtfully. "I've tried. A few starts that didn't quite go anywhere. But..."

"This is the one," I declared, which damn near shocked the bejesus out of me, and made Styles' eyes glimmer with electricity.

"That's my girl! I mean... yes, alright!" This time, the high-five landed on the first try, and honestly, it slapped.

Hours passed while we worked, losing track of the time. Daylight faded to as dark as night could get in the city of spotlights. I hadn't even checked my phone, but when I finally did, I realized that Griffin would be heading to bed soon, if he wasn't waiting up for me.

Styles and I wrapped up our working session and started to gather our things. I tried not to notice how reluctant I felt to leave, the perfect half-moons of his cuticles, or how deep his dimples got when he was really happy.

* * *

When I finally got home, Griffin was still awake, lying down on the couch with the TV on.

"Griff?" I called out to him as I closed the door behind me.

"How was work?" he asked, sitting up and making space for me next to him on the couch. I went and sat next to him. He looked tired, but happy to see me, still wearing what was becoming a perma-grin on his face, clearly having had a good day at work himself. For me, calling it *work* felt strange, because nothing felt *worky* about it.

"Good. We're setting up a meeting with some development

people about the web series."

Griffin raised his arms and threw them around me. "Whoa, Car, that's huge." I wrapped my arms around him too, careful not to bonk him with the snow globe in my hand. As the hug finished, he took off his socks and then leaned into me for a snuggle. "Oh hey, you got your souvenir!" He pointed to the snow globe in my hand.

"Styles gave it to me. To keep me inspired." I rolled my eyes dramatically so Griffin would think I didn't think too much of it. He picked it up and gave it a gentle shake, watching the snow swirl around inside it and settle on the palm-lined street beneath the Hollywood hills.

"There's a lot going on," he observed, his mood becoming more serious. I looked at him, wondering if he was referring to the snow globe, or making a deeper observation about our move to California. "What do you mean?" I asked, having a pretty good idea exactly what he meant, but needing him to tell me in his own words.

"Sometimes I just wonder if it's too much at once. For both of us."

"You think I'm maxed?"

"You're juggling a lot. I'm proud of you, but I don't want you to burn out."

I studied his face. "And what about you?"

"I'm adjusting to the move."

"It seems to me like you've adjusted pretty well. You haven't stopped grinning since we got here."

A pause. A big one.

"I'm adjusting to the move to the background of your new life."

Ouch. Not Griffin metaphorically bonking me with the snow

globe instead. If I were a cartoon character, a rotating ring of dizzy stars would absolutely have appeared over my head. I sat there speechless, waiting for words to form that would bring us both some reassurance. But before they could, my phone buzzed with an email notification. I glanced at it and immediately winced.

Missed Appointment: Paige 6 PM

"Oh, shit. Fuck."

"What's up?"

"I missed a therapy appointment today."

Griffin read the look on my face, and immediately went into support mode. "I know those furrowed brows and what they mean. Don't be so hard on yourself, it wouldn't be the first time, right?"

I knew what he was trying to do, but my head still hurt from the previous bonking. "I just thought I was rewiring, to put it in your terms. But I'm not. I'm still a mess."

My eyes filled with tears and despite my best efforts at holding them back, they spilled over my cheeks and all I could do was drop my phone on my lap and lean into Griffin with my hands over my face.

He didn't say anything. He just moved behind me and began rubbing circles with his thumbs between my shoulder blades where he knew I carried my stress.

"I'm trying so hard," I whispered.

"I know," he said. "I see it."

I wiped my eyes. "Maybe you're right. Maybe it's all too much. I don't want you to feel like you're playing second fiddle."

"Or third fiddle?"

That made me laugh, which made me cry again, which made him pull me into a soul-healing hug. "I'm sorry, I didn't mean to upset you. It's just taking some getting used to. And it won't always be like this, right?"

"Right," I said, my face buried in his shoulder. But as he held me, I felt something wobble. Kind of like that earthquake from the other night, except this time it was definitely on the inside.

Chapter 24

Styles had made it sound so simple. The next step was to pitch *Sixty-Six* to anyone who might give us a production budget, a team to make it happen, and hopefully, distribution. The way he had said it, I was under the impression we'd be having that meeting imminently, but unfortunately, that was not the case.

Despite the anguish of learning that production companies weren't exactly clamoring to win the web series, in retrospect, it was a blissfully creative period that strengthened our belief in the project and gave us time to polish our pitch.

Styles' agent, Rich, was eventually able to schedule us a meeting with a network that was about to launch a new streaming service. The meeting was at a production studio building in West Hollywood. As we approached, I very nearly stepped back from its shadow. Even thought it wasn't that tall, it was as if the building had specifically been designed to appear as intimidating as possible.

"You'll be fine," Styles said as we rode the elevator to the fifth floor. "Just be yourself. That's what they want to see."

"What if that means having a panic attack in front of people who can determine the trajectory of my entire career?"

"Then you'll be super memorable."

"Oh God, that's even worse. They'll tell jokes about me to all their friends and colleagues and I'll never be able to show my face around these parts again."

"Maybe," he said, flatly. "What? It happens."

I looked at him with fear in my eyes and trepidation in my heart. "What if I blank out and forget everything?"

"You know this story better than anyone. You got this, I'm telling you."

The meeting was surreal. There I was, pitching a story I had originally written for no purpose other than to appease an intangible force from another plane of existence, to a room full of executives like some kind of *professional.* The executives sat across from me asking detailed questions about my vision for the series. Meanwhile, I tried not to get distracted by the wall behind them, which was covered in posters, awards and shiny industry plaques that made it very clear these people knew what they were doing.

"What we love about this concept," said the woman who'd introduced herself as Mona Willinger and seemed to be the person whose opinion mattered most, "is how it uses a balance of comedy and drama to explore really fundamental questions about the human condition."

"That's exactly what I was going for," I said, which was true but also felt like I was responding to an ambiguous horoscope prediction, like 'yes, that's totally me, how did you know'.

Styles, sensing my mind had indeed gone blank, stepped in with a clear head. "This has mass audience appeal. With the right backing, budget, and creative team, we can make something that resonates and really sticks. I seriously think it has binge-and-rewatch potential."

Mona turned to look at one of the men whose name did not register in my brain, and nodded. "We'd like to commission the pilot," he said. "With an option for additional episodes if the pilot tests well."

I waited for *the catch*, but there was no follow-up. *Was that... it?* I looked at Styles, whose dimples gave away his reaction despite trying to keep his composure. He turned to me and nudged me with a nod.

"Thank you. That would be incredible," I managed.

"Great. We'll have contracts drawn up by the end of the week."

As of that moment, something I'd created in my head had officially been invited into the real world. There would be contracts and deadlines and other people's money being invested in my project... *our project.*

As we left the meeting, I felt like I was floating up off the ground. I swear I remember Styles grabbing my hand to pull me back down, but that might have been a hallucination. While we waited for the elevator, Styles opened his mouth to say something, but I hushed him.

"Not yet," I whispered. "Wait."

We rode the elevator down in an electrically charged silence, my mind riding a rollercoaster of thoughts and emotions. You know how sometimes you can tell when a core memory is in the midst of forming? This was definitely one of them.

Once we were down to the main floor and had hurried out of the building, I was finally ready to process externally.

"Holy shit!" I bounced with clasped hands in front of the revolving door, blocking other people from going in or out with my total lack of spatial or social awareness.

"I was going to say, you nailed it!" Styles started bouncing with me, putting his hands on my shoulders amicably.

"I mean, I just kind of agreed to the things they were saying. I wasn't even sure they were getting it. You totally sold it."

"To be fair, I've tried that approach before with no success. But that doesn't make it any less true."

"Well, it worked."

"Stop giving me the credit, we're here today because of you."

A little more bouncing and quasi-maniacal laughing ensued, punctuated by a righteously (and rightfully) annoyed "Excuse me!" from a woman who was also trying to leave the building. She sniffed at the pair of us while she iced us in her wake.

"What's her problem?" I asked.

"She didn't get her pilot greenlit," Styles said, smugly.

I was buzzed, like I had been injected with pure, concentrated sunshine and rainbows. We bounced and laughed all the way to the car, and I realized that not only did I feel high, I felt a new sensation. Not scared. Not pretending to not be scared, just... 100% *me*.

* * *

I was starting to get the hang of interacting with *Los Angeles people.* It was enlightening in that stereotypes were often both confirmed and shattered in the same instance. By that, I mean that some of the clichés were kind of accurate, but the people living them were far more layered, real, and interesting than you might imagine. Kind of like finding out a movie was way weirder, funnier, and more nuanced than the trailer let on.

Take Willow, for instance. When I first met her at River's pool party, my brain short-circuited. I had never met anyone who was a 14,659/10 before. I didn't even know the scale went up that high. She was too perfect to be real. That impression led to an assumption that someone like her would never, could never be more than mere acquaintances with someone like me.

As I got to know her better, I realized how unfair that was, and that it said more about me than it did about her. She was so unbelievably nice. She made an effort to include me in social gatherings, introducing me as her new-in-town writer friend, the one she met through River Deane. She pumped me up and pushed me to talk about my projects. Her friends were lovely, too. I appreciated her attempts to draw me into her social circle, even if it didn't really stick.

The animal rescue operation she ran out of their house was the real deal. She would routinely wake up at 3 AM to bottle-feed orphaned kittens and spend her weekends setting up custom enclosures for dogs with trust issues. Her social media was full of before-and-after photos of animals she'd rescued, fostered, rehabilitated, and found homes for, which made me feel grateful that people like her were out there doing that kind of work. And made me feel like I could be doing more.

Which led to me doing exactly that. I became a regular fixture at her rescue adoption events, and even accompanied her on hunts to help her trap abandoned pets she received tips about.

"She's basically a saint," I explained to Griffin during dinner after spending an afternoon helping her socialize a litter of hissy feral kittens. "Those furry babies had murder on their minds, but she didn't take one single hiss personally. Her patience and tolerance for spicy kitten diarrhea is astounding. I don't know how she does it."

"Maybe that's why she married Styles," Griffin replied. "He seems like he needs someone who will take care of his shit so he can focus on his career."

I was surprised at Griffin's venom. "Well, that's unnecessarily harsh, don't you think? They've been good to us."

He looked instantly regretful. "You're right. I'm sorry. I shouldn't have said that." He pushed his half-finished meal away slightly, as if he had ruined his own appetite.

But truth be told, there was likely something to what Griffin had said. Styles and Willow were the dictionary definition of the opposites-attract concept. I got the sense that they balanced each other, but that it might not take much to unbalance them, potentially resulting in their mutual destruction. It would all depend on how they handled their own emotional baggage. But that was none of my business.

* * *

My emotional baggage, on the other hand...

The high from winning our 'greenlight' for the web series was keeping me abuzz as we forged ahead with the pilot. It was a feeling I never wanted to let go of. And if I felt it level off? I just had to relive that day in my mind. Shake the mental snow globe of it, so to speak. Mostly to go back to the celebration part. But it worked. My intoxication level would bump right back up again.

But I had to be careful. The feelings were almost too good, and that was dangerous. Just when I felt like the real me was finally starting to emerge, it came with this massive price tag of feelings I shouldn't be having. I couldn't afford the consequences of going all in on that big ticket item. I had a choice to make. I could:

1. Continue to let the feelings grow in support of the best creative work I had ever done with someone who made me feel like the most authentic version of myself yet, thus risking my relationship with the person who was the guardian of everything else, or...

2. Mask up and put a lid on the fuzzy-wuzzy twitterpated emotions in the name of fidelity, knowing it might stifle the vital air supply I needed to fuel my emergent creative spark, finish the web series, and become the *me* I always dreamed about.

Hannah, of course, smelled what was cooking like it had wafted across the continent and directly into her otherworldly attuned nostrils. She texted me out of the blue one night while I was enjoying a glass of rosé in the bubble bath, listening to an album that Styles had recommended. She'd pulled a basic three-card spread for me, and the signs were clear.

"The Queen of Wands, the Seven of Cups and the Two of Swords. You know what this means, don't you?"

"That I need to go shopping to round out my kitchen cupboards?"

She called me. This was too big for text messages.

"It means you have a very big choice ahead of you, but your head is in the clouds. The Queen of Wands is saying you're on fire and driven with passion, inspiration and creativity. Then the Seven of Cups, it's literally the card of daydreaming and wish fulfillment, but it also means indecision. And the Two of Swords. Babe. You do not have all of the information. You're going to have to listen to your gut, and frankly, your guts are a bad influence on you."

"Wow. That's... I mean... you're not wrong."

"Spill it."

"I can't really...," I turned the music up and my voice down, and slunk a little lower into the tub. "It's just stuff about work, you know?"

"I thought you said it was going well? You got a traffic ticket for your TV show?"

I smiled. Hannah understood things on such a deep level that the outer layers were all just window dressing to her.

"Yeah, the web series pilot was greenlit, it's great news. And I feel like I'm rewiring, Han. Changing. For the better, I hope."

"You hope?"

"I do have a choice to make. It's just that whichever way I go, I feel like I'm going to win and lose at the same time."

"That's life, babe. And look at you, living it. I'm a little envious. But you got this. Just don't do anything rash or ill-advised."

"Well, what advice do you have?"

"That's it. That's the advice."

"Thanks. This actually really helped. I think I know what I have to do. Maybe there's something to this tarot stuff after all."

"The signs are where you look for them."

"You have no idea how much I appreciate you. I mean it."

"I know you do."

* * *

When my bath was finished and I was in a suitably relaxed

state, I crawled into bed next to Griffin, who was propped up on his pillow, scrolling on his phone.

"Good bath?"

"That clawfoot tub is nice to look at but not a lot of room in there to stretch out."

"Dagnabbit," he swore.

"Consarnet," I replied.

"Such profanity from a supposed lady."

God he was so funny. I loved when we swore like old-timey coal miners.

"I love you, Griff." We said it every day, but this time, it was loaded with so much more than he could possibly know. It contained within it a choice.

"I love you too, babycakes."

Chapter 25

And so, the mask I had removed to make room for this new version of me went back on. In dropping it to open myself up to the flow of inspiration and creativity fueling the lifeforce of *Sixty-Six*, I had let myself become too vulnerable. And now look at what was happening. I needed to pop the lid back on that can of worms.

I told myself I was just being professional. But it wasn't just about protecting my marriage or my career. It was about managing that liminal space between who I was and who I was *becoming*... and which one of those versions of me I could ultimately live with.

It didn't affect things with River much. Some say "never meet your idols", but in his case, whatever *lust from afar* fan-girl inclinations I had before meeting him had been replaced by just admiration of his craft, a feeling of camaraderie, and hoping I'd measure up to his expectations. Despite that, I still couldn't seem to make it to our studio appointments on time, or sometimes at all, because *I am a dick*, apparently.

The real impact was with Styles, obviously. I had to start suppressing myself during our working sessions, which felt like actively starving a fledgling creature in its infancy, crying for nourishment and attention. If *Sixty-Six* had a voice, it would probably have sounded a lot like Audrey II from *Little Shop of Horrors*. Holding back meant that the thrilling butterflies of working together now felt like an overly sensitive car alarm that would not shut off. Funny how doing the right thing made me feel worse, what the fuck was that all about?

And what was even worse than that, the shared frequency we had been on? There were still the occasional moments when we were picking up each other's vibes, but those moments had become fleeting among all the static and interference that had moved in. I couldn't really tell if he noticed me pulling away, trying to create some distance, while still trying to hold on to the exhilarating stream of inspiration and creativity we were wading in together. It was agony, and I sincerely hoped he was oblivious to it.

But it was the right thing to do. Of course it was. Still, maintaining that intentional distance took energy, and I felt my battery starting to drain again. It left me wondering what was really more important: giving in to the growing needs and desires that the web series demanded, or letting it take a back seat to my bigger life commitments. I didn't know the answer. I only knew that the internal tension between changing and staying the same was getting harder to endure.

So, when Willow invited herself and Styles over for dinner, I had to prepare more than just the house to receive our guests. Though I will say it was clear that she never once in her life worried about whether she had enough matching plates and utensils to make a table setting look like a dinner party and not a garage sale.

She'd dropped by Styles' office where I was working on the pilot script revisions and Styles was in the studio recording his next episode of his podcast. She brought a wild arrangement of bright flowers for the reception area and some insanely huge cookies that were basically little cakes. Can I just say, we need to stop calling those abominations *cookies*, it's an egregious misnomer.

"Heya," she sang, popping her head into the writing room as she wandered through the office distributing botanical cheer and baked goods to all, like a domestic goddess on her rounds. Once she'd greeted the receptionist and production crew who were flitting about, she made her way over to me with a "cookie" and an inquisition.

"What are you and Griffin doing tonight?"

I looked up from my laptop, where I'd been staring at the same paragraph for approximately eight million minutes while trying to figure out how to reference the lyrics to the Beatles' *Tomorrow Never Knows* without referencing the lyrics to the Beatles' *Tomorrow Never Knows* in a story about kids discovering 1960s music for the first time.

"Probably the usual," I said. "Ordering takeout, debating what to watch, and then falling asleep on the couch."

"Perfect. Mind if Quinn and I come over? I have this amazing chickpea pasta recipe I've been dying to try out on people who will eat carbs. And I want to meet your cats! They were so afraid to come out on your move-in day."

"The cats have definitely taken ownership of the place," I laughed. "But I should warn you, Clover is very butt-forward. If he likes you, you'll be brushing his floofy tail out of your face pretty much all evening. And Daisy will insist on being the centerpiece on the dining room table while we're eating. Not very sanitary, but I don't make the rules, she does."

"Listen, I was up most of the night stroking orphaned kitten butts to get their little poops out, so I can handle Daisy and Clover being perfectly normal house tyrants."

Ugggghhhhh. I guess there are people who keep their homes in *ready-for-whoever-just-happens-to-drop-by-tonight* condition, but I'm not one of them. Unpacking from the move had become a bit of a nightmare task for me as each unboxed item clashed horrifically with the house's very specific décor. As a result, I went into unpacking paralysis. It was an ongoing daily struggle to not chuck everything in a closet and order an entirely new set of everything to match our new habitat.

As a result, a lot of boxes still lay around, providing ample opportunity to trip over or stub toes on them. I had started to believe that if I left them there long enough, my muscle memory would eventually adapt.

"Are you sure? I mean, I know we should be unpacked by now, but the house is still kind of..." I gestured vaguely, hoping she'd understand that I meant "not ready for visitors, even if they are bringing carbs."

"I know it's last minute, don't trouble yourself with making things perfect. Unpacking is the worst. I still have a box somewhere that I never unpacked after Quinn and I bought our house. I have totally forgotten what's in there and I'm living without it just fine. I feel like it's good luck, or something?"

"What time works?" I asked, because my brain can move from denial through bargaining to acceptance in record time if I think it'll make someone else happy. I knew Griffin would be fine with it, his family practiced a drop-in lifestyle, and he was flexible like that. My ill-equipped domestic side however... she was going to hate me.

"Seven-ish? And don't worry about cooking. I'll bring everything. You just provide the roof and the company."

After she left, I sat at my laptop trying to process the fact that I now had *people-coming-over-for-dinner* plans, whereas mere moments ago, my evening plans involved not having plans. Styles bumped into Willow on his way in, and her way out. I watched them share a sweet smooch, but thankfully I was too preoccupied with my new predicament to notice the pang of jealousy (that would hit later).

"You look dazed. Everything okay?" Styles asked, when Willow had left the building. He was setting his laptop down across the table from mine and plugging it in.

"Willow just invited you both over for dinner tonight."

"She told me she might do that. I know it's last minute, but she wanted it to be casual."

"You didn't think to mention it?" I snapped. Styles stood up and stepped back.

"She wanted to ask you. I didn't think..." He looked shocked and a little hurt, and I instantly felt a wave of remorse that was like that time when you were a little kid and you crushed a bug to see what would happen and its guts came out and then it wasn't moving anymore and you learned that acting without thinking can injure.

"I'm sorry. I don't know why I snapped like that. I'm really glad you guys are coming over."

In truth, of course I actually *did* have an inkling as to why I snapped like that. Holding back, however necessary, was so freaking hard. I had liked who I was becoming with Styles, and forcing myself to roll back to what felt like an outdated version was making me act kind of glitchy.

"It's alright," Styles relaxed. "We've been working so hard.

We'll kick off our shoes and let off a little steam tonight. It'll be fun."

"Yeah," I smiled back. "But do you mind if I check out a little early today to tidy up? I know Willow said not to worry, but there are legit safety concerns."

Styles laughed. "Hey, I'm not your boss. I'll see you tonight."

So much for creating distance.

* * *

How to Clean Your House for Guests While Having a Complete Mental Breakdown

Time required: 5 hours to accomplish 45 minutes of actual cleaning.

1. Survey your living space critically as if your entire social worth depends on the total absence of cat hair in a cat-occupied home and the strategic placement of decorative objects you usually ignore.
2. Begin by organizing one small area perfectly. Spend 90 minutes on a single shelf while the rest of your house looks like it was ransacked by the FBI in an episode of any show you've ever seen with the FBI in it.
3. Panic-clean by shoving all moving boxes regardless of how unpacked they are into closets, under beds, and into that one room you'll forbid your guests from entering.
4. Realize you have no idea what normal people keep on their coffee tables. Frantically Google "what to put on coffee table" and spend 30 minutes rearranging the

same three objects like they're going to be judged in a competition where losing means you'll be hunted to death for sport.

5. Clean the bathroom mirror until you can see your anxiety reflected in flawless detail.
6. Survey your artificially clean and organized house and have an existential crisis about whether you even deserve friends. Pre-emptively exact judgment upon yourself to protect yourself from... what, exactly? Opinions you'll never know about and are none of your business?

Safety warning: May result in exhaustion, resentment and the damaging belief that domestic perfection makes you worthy of friendship.

* * *

By the time Willow and Styles arrived at 7:15 PM (fashionably late, as befitted people who understood social timing), I had managed to transform our house from moving box infested safety hazard to an aesthetic that boasted "the complete lack of cohesion *is* the aesthetic." It almost looked purposeful.

Griffin, meanwhile, helped to handle the psychological preparation by opening a bottle of *getting ready wine* to make me worry a tiny bit less.

"It looks great, Car" he said, scanning our living room and giving an enthusiastic thumbs up, the real-life version of clicking "Like" on it.

"Who can make a hot pink couch work with muted blue and brown plaid throw pillows? Only us."

"Hell yeah," Griffin clinked his wine glass against mine. I

subtly nudged the Hollywood snow globe forward from its spot on the fireplace mantle so that it was the star of the ledge's assorted knicks and knacks.

Griffin noticed. "It would all fall apart without that centerpiece."

"Touché."

The doorbell rang before I could make any further adjustments. Willow stepped through our door carrying what looked like enough groceries to keep this dinner party going for three days. Styles was behind her with a bottle of wine that had dust on it, because wine bottles you bring to people's houses can and should be dusty, but the houses where the wine bottles are brought must not be.

Griffin brought out the wine glasses along with his easy style of host energy and house pride. It didn't matter to him that we didn't live in a mansion like River Deane's. Griffin knew his way around a dinner party (unless there was a pool involved, but thankfully, that wasn't a concern this time), and he was going to host the shit out of this one. I was grateful he took on the responsibility so I could try to relax a little.

"Welcome back to Becker Manor," he said, his arms extended. "Please avoid opening the closet door next to the main floor bathroom if you prefer not to be crushed by falling boxes."

"It's still lovely, even with all the boxes put away," Willow giggled, looking around our place and showing zero sign of disgust. I mean, this frickin' woman. She was the epitome of poise, grace and humility. She said all the right things. It was impossible not to love her. Within thirty seconds of entering the house, both Daisy and Clover were already rubbing against her legs like they wanted to go home with her.

"Hi babies, aren't you beautiful!" she cooed as she bent down to put a bag on the floor and pet little Clover's purring head. Styles picked up the bag and took it into the kitchen.

"I hope you don't mind, but we're going to take over your kitchen for a little while," he admitted.

"You cook?"

"I take instructions," he laughed. Willow ripped herself away from the cats and joined Styles in the kitchen as the two of them began organizing the ingredients. Griffin put on a little mood music, a local band from back home that he was buddies with.

"Bet you never heard of these guys," he bragged.

Indeed, neither Styles nor Willow had, and we got on with the business of making merry in our little mismatched house. As I cleared a space on the kitchen table, I noticed two little plastic cocktail swords crossed perfectly on a napkin. *They still make those?* I thought. They were for the olives Willow had brought for her appetizer plate.

My brain flashed instantly to Hannah's warning. *The Two of Swords. You don't have all the information. You're going to have to listen to your gut.*

I uncrossed the swords so they lay parallel to one another in kind of a 69 formation. But the unease lingered just enough to remind me that nothing is ever just what it seems.

Chapter 26

The meal was delicious. Of course, Willow was also going to be an excellent cook. Was I secretly hoping that she'd scorch the sauce, or leave out an important ingredient, or forget she was cooking on an electric stove top instead of gas? I mean... maybe a little, for like, a nanosecond, because the moment I imagined it, I felt really, really bad about it.

I then imagined how things might have gone if I was the one cooking over at their place, and that scenario ended with a call to 911 and the fire department being dispatched and OMG, the rescue animals!!! I didn't even realize I was crying at the dinner table and when Griffin asked if I was okay, I made up some lie about biting into a whole peppercorn, and then Willow felt really, really bad about that.

I had to give her credit. She had worked so hard at overcoming her self-proclaimed misstep at River's pool party. At this point, it had become futile to envy her for literally anything. It would be unsatisfying, and such a waste.

When the brouhaha about my unexpected tears had subsided, the dinner conversation relaxed once more, and I did my best to get my shit together, as if I hadn't just accidentally burned down my friends' house in my mind.

"I love your reckless waves, Cara," Willow commented.

I didn't know how to respond. *Reckless waves?*

"Your hair. It's so effortless. Like you just woke up like that. It takes forever to get mine to do anything even close to that."

"Oh, it does this when I forget to wash it."

Griffin nearly choked on his wine, stifling a laugh. I was instantly aware of my faux pas and felt a rush of blood to my cheeks.

"Just good genes," he clarified, rubbing my back.

After dinner, we ambled outside to the backyard. A little after we'd moved in, we managed to score some patio furniture from a garage sale in the neighborhood. Four patio chairs and a couple small side tables, as well as a basic backyard fire pit. The chairs were evenly spaced around the fire, the same distance apart, in a four-pointed north-west-south-east arrangement. Griffin had strung some basic patio lights as a finishing touch. It was practically the exact setup we had back home, and there was no affectation about it. It was my favorite "room" in the house.

The sun had set at this point, but the moonglow and the artificial city light prevented the sky from achieving true darkness. Regardless, the fire was Griffin's domain, and it was quickly ablaze under his expertise.

"This is so nice," Willow said, lying back in her chair. "Very peaceful."

"It feels a bit like being at camp," said Styles. "In a good way."

It was a coolish night, and Willow was rubbing her bare arms for warmth. Griffin reached into the deck box and handed her a light blanket and then one to me. They leaned toward each other in their patio chairs, deep in discussion about the benefits of massage therapy for traumatized rescue animals. Styles and I listened to their conversation for a few minutes before beginning our own.

"There's something I've been meaning to ask you," I warned.

"Uh oh. What's that?"

"How did you get the nickname "Styles"?"

He tossed his head back and laughed.

"I wasn't expecting that at all."

"I mean, I assumed it's because you dress well. But lots of people dress well. This is LA."

"Well, the nickname does predate my arrival here."

"Oh! And here I thought you were a homegrown hero."

"Nah. I'm from up north."

I sat forward in my chair.

"Up north where? Washington? British Columbia? Frickin' Alaska?"

"Ukiah."

I squinted my eyes to recall all the California geography I had gleaned since we'd arrived, and scoffed at his definition of *up north*.

"Ukiah, *California*? Dude, is that even northern California? It seems more... mid."

"Oh, it's definitely mid," Styles laughed.

"Touché," I conceded.

Across the fire, I watched as Willow picked up her empty wine glass, and Griffin picked up the wine bottle to refill it, only to find that the bottle was also empty. He asked if she wanted another glass and she said she did, but as he got up to go into the house, she followed him inside to use the bathroom.

"But the nickname, though," I reminded Styles. He hadn't answered my question.

"Right. Well, it's sort of embarrassing."

I waited on the proverbial edge of my seat.

"Remember the movie *Teen Wolf*? The original one, with Michael J. Fox."

"Oh my God. Yes. Of course."

"I was like ten years old when that came out. And Michael J. Fox's friend, the one with the sunglasses, I thought he was the coolest guy."

"*Surf's up*," I smirked, giving a hang ten sign, remembering the van-surfing scene and putting two and two together.

"Exactly. I started wearing sunglasses indoors, everywhere I could get away with it. My teacher kept taking them away. The kids at school started calling me Styles, and it stuck."

"Please tell me you were not the '*Stiles from Teen Wolf*' of your high school."

"I absolutely was not."

"Thank goodness, or I'd have to call this whole arrangement into question."

"Fair enough."

"Wasn't it Stiles with an 'i'?"

"Could be."

"Styles with a 'y' is better. Pretty sure nowadays we would call that character problematic, anyway."

"Come on, I was ten. I didn't know any better."

"Apparently neither did anyone else in 1985. No judgment." I held my wine glass toward Styles for a clink, and he responded in kind.

The moon had moved up in the sky since the last time I checked. The fire crackled in the pause in our conversation, and I realized that Griffin and Willow had not come back outside yet.

"Where did they go?" I asked, glancing into the kitchen through the patio door window, but not seeing anyone.

Styles followed my gaze. "Inside, I think? Maybe they went to get more wine?"

"How long have we been talking?" I asked. I checked myself to make sure the barrier I had put up to keep Styles beyond arms' length for propriety reasons had remained in place, and as I fast-forwarded through the evening's various conversations, I was relieved to find it still intact.

"I don't know. Twenty minutes? Half an hour?"

I felt a flutter of anxiety and wondered if I had missed something. Maybe I'd stepped over the barrier without realizing it. It wouldn't be the first time I zeroed in on one person or conversation to the exclusion of all others. I hoped I hadn't been unintentionally rude.

"Do you think they're okay? Should we go check on them? Maybe something's happened."

"I'm sure everything is fine," Styles said, seemingly unconcerned. I was probably just being paranoid, was the subtext, whether Styles meant it or not.

In the lull of our conversation, I let myself become hypnotized by the fire. But as the minutes stretched on with no reappearance by Willow or Griffin, I found myself fighting the intimacy of being alone with Styles in my backyard.

The magical little patio lights, which normally would fill me with a serene wonder, began to feel overly romantic. *Whoosh.* A wave of feelings hurtled toward me like an emotional tsunami, and I was afraid my hastily constructed internal barrier wall would be no match for it. The silence was begging to be filled, and if I wasn't careful, a goddamn sonnet might burst forth from my lips. My throat was tight with it.

I cast a covert gaze over at him, hoping to catch a sign that he was about to buckle under the same wave. He seemed lost in his own thoughts, gazing intently at the fire like he was contemplating the mysteries of the universe. I tried to tune into our frequency but didn't find him there. Nothing but a lonely hiss of distant static. He was clearly on another plane of existence, one that had nothing to do with me or the imminent unbattening of my hatches.

At that moment, Styles stirred from his trance and stood up. "Hope there's not a lineup for the bathroom," he chuckled nervously, and started toward the patio door. There was an urgency to his demeanor that broke the onslaught of my internal emotional wave, and I immediately dropped back into the physical world where there were other more earthly concerns.

"I think I'll check on the wine situation," I followed, sensing that there was something more to his movement than heeding the call of nature. Maybe I wasn't just being paranoid after all.

Now, this next part is a little hazy, because it all happened so fast. Here's what I remember.

The sound of us coming into the house seemed to trigger an abrupt response from upstairs. It was the unmistakable sound of rushing footsteps, followed by a door slamming.

On the main floor of our house, there was no one but Styles and me and the cats, who were snoozing quietly on the couch. But why would Griffin and Willow be upstairs? We had a bathroom on the main floor. The one upstairs was an ensuite, in bedroom-land.

You know in horror movies when there's a scary noise and there are the people who have to go and investigate? The ones who make you yell and throw popcorn at the screen because who does that? Who willingly goes toward the scary thing, toward their most certain and untimely demise? Well, in this horror story, it turns out Styles is the one you want to yell and throw popcorn at. *Turn around you moron, nothing good will come from this. Count me the fuck out.*

Styles blew past me through the hallway and stopped briefly at the bottom of the stairs before racing up to see for himself whether his worst suspicions were true. I trailed after him, remaining at the bottom of the stairs, unable to make myself go any further.

Willow appeared at the top of the stairs just as he arrived. She looked surprised, slightly disheveled, guilty, and distant, like she was formulating a defense or apology, I couldn't tell which. They locked eyes with a pause that contained an entire conversation concentrated in a silent language that belonged only to the two of them.

Styles then turned and raced down the stairs like he was running for his life, blew past me on the landing, and ran out the front door. Willow went after him, but she wasn't fast enough to catch him. I heard the sound of his car engine followed by the screech of tires tearing out of our driveway. Then Willow's voice, calling his name... *Quinn!* If only he had more syllables and hard vowels in his name, maybe an echo of her cries might have reached him, but I suspect it wouldn't have mattered.

That's when Griffin emerged, wearing the same "I know what this looks like, but I can explain" expression that Willow had on. Up until that moment, the only thing I knew for sure was nothing. Total uncertainty had blocked me from having any emotion other than a sickening case of nerves.

But not for long. The inevitable shockwave reverberated through my body, and a sob rose in my throat. I wished I could storm out like Styles, but it was *my* house. Since I lived there and couldn't fathom where else I would go, all I could do to escape was retreat to the backyard, so that's what I did. I tried not to make any crying noises. Through my tears, the patio string lights looked like one of those bokeh lights photos that were cool in the 2010s.

I don't know whether Griffin was intending to come and find me outside or not. From the backyard, I could faintly hear his and Willow's voices in an argument, but it was too muffled to make out their words. This was followed by the sound of the front door slamming shut and then Griffin's car pulling out of the driveway, presumably to drive Willow home and continue the discussion without the risk that I would overhear.

I was alone at the house, but I couldn't make myself go back inside. Going inside would mean confronting whatever evidence of their activities might still be lingering. It meant opening Schrödinger's Box, or Pandora's Box, or whatever metaphorical box was sure to unleash a grim new reality that I did not want to confront.

So, I stayed outside, curled up in a patio chair, wrapped in my blanket. Avoiding the reality of the situation meant only one thing. Looping on endless variations of possible scenarios of what might have happened, which would paradoxically bring me equal amounts of comfort and anxiety. I know it makes no sense, but both were somehow better than finding out the truth, whatever it was.

I closed my eyes to let the rumination loop take me. Along

with it came the oddest sensation of being blanketed by gently falling, fluffy glittering snow. It wasn't cold or wet, or uncomfortable in any way. In fact, it felt almost like being tucked in by something otherworldly.

The last thing I remember before I fell asleep was wondering exactly how much of the evening's events were my fault. *How far back would I have to go to stop it? Was there any possible way to wake up tomorrow and go on like none of this had happened?*

Chapter 27

I woke up the next morning as the sky was brightening, still in my backyard, snuggled up with a blanket and using another one as a pillow. I had forgotten to turn the patio lights off, and now they reminded me of straggling party guests who'd stayed up all night, still buzzed but could totally crash at any moment. My body ached from the hours spent contorted in an unnatural position. Whatever sleep I had gotten had been fleeting at best. I checked the time on my phone. 6:18 AM. The battery was close to dead.

Griffin would be getting up soon to make coffee and get ready for work. I desperately needed to pee, but my stomach tightened and I felt nauseous thinking about going inside. I was still furious but also craving comfort from him, which was confusing as hell and a bubbling emotional cauldron I couldn't handle. I'd have to wait until he left. That was all I could do.

I tried to push my urinary needs out of my mind. I closed my eyes and thought of Styles, hoping he had made it home safely. Should I reach out? See if he's okay? Send him a text and then watch my phone battery inevitably die and wait with sickening, anxious uncertainty for the coast to be clear so I could go inside and charge it to find out if he had replied?

The thing about the blast radius from the previous night's hand grenade was, how do you even triage whose care is the priority? The person whose wounds are so visibly horrific that the immediate response is to stop the bleeding, or the person who is bleeding internally and may succumb to an injury no one can see?

Styles' situation was particularly sensitive, given his status as a "famous-adjacent" person. He wasn't exactly tabloid fodder, but between his podcast and Willow's post-modeling animal rescue persona, they had just enough visibility to make a messy story go viral. My urge to reach out to him was tempered by not having a clue how to deal with the potential fallout. What exactly was the etiquette in a situation like this?

At 7 AM my phone's wake-up alarm went off, quickly followed by a reminder I had set myself:

River @ Burntree 10 AM

And then my phone died, as expected, spawning a feeling of frustration that I'd be alone with my thoughts again until it was "safe" to go into the house. Unfortunately, the rational part of my brain didn't feel safe enough to rummage through, either. I toggled to my imagination, and scanned through the various scenarios and daydreams cataloged there like a self-soothing fantasy jukebox, but none of them felt right. I was looking for comfort, but it was like my brain had set up an "access denied" barrier on anything that wasn't anxiety fodder.

So I catastrophized instead. That's how some of my best fantasies have started, with everything going wrong first before I can get to the happy place. Like I have to walk through all the worst-case scenarios before I'm allowed access to comfort or pleasure.

My brain queued up a montage of tragic outcomes, and I pressed the proverbial play button. There I was, floating above a sea of tasteful floral arrangements and distraught loved ones, watching my own funeral. Don't get me wrong. It wasn't *that kind* of a thought. Just one of those bizarre rituals where I imagine what it would be like if I disappeared, just to see who would notice. It's dark, I know. But sometimes that's the only way to the door of catharsis.

* * *

And of course, I lost track of time. There were a lot of catastrophic outcomes to imagine. Once I'd buried myself, I had to mentally map out an untimely and tragic end for everyone else involved. Oh God. I know how that sounds. I'm not a psychopath, and these were not plans, I promise. I just needed to clear the wreckage before I could even start building toward a happier ending. If that makes any sense at all.

When I awakened back to reality, I noticed the sun's position in the sky and it dawned on me that it was no longer dawn, and Griffin had long since left for work. I flew into the house, grabbed my phone charger, chucked it and a protein bar into the passenger seat, and proceeded to hurl myself through space (and, I hoped, time) to get to the studio as fast as I could.

* * *

My late arrival at Burntree studio was met with visible agitation from River. *He's so mad at me*, I thought.

"I just heard from Magda," he said, while nodding at my arrival. You remember Magda? She was at that fateful pool party at River's house. I didn't know it then, but Magda was the producer of Styles' podcast.

"Styles didn't show up to record the podcast today." With no missed uploads in the six years since Styles had started podcasting, this was obviously concerning.

River continued. "She waited two hours for him. He's not answering his phone. So, I called Willow. She said he never came home last night."

I felt my stomach tighten. "Never came home? As in, at all?"

"As in, she was up all night waiting for him, but he hasn't showed. She's been calling him constantly since last night."

"Any idea where he might have gone?" I asked, even though the answer was obvious. Of course we didn't know, or people wouldn't be looking for him.

"No idea. Willow's going to call the police if he doesn't turn up by noon. He and I had plans to play pickleball later, but..." River trailed off, and I could hear the worry in his voice.

"What even happened last night?" River asked. "I thought y'all were having dinner or something."

I hesitated. "Uh... yeah, they came over."

"Maybe they had a fight after. But it's not like him to just take off like that."

I sat staring at my hands as I picked at my cuticles, still trying to figure out exactly how much of this was my fault.

If Griffin and I hadn't moved to LA. If I hadn't started working with Styles. If I hadn't made Griffin feel like he wasn't a priority. Styles would be in his studio right now, prepping a podcast, gearing up for pickleball, maybe planning a date night with Willow. Not vanished somewhere in the greater Los Angeles area.

The guilt was crushing. I'd spent most of my life trying to make things easier for people, trying to keep my own emotions contained so as not to become a hazard for others, and yet, my mere presence in other people's lives still managed to lead to disaster. I was a homewrecker by proximity.

"Did you try calling him? Maybe there is a reason he doesn't want to talk to Willow."

"Yeah, I tried calling. I can't get him either."

I remembered my phone charger and plugged it in. The screen turned on and as the battery jumped to 1%, I tried calling Styles myself, though I wasn't sure what I would say if he answered. *Hey, just wondering if you're okay, and also sorry if I accidentally ruined your life?*

The call went straight to voicemail anyway, which meant either his phone was dead, he'd turned it off, or he was deliberately avoiding anyone who might want to discuss the previous evening's events. All of which were plausible scenarios. I was about to leave a message, when I was informed by his automated voicemail service that his voicemail box was full. My mind started spinning again.

Where would Styles go to disappear? Not back to Ukiah, that much was clear. Maybe a motel. A friend with a cabin. Maybe he was parked somewhere, staring at the ocean, trying to decide if this could all be fixed with a conversation or if it was an irreparable catastrophe.

Or maybe something had actually happened. Maybe he'd been in an accident. Maybe he was in a hospital, unidentified.

Oh God.

River was pacing, which I had peripherally noticed. But he sure as shit noticed that I had gone catatonic, staring out into space, picking my fingers 'til they bled, because he practically shouted my name to get my attention.

"Earth to Cara! Are you there?"

Startled, I blinked back to the present.

"Um, yeah, sorry. I guess I'm just... worried."

He opened a drawer in a desk and pulled out a first aid kit.

"Your hands... here," he said as he offered me a band-aid for my bleeding fingers.

The worry was sickening. I searched for Styles on our frequency, to try and connect with him there. I needed him to be okay, but I was overcome by the fear that I was part of the reason he might not be.

"Anyway," River said. "I don't think we're going to get much done here today. You might as well split. We'll rebook when this blows over." His voice cracked, and my eyes stung in response. I went out to my car and sat in the parking lot, unable to move.

Chapter 28

We'd been trying to keep track of the days on the island, but time had started to slip. Months had passed, that was all we knew. Every morning, Styles and I went to the beach to check that our SOS signal, arranged with rocks and whatever other island debris we could find, was still intact.

Our clothes were falling apart, and we took turns washing them in the waterfall pool. Our hair had gone feral. The hairbrush we found in the backpack was missing bristles and kind of gnarly, but Styles had started braiding my hair to keep it from tangling too badly. I savored every second of it, even if the intimacy of it was based on survival, not romance.

We were sunburned, mosquito-bitten, and rapidly thinning out, our clothes hanging off us in disappointing ways. But we continued our daily routine, which was to gather food and water, reinforce our shelter, and watch the horizon for signs of potential rescue.

Our conversations grew more philosophical as the days passed. We swapped ideas for creative projects, made lists of movies and books we'd consume if, or when, we made it home. We never strayed too far from camp, just in case a plane flew overhead, and we had to run to the beach, arms flailing, screaming at the sky.

Hope of being found kept us from crossing the proverbial line.

That, and the questions that lingered between us but never got asked out loud. What would happen if we were rescued? Would we go back to the way things were? And did we even want to be rescued?

At night, we lay side by side in the shelter, arms wrapped around each other for safety and warmth (or so we told ourselves). The jungle teemed with hazards that could strike at any moment, like snakes, spiders, and who knows what else. But there was also a strange peace and a sense that no matter what came for us, we'd face it together.

And that's when I asked the unaskable on the outside of my head.

"What's the first thing you'd do," I asked, "if we got rescued tomorrow?"

He didn't answer right away. I heard him breathe, slow and steady.

"I don't know," he said finally. "Go quiet for a while. Work on trying to put this all behind me."

"Even me?" I whispered.

He was quiet again. "Especially you."

I didn't know what I wanted to hear. But it definitely wasn't that.

I turned slightly, pressing my forehead into his shoulder, letting the night noise distract me.

And then, with uncanny timing, a low hum overtook the rustling of jungle leaves and chirping insects. We both sat up, instantly alert. The unmistakable sound of an engine in the distance grew louder overhead. Styles jumped to his feet. I followed, my heart pounding.

We burst from our shelter and tore across the sand, past our low-burning campfire, toward our SOS signal with our arms waving wildly and our voices screaming with hope and desperation.

The moon was out, but it was dark, and the low-flying plane went over us too quickly. It passed, and the sound of it faded as the familiar sounds of the island returned.

"Do you think they saw us? Our SOS signal? Our fire maybe?" Styles asked, still watching the sky. His voice cracked slightly with a fragile hope leaking out between the syllables.

"Maybe?" I said, because what else could I say?

His whole posture shifted. His shoulders squared and that ambitious focus returned to his eyes. "They saw us," he repeated, more firmly now. "They're looking for us. Now they know where we are. They'll come back."

He looked so certain, and so lit up by the idea of rescue, return, and the restoration of real life that I nodded along, pretending I wanted all of that, too. But inside, something wilted. If they came back to get us, everything would change. All the closeness that we had forged in seclusion, along with the permission to be more than we were allowed to be, would all just vanish.

I stood beside him, scanning the empty sky, and tried to will myself to want to be found.

* * *

The sound of my phone ringing yanked me back to reality. I was still in my car, which was now sitting in my driveway with the engine switched off, but I could not recall the part where I drove home. River's name appeared on my phone as it continued ringing urgently. I could just tell that the news wasn't good. I answered.

"Willow just called the police," he said. "It's been over twelve hours. They're treating it as a missing person case."

I felt like I'd been punched in the stomach. *Missing person case* meant this wasn't just Styles taking time to process his feelings. This would likely end up on the news, with helicopter footage and search parties and people speculating about what could make a successful, well-regarded podcaster vanish without a trace.

"Oh God. Is there anything we can do?" I asked, though I wasn't sure what we could do that the police weren't already doing better.

River let out a long breath. "I don't know. I'm still trying to wrap my head around it. Something doesn't add up. What are y'all not telling me?"

I hesitated. On one hand, I was relieved that Willow hadn't given River the details of the previous night's events. On the other, now it was up to me to decide how much information to share. And I wasn't even close to finished processing it myself.

"It's... um... complicated," I said, aware that I was shutting River out.

He was quiet for a moment, like he was thinking carefully about what chess piece to play against mine. "If you think I'm oblivious to the current dynamics between the four of you, then you must not think I'm very perceptive."

Ouch. I opened my mouth to speak, but nothing came out.

"And you know that Naomi and Willow are friends, right? They talk. And Naomi talks to me. I know all about Willow's adventurous leanings."

"Did Styles ever mention it?"

"Nah, he keeps his cards close."

I felt a sudden flash of quiet embarrassment. How narcissistic had I been to think that all of this, *any of this*, was actually about me? I suppressed a lump in my throat, basically swallowing a ball of heartburn.

"Did Styles say anything to you?" River asked. "Before he left?"

"Uh... no." I tried to recover. "It happened so fast. He looked devastated. And lost."

River and I hung up, and I hurled myself out of my car and went into the house. I sat down on the living room couch and tried to figure out what I was supposed to do with myself, the acid of worry and helplessness eating through my core.

Griffin, who I hadn't seen since the previous evening's fuckitude, came home and found me there twenty minutes later, staring at the snow globe on the mantle like it might suddenly become a crystal ball and give me the answer.

"What's wrong?"

Are you fucking serious right now? Did he really not get it? Did he not understand that he and Willow had set off a nuclear emotional chain reaction that led to one of our friends disappearing into the Los Angeles wilds without a trace?

Griffin just stood there, looking at me like the only thing worth noting about last night was that the cat threw up on the carpet.

"Styles is missing," I said, flatly. Having to explain the whole situation to him as if he had not been there and had not contributed to this mess was triggering a fury inside me I had not felt since... well, I didn't have a reference point. All I knew was that I was more distraught about Styles being missing than I was about whatever transgressions Griffin had committed.

As I explained, trying not to raise my voice but failing, Griffin listened intently, asking all the practical questions about when Styles had last been seen and whether the police had any leads. He was being supportive and rational and everything you'd want in a partner during a crisis. And it was making me even more livid.

But I could see something else in his expression that looked like the beginning of an uncomfortable realization. Was he gearing up to admit his own guilt? Or maybe that was just me projecting onto him.

"Car," he said finally, "you know this isn't your fault, right?" He was right, and deep inside a dark crevasse in my soul, I knew it. If this wasn't my fault then, maybe that meant that the whole world didn't revolve around me. Bad things didn't just happen left and right because of my internal monologue or overthinking or daydreaming things that I shouldn't. You'd think that would make me feel better, but actually, the idea that I wasn't the cause of everything bad was deeply unsettling, because the alternative was much, much worse.

"No, it's yours!" a diminutive voice cried from deep inside the crevasse. I almost yelled it aloud to Griffin, but I stifled it. I couldn't say it. Because acknowledging to him that it wasn't my fault meant admitting to myself whose fault it really was. And that meant talking about it for real, and I, teetering woozily at the edge of the bottomless crevasse in my soul, wasn't ready for that. The grassy, flowery area surrounding the crevasse had a name, and its name was Denial. And so, I took a metaphorical step back onto Denial's safer, more stable ground.

"But if we... if *I* hadn't come here..."

Griffin sat down next to me on the couch, the detritus from our dinner party still on display in the room around us.

"You aren't responsible for Styles going missing, you know that."

Stop it, Griffin! Denial, don't fail me now. "But I'm connected to it. My presence here is somehow making everyone's life more complicated."

"Or maybe everyone's life was already complicated, and you're just here to witness it."

His words echoed River's, and the reassurance was oddly comforting. I looked at him, my Love with a capital L, who'd uprooted his entire life to support my dreams, and my anger began to soften. Even if I admitted it wasn't my fault, the truth was that I still had to contend with my own inner conflict and guilt about my feelings for another man, and those were certainly all on me.

"What if something's really wrong?" I asked. "What if he's hurt, or..."

"Then we'll deal with that when we know more. But right now, the only thing we can do is hope he's okay and help however we can."

Griffin was right about that too, of course. But being right didn't make the anxiety any easier to handle. I spent the rest of the day refreshing news websites and checking my phone for updates about Styles. I tried to distract myself by working on *Sixty-Six*, while simultaneously worrying about whether I'd ever get the chance to finish it with him.

By evening, there was still no word. The missing person report had gone public, and Styles' face was on local news websites, described as a "creative entrepreneur and well-known host of the popular podcast *Making It*" who had disappeared under "unclear circumstances." The comments sections were filling up with speculation and theories, because the real-life heartbreak of a human being with even minor celebrity status is obviously, and cruelly, a form of public entertainment.

I was checking his social media accounts obsessively, looking for any sign that he might have posted something that would give a clue about where he'd gone. But his last post was from two days ago, a photo of his studio setup with a caption about being excited for an upcoming interview, the one Magda had said he hadn't turned up for.

That night, I lay in bed listening to Griffin breathe and trying not to think about all the ways the situation could get worse. But my brain, apparently committed to finding the most anxiety-provoking possible scenarios, kept cycling through possibilities: car accident, medical emergency, complete psychological breakdown, decision to disappear permanently and start a new life somewhere else.

Or maybe, whispered the part of my mind that had been crafting elaborate fantasies about him for far too long, *maybe he was somewhere thinking about the same kinds of things I'd been thinking about.*

Maybe he was trying to figure out what it meant that Griffin and I had walked into his life just as Willow was suggesting they open up their marriage. Maybe he was sitting in his car somewhere, staring at his phone and trying to decide whether to call me.

Chapter 29

I lost track of how much time had passed since the plane had flown over our island, but it felt like an eternity.

In the days immediately afterward, Styles was sure we were going home. He practically camped on the beach next to our SOS sign, staring at the sky in a heightened state of hope and expectation. Every afternoon, I brought him water, the ratty towel to cover his exposed skin, and gentle reminders that while turning bright red might make us more visible from above, sunstroke wasn't going to help our rescuers get here any faster. He'd just wave me off and say, "Any minute now."

His optimism was either admirable or delusional, but it was also contagious. Together, we started preparing ourselves for the inevitable press interviews and fame. We even got our "story straight" so that when it hit the news that there were two survivors of the plane crash that was believed to have killed all other passengers and crew, we'd stand in unwavering solidarity about our survival story, the parts we wanted the world to know about.

But nobody came.

And then one afternoon, I found him sitting alone on the beach at the water's edge. His arms were wrapped around his knees, shoulders hunched, looking out at the horizon. When I got closer, I saw that he was crying. This was not the stoic kind of crying you might imagine, with subtle tears glistening down his face. No, we're talking full, ugly sobs with his nose running and limited places to wipe it. His tattered and dirty tee shirt and boxer shorts were already gross with snot.

It was devastating to watch, and I had no idea how to console him. I just sat on the beach beside him quietly, because other people's heartbreak is a slippery slope to my own. I did unclasp my bra from under my shirt and pull it out my sleeve, handing it to him to wipe off the next load of snot (my already insubstantial 34B rack had deflated from borderline starvation, the bra was just a remnant of social decorum at this point anyway). He accepted it and blew noisily into it, as if it was just a regular square of facial tissue and not my heart.

"They're not coming," he said, after a while, his voice sounding cracked and raw. I wanted to tell him he was wrong. That any minute now, a helicopter or a cruise ship or a guy on a paddleboard from a neighboring resort island would show up. But I didn't, because he was probably right.

When the sun started to set, I wasn't sure if he was planning on coming back to our camp. Getting the fire going was usually his thing, but if I didn't start it soon, we'd lose the light. He stayed by the water for a while longer as I got ready for dark. Eventually, he drifted back and sat down beside me, looking tired and crusty.

"That's a good fire," he said as he sat down next to me.

"Thanks, I learned from the best." I bumped him with my shoulder.

"Everyone thinks we're dead," he said.

"Yeah," I replied. "Honestly, I'm kind of amazed it took them this long."

He gave a weak chuckle.

"This is our life now," I said, poking the fire. "We've gone full

Survivor, minus the camera crew and the social backstabbing."

"We should've known," he said. "It stopped being about getting rescued the second that plane whizzed over us like we weren't even here."

He turned toward me, and for the first time since his breakdown, he looked steady. Hollowed out, maybe, but clear.

"So, what do we do now?" I asked.

Styles didn't answer. He reached for my hand slowly, and held it. I didn't pull away.

"Like you said, we live here now. I guess we stop pretending we're still trying to get home."

In that moment, having become each other's emergency contact on an island with no phone service, we both felt the wind change direction. Initially, it made me concerned that a hurricane might be coming, but my fear was quickly doused when he leaned in and kissed me gently, almost apologetically, like he was sorry for leaving my snot-filled bra on the beach.

"This might be a bad idea," I whispered, between kisses.

"What makes you say that?" he asked.

"There's a pretty good chance that living on this island has given at least one of us Hep A."

More kisses.

"Well, we share pretty much everything, don't we."

Kiss.

"It was only a matter of time," I conceded.

"Let's make it worth it."

When his hand came up to brush my cheek, I felt a bolt of electricity zap through me, and when I pulled the hem of his shirt up over his head, he didn't stop me. This wasn't going to solve anything, of course. But with all hope of rescue gone, we came alive all over again, ironically, with surrender. About damn time.

* * *

"Cara."

I must have finally fallen asleep, because the next thing I knew, it was morning, and Griffin was saying my name and tapping me gently to pull me back to consciousness without startling me.

"They found Styles," he said cheerfully, meaning it was the good kind of being found instead of the other kind. Styles may not have been Griffin's favorite person, but he would never have wished for anything bad to happen to him.

"He's alright?"

"Yeah. They found his car parked at some overlook in the hills. He'd been sleeping in the backseat."

I felt every muscle in my body relax simultaneously. "Thank goodness. How did you find out?"

"River texted the group chat. Willow went to pick him up. He's taking a few days off from work, but he's physically fine."

As Griffin got ready for work, I lay in bed processing my relief. Styles was safe. He was going home to his wife, and they were going to talk about... what, exactly? It occurred to me that I didn't have a clue what they would talk about. I had been so focused on his disappearance that I'd completely avoided thinking about how I would even talk about it with Griffin.

And now that I knew Styles was okay, my nervous system had enough capacity to redirect its full, undivided attention to the matter that would have been my number one concern if someone hadn't gone temporarily missing in the hills of Los Angeles. *What in the actual fuck had happened between Griffin and Willow?*

Griffin was still acting like it was no big deal. Like maybe they'd just gone upstairs to look for a charger and accidentally got trapped in the most private region of the house for almost an hour. But surely, he must have realized that it was big enough to make Styles flee his entire life. That it had detonated something that could have ended in disaster.

And yet: no apology. No explanation. Just going about his daily business as if there was no reason to get all bent out of shape, as if his calm demeanor could hypnotize me into forgetting what had set this crisis in motion. I wasn't ready to deal with it then, but now that the crisis had been averted, I suddenly had the capacity to attempt mentally answering that question in as much gory and devastating detail as I could muster.

All the ways Griffin could have betrayed me. All the uncomfortable truths I hadn't let myself fully absorb. There was a lot to explore. I was almost giddy at the volume of pathways I could take. Because if I was going to confront Griffin, I needed to be ready for what he might admit, but also for what he might not, and what that meant for me.

* * *

How to Pre-emptively Overanalyze a Confrontation

Materials needed: One ambiguous romantic situation with multiple possible entanglements, a partner who is either unbelievably oblivious or secretly a sociopath, and at least three worst-case scenarios ready to deploy at a moment's notice.

1. Mentally rehearse every version of the impending conversation. Make sure to break your own heart in at least half of them. Use an entire roll of toilet paper to wipe the tears.
2. Decide on the most likely conversation scenarios and prepare for the inevitable.
3. Construct a detailed visual flowchart of possible reactions, complete with backup scripts in case he cries, stonewalls, or says you look cute when you're angry during the confrontation.
4. Briefly consider just letting it go, then spiral into shame for even thinking that, followed by rage for all the work you're doing by even planning this conversation.
5. Pack a bag, just in case.
6. Lie awake in the wee hours waiting for the right moment to have the conversation.
7. Practice storming out of the house dramatically with the intention of becoming a missing person case yourself, while idling in your driveway with a new full roll of toilet paper.

Warning: Side effects may include heartburn, nausea, sweating, and a strong desire to get vomitrociously drunk, fall asleep on the cold bathroom floor, and wake up with zero problems solved.

* * *

Three days. That's how long it took me to work up the courage to spark the dreaded confrontation. It might have taken longer if it weren't for the infuriating sound of the coffee grinder at maximum volume before I'd had my coffee. Seriously, who decided coffee grinders should sound like that?

"Alright," I said, stomping into the kitchen and cornering Griffin by the coffee maker as he tapped the "brew" button. Nothing says "let's get fucking real now" like trapping someone next to a filling carafe of scalding liquid. "We need to talk about the other night."

Griffin's shoulders hunched forward as he let his body lean against the wall. There was nowhere for him to go that didn't involve climbing over or under the kitchen table to get away from me and incriminating himself in the process.

"Well... it was kind of funny, actually..."

He smiled. I didn't.

"I was refilling our wine, and Willow went to the bathroom. I heard Clover making that chirping sound he makes, you know, when he thinks he's spotted a moth or a ghost or something."

A cat story. Really.

"She brought over some catnip for the cats," he continued. "But she forgot it in her tote bag. Clover must have caught a whiff of it because he jumped right into that bag. But I guess he found something else more interesting."

Now Griffin's neck and ears turned pink. He crossed his arms and put his hands into his armpits.

"It was a pair of her underwear. You know, panties."

I glowered at him on the outside of my face so as not to break the illusion that on the inside I was rapidly scanning through all the reasons women might carry underwear in our totes. It wasn't really a particularly scandalous thing to do. I had done it myself. In fact, it was not uncommon for me to bring an extra pair of undies with me whenever I was hanging out with

Hannah, for instance. She made me piss myself laughing in public more often than I care to admit.

"Alright, so..." I nudged him to continue.

"So, Willow came out of the bathroom just as he was sprinting with the underwear in his mouth up the stairs."

"And..."

"She chased him up there, and I just instinctively followed her."

I thought for a moment. "To retrieve the stolen panties."

Griffin nodded, his eyes searching for a place to land other than mine.

"But you were up there for a long time. Longer than it takes to dig out a pair of undies from a cat's stash."

"We just got talking."

"In our bedroom. With the door closed. For forty-five minutes while Styles and I pretended not to worry about it. What were you talking about, Griff? That Clover has a penchant for silk and Willow should really bring cotton undies over next time?"

The coffee maker beeped as the final brewing sounds sputtered. Griffin quickly grabbed his mug from the kitchen counter and began to pour. He then set the carafe back on the coffeemaker's warming element. "We talked about you and Styles, okay?"

Of all the scenarios I'd imagined, I had somehow not conjured this one. I had done so much prep work for this conversation, and to find that I had not considered this angle made me even angrier. I felt like I was in some wretched sitcom nightmare, listening to the live studio audience gasp in hushed tones. And Griffin was still standing between me and my first cup of coffee of the day.

"What about us?" Funny how a word like "us" can suddenly become exclusionary in certain contexts.

Griffin took a sip of his coffee. Without taking my eyes from him, I reached for the cupboard above, opened it, took a mug, and nudged him back against the wall to fill it myself from the carafe, while I waited for him to enlighten me.

"Just how simpatico you are. How much time you're spending together on your project. I don't think either of you can see how much it impacts *us*."

There was that word again, and having positioned it in a way that excluded *me* felt like another kind of betrayal. And it was then that I realized I had no answer or defense that wouldn't sound like an excuse loaded with hidden implications. Instead, I took a sip of coffee and went in for the kill shot.

"So, you decided to get even."

"No, it wasn't like that."

"Then what was it like? Because from my vantage point, it looked a lot like you and Willow decided to have some kind of intimate, ill-advised *moment* at the worst possible time, in the worst possible room, with the worst possible consequences."

Griffin rubbed the back of his neck, thinking carefully about his next words.

"It wasn't planned."

He wasn't telling me everything. I wasn't going to nail this down with targeted strikes. I took a page from the book of Paige, and cast a wide, ambiguous net to draw out the truth. "Maybe not, but are you telling me opportunity knocked and you didn't answer?"

A deep red flash of remorse on his face. I knew I had him, and that felt fucking terrible. He sighed. "What do you want me to say? That this was all my fault?" he asked. "You're right. I wasn't thinking."

Wait. Was that it? Was this the closest thing to an admission or apology that I was going to get? We both chugged our coffee. I was desperate for the sweet hot caffeine infusion. He was going to be late for work, but he stayed put.

"I don't want anything to be your fault, or mine, or anyone's. I want you to say that we're okay. That we didn't come all the way here to come apart." My eyes welled up and I turned my face away to hide them from him and hope they wouldn't spill over.

Griffin took a step toward me and reached his arms out, pulling me toward him with a hug that radiated love. I was powerless against it. He held me tight while I dampened his shirt with my tears, my throat in knots.

"We're good," he said, just barely above a whisper, choking back his own emotions. We stood there holding each other for a few minutes, until I was finally able to speak again.

"What now?" I asked, still clinging to him.

"Well, everything turned out alright, didn't it? I guess the dust will settle and we'll just get back to normal."

I wasn't so sure about that. "But what if Styles can't handle working with me because every time he sees me, he's reminded of whatever happened between you and Willow?" Griffin tilted his head a little and cast me a weird look, like I had conjured up a premise so ridiculous and unlikely that it might just have a shot at being a blockbuster movie starring Nicholas Cage.

It was pointless to try and make it make sense to him. But I knew that while Styles might no longer be physically missing, if our shared frequency and the source of our creative connection was lost, it wouldn't just be a work problem. It would be a grief that would be much harder for me to explain.

Chapter 30

"How are things going at work?" Paige started our conversation through the laptop screen. I had missed our last virtual session for reasons of a distracted nature, so she wasn't fully caught up on how things were unfolding. Just thinking about all of the dots I'd have to connect for her to make sense of the most recent events made me want to ghost her.

She waited patiently for my response, as always. I stared at my laptop screen, wondering if there was a way to convey my full-body cringe response through video chat without actually having to articulate why. But nope. Paige was a very skilled therapist, but she was not telepathic, unfortunately.

"Oh, you know. It's very collaborative and appropriate. No emergencies. Absolutely nothing that might have ended up on the news or TMZ. And I'm definitely not having forced proximity fantasies about anyone I work with or anything like that."

Paige's eyebrows inched upward.

I sighed. "Fine. There *may* be a mild emotional subplot. But I'm handling it quietly in my own brain where it belongs."

"Are you sure?"

"Well, I haven't declared anything out loud or climbed ravenously over a desk toward anyone, if that's what you're asking."

"Are you having intrusive thoughts about this person?"

"Define intrusive. If you mean the occasional imaginary scenario where we realize we get each other but don't belong together in real life so I strand us on an uncharted tropical island together, then, yes. A few."

"We've talked about this. When you're under stress, you tend to escape into fantasy narratives. Your imagination is one of your strengths, but too much of a good thing can also be a sign of dysregulation."

"Right. The whole maladaptive daydreaming problem."

"It's only a problem when it starts interfering with how you're engaging in your relationships. Even if it's just impacting you emotionally, we want to pay attention to that."

Styles definitely had my attention. "I'm not proud of it," I said. "It's just how I process, right? Through extremely vivid fantasy sequences with fully scripted dialogue and... the odd sex scene."

Paige smiled. "Which you're aware of, and naming. That's the work."

"Cool. So, the work is owning my thoughts but not acting on them. No problem. You know I love Griffin, right? It has nothing to do with him."

Paige nodded. "I believe that. And I also think love and longing can live side by side. You can love Griffin and still feel drawn to someone who reflects an emerging part of you that you're growing into."

She paused, then added, "No one can take your thoughts away from you, and having them doesn't mean you're unfaithful. It means you're human and going through something, which is often a sign of an impending growth spurt."

Paige leaned forward slightly. "You've made progress with this before, Cara. But we've also never tested it under these conditions. You have a new career, there are high emotional stakes involved, and there is a lot of ambiguity."

"It honestly feels like this has the potential to be my supervillain origin story."

Paige laughed. "We're all the hero of our own stories, but unfortunately, we're all also the villain in someone else's."

* * *

Styles and I were scheduled to work on *Sixty-Six* the following day, but, as anticipated, he decided to take a mental health day. I probably could have used one too, but I knew that I would just end up in a daydream spiral and was honestly feeling a little exhausted from the inside of my own head. Instead, I called River to see if he was free, and that's how I ended up at his home studio, trying my best to get back to rewiring this brain of mine for the better.

But River wasn't his usual relaxed self either. Seeing him in an agitated state gave me that sick feeling inside. You know, that *Star Wars* "disturbance in the force" feeling? There was no joking around, no inspired discussions about lyrics or harmonies. We did get a lot done, even if it seemed like River was somewhere else mentally the whole time. *Holy shit. Is that what it's like being around me?*

It was kind of driving me nuts, and I felt an overwhelming urge to clear the air. "Riv, how much do you know about what happened the other night?" I asked him the next time an awkward silence invaded our momentum.

River looked up from his guitar. He appeared unimpressed,

but not necessarily annoyed. "I talked to Styles last night. He told me everything. He was pretty shaken up." Styles had talked to River, but not to me. Cue my puketronic digestive reactions bubbling up.

"Everything being...?"

"Well, I already knew that Willow was trying to convince him that finding a couple to swap with would be fun. They had some discussions about it and landed on a hypothetical, 'sure, if these planets align and the magic 8 ball says yes during a meteor shower, then let's do it'. Naomi had told me that much."

My guts churned. "Uh huh."

"Willow told Naomi that there was some attempt to realize that hypothetical, but the decision wasn't unanimous. That must've been weird."

"You have no idea."

"Anyway, what Styles did tell me was that Willow and Griffin ended up alone together in your bedroom the other night, which was enough to make him head for the hills in search of solitude. And since he's returned, I guess Willow hasn't exactly been forthcoming about what happened..."

What happened.

"...and now he's in this mixed-up headspace about it all."

What happened.

"How are you about all this, by the way?" His tone warmed slightly, and I thought I detected a note of empathy under whatever it was that was dominating his mood. "This has got to be rough on you, too."

I deflated into the studio couch. "I'm starting to think maybe I should pack up and go home before I wreck everything."

He froze, mid guitar strum. "You mean quit?" he asked, incredulously.

"I mean, it makes sense, right?" I asked, trying to sound casual instead of like someone whose entire identity hinged on his answer.

River stared at me like I'd just suggested we burn down his recording studio and join a circus. "Why would you quit?"

"Because my presence here seems to be wreaking havoc on people I care about. Maybe if I went back to Niagara Falls, everyone's life would go back to normal."

"Cara." River put his guitar down and turned to face me. "Do you like being here?" His voice was firm but gentle.

"I love being here. This is the first time I've ever actually worked toward putting something I created out into the world, and it's all because Styles believes in it... believes in me."

"What about me? What about *our* thing?" he asked, hurt subtly inflaming his eyes.

"You know what I mean. This is *your* thing."

I thought I detected a barely audible growl sound. "Did Styles tell you that?"

"Yeah, Styles might have framed it that way... but... I'm just..."

"You're not *just* anything. This record wouldn't be happening right now without you."

My guts went full hurricane as I stared at him, speechless.

"And you want to give all this up, and all of that other stuff up, because other people are having personal problems that have nothing to do with you?"

I desperately wanted to say the right thing, scanning my brain for a response that mirrored his level of emotional maturity, while pretending I wasn't melting down internally.

"Because I feel responsible," I said, finally. "Like maybe moving here disrupted some kind of cosmic balance, and now everyone's life is more complicated because I selfishly wanted to pursue my dreams."

"Life is complicated," River leaned back in his chair, analyzing me with his entire being. "You really think you're responsible for all the bad things that happen around you?"

"But what if..."

"Cara," River interrupted, "if you quit now, *that* would be disruptive for everyone, including me, including Styles. And I think he'd be the first person to tell you that his problems aren't a good reason for you to abandon your dreams. You have as much right to them as anyone else."

I felt a knot loosen in my guts. "So, you think I should stay?"

"I think you should stay, but not on my account, and not for Styles, either. You should stay because... it's like you're here for a reason. I don't mean it like that 'everything happens for a reason' kind of thing. This isn't some cosmic bullshit. Whatever led to you deciding to move here, *you* decided. We might be part of what made you decide, but you'd do just fine here without either one of us.

It was like something inside me was being torn in two. I felt a strong step away from the version of me that was holding onto the idea that everything was my fault, toward another version of me that was starting to realize the world didn't revolve around me. That my mere existence in the world wasn't interfering in everyone else's normal everyday life. I might be messy, but so is everyone else, all around me, with or without me.

And even though that realization had been brewing for a

while, I gave River the credit. "Has anyone ever told you that you're annoyingly insightful?"

"It's been said. Just be warned that this whole ordeal could inspire another new song." I laughed, remembering what Naomi had told me.

River was right, of course. But being right didn't make the situation any less fucked, and it definitely didn't resolve the fact that I was going to have to figure out how to be around Styles when he was ready to get back to work.

* * *

How to Maintain Professional Boundaries While Secretly Hoping Someone Will Cross Them

Prerequisites: One inappropriate attraction and a metric fuckload of denial.

1. Resist the urge to smile, laugh, touch any part of them, or look directly into their eyes. They'll probably think you're pissed at them, but maybe that's for the best.
2. Talk only about work, traffic or the weather. If the conversation steers into more personal territory, answer your non-ringing phone and say "Sorry, I have to take this."
3. Avoid wearing any outfit they have previously complimented you on. If wearing *that top* is unavoidable for laundry reasons, cover it with your frumpiest sweater.
4. Keep your distance. If you can detect how goddamn good they smell, you're too close.
5. Dream up scenarios where they confront you about your

nonchalant standoffishness and confess their feelings first, absolving you of responsibility for any boundary violations.

6. When they respect your boundaries perfectly, feel simultaneously relieved and devastated.

Note: Following these steps may lead to feeling like you've been dumped when you're the one doing the dumping, completely unbeknownst to anyone but you.

* * *

I wasn't sure how I'd find Styles when I rolled up to his studio for our first working session since the dinner party. When I walked in, his laptop bag was on his desk, and I could hear him making a coffee in the kitchen.

As I tentatively began setting up, he came into the writing room and greeted me with that familiar charismatic smile and gleam in his eyes. Setting his coffee mug down, he pulled his laptop out of his bag and began setting it up like it wasn't his first day back after his nervous breakdown. "Are you ready to get back to work on *Sixty-Six?*" he asked, hopping right to it. "Because I've got some new ideas, and I think we can build out some of the more lovable side characters."

While everything that had happened since the dinner party remained unsaid between us, we somehow managed to slip back into our comfortable work groove again. In some ways, our mutually unspoken decision not to talk about it kind of freed us to focus on our work. It didn't feel weird at all. Actually, it felt like we had passed some kind of test, or earned some kind of badge together.

I had been worried for nothing, as usual. Everything just clicked right back into place, and as we worked, we found ourselves on our wavelength again, the two of us wading together in that same creative stream that made the web series feel like it was part of our shared destiny. There was no place I wanted to be more on that day than at his studio working together. We had survived.

* * *

My phone buzzed around midnight, because apparently Hannah's psychic abilities don't care about things like the time of day. I was still awake in bed, scrolling on my phone, while Griffin sawed logs next to me. Her text message had cortisol spike vibes.

"You don't tell me anything but your energy is LOUD. My crystals are practically screaming your name. You OK babe?"

Hannah's crystals had better intuition than a mother wondering why her toddler is so quiet. I texted her back.

"Just busy. You know how it is when dreams come true. It turns out they require actual work."

Hannah's name flashed on my phone screen, escalating from text to a full-fledged phone call. I slipped out of bed quietly and down the stairs to answer. She didn't even wait for me to say hello.

"That's not what my cards said. What is going on? I pulled five different spreads and the Three of Swords showed up every time."

I didn't know what the Three of Swords meant, but since it was the next one over from the Two of Swords noted earlier, I assumed it must be bad.

"Ah yes, the Three of Swords. Very sharp. Pointy."

"Cara Nicole Becker, do not do that thing."

The fact that she'd used my full name meant she was switching from friend mode to intervention mode. I wanted to yell out that little pieces of cardstock with pretty pictures on them would not be the boss of me, but I fought back the urge. She was caring for me in her love language, after all.

"Sorry, Han. I'm listening."

"Not just that. The Fool, too. Normally I'm excited when The Fool turns up, jumping naively into the great unknown, but when The Fool turns up with the Three of Swords, I worry about how things are going to turn out. It reeks of heartbreak. Betrayal, even. And a hard landing."

"What should I do?" I asked.

Hannah sighed. "Only you know the answer to that. I know you're not going to give me the deets. Just know that The Universe doesn't send things you can't handle. Whatever happens, you'll be okay."

My chest tightened with emotion. How did she always know exactly the thing I needed to hear even if I didn't want to acknowledge it?

"Your implements of witchy divination are fucking nosy, you know that?"

"They're just looking out for you. Just don't shut me out, okay? If you need to talk, I'm here. You know I got you."

"I will, I promise."

But we both knew I wouldn't. Not because I didn't trust her, but because I still wasn't sure if I could trust myself.

Chapter 31

"Let's do a creators' retreat."

I don't know if I can convey the excitement that shot through me upon hearing those words. As if living in LA and working on not one but two creative projects with actual professional creators hadn't been enough to convince me that I'd made it, this put me over the top. I'd finally leveled up.

If someone had invited me to such a thing in my old life, that old version of me would have scoffed. *Yeah, right.* I didn't belong at a thing like that. Obviously, they'd be inviting me as some kind of wannabe mascot to make fun of me. And yeah, I could have gone on my own creative retreat, just me. Why not? That version of me would have daydreamed about it, for sure, but to actually do it? There was no task initiation button in my brain for that. And if I somehow did end up doing it, I'd probably just end up being the butt of my own joke there, too.

But now it was different. I was doing real creative things, working toward actual goals. I didn't have to fret about doing things that *real creators* do, because I had crossed the previously unattainable boundary into *real creator* territory. I had visions of a small but passionate group of us... me, Styles, River and our production teams, blending our ideas and inspirations and conjuring new and exciting things for the future in a relaxed setting with no rules, creatively speaking, at least.

* * *

The development on *Sixty-Six* had been going spectacularly well, in spite of everything. But just when I was starting to believe we might actually pull this thing off, the inevitable, proverbial bomb went off.

It had been some time since we'd heard from the streaming platform. We'd submitted the pilot script for review, but the contracts we were supposed to sign never materialized. When Styles called to check on how the review was going, he learned that the pilot had been promptly and quietly shelved. The green light skipped amber and went straight to red. The budget promise was revoked, with no polite euphemisms about "timing" or "fit." All they gave him was a mild, generic apology and a definitive *no*.

The news knocked the breath right out of my body. The sensation of a room spinning and then going dark is not new to me, but this time it felt like I had been given a terminal diagnosis. Styles pulled up a chair next to me in his office (*our* office) and moved the pile of assorted cords, cables and other studio crap that lived on it so he could sit. He leaned forward, clasped his hands, cleared his throat, and delivered the message with the meekest voice I had ever heard wisp out of him.

I hadn't let myself imagine this outcome. But I should have. I should've known that something this good, this improbable, couldn't last. How could I have let myself get sucked into the idea that the universe was suddenly in my corner, fulfilling all my wishes like a genie whose lamp I hadn't even rubbed. I hadn't earned any of this, and I had taken it for granted.

Rousing from the knockout was like waking up in a back alley feeling like my soul had been ravaged. I finally managed to lift my head from the desk where I had laid it, my eyes wet with tears. Styles raised his head to meet my eyes, and he somehow looked even worse than I felt.

"I feel like such a fool," he said, shaking his head.

I had this mental flash of an image of Styles illustrated in a Victorian art nouveau style taking me by the hand as we leapt off a cliff together, only to realize halfway down that the water that was supposed to catch us below had dried up and our exhilarating cliff dive had turned into a plummet to certain disaster. *The Fool. Holy crap, Hannah.*

"You can blame me," he continued. "I was so sure we had this in the bag," he said, slumping back over. He rubbed his eyes and mumbled. "You uprooted your whole life for this... and now there's no show."

My free fall toward the bottom of the abyss continued, threatening to launch my last meal out from whence it came. "So, that's it? It's just over?"

Styles was silent except for his breathing, which sounded a bit heavy and uneven, like he was out of breath from doing mental calisthenics. Then he sat up suddenly, looking clear-eyed and determined.

"I'll fund it myself."

My jaw dropped. "What the what?"

"I've been putting money aside for my *someday* project. But I believe in *this* project. It'll be harder to do it without industry support for sure, but we can do it. It doesn't have to be over."

Apparently, he had enough tucked away to get us through

continued script development and maybe even some early production work. Not enough to fund an entire season, but enough to inspire someone else with money for a project like this to come on board.

I couldn't believe what I was hearing. "You seriously want to put your own money into this?"

He nodded. "If you'll let me. It just means I'd be more than a producer. I'd be the executive producer, too. I already have an LLC for the podcast. *Sixty-Six* could live under that umbrella."

It was a no-brainer. After all the recent events, after all the what-ifs, what-the-fucks, and other emotional landmines, the idea of the web series being over felt like more than I could bear. *The Universe won't give me things I can't handle, my ass.* Styles' offer to fund the project himself was the lifeline I desperately wanted. It was one of the easiest yeses I ever said.

* * *

Which brings me back to his idea for the creators' retreat. He described it as a weekend away to reset, regroup, and figure out how to approach this next phase, away from the pressures of the LA scene. We would be able to unplug from the chaos and focus on the creative side of things without businessy distractions.

"The theme will be *there's no such thing as a bad idea*. We'll brainstorm, write, strategize, get our momentum back."

"So, who all is coming?" I asked, as if the invitations had already been sent and accepted. I had originally imagined the retreat including everyone in my creative orbit. I was uncomfortable with the competitiveness between River and

Styles for my creative attention, and enamored with the idea of bringing them back together, along with merging everyone else who was involved in our projects.

Styles' podcast producer, Magda, had stepped in as an assistant on *Sixty-Six*. Our animator, El-Jay, was already working on the character design and storyboarding process to develop the pilot. And River's producer, Darian, was a maestro of creative ideas. I wanted us all to gel like some kind of artist collective, minus the toxic Andy Warhol energy.

"The core *Sixty-Six* team," he smiled, extending his arms as he did when he was enthusiastic about something. I was about to suggest expanding the invitation in River's direction, when he continued. "I was thinking we could rent a cabin somewhere in the mountains. Something rustic, where we can let our creative juices flow naturally."

With or without River and Darian, it did sound awesome. I'd seen almost nothing of California beyond Los Angeles since we'd moved. And since spending a weekend in the mountains writing was exactly the kind of thing I imagined real writers do, and I was one of those now, my answer was a resounding "duh, of course."

* * *

I overpacked. In my old life working from home, I could go a whole week with very few costume changes, but being surrounded by so many stylish and fashion-conscious people in LA had definitely had an influence on my closet. I wouldn't say shopping trips with Naomi were a regular occurrence, but I can't say I didn't let her style me from time to time.

Not that I wore most of what I bought on those shopping

trips. More like I bought things I *could* wear in LA, even if I still probably *wouldn't* and inevitably *didn't*. But what if I needed an outfit for a last-minute prestigious awards ceremony? I couldn't daydream a red-carpet worthy gown onto my body. I called it being ready, just in case. Paige called it "paying the ADHD tax."

So, that Friday morning, I lugged my overstuffed weekend bag containing enough options to handle every possible weather and cabin fashion situation to the office in readiness to embark on our team mountain retreat road trip at the end of the workday. When I arrived, Styles and Magda were busy in the studio auditioning voice talent for the web series characters, so that left only El-Jay and myself in the main office.

El-Jay was working with his headphones on, as he typically did, and the quiet in the office was super distracting. Something felt kind of off. He didn't have a weekend bag under his desk. Maybe it was in his car. I figured we'd all carpool with Styles, but it wouldn't be surprising if others wanted to drive themselves, I supposed.

Rather than just ask him (OMG, like ask someone something instead of making up four-trillion scenarios in my head? Are you serious?) I eavesdropped on his intermittent phone conversations, listening for any mention of the creative retreat. Nada. But he did say something about meeting his buddy at a jazz club that night. *What the actual fuck.*

At that point, I started to wonder if I'd gotten the date wrong, or if I'd daydreamed the whole idea myself, or if I had hallucinated it, finally having my impending break with reality.

At 4:30, I watched El-Jay pack up his desk and head out for

his jazz meetup. Then Magda came in from the studio, her purse slung across her chest, making a beeline for the door. I jumped in her way.

"Magda!"

"Cara, hey, I guess you want to know how the auditions went?"

"Oh, yeah, of course."

"I have to run, but Styles can fill you in. A few good candidates but we'll keep auditioning. We'll put a shortlist reel together for you to review. Gotta run!"

"Wait!" I exclaimed, not letting her pass. She paused, looking impatient to get on with her weekend, which confirmed my suspicions, but I had to ask her anyway, just in case I was reading everything wrong, which was not only possible but likely, given my history of misreading situations.

"Are you meeting us at the cabin tonight? Driving up yourself?"

She stared at me blankly. "Cabin?"

"You know, the creators' retreat."

"What retreat?" she asked, looking confused, and a little left out.

The alarm bells I had been suppressing finally went off in my head. Either Styles had forgotten to invite anyone else to the retreat he'd organized, or he'd deliberately arranged a weekend getaway for just the two of us and somehow failed to mention that rather significant detail during the planning conversation.

Neither possibility was particularly comforting.

And so, as Magda left the building, I sat at my desk and stared at my weekend bag, contemplating whether it was too late to develop a sudden case of food poisoning or a UTI.

It's not that I didn't want to go, exactly. I mean, you *know* I wanted to. But we had just gotten over the most recent drama. All I wanted was a period of sustained peace. And sure, a cabin in the mountains sounded peaceful, but... do I have to even say it?

Styles emerged from the studio with a pep in his step and an excited look on his face. He practically skipped over to me as I stood with my arms crossed and my eyebrows as furrowed as I could make them.

"Ready to go?" he asked, practically dancing past me toward the door, car keys in hand, keeping his head turned to me as if I would just automatically follow him. "I see you have your bag. Mine's in the car. Our chariot awaits!" He made a grand gesture with his arms, you know, the kind that could knock you into a nearby pool if you weren't expecting it.

The previous version of me, the people-pleaser who went along with everything to make everyone else happy, might have just smiled and said yes. But this new version of me, she had something new that I wasn't entirely familiar with, but was undeniable. A quiet resistance? Guts even?

Even though I knew the answer, I gave Styles the chance to come clean. "So, um, where is everyone else meeting us? At the cabin, or are we picking people up on the way?"

Styles' expression shifted from enthusiastic to carefully neutral. "Everyone else?"

"The *core team.* It's a creators' retreat for *Sixty-Six,* after all."

"Oh." Styles ran his fingers through his hair and exhaled a deep breath. "I guess I should have been clearer about that."

Now, in my experience, when someone tells you they "should have been clearer", you're generally dealing with a harmless miscommunication, unless a deliberate ambiguity was in play, leading to inadvertently agreeing to something significantly more complicated than you realized. And given my track record with accidentally agreeing to complicated situations, I was bracing for the latter.

"Clearer how?" I asked.

"The core team is us, isn't it? You and me?" While Styles and I certainly were in charge of the show's direction, I couldn't imagine being able to finish it without Magda, El-Jay, and the other talent who were being auditioned to come on board. How could the core team be *just the two of us*?

Thus began an earworm that threatened to portend my slow descent into anxiety-induced madness. This had all the signs of not just being an innocent writing weekend in the mountains, but the opening scene of a horror movie where the characters make increasingly ill-advised choices and the last one standing ends up screaming in the rain covered in blood. Which, knowing me, was still entirely possible even if the weather held up. Thankfully, I had packed an outfit for that.

"I can cancel," Styles said quickly, reading the incredulous expression on my face. His tone switched to a stilted professionalism, like an invisible but palpable wall suddenly formed between us. "I should have been explicit about the invitation list. If you're not comfortable with it, I completely understand. I can go by myself, or we can reschedule for another time with everyone, the whole team."

He was trying hard to hide behind this professional barrier he just put up, but wasn't doing a very good job. Instead, he looked apologetic and deflated, which kind of killed me. He put his car keys down on the desk near me, and sat down in the chair, leaning over his knees, waiting for me to put the final kibosh on the plan.

The rational part of me was drafting a polite decline. But the other part, the one that had been quietly screaming for exactly this in a long running fantasy, was louder. Out in the wilderness with fire, bugs, and a pretend sense of "roughing it" to survive, with someone who not only saw me in a way that no one else had, but was pretty much consuming my every waking thought. Would it not be crazy to graciously accept this level of wish fulfillment as a blessing from The Universe?

"It's fine," I heard myself say, wearing my most impenetrable mask of nonchalance while I internally flailed around in a stew of indistinguishable emotions. "We should get on the road, before it gets dark." *OMG what was I doing?*

Styles' face lit up with relief and excitement that also almost killed me. "Are you sure? Because I really didn't mean to create an awkward situation."

"I'm sure," I said, hefting my weekend bag over my shoulder. "Besides, Griffin will be disappointed if I go home and interrupt his 'me party' weekend with the shitty pizza he loves and his video games."

Styles swiped his keys up from the desk and whisked me out the door to our proverbial chariot, his hybrid SUV. As we got on the road toward the mountains, I continued to examine the situation for an ulterior motive, and convinced myself there couldn't be one. In the face of previous temptations, Styles had always acted appropriately. This was fine, a perfectly normal thing that creative colleagues do. When Hannah had said *I got this*, in regards to The Universe dealing me wild cards, I figured this was my chance to prove it.

I shut down the big black sinister butterflies that fluttered inside me as we finally moved through traffic out of the city. I stared out the window and felt myself swirling with happy anticipation of our planned creative reset for the project and for my mindset. Cara 2.0 had earned this.

Chapter 32

The scenic evolution on the drive to the cabin was astonishing. Being from Niagara Falls, I guess I had this idea that being surrounded by natural wonders that others from around the world flock to, meant I'd seen the best of what this continent could offer. I had spent all this time immersed in a high-energy cityscape and was only now venturing out into what reminded me of a sunset flipbook. The undulating terrain was bathed in that trademark California golden light with contrasting purple shadows. Let's just say it was equal parts breathtaking and humbling.

"Okay, how is it *this* pretty?" It was more of an observation than a question. Palm trees soon gave way to pine trees, silhouetted against a sky painted in shades of orange and rose that reminded me of an early 1900s impressionist landscape painting.

"One of LA's underrated perks," Styles said, sucking up the last dregs of his soft drink from our drive-through dinner. "You can go from gridlock to national park tranquility in under two hours."

I couldn't help noting the irony. Styles had just finished his impromptu "solo retreat" to confront his feelings or find himself or whatever it was, and now here we were, heading out to the mountains. Like the cure for running away was apparently more running away. At least this time we were prepared with road trip snacks.

A lot had gone unsaid between us, especially regarding recent events. Those unspoken words echoed loudly in my head during the moments of silence as we drove, in between bursts of light conversation. He hadn't brought up the night he went MIA or what came after, and I hadn't asked. But we both knew it was all there under the surface.

He was calm and focused while driving. It seemed to me that he had clearly decided this weekend was going to be all fresh starts and no flashbacks. Maybe that was healthy. Maybe that was what I should have wanted, too. But after a particularly long stretch of uninterrupted silence, the question slipped out before I could stop it.

"Are we going to talk about it?"

Styles glanced at me, then back at the road, a tiny smile forming on his face that allowed just a hint of a dimple to form, which gave me the impression of sunlight poking through a storm cloud.

"Talk about what?"

* * *

The cabin and its accoutrements were exactly what I'd order from a vacation house menu or one of those memes where you pick the items from each line to build your perfect wilderness retreat. Log cabin exterior surrounded by forest: check. Wraparound porch with rocking chairs: check. A wall of windows looking out onto a calm lake surrounded by evergreen trees fencing in a range of huge purple mountains:

check. Pine interior with a large fireplace and comfy couches strewn with blankets: the final check.

It was rustic and charming, and if you're like me, then you find that aesthetic utterly romantic, even in the most platonic of situations. Every nook and cranny of the place begged to bear witness to deep conversations while wrapped in blankets and nursing mugs of steaming hot chocolate.

There were just enough exposed beams and firewood to remind us we were there to pretend we were roughing it. But it also had a strong Wi-Fi signal, for when our creativity required googling obscure facts about 1960s music for our dystopian pop culture web series, as the case may be.

"Why don't I live here?" I asked myself out loud, hauling my weekend bag into the cabin and trying not to think about how this entire scenario looked like it had been curated by my own romantic subconscious.

"Yeah, I could get used to this," Styles chuckled.

"I'll take this one," I said quickly, claiming the small bedroom on the main floor before the sleeping arrangements could become a topic of discussion. It was a strategic choice, situated next to a bathroom. Hopefully it meant reducing the likelihood of any middle-of-the-night encounters while searching for the toilet.

Styles wholeheartedly accepted my choice. "Well, I was willing to flip a coin for it, but sounds good. I was hoping for the big one with the ensuite bathroom anyway," he shrugged happily before heading upstairs with his stuff.

By the time we'd unpacked and uncorked the inaugural bottle of wine, the sun had set behind the mountains, and the warm glow had faded to monochrome dusky darkness with a moon bright enough to illuminate the path to the fire pit. It was on a low hill by a rocky cliff edge, surrounded by Adirondack chairs that faced the lake. My heart suddenly pined with a homesick longing that I hadn't felt since we moved. I didn't even know loons lived in California, but a quick Google search confirmed I wasn't hallucinating a ghost bird calling.

"This is ridiculous," I said, sitting in one of the chairs with my glass of wine. "It's like a commercial for prescription-level relaxation."

"Ask your doctor if Mountain Cabin Retreat is right for you," Styles quipped in a television announcer's voice. I watched him skillfully light the fire, a satisfying confirmation that he knew his way around a campsite, and that my island survival fantasies were plausible in at least that one aspect.

"Side effects may include jerky cravings, a need to point out constellations, and campfire hypnosis," I continued.

"Do not operate heavy machinery while under the influence of Mountain Cabin Retreat," he added.

We wrapped ourselves in the cabin's designated outdoor wool blankets that smelled like that weirdly pleasant combination of bug spray and wood smoke, and I had to admit that despite my anxieties about the unexpected twist in the weekend's plan, it was pretty hard to imagine wanting to be anywhere else.

"Where do you want to start?" Styles asked, pulling his laptop computer onto his knee and opening it up. "Pilot script revisions? Or brainstorm something new?" It felt a lot later than 7 PM, but it was early enough that we could absolutely get some work done before turning in for the night. I felt myself cringe a little at the realization that I had left my own laptop inside the cabin.

I hesitated to answer, staring into the flames. While I was happy that Styles had revived our project through his self-funding idea, doing so at his own expense did make me feel a little unsettled. He had assured me that funding it under his existing LLC would make things easier, but it had gotten me thinking about ways we could reduce our upfront costs.

"I've been thinking about the way we approach things, now that we're going all indie-style," I said.

"It's exciting, isn't it? We might not have the same resources, but in some ways, we have more power."

"Right. So... since we're now the kind of operation that can make our own calls, I wanted to pitch an idea."

"Give it to me."

I took a breath. "What if we brought River in? For the music."

Styles was quiet for a moment. "For *Sixty-Six*? It's not really... country though, is it?

"He has more than country in him. You heard his new direction. He could lean into that new neo-psychedelic style, and it could help shape the tone, the emotional palette. He gets it, you know? And he's already kind of invested, in a weird backseat kind of way. I don't know. I just keep hearing him on the soundtrack."

Styles leaned back, thinking. "I mean, he might be less expensive than licensing the original tunes or even covers, that's true. But do you think he'd want to take it on?" he asked.

"I don't know," I admitted. "I haven't mentioned it to him yet. But it kind of seems like a no-brainer."

He nodded slowly, poking again at the fire. "Yeah. You're right. I could see him liking the idea."

There was something else in his expression then. It was hard to pin down what he was thinking, but for just a quick second, he seemed a bit tense. I hadn't considered how bringing River in might affect our dynamic, but it made the most sense.

"I just..." Styles said, carefully, "don't want him to feel like I'm using his friendship to save my ass."

"I'll ask him," I said. "And River's smart. He knows what's worth his time. If it's not a fit, he'll say no."

"That's true," Styles murmured, finally smiling. "But if it is a fit..."

"His name attached to it might give us more cred."

That brought a glimmer to Styles' eyes, briefly. "It might change a few things," he said, carefully.

"I know," I paused for a moment like I was calibrating, "but *Sixty-Six* didn't begin its life as a web series anyway. It started as a novel. So, if it evolves again, doesn't that just mean it's still finding its final form?"

We sat with that for a moment, the idea of River's voice breathing a different vibe into the story. If he agreed, then *Sixty-Six* might actually have a snow's chance in Helsinki to become a reality.

"To recalibrating," Styles mused, raising his wine glass.

"To moving forward," I said, raising mine.

Styles clinked his against mine. "To surviving the apocalypse and turning it into art."

The fire was dying down, and the temperature had dropped enough that I was grateful for the wool blanket keeping me warm. I thought about letting myself drift off in the chair by the fire, but then remembered my recent outdoor chair sleeping experience and how cricked my neck was the next morning.

"I should probably get some sleep," I said eventually, though I was reluctant to end such a pleasant and productive evening. "Tomorrow's going to be a long day of revising the scripts."

Styles looked at me for a moment without saying anything. It felt like he was deliberately trying to hold me in place with his intense but slightly bemused gaze. I looked for signs of Morse code in his blinking, but he broke his gaze to poke the fire just as I was about to ask him, "What?"

"Well, g'night then," Styles said gently. The way he said it made me wonder if he was also reluctant to call it a day, or if I was reading too much into a perfectly normal expression of friendly camaraderie.

* * *

I. Could. Not. Fall. Asleep. Not that this was surprising or abnormal for me. But damn, I had hoped the peaceful setting would ease my mental activity just a little, for once. I tried to focus on the sounds of the surrounding mountain landscape and the way the cabin creaked when the winds swelled.

But instead, my mind wandered to Griffin, and I caught myself replaying our conversation about the retreat in my mind. It hadn't been particularly dramatic, which might have been exactly the reason I felt so uneasy about it in retrospect.

* * *

"Styles is planning a thing this weekend for the whole Sixty-Six

team. It's up in the mountains, isn't that rad?" I said casually while licking a spoon of crunchy peanut butter.

Griffin looked up from his phone. "Like a work trip?"

"Yeah. Kind of a working retreat. Just a couple days to refocus and try to figure out how we're going to approach the project now that the pilot's been canceled."

He nodded. "Everyone going?"

"That's the plan," I said. I thought it was true at the time.

Griffin nodded. "Yeah, that is rad." He looked at me with a tinge of jealousy. But I knew this jealousy. This wasn't possessiveness. This was the facial expression of a man who could use some mountain retreat time himself.

"I could find out if there is enough room for you, too," I offered.

He thought for a moment. "Well, it would be nice to get out of town for a bit, but... that's okay. I'd probably just end up being the team massage therapist all weekend," he laughed.

"That's a distinct possibility," I agreed.

"Thanks, anyway. The cats and I will just order a bunch of pizza and rewatch 'House' episodes."

"Daisy's favorite!"

Griffin scratched the top of her head while she purred on his lap. But it was no joke that she had an interspecies crush on Hugh Laurie. I'm sure she would have left us for him if he'd walked in the door.

* * *

I hadn't told Griffin the plan had changed, and now the guilt was driving me bonkers. It wasn't guilt about anything I'd done, because I hadn't done anything. It was guilt about the thoughts I was having. The way Styles had looked at me when

I mentioned bringing River in. The way he'd said good night like he meant something more than just good night.

I replayed the conversation with Griffin several times, enough to make sure I hadn't missed anything, until I drifted into a certain tropical island survival scenario from where it left off.

* * *

Where were we? Right. Kissing like we were thirsty for each other's saliva. As we pulled off our clothes, I was aware of how, up until this moment, we had been very careful about maintaining modesty. We didn't belong to each other then, and so it was only right to halt any temptation by keeping that aspect of social decorum in place. But now, getting naked in front of him, outside in nature, was the most electrifying feeling. It might've been hot and humid, but our nipples clearly hadn't gotten the memo. No breeze, no chill. Just immediate enthusiasm for what was about to come. Pun very much intended.

Dusk had given way to dark and the firelight was more romantic than it had ever been. But my view of Styles was only of his outline lit by the orange flames. I wanted to see him, all of him. Not just soft shadows on his skin. And so, with a quick flip of an imaginary switch, we were suddenly bathed in glowing daylight.

I knew what was going on, but Styles didn't, and obviously it caught him off guard. He raised his head and squinted at the sky. "Wasn't it getting dark?"

"I hadn't noticed," I said, and pulled him back to me.

We'd built a life here. Well, a fantasy life, which despite the lack of creature comforts was as structurally sound as it could have been. But now, with the hope of rescue officially gone, we could commit to it fully.

The pile of palm fronds beneath the multipurpose towel that lined our shelter bed now scattered under our dramatic movements. I felt myself surrender to Styles' touch as his hands slid up my waist. I felt his breath on my ear, and shivered at the feeling of his lips and tongue on my neck. My back arched so strongly I wondered where this ability was when I was doing yoga classes and went home needing Griffin's skilled hands to undo the damage.

Griffin. Nope, not here, not now.

"You taste salty," Styles said softly.

I laughed. "Your beard smells like smoked coconut and... something tangy."

"That could be grub juice. One exploded when I bit into it earlier."

"Gross!"

"I thought I washed it all off, sorry."

"It's delicious on you." I admitted, taking my turn to devour him. I moved down his body, kissing as I went until I arrived at his waist, anticipating what I'd find there. While I had always found his salt and pepper hair to be sexy, especially with the face-framing silver wisps that now matched the growth of his island beard, I didn't realize just how much I'd be into his mess of gray pubes. Not that they were the main attraction, by any stretch. Now it was his turn to arch his back as I took him, as much of him as I could fit, in my mouth. His impressive size required some creative tonguework, but he seemed to approve. That little groan he made... I almost shattered into a million horny little shards.

And then there was a sound, like a rustle from the trees that we had not heard on the island before. We froze. Styles sat up slightly, his ribs visible through his skin, his belly folding taut at the navel. His eyes scanned the jungle's edge. "What was that?"

"Just the breeze, I'm sure," I whispered, going back down on him.

"There's no breeze," he observed, accurately. More rustling sounds, and then suddenly a sharp EE-EE-EE noise that definitely wasn't wind. "Okay, that was not the breeze. Was that a... are there monkeys on this island?"

"Maybe," I tossed out nonchalantly, while resuming my activities at his pelvis.

"Maybe? Since when?"

"It's not important."

I don't know why my brain does that. Messes with my immaculately constructed scenarios so that I can't even have the perfect moment I've been planning and scheming and slow-burning toward in my imagination. Why monkeys suddenly appeared is not for me to say, only that now they were there, and I was going to do my best to ignore them and finally get the satisfaction I was craving.

A black spider monkey emerged from the treeline carrying something. It was the toothbrush from our serendipitous backpack discovery. He looked like a tiny pirate with stolen booty. Another monkey perched on a rock, wielding our revered pocket tool. A third was doing what could only be described as interpretive dance on a piece of driftwood.

"Are they going to watch us?"

"I don't think they care. Do you care? I don't care," I said with my mouth full, intent on maintaining the full length and breadth of his attention.

"Wait. Is that one wearing your bra on his head?"

I was done with all this monkeying around. No more distractions. My hand took over where my mouth had been while I maneuvered back up to his lips and kissed him like both of our lives depended on it. A monkey shrieked from a branch overhead. Whatever.

Styles wrapped his arm around my back to my side and expertly flipped me over, kissing me all the way down my body until he arrived at my pelvic region. I was suddenly aware of my own pubes, which had grown in since our arrival with no blade to keep them in check. He didn't seem to mind.

I gasped at the softness of his tongue between my legs. A screeching EE-EE-EE sound came from the trees.

"Do you want me to get rid of them?" Styles asked, in between licks, his voice low and soft, like his tongue

"No," I gasped. "It's fine. Just, don't stop."

When he finally went inside me, I felt all the bliss I had anticipated. My body was flooded with a sudden surge of all the endorphins known to humankind and maybe some undiscovered ones. We found our rhythm, moving together and against each other as the sensations intensified.

A pair of monkeys chittered close by, fucking on the driftwood log that marked the entrance to our camp, pounding in an accelerated rhythm all their own. I blocked them out, and along with them, the rest of the world disintegrated around us.

"I'm so close," Styles whispered. I was, too.

Chapter 33

CRASH.

A loud clattering sound, very much not in my head, jolted me upright in bed. I was disoriented, but as my eyes adjusted to the darkness, I realized that I was looking at a ceiling. Not a palm tree in sight, and thankfully, no monkeys. I was in my cozy cabin bedroom.

The crashing sound came again, and this time I identified it as being in the kitchen. The fantasy had slipped away, but my heart was still hammering in my chest, now out of terror rather than the excitement of what was happening in my imagination. Adrenaline pumping, I reached for my phone.

It was 2:18 AM. I considered the possible reasons for the crashing sounds in the kitchen. It was either a clumsy mountain cabin burglar in desperate need of metal cookware, or Styles indulging a middle-of-the-night urge to test the quality of the frying pans by standing on the counter and dropping them.

I remained sitting up in bed for approximately thirty more seconds, trying to determine whether I should A) pretend I hadn't heard anything and let Styles give me the frying pan report in the morning, or B) hide under my covers and hope that if it was actually a burglar, they'd be satisfied with whatever they found in the kitchen and wouldn't feel compelled to expand their criminal activities to my bedroom.

Option B was the most enticing, because as we've seen, I'm a big fan of ignoring shit until it either goes away or becomes the only option. But I was trying to rewire my brain, not be that person anymore, so I did the hard thing and got up to find out what was going on, hoping that the frying pans were of good enough quality to knock out a mountain cabin burglar should the need arise.

I found Styles in the kitchen, lit only by the flashlight of his phone, inspecting his expensive metal water bottle for dents. "Sorry," he said, looking mildly embarrassed by his normal human accident. "I couldn't sleep, came out to get some water. I was trying so hard to be quiet, so naturally I dropped it twice."

"It happens," I said. "That's a pretty big dent there."

He sighed. "Two of them. And I just got this bottle." He proceeded to fill it as carefully as possible so as to avoid any further crashing and smashing. "I don't suppose you have any tips for how to beat insomnia?" he asked. "Because lying in bed staring at the ceiling while my brain cycles through every stupid thing I've ever said doesn't seem to be working."

Been there, done that. "I wish I could help, but I'm having the same problem."

Styles screwed the cap back on his water bottle and moved toward the living room, which had gotten chilly. "Want to sit by the fire for a while?" he asked, picking up the electric fireplace remote and switching it on. "Maybe a change of scenery will help."

I followed him and sat at the far end of the couch, pulling my knees up to my chest. He sat at the other end, leaving a fair bit of distance between us. We quietly watched the fake fire for a few minutes, until Styles received a text message. He picked up his phone and reacted with identifiable surprise.

"Who's that?" I inquired, feeling simultaneously nosy and that it was none of my business, as well as weirdly and inappropriately jealous about whoever was texting him at this time of the night.

"It's Delphine, my daughter," he revealed. "I almost never hear from her, except when she wants to blame me for someone calling her a nepo baby," he grumbled before continuing to vent. "I like to remind her she could have stayed in college, chosen any career she wanted."

"You don't choose the influencer life, the influencer life chooses you," I joked. He half-smiled, the dimple on his left cheek appearing briefly before he went serious again. "She's at some party and just dumped her boyfriend," he said, looking serious.

"Timo," I said, remembering her boyfriend's name.

Styles nodded. "She must have meant to text someone else. She doesn't talk to me much." He looked like he was trying to think of the right reply, tapping words out on the phone keyboard and then hitting the delete button repeatedly.

"How come?"

Styles stared at his phone for a second before looking up. "She blames me for her mother's death." He said it kind of flippantly, shrugging his shoulders and shaking his head while gesturing with a dismissive wave of his hand, but it still landed heavily. I didn't want to be the jerk who asked him to explain the details, but holy crap did I want him to explain the details.

"Um... what happened? If you don't mind my asking. You

can tell me to take a hike if I'm out of bounds."

He winced, then obliged. "It was our ten-year anniversary. Delph was eight at the time. She wasn't there when it happened, she was at her grandparents' house," he clarified. "I wanted to do something special for Michelle. I'd heard about this hike up to a lookout that was supposed to have this incredible sunset view like nowhere else. It wasn't a long hike, and we'd have plenty of time to get back down before it got dark, but to get there you had to go off the main trail. I had this idea that we would hike up there and have this romantic moment. I brought champagne in my backpack and everything.

"When we got to the lookout, the view was even better than I pictured it. We took some selfies, then I was taking photos of her in front of the view. She looked so beautiful."

He paused, searching for the words. "There was this narrow ledge with a steep drop. I didn't ask her to step on the ledge, she did that all on her own."

I covered my mouth with my hands to stop my heart from flying up my throat and out of my mouth, sensing exactly where this was going.

"When she fell, all I wanted to do was go after her, but there was no safe route down on that side. I scrambled back down the trail to see if I could see her. Maybe she was okay, maybe she wasn't hurt that bad and I could get her out. But I couldn't see her. I called out to her, but she didn't respond. There were some other hikers and they heard me yelling. They went for help, but..."

He changed his tone suddenly to hide his emotion, but his voice was still thick. "Anyway, you can't go up there now, they've fenced it off."

"Oh my God. I'm so sorry. I can't even imagine what that must have been like." And then I flashed back to him jumping in to rescue me, a virtual stranger to him then, from six feet of water at River's pool party, and understood him in that moment in a way that I couldn't back then.

And as if he knew exactly where my mind had gone, he followed me there.

"You know, I keep thinking about that dinner party. Not yours. I mean, yes, yours. But mainly the one at River's. The day we met."

"That was a memorable evening for sure," I agreed. *Understatement of the year.*

"When Willow called us inside to chat, I just knew she was going to... go there. We'd talked about it before."

"So, you weren't surprised?" I asked, remembering what River had told me.

He shrugged. "I was hoping it was all just talk and that the hypothetical aspect, talking about it and thinking about it would be enough for her. I mean, she can do whatever she wants in her own imagination, right?"

I shivered, even though the fireplace had sufficiently warmed the room. "Totally," I said. The feeling that he was somehow inside my head intensified. *Had I been discovered?*

Styles stared into the electric fire intently. "Do you ever wonder what would have happened if we'd said yes?" he asked.

He went there. He asked the question out loud like he wasn't afraid of splitting our timeline, leaving me with the responsibility of answering and deciding which one we'd end up in. I was on the verge of leaving my body. The only thing I could do was try to come up with another hypothetical play.

"I mean, in some parallel universe, maybe we did say yes," I said, trying to keep my voice light and philosophical. "Maybe there's a version of us somewhere that made a different choice and is dealing with those consequences."

"Yeah. Or like, in that universe, maybe we weren't strangers who barely knew each other. Maybe we already had some kind of connection that made the whole thing seem less insane than it did at the time."

There was something in his voice that made me look at him more carefully, wondering whether this was all just talk, or if he was laying the groundwork (the palm fronds, if you will) for something more.

"It did seem pretty insane at the time," I said. "I remember thinking that recreational spouse-swapping was maybe not the best way to get to know people at a BBQ. I'd like to think that if we rewound to that moment, I'd make the same choice all over again."

"It was the right choice *then*. But *now*..." Styles trailed off, and the silence that followed was loaded with all the conversations we hadn't had and all the boundaries we'd been carefully minding. "Now it doesn't seem quite so insane."

The electric fire made an artificial popping sound, just as he crossed the line between theoretical discussion and dangerous territory. This was the moment where I should probably have redirected the conversation back to safe topics like work, or mountain cabin burglars, or literally anything that didn't involve acknowledging what I had been feeling.

Instead, I heard myself say, "No, it doesn't seem quite so insane now."

"You look cold," Styles observed, noticing that I was still hugging my knees, more for emotional comfort than actual warmth.

"A little," I lied. He moved closer on the couch, close enough that we could share the throw blanket that had been draped over the back cushions. He pulled it over the both of us. "Better?"

I mean, sure, it was better, in terms of amplifying the electric energy I was feeling between us, but also significantly worse in terms of my ability to keep my shit together. How was I supposed to maintain an appropriate amount of emotional distance from him when I had been fantasizing about him in bed less than an hour earlier? The blanket was like a cocoon of security that felt both innocent and charged at the same time.

"Better," I said, though being close enough to smell him and feel the warmth radiating from his skin was almost enough to make my heart pound out of my chest cartoonishly. We sat in silence like that for a while, just staring at the fireplace while the air between us hummed with electricity, trying very hard not to acknowledge something that was becoming increasingly difficult to ignore.

Styles gave my hand a quick but gentle tap. Maybe to check if I felt cold, maybe just a friendly gesture. But when I looked at him, I found myself staring directly into his eyes, and there it was. An expression I had imagined hundreds of times, staring back at me in reality.

His face hung only a few inches from mine. He reached up and took my glasses off, setting them on the coffee table. I should have pulled back. I should have made a joke about not being able to see. I should have suggested we go back to our separate bedrooms to try to get some sleep so we could be productive and creative in the morning.

Instead, I closed the distance between us and kissed him. His mouth was soft and his tongue touched mine tentatively at first, and then the kiss intensified, breaking only briefly as our sleep shirts went over our heads and our pajama bottoms were pulled down our legs, and thrown onto the floor.

He was different from how I had imagined him. Nothing like the fantasy. Better, because it wasn't all me, pulling the strings. There was no resetting the scene. No imaginary monkeys. Just this version of the timeline, unfolding in ways I couldn't anticipate or control.

He surprised me with touches and flicks and licks that were new to me. Gentle nips and pinches that when released, sent waves of pleasure throughout my body. I was mildly concerned about the wet spot that was forming beneath me on the couch, but not enough to overtake how fucking good he was making me feel.

I wanted to stroke him in return, but every time I reached for him, he gently moved my hand with an insistent "you first". Which only made my craving stronger. I imagined going down on him, tasting him, exploring him with my tongue, when he came up from down below and his mouth found mine again. It tasted... sweet. But a specific kind of sweet. Marshmallowy. No, s'moresy. And there was something in his mouth. He transferred the small object to my mouth with this tongue.

"Is that... a jellybean?"

I heard the crinkling of a plastic candy bag as he pulled back, kneeling on the couch between my legs. He smiled slyly as he pulled another jellybean out of the bag in his hand and placed it in my bellybutton.

"Jelly belly. Camping flavored."

"Wait, when did you..."

"You were so enthralled you didn't even notice me grabbing these off the coffee table and opening them," he laughed, before ducking back down to tongue the jellybean out of my bellybutton.

"Mmm. Hot chocolate."

"How do you know it's the hot kind?"

"Oh, trust me. It's hot."

I reached for the bag with an imploring, "Can I have another..." but he pulled the candy away and held it over his head, with a playful smirk on his face and a twinkle in his eyes.

"Hey, what happened to *me first*?" I whined, impishly.

"You're right," he conceded, and inserted a jellybean into his own bellybutton for me to extract.

"I just need to move this out of the way," I said, reaching for his magnificent hard-on, which was pointing happily upward and outward.

"I'll allow it." He let me nudge it to the side, and I proceeded to extract the jellybean with my mouth.

"What did you get?"

"Belly button lint," I joked.

"What?! I cleaned it out before bed," he insisted, pulling his navel open with his thumb and index finger to inspect it. Which gave me the opportunity to grab for the bag of jellybeans in his other hand, but when I did, he jerked his hand back, sending the jellybeans flying everywhere.

Thus began the hottest, sexiest, funniest, nakedest food fight I've ever had the undisputed pleasure of taking part in. But it wasn't too long before the laughter from the silliness of jellybeans in various orifices gave way to even more delicious indulgences.

"I just found the best tasting bean of all," said Styles, letting his finger take over his flickwork briefly before going back down for another taste.

Eventually it was my turn to bring him to the brink, his blissful gasps and moans an enthusiastic guide toward the next stop on the way to our ultimate destination. He slipped inside, and then, after syncing our bodies in a deep, undulating rhythm, we finally came together in a carnal connection that made my head spin with a mix of endorphins and emotions that exploded like fireworks all throughout my body. It wasn't a sugar rush, I can tell you that much.

Later, entangled with each other under the throw blanket as the electric fire flickered on, I drifted off to sleep with Styles' warm breath on my shoulder, a vague splintered feeling in my chest, and a wish for a "universal remote" that would let me pause time.

* * *

I woke from a dreamless sleep with no idea how much time had passed. It was still dark. Styles shifted behind me. I stayed still, breathing slow, pretending I was asleep. He didn't say anything. No hand on my arm. No whisper of goodnight. Just the soft rustle of the blanket lifting, a creak of the couch as he stood, and careful, quiet steps across the floor.

I kept my eyes closed as he crept away. The fireplace was still on, but it felt like all the warmth had left the room. I had this unsettling awareness of the space next to me where he'd been, now vacant. I felt powerless, like I'd given up control of my story to someone else.

* * *

The next morning was exactly as awkward as you'd expect. I wasn't prepared to talk about it, or not talk about it, or for anything, really. After shuffling back off to my bedroom to leave behind the feeling of being left behind, I had been too restless to sleep. Not even a daydream. The word "fuck" had been playing on a short-circuit loop in my head for the rest of that night.

I did not want to leave the security of my room that morning. Whatever was going to happen on the other side of that door, I wanted no part of it. I wanted only to live in my Schrödinger's Box of a bedroom in liminal space until someone, preferably a cannibalistic mountain man with cravings for city flesh, kicked the door open and dragged me out.

When I finally went out to the kitchen, Styles was already there, leaning on the breakfast nook, resting his chin in his hand, and staring into a mug of coffee. He looked like hell. Which was exactly how I felt.

"Maybe we should head back to LA today instead of tomorrow," Styles suggested, his voice gravelly and barely louder than a whisper. As I approached the nook, he gently pushed a steaming mug of abyssal darkness in front of me. I was suddenly aware of a sour bile taste in the back of my throat. I tried to clear it away.

"Probably a good idea," I agreed half-heartedly. My stomach in knots, I tried to wash the sick feeling down with coffee.

But I did not want to go home. I wanted to go back to bed and imagine a reality where we slept through the night and woke up that morning bright-eyed and bushy-tailed and ready to connect in the way we had intended, on our work together, over our shared creative wavelength.

Styles swallowed the remaining contents of his mug, and fled back to his bedroom, leaving me again to wallow alone, as if he hadn't made his point the first time.

Chapter 34

The drive back to Los Angeles was the longest two hours of my adult life. Every attempt at normal conversation was quickly throttled by the elephant in the car who took up so much space there was barely any room to breathe, let alone speak. Not that I actually wanted to talk about it, but the part of me that equates silence with rejection was screaming, crying, throwing up.

I had about a zillion tabs open in my brain, all glitchy Google searches for "What the fuck do I do now?" with conflicting responses that did nothing to answer that question. I was scanning the tabs for the right way to respond in case he decided to bring it up, but the words fell out of my mouth instead on impulse.

"Are you going to tell Willow?"

Traffic was quiet and the road was clear. We had a long stretch of road ahead of us. But Styles' reaction was to hit the brake. My head hit the back of the passenger seat. Not whiplash hard, but enough to startle me.

"Sorry. Thought I saw a lizard," he lied. Several excruciating minutes later, without answering, he threw the question back to me.

"Are you going to tell Griffin?"

"I don't know," I croaked, the words barely audible.

We drove the rest of the way in silence. I tried to find a daydream, but it was like the catalog had been locked up, or corrupted. I couldn't access anything, not even something basic or soothing like mentally painting the landscape or planning how to disappear and start a new life in Siberia. There was only static, and the word "fuck" playing on an incessant loop.

Do you know what it's like to have your dominant coping method break down when you're on the edge of an emotional meltdown with nowhere to run or hide? Well, it fucking sucks. I stared out the window, hoping to find peace, but all I found was a scenic blur that reminded me how much closer we were getting to the city, and that I still had no clue what the hell to do when we got there.

When Styles dropped me off at my house, I managed to squeak out a delicate, "See you Monday?" but he drove away without responding. Another kick to the gut that I was already giving myself anyway and didn't need from him.

As I stood in my driveway watching his car disappear, I realized that I was about to walk into my house and pretend to be the same person who'd left for a creative working retreat the day before. I had blown right past my upgrade to Cara 2.0 and crash-landed at Cara.wtf. Control-Alt-Delete was not going to save me.

I hesitated in front of my door. It was Saturday morning. Griffin was going to ask why I was home so early. And I didn't have a solid plan for how to answer that question. All I knew was... *Fuck.*

* * *

And that was how I ended up back in Niagara Falls, falling well short of meeting any of my LA trial period goals. Turns out, if you give me the chance, I'll blow all my chips on one spin of the roulette wheel, even with the deck stacked in my favor (and mix my metaphors while I'm at it). Not exactly the outcome I had wished for. Triumphant heroine, I was not. Instead, all I had succeeded in doing was wreaking havoc on the lives of those around me, achieving my supervillain era.

Griffin and I Separated with a capital S, the direct result of me confessing about the retreat. I had to tell him the truth.

For him, because there was no timeline in the multiverse where I could look him in the eye every day knowing what I'd done. He was my anchor, the thing that kept me from floating away like some anxiety-riddled helium balloon, and he deserved the truth even if it meant I had to let that anchor release me.

And for myself, because I was tripped up like a broken record, unable to process, or think, or move forward in any kind of meaningful way. Even knowing what it would cost, I needed to move the needle and get past the fuckitude I had mired myself in. I didn't know if it could be fixed. All I knew was that I couldn't stay frozen like that.

His subdued reaction was worse than the rage I deserved. Griffin was never one to do explosive anger, it was just not in his emotional repertoire. Instead, he just completely deflated, because I had punctured him to the core. He didn't yell or throw things or demand explanations. He cried, like a lot, and there was nothing I could do to soothe him, because I had inflicted the wound. I basically became a ghost to him in our LA house, unable to get my message of regret and sorrow through to him, while he walked right through me, chilled to the bone.

The fallout with Styles, Willow, River and Naomi was also devastating. It wasn't just about the projects. They were my friends. They believed in me when I barely believed in myself. Losing them didn't just feel like my creative dreams imploding. It felt like I had punched an irreparable hole in the fabric of the universe that was widening into a chasm that would swallow me whole, alone, cut off from any source of any healing light or love.

* * *

I used to make fun of Hannah for saying things like that. "Healing light and love," she'd sign off her emails, a gentle New Age blessing. But the truth is, I was desperate for both. Maybe that's why, from the cocoon of a blanket fort I had constructed in the LA house guest-room-turned-home-office which had become my primary domain, I called her. On the phone. If you've ever met me, you know I NEVER do that.

It was 12 AM California time, which made it 3 AM Niagara Falls time. She picked up on the first ring, her voice warm and drowsy. "Hey you."

"I'm sorry it's late."

"It's not that late."

"I need you to know, I'm the worst person who ever lived. Worse than the worst."

"Oh babe," she said gently. "What happened?"

"I don't want to say. Can you... give me a reading or

something?"

There was a rustle, the sound of her moving to where she kept her cards. "I mean, I can, for sure. But the cards won't tell me what's actually going on. Only you can do that."

"But what about the Tower, and the Three of Swords...."

She gave a soft laugh. "It's true. They've been saying something big was coming. They don't say what. That's all you."

So, I told her. As much as I could, through tears and snot and gasping through sobs for words. Everything, from the very beginning. The truth about the album with River, and the web series with Styles. The questions surrounding Griffin and Willow. The onslaught of feelings for Styles, the fantasy I let blur too far into reality, the night of unbelievable sex at the mountain cabin, the confession to Griffin, and the aftermath of it all. The unraveling of my life one daydream, one justification, one impulse at a time.

I hated saying it out loud. Every syllable was drenched in a pool of slobbering shame. If a picture is worth a thousand words, the one I described was an unintelligible word-slurry of all the ways I'd screwed everything up.

"Everyone hates me now. I deserve it, too," I bawled.

"Cara," Hannah said softly when I finished. "I love you."

"Why? How? Look at what I've done."

"You know I do. That's why you called me. I wish I could make this all go away for you. But that kind of magic doesn't exist. And I can't pretend I know exactly how this is all going to end up. But I do know that the cards don't predict what will happen. They help you figure out where you are and where you still have power."

"It doesn't feel like I have any power."

"You do though, always."

There was a long pause on her end, then I heard the shuffle of her cards. I braced for a fate worse than The Tower.

Hannah cleared her throat. "Um, so, I've pulled the Death card."

"WHAT?!"

"Don't freak out, it doesn't mean what you think it does," she tried to reassure me, unsuccessfully.

"I have a headache." Clearly that was the first symptom of my untimely end.

Hannah's voice was soft. "It's not literal. The Death card in tarot is about endings in general. And what happens when something dies? Something new grows out of it."

"It's like you're telling me this is a good thing."

"Only you can make it a good thing, or a bad thing, that's entirely up to you. That's the power you hold."

Despite Hannah's attempt to soothe me, powerful was the opposite of how I felt. My headache grew, and I summoned my last drop of power to take a painkiller. I fell asleep in my cocoon with her voice echoing in my head. In the morning, a bit surprised to find I was still alive, I checked my phone to see if any sign of hope had texted me back, only to be disappointed.

* * *

Styles was ignoring my texts, my emails, my calls. It didn't matter if I approached him as a working colleague, a friend, or that splintered version of me that did the unthinkable. Styles had retreated behind an impenetrable wall.

I didn't know what he'd told Willow, if he'd said anything to her at all. It didn't feel right to reach out to her. Asking River wasn't much help either. I'd kept things vague. Just, "Have you heard from Styles? I really need to talk to him." His responses were also ambiguous, almost suspiciously so, and terse. Mostly of the "IDK" variety.

So, I'm embarrassed to admit I found myself entering stalker mode, frequenting locations that Styles had introduced me to. Parks we'd met at, coffee shops we'd worked at, bars we'd hung out at. I wasn't trying to harass him, though it felt exactly like I was some kind of unhinged ex. I just needed to know where we stood. I had hoped we could salvage our work, that *Sixty-Six* was somehow bigger than us. He'd always made it sound like it was, and he had made me believe it, too.

I finally found him quickly grabbing a coffee to go at his least favorite coffee shop, the one with the weak watered-down coffee, closest to his studio. He looked mortified to see me.

"Styles..." I said, catching him at the pickup counter. "Can we talk? Please?"

His gaze shifted all over the place, anything to avoid looking at me. He exhaled strongly, somewhere between a sigh and a huff.

"Okay," he relented, finally, looking down at his shoes. We moved over to a table nearby and sat. He looked at his hands, fidgeted with his wedding ring, while I sat on my own hands to avoid a skin-picking bloodbath.

I wanted to know how he was. That he was okay, working through it or whatever. I was desperate for a smile, a nudge, some flicker of the old him, but all he gave was melting ice sculpture. If I started asking him the "How are you doing?"

kinds of questions, I might lose him to a puddle on the floor before I could get the information I was seeking.

"We need to figure out what's going to happen with the web series," I said, leaning toward him. He did not lean in my direction.

"I think it's pretty clear what's going to happen. Nothing."

My stomach dropped. I swallowed, trying to process the word before I repeated it. "Nothing?"

The barista called his name, and he jumped up to fetch his coffee. I thought he might bolt, but he sat back down, still avoiding my gaze. I thought I detected something wet on his cheek, which he wiped covertly, and he sniffed subtly as he sipped his coffee.

"But we spent so much time developing it. What about all the work we did, the character bibles, the sketches, all the episode scripts we wrote, the outlines, the incubator of unripened ideas... It can't all just evaporate."

"It's not evaporating. It's just... over."

I felt a chill move through me along with the realization that I had been naïve about everything. "Well... okay. Then I'll finish it myself. I'll figure it out, maybe I can find another way to make it happen."

"Cara." His voice had a peculiar tone about it. Sorrowful, but careful at the same time. "You transferred ownership of it to me when you agreed to let me finance the project. It's owned by my LLC."

"Well, then give it back," I said, angry that he'd act as if there was just no way. "If it's really over."

"It's not that simple."

And there it was. Months of collaborative creative work. Some of the best moments of my life. Moments when I'd felt like I was doing something that mattered with someone who was as passionate about it as I was... All for nothing.

"So that's it? Everything we were building together just... belongs to you now?"

"I'm sorry. I really am. But I think a clean break is better for both of us."

That was the last real conversation we had. After that, Styles slipped back behind his wall, and I let him. What else could I do? He'd decided the only way he could deal was by pretending I'd never existed. Which, honestly, I could not blame him for, even if it made me feel like I was being obliterated from his life with the totality of a natural disaster.

I knew then what I had to do. It was time for me to leave.

* * *

The next step was to break the news to River, who, it turned out, had strong opinions about my sudden departure. I found him at Burntree, jamming alone in a session I'd forgotten about, showing up at the last minute like a student arriving just in time to fail the final exam.

"So, you're running," he said, not bothering to look up from his guitar, strumming the chords to our best song, *Riptide*. "That's your grand solution."

I perched on the edge of the couch with a lump in my throat. It felt like I was breaking up with him. I guess I was. "I can't stay, River. It's time I went home."

"You've been talking about giving up and going home since you got here." I couldn't argue with that. Instead, I just stared at the floor.

"Guess you finally created the excuse you always needed." He looked at me, and I felt the full weight of his disappointment. It was like being silently judged by, say, a beloved English teacher after handing in fan fiction instead of your final essay. Which I had done, but this felt much worse.

"What about all this?" he continued. "These songs we're recording? They aren't charity work or friendship favors. They're the real deal. And you're just leaving me with the unfinished pieces."

"You think I don't know that?" I snapped. "I've already run this guilt trip on myself a hundred-million times. I'm just trying to get out with the least amount of collateral damage."

He was quiet for a moment, picking at his guitar strings, while I picked at my thumb until a strip of flesh tore free and blood pooled at the edge. I put it in my mouth to suck the wound.

"Think about why you really came here. I don't mean to record music with me, or to work on a web series with Styles. You were looking for something. And maybe you found it, and that's what's really scaring you."

"What's scaring me is that everything feels so out of my control. But if I leave now, I know what happens next."

"It's over."

"Exactly."

It may not have been what I really wanted, but it was certain, and that was better than the uncertainty that faced me. River set his guitar down. "I believed in you," he said softly, and that, more than the disappointment, more than the judgment, was what nearly destroyed me. "If you leave now, you'll never know what could have happened."

A wave of physical pain rippled through me, leaving in its

wake the promise of the only type of fulfillment I knew how to achieve. "I can only imagine."

Chapter 35

The move home was frigid, both figuratively and literally. Pulling myself out of the sunny warmth of Southern California and landing with a cold hard thud back in moody Niagara was fitting, given the circumstances. The house was exactly as we'd left it. Kind of a museum exhibit of my former life. Messy as fuck, and everything seemed smaller and shabbier somehow. It all felt so surreal and hollow without Griffin.

I could almost see the ghosts of us from before we left, packing in a frenzy, half-panicked and totally unprepared, not giving a shit about what state we were leaving the house in for future us. If only those ghosts had paused for a moment, they might have caught a glimpse of the shape of only one of us returning.

The cats came home with me. We'd both agreed that it was for the best, even though the thought of depriving Griffin of their comfort was fucking awful. Those murder-mittened little scoundrels had shredded too many corners of the expensive LA rental couches and vomited on the fancy rug too many times. Bringing them home had been a practical decision, but now Griffin was missing them like he had lost custody of his precious children.

Like a good long-distance cat dad, he requested daily updates and I obliged, trying to make him laugh with anecdotes and blurry photos. It was the only part of us that still felt *together*. Our conversations never ventured beyond the cats. We didn't talk about our separation, the house, our heartache or what the future might hold. But the cat update exchanges were something I could cling to.

"How's Daisy? Is she happy to be home?" My heart just about leapt out of my chest whenever a cat inquiry text message would appear with Griffin's name attached to it.

"It's like she never left. She's back to meowing into that corner of the bedroom again."

"I need proof." Cue me sending a thirty-second video of Daisy-cat yowling into an empty corner.

"I swear to God it's like she's talking to another cat in that same corner in another dimension."

"I believe it."

"And what about Clover? What's he up to?"

"He misses you so much, Griff. So does Daisy. And so do I."

I stared at the screen, waiting for the little bouncing dots to appear that meant he was texting, that he might say something more that would collapse the space between us. The dots appeared, then disappeared. Then they came back, and then they vanished again.

And then, after an hour of me checking my phone, unable to do anything but wait, just lying on the couch looping on a daydream of him walking in through the front door and throwing his arms around me telling me it was all going to be alright...

"I miss them too. Cuddle them for me and tell them Daddy loves them."

The separation wasn't meant to be final. The plan was for him to stay in LA to finish our lease on the rental house, but also to get some space, and figure out whether forgiveness was possible. The hope was that he would come home when the lease ended, and we'd see where we stood after some time apart.

Which sounded mature and reasonable when we discussed it, but felt like abandonment now that I was actually living it, however much I deserved it.

So, there I was, back in my old house with the cats and a suitcase full of California clothes that Naomi had styled me in during our shopping excursions. I would never dress so fashionably in this small town, not even during summer.

Late at night, when the cats were hunting for hair elastics, I lay awake replaying everything in my mind and assessed the damage. Once I had sufficiently ruminated on the breakups, not just with Griffin, but with all of my LA friends, then my mind would drift to the unfinished projects. I was clearly destined to never finish anything creative, not even when sharing the work with others. When that mental doomscroll was over, I would spiral about losing all my progress on the new version of me I was working on. For a short time, I'd been someone who belonged in recording studios and writing rooms, someone whose ideas mattered, who deserved to be there.

And then I thought about what Hannah had said, about power. As in, did I actually have any? I was starting to believe that all of this had happened through the sheer force and will of my imagination. That a lifetime of daydreaming and fantasizing had somehow manifested into something real. If I could make that life happen through pure and simple and endless wishful thinking, maybe I could undo the wreckage the same way.

I know how this is going to sound, but I really tried that. I spent entirely too much time trying to daydream my way out of what I'd done. I constructed alternate timelines where the retreat never happened, where I made different choices, where I somehow managed to not destroy everything good I'd stumbled into. I was convinced that if I could just visualize the right sequence of events, I could retroactively un-cheat on my husband and un-ruin my friendships and un-delete my creative awakening.

Turns out reality doesn't respond to wishful thinking the way fantasy does. The damage was done and it had echoed across all dimensions of my actual life. I'd lost the version of myself I'd briefly been brave enough to become. And for the first time in my life, no amount of elaborate daydreaming, not even my best mental rewrites, could bring her back.

* * *

How to Undo a Life-Altering Mistake Using Only the Power of Wishful Thinking

Equipment needed: One catastrophic error in judgment, unlimited imagination, and a complete misunderstanding of how linear time works.

1. Immediately begin constructing alternate timeline scenarios where you made different choices. Focus on the exact moment everything went wrong and visualize yourself noping it super hard.

2. Dedicate three to four hours a day to daydreaming sessions where you rewrite history, including dialogue improvements and better outfit choices.
3. Research quantum physics and parallel universe theories that support the notion that somewhere in the multiverse, there's a version of you who didn't screw everything up. Feel temporarily comforted by this completely irrelevant information.
4. Write a letter to yourself in the past, before you made the mistake, with a serious warning about the consequences, and leave it in the pocket of the jacket you were wearing on your way to make the mistake. Watch *Back to the Future* again to live vicariously through that plan actually working.
5. Create complex mental scenarios where your mistake somehow leads to a happy outcome, like a romcom where the initial disaster was actually the universe's plan all along. Frame this as positive thinking rather than utter denial.
6. Lie awake at 3 AM bargaining with the cosmos, offering to trade various body parts or years of your life for a do-over.

Warning: May lead to the gradual realization that your imagination is not, in fact, a time machine. Not recommended for those who prefer their coping mechanisms to be based in reality.

Important disclaimer: This method has a 0% success rate but a 100% guarantee of making you feel temporarily better while ultimately solving nothing.

* * *

After exhausting my repertoire of metaphysical time-travel techniques with the predicted 0% success, I decided to try something revolutionary: actually dealing with my life like a responsible adult. This involved what is known as *getting your shit together*, which tends to happen when you finally get sick of your own bullshit.

It was a nebulous endeavor, so fucking vast and ambiguous that I couldn't even come up with a list of steps for how to tackle it (I know! As if!). So I concentrated on starting with just one: getting a job.

My attempts to get in touch with Gunnar to see if he was willing to give me another chance were met with silence. I eventually gave in and accepted my Uncle Keith's offer. As expected, the content was intensely dull. Standard operating procedures for the warehouse. Writing so boring it made me consider learning how to draft it in another language and then translate it back to English just to make it at least somewhat more interesting.

Boring was safe, at least. And he let me work from home sometimes, so that was something. It may not have been inspiring, but it was kind of like doing emotional rehab, even if I was practically narcoleptic at times.

But I was determined not to fuck things up anymore. I went full accountability nerd, with color-coded calendars, tracking spreadsheets, motivational sticky notes that said things like "You can write about locking and tagging broken forklifts without having an existential crisis." I was working out some seldom-used mental muscles. It weirdly felt like I was "getting clean", at least during work hours.

In my off-work hours, my reward was falling off the wagon into the addictive wasteland of my daydream world. You know, recreationally.

Chapter 36

For someone who was actively *not* trying to get in touch with her former friend and creative partner, I sure was doing a lot of thinking about him trying to get in touch with me. It was like I wanted the chance to ghost him back, for him to know that whatever he was going through, I was going through it worse, without having to say a word. He was done? Well, so was I, obviously.

I'd find myself staring into space, waiting for a text that wasn't coming, mentally crafting a response that I was absolutely not going to send, because I was over it. SO over it. I would freeze Styles to the bone with my silence. I practically salivated for the chance.

And while I waited, I hurt him back the only way I knew how.

* * *

After what felt like eons of denial, pretending we were just friends trying to survive the inhospitable natural world to get home to the loves of our lives, only to realize there was no hope of rescue, we had done the deed. Now it was the morning after, and Styles and I had woken up intertwined around each other, raw and blissed out from the most incredible sex I could possibly imagine, if you ignore the spider monkeys. I was only slightly aware of him getting up from our bed of palm fronds, giving me a tender kiss on the cheek as he climbed over me and ambled to the designated pee zone to empty his bladder.

The sun was warm, there was a soft breeze, and the post-sex glow was still emanating from my body. I felt the lovesick waves ripple through me as Styles emerged from the ocean looking like the Sexiest Man Alive: Plane Crash Survivor edition. I lay there gazing at him as he peed, letting our blanket-towel slide off me and making no moves to cover myself up with it.

When he returned to the camp, he handed me a carved-out coconut shell which had collected a bit of rain overnight. The island survival fantasy equivalent of handing me a cup of hot coffee. "You good?" he asked, brushing my hair from my face. His eyes sparkled and his smile took me all apart and then put me back together again.

I smiled back, dazed. "I'm perfect."

Believe it or not, it was a lie. The truth was, I could feel something down below. A dim ache in my abdomen, and the familiar twinge of urinary urgency. Clear signs of a urinary tract infection. Because OF FUCKING COURSE. Not even in my wildest dreams could I have mind-blowing sex without my urethra having a hissy fit about bacteria getting rammed in there. Getting them after sex was so common for me that I had a 'refills forever' kind of prescription back home.

If you've ever had a UTI, you know the drill. You feel the twinge coming on. You deny it. Maybe it'll go away on its own. Sometimes it does. Sometimes slamming it with unsweetened cranberry juice does the trick. But usually not.

Usually, after ignoring it for too long, it reaches the point where the discomfort is no longer bearable. You want to punch yourself in the crotch. You curse the universe. You writhe in pain a little longer, trying to shore up the energy needed to get yourself to a doctor, so you can squeeze out some pee into a cup in exchange for sweet antibiotic relief.

And it's that easy. As quickly as it came on, it starts to recede, and you THANK FUCK you live in a modern society with access to lifesaving medicine.

Unfortunately, I did not have that option. Approximately two hours later, I sat hunched in the shade of our DIY lean-to, clutching my lower abdomen and realizing with hopeless dread that this UTI was coming on with a vengeance.

"Oh my God," I groaned.

"What? What is it?" Styles rushed over to me, his hands hovering over me like an unwitting reiki master.

"I think I have a urinary tract infection," I said, trying to pretend I was not on the brink of pee-related death. "It's like peeing razor blades. I could shave your beard clean off with it."

He paled. "Shit, aren't those painful?"

I groaned in acknowledgment.

"Willow had one once... antibiotics cleared it up super fast."

"You're right. Could you pop over to the pharmacy real quick?"

The realization appeared all over his face.

"Shit."

Styles went into full panic caregiver mode, trying to concoct a treatment from whatever he could find. He tried everything, from boiled leaves to crushed moss, to a moldy coconut he insisted might have antibiotic properties.

"Mold is penicillin, right?" he asked, proudly handing me what looked like a mashed-up chunk of jungle refuse.

"You want me to eat this?" I muttered. But there really wasn't *an alternative. I had to take a chance that it might help. Spoiler alert: it was vile, and I threw up a few minutes later, with the opinion that if I was going to die like this, I'd rather not have tasted that.*

He stayed next to me, massaging my abdomen and periodically fanning me with a palm frond while I moaned about my imminent demise and how unfair it was to get a UTI in my own fantasy.

"It hurts so much," I whimpered.

"Hey... hey..." he said, crouching beside me and taking my hand in his. "You're going to be okay. I'm here."

I could tell that he meant it. I could see concern and tenderness in his face.

"Can you die of a UTI?" he asked, "you know, if it doesn't get treated?"

Thanks for asking the burning question, dear. "Maybe not from the UTI, but it can lead to a kidney infection, and I'm pretty sure that can have some dire consequences, like sepsis." I curled up with my head on his lap. "I just want you to know," I whispered, "if this is how I go... you rocked my world last night."

He laughed, sincere and startled, and then caught himself with a gasp. "Jesus, Cara."

* * *

I jolted back to reality in Paige's waiting room, the urge to pee reminding me that I was not, in fact, dying of a UTI. I was just early for therapy, which was either a minor miracle or a side effect of my *getting my shit together* efforts (ask your doctor if *Getting Sick of Your Own Bullshit* is right for you). I considered holding it, but decided against tempting fate. Holding my pee *was* a surefire way to actually give myself a UTI.

After having satisfied the call of nature, Paige called me in to her office. This was my first in-person appointment since before we had gone west. I was comforted by the fact that everything looked exactly the same. Still, I was churning inside about our imminent conversation and the forthcoming admissions of guilt. I sat down on the same old couch that was so comfortable it could disarm you into spilling your guts about all your crimes. The truth-telling couch.

"So," Paige said, in that calm, patient tone of hers. "What are we unpacking today?"

I put my hand to my forehead as if to rub out a headache. "Well, my suitcase is full of stank-ass shame and dresses I'll never wear again."

"Let's start with the shame."

I sighed. "I blew up my life. Griffin's still in LA. He and I are... separated." I watched her expression closely, waiting for her to react with shock, pity, even judgment. But she only nodded with the same measured compassion she used for everything we talked about, whether it was a life-altering mistake or me ruminating over a mean social media comment.

"We still text," I continued. "Usually just about the cats. He misses them, so I send him photos and little updates like we're co-parenting in some feline custody agreement. It's not nothing. But it's not... us."

"That's a big change," she said gently. "Do you want to talk about what led to it?"

I picked at that loose thread on the couch cushion. As comforting as it was that it was still there, it was also annoying. "Not really. It's complicated. I made some bad decisions. Like... mythologically bad. And I didn't just hurt him. I wrecked a lot of things and hurt a lot of people I care about.

And now he hates me. Everyone hates me."

Paige did her best to hide her frustration with me. *Everyone hates me* wasn't exactly new territory.

"The truth is, you don't actually know what they think, and there isn't anything you can do about it anyway. The only thing you can control is yourself, so let's stay focused on how *you* feel."

She waited while I slid into and then snapped myself out of a quick daydream of her shaking me by the shoulders and slapping me in the face. I knew she wanted to.

"Everything was going so well. I felt... like I was stepping into this new version of myself," I said slowly. "Like I was turning into this bold, creative, confident person who belonged there. And then I fucked it up. Now I wish I could revert back to an earlier place in time. Erase everything that happened since the concert trip."

Paige tilted her head. "Let's pretend that's possible. Are you sure that's what you really want?"

"Maybe not erase everything. But just... go back to normal, the old version of me. But when I try, it feels like it doesn't fit anymore. I don't know what to do."

"I'd say that means you've made progress."

I looked at her, incredulous. "How is blowing up my life and the lives of people I care about progress?"

"I know it seems counter-intuitive, But I don't think there's a normal to go back to, Cara. You've changed. All the things you experienced in LA, the good, the bad, the complicated... they happened, and they changed you. Even if you could go back, it wouldn't be the same as it was. That version of your life doesn't exist anymore."

I hated how I knew she was going to say that and how right

she was.

"You can't go backward," she continued. "You can only go forward. There is no erasing what happened. All you can do is learn from it, and try to build something new with it."

"That sounds exhausting."

She smiled. "It's also empowering."

There was that word again, *power*. Hannah had used it, too. But empowering wasn't a word I would've used to describe my current emotional state. And yet, hearing it again made something click inside me. I thought about that version of myself I'd briefly been in LA. Maybe she wasn't gone. Maybe she was just... waiting, underneath the guilt and the regret and the boring-ass Uncle Keith job.

"I mean... maybe... but I feel so stuck. How do I even move forward?"

"You could start by journaling. A lot has happened, and most of it you haven't even told me. And that's okay. Tell it to yourself. It might give you some relief and help you process so that you can take the next step."

Ding ding ding ding ding! Why hadn't I thought of that? If I'm a writer, I could just... write. For no one else but me.

* * *

I left Paige's office feeling untethered, like it was taking all my effort to not just float up off the ground and into outer space without any type of life support system. It would be a fitting end, though, right? My obituary would be something like: *Cara spent her life with her head in the clouds. Her head is now reunited with the rest of her body. In lieu of flowers, please send donations to the National Space Cadet Foundation.*

On the drive home, I tried to remember what Paige had told me for the zillionth time. That other people's feelings about me were none of my business, that I couldn't control what they thought, that their silence was information, but not necessarily about my worth as a person. I thought of Griffin, Styles, River, Naomi, and Willow. It took all my strength to not collapse into a sobbing mess onto the steering wheel in the middle of the road.

I had to let go. Which sounds simple when you write it in a sentence, or even consider it as a thought. Actually doing it felt damn near impossible. Letting go meant accepting that I couldn't fix it, and that I couldn't go back to retrieve what I'd left behind.

But maybe letting go also meant something else. Maybe it meant accepting that the version of me I was becoming in LA wasn't just a temporary character I'd been playing. Maybe she really was still with me inside somewhere, just hiding, needing a new reason to emerge.

Frankly, I had just about reached the maximum level on the *Sick of My Own Bullshit* meter. I was almost ready. There was just one more thing I needed to do first.

Chapter 37

I was dying.

The pain had intensified from "Owwie, it's achy and burny down there," to "Holy fucking shit, a demon is trying to bust its way out of my lower back with a hammer." I recognized this escalation. I'd had a kidney infection once before, back when I thought I could ignore a UTI out of existence. Don't ever do that, it's the absolute worst.

Styles hovered above me with wide eyes and a panicked energy. "It's getting worse?"

I whimpered in response, which he took as confirmation.

"I'll find something else to fix it," he said, scanning the outer edge of the jungle for ideas. "There's got to be something on this island that can help."

"We tried that already."

His eyes were wild with worry. "But I... this can't be what happens. This is your daydream, can't you, I don't know, insert a deus ex machina here or something?"

"What, like a medical kit containing antibiotics washes ashore?"

"Yes! That! Do that!"

I tried to lift a reassuring hand to his bearded cheek. It flopped somewhere near his knee. "I thought of that, but... I'm sorry. It's just, not how this story goes," I whispered.

I was sorry, but also not. A fit of cry-laughing overtook me. My fever was rising fast, and I knew this particular brand of delirium. It came with hallucinations and profound observations about the nature of existence. Also, nonsensical word salads.

"Listen to me," I croaked. "Watch out for those pine trees crossing the road. And tell the dolphins... the nachos are theirs now."

Styles knelt beside me, putting his hand on my forehead. "You're burning up. I need to cool you down."

He made a sound that was somewhere between a sob and a laugh, and then scooped me up in his arms, bridal style, which would have made me swoon if I wasn't actively trying to give up my corporeal state out of spite.

He carried me into the ocean, allowing the cooler-than-air-temperature water to lap over my skin. The heat in my body almost seemed to hiss against the saltwater and I felt, for just a moment, like I might be okay.

Styles held me there, mumbling things I couldn't quite make out. His voice cracked, and I almost told him to stop trying to save me. That I was doing this because of him, after all. That this was the only way I could get him to feel the loss I'd been feeling since the moment he unfriended me in real life.

After a while, he brought me back to our camp. My fever broke that night. I felt clear-headed enough to string together a coherent thought. "I'm so thirsty."

Styles looked hopeful again. He handed me a hollowed-out coconut shell filled with fresh water from the spring, which I swallowed quickly. He then tucked me in on our palm-leaf mattress, kissed my forehead, and said, "You're going to be okay, I can feel it."

I drifted off with his arm around me and the jungle humming nearby, and the last thing I thought was 'This is possibly the most demented revenge fantasy I've ever conceived.'

The next morning, I was dead. Styles found me still, cool to the touch. He shook me, and said my name a bunch with increasing volume and urgency.

When I didn't stir, he crumpled beside me, his head on my chest, like I was still his and we weren't just figments of my broken imagination. He sobbed quietly into my lifeless cleavage. His outpouring of grief was a form of intimacy so intense it rivaled our sexual adventure. It was the closest thing to love that this fantasy could conjure.

I know this because I was hovering somewhere just outside my own body, watching him, crying and mourning myself along with him, because somewhere inside me, I wasn't just mourning him mourning me. I was mourning her, too.

* * *

I flung myself out of bed the next morning like the house was on fire. But it wasn't the house, it was all me, with more energy and motivation than 97,306 *Energizer Bunnies.*

I knew exactly what to do with this energy. All these day-dreams weren't just unproductive wish fulfillment garbage. I mean, yes. They were. That's exactly what they were. But they didn't have to stay that way. Instead of looping and spiraling and getting stuck, I would clear my head to make way for whatever was next.

For what might have been the first time ever, I actually did my therapy homework, the journal that Paige had suggested.

But I didn't just log recent history. That was certainly a part of it, but retelling those events was not the interesting part. It was like scaffolding for something else.

I journaled the plane crash fantasy as if it had all actually taken place. My hand ached from hours of scribbling. It wasn't well-worded, or coherent, even. But I was getting it out of my head, onto paper, where I could either crumple it up and throw it away, or file it as therapy homework. This was a clearing out. It didn't have a shape. It didn't need to.

There were other things in my head that needed purging too, before they fermented into something toxic. Ideas from the web series that would now never see daylight, conversations in my head that I desperately wanted to have with Griffin, scenes about getting in touch with River, and even Willow, to try and make some kind of amends. Things I wished for but couldn't have without making an even bigger mess.

I wrote the hottest garbage you can imagine. Pure stream-of-consciousness, disheveled word vomit. An utter mess that, if personified, would look exactly like I did: mismatched socks, gross hair, tee shirt with a hole in it, and something stuck between my teeth that I'd been tonguing instead of flossing to remove.

None of it meant anything, but holy shit, did it feel good to get it out.

It didn't stop the daydreams. If anything, it fueled them with purpose. Under the surface, it had all been about distraction, escape, and protection, but now I didn't have to feel guilty about them. I could lean into whatever absurd, dramatic, softcore scenarios I wanted. It was therapeutic as hell.

* * *

Griffin came home without warning. Just opened the front door like he was just coming home from work, which, technically, he was. I was in the kitchen, wearing only a tee shirt and a pair of his worn-out boxers that he'd left behind, microwaving tea I'd forgotten about for the third time that morning.

"Hey," he said, as if we hadn't been separated for what felt like an eternity.

I didn't say anything. I just walked right up to him, threw my arms around him, and kissed him like I had something to prove, because I did.

We didn't talk. I mean, we couldn't, because our mouths were otherwise engaged. My hands were already under his shirt as he kicked the door shut behind him. There was some stumbling, and a crash as we knocked the stuff off the hallway side table.

"Wait," I gasped, in between kisses. "We should talk."

"This is me talking. I'm telling you everything," he said, kissing me again.

"No, like really talk. We have a lot to... oh my God, yes, there."

He found the spot behind my ear that switched the thinking part of my brain off and turned the Discovery Channel part of me on. I pulled his hoodie off like our lives depended on it. Those freckles on his arms, goddamn. I wanted to renew my vows with each and every one of them.

He pulled back to look at me with a half-sorry, half-feral expression while continuing to undress me. "I messed up," he said.

"I messed up worse," I said, undoing my bra.

"No, I definitely messed up worse," he insisted, putting his face into my boobs and inhaling.

"I cheated on you emotionally and physically," I reminded him, unzipping his jeans.

"I slept with Willow," he said, sliding my underwear down my legs. "A lot."

I paused and stared at him. "How much?"

"She came to the clinic once a week..."

"Griff, oh my God. You are so much worse than me."

But I was too horny to be mad. I dropped to my knees and pulled down his pants.

He gasped as I took him in my mouth. "This is the weirdest foreplay ever," he groaned.

It wasn't long before we were both naked on the hallway carpet, all over each other trying to undo recent history with our bodies. He rolled onto his back and I got on top, taking him inside me with every single one of my senses, and a few more that I'm not sure have been identified by science yet. Riding him in that position, I opted for a little power play.

"Did you do that thing I like?"

"What?" he said, gripping my hips and guiding me to increase the speed of my thrust rhythm.

"The thing. With Willow. I want to know."

"Oh. Really? Well... uh, yeah, but... she wasn't into it."

"Does she not have nipples?"

"She told me to do this, instead." Griffin put his arms around me and flipped me over onto my back. Putting his mouth between my legs, he began to hum a tune.

"Is that... 'When You Wish Upon a Star'?" The vibration was nice, but I couldn't help laughing.

"It's all I could think of," he admitted, laughing as well. He moved back up to my face and began to kiss my lips. But I wasn't finished yet.

"What else?" I asked.

"Are you sure you want to know..."

"I'm as surprised as you are, but yes."

"Okay... she licked my nutsack."

"You never let me do that, you said it tickles!" I was incredulous.

"Not if you do it like this..." He demonstrated on my neck, using the flat part of his tongue like he was lapping at an ice cream cone. I instantly pushed him over so I could practice the technique on him, and he made sounds that almost exploded my insides.

"Now ask me," I demanded, while I continued licking.

"Cara... I..." his breath caught in his throat.

"Please, Griff, " I pleaded.

"Did he... did you..." He wasn't able to get the words out, but that might have been because I was stroking him while licking his nutsack better than Willow ever could have.

"Did we what?" I asked, now kissing my way up to his bellybutton and licking him there while continuing to stroke him.

"Did he make you..."

"Uh-huh."

"He did?"

"M-hm."

"Well, I'm going to make you..."

He didn't need to finish the sentence. He put his hands on my head and gently pulled me back up to kiss my lips, and I straddled him once more, taking him inside me and gripping him with my Kegel power while thrusting in my own rhythm, while Griffin did the thing I like to my nipples.

Finally, it was his turn, and as we finished in a tangle of limbs and hair and gasps, we forgave each other, at least on a physical level. Afterwards, we lay in each other's arms staring up at the textured ceiling like we were gazing at our own little galaxy of constellations.

"Good talk," I said.

"Good talk," he agreed.

* * *

If I ever wanted one of my daydreams to actually come true, it was that one.

Chapter 38

The journaling experience was certainly cathartic in the moment, but once the purge was complete, I just felt kind of empty. Maybe that was the point, but ultimately, the goal was that it was supposed to make me feel better. So why the hell didn't I feel better?

I'd expected to feel lighter, like after a good cry or a breakup haircut. Instead, I felt itchy and restless, like I'd cleaned out my hobby-hoard closet only to find that the floorboards had rotted and needed to be ripped out. Clearly, there was more work to do.

I kept staring at the pile of messy, tear-streaked journal pages, wondering what I was missing. I tried to read it to see what I had left out, but all I could see was self-indulgent rambling that made no sense.

That's when I started thinking about burning it. Maybe that would give me the closure I was looking for. I could invite Hannah over and make a release ritual out of it, set fire to the pages in my backyard fire pit. She'd know all the right things to say, maybe even cast a spell to release me from the burden of what was in those pages.

But every time I thought about destroying it, something inside me screamed *DON'T*. Like maybe there was something buried in the mess that I needed to keep. So, despite being disappointed and unsatisfied with the whole journaling thing, I hung onto it for completely unknown reasons.

I just kind of got on with my life, trying to fight the heaviness. Maybe that's why I decided I needed a new bag. You know, the perfect bag that not only met all my aesthetic criteria, but that represented me as a person, with the ability to carry the extra weight in my heart and soul. Sadly, I now know that such a bag does not exist, and I have a trillion bags to prove it. But on a shopping trip searching for it, I bumped into an old friend from high school. I was sure we were friends on social media, but couldn't recall anything about what her life was like now.

"Cara Lavallee, is that you?"

"Wow, Julie, hi! It's Cara Becker now." Julie Whatshername was *so not* a bitch. Is that a normal way to remember someone from high school?

"I almost didn't recognize you!" she squealed, and we embraced in a quick hug.

"You look exactly the same," I said. "I mean that in a good way, like look at you. You're glowing."

"Aw, thanks! The kids are getting so grown up, but somehow they keep me young!" she beamed. "What about you? I heard you moved to California or something? Are you just home to visit? I always thought you'd be a famous author or filmmaker or something by now."

Those were some of the nicest words she could have said to me, and yet they were almost too much to bear. I summoned all of my energy to not lose it at her devastating kindness.

"Uh... just a rumor, I guess. Griff and I took a weekend trip there a while back. Funny how something like that gets warped."

"The telephone game can't be stopped," she laughed.

I was fighting back the urge to collapse and cry on Julie's soft, inviting shoulder, but resisted with everything I had.

"Well, it was so good to see you," I said, my throat tight.

We hugged again, promised to keep in touch, and even loosely planned a get together sometime in the not-too-distant future which, predictably, would never materialize.

After she left, I beelined to the nearest changing room with the bag I was trying on. It met almost all of my criteria except I needed one in every color, and I couldn't afford to pay that much ADHD tax.

And then came the waterworks. Like, loud, to the point where I could barely contain the sobs. I fully expected a store employee to come knocking and check on me, but thankfully, I was left alone to wallow in my sadness.

When I was no longer gasping for air, I slumped against the dressing room's cool wall and let my eyes shut to block out the world.

* * *

I barged into Styles' studio with my journal in my hands, and slammed it onto the table in front of him.

"Fine, you can keep Sixty-Six. I'll make something better, that doesn't need your input or your money. And guess what? It gets a goddamn book deal and wins an award and then gets adapted into a movie that I write the screenplay for, with an A-list cast and the critics love it and it has a 99% audience rating and it wins all the Golden Globes and all the Oscars in every category, including Best Screenplay..."

* * *

I jolted from my daydream and looked at my red, wet, puffy face in the changing room mirror. Holy shit. Maybe I really *wasn't* finished.

Once home, I promptly went back to my pile of word vomit. Getting it out of me had only been the first step. I couldn't just throw it out, or burn it, or let it languish in my filing cabinet with all my other abandoned scribbles. It had a purpose. And while I didn't quite have a clear picture of what that was, I knew I needed to take another step with it. I would polish it, to the best of my ability. I wouldn't try to make it a masterpiece. I wasn't delusional enough to think any awards were actually in my future. But I would give it a shape and tell it in my voice.

Honestly, going back through what I wrote was utterly embarrassing. I never cringed so hard in my life. If people who knew me read it and found out the kinds of things I think about, I would have to fake my own death and move to the Falkland Islands.

If I was going to turn my journaled maladaptive daydreams into a novel, I had to be super careful about it. Trying to distinguish the fantasy from reality wasn't as easy as it might sound. I had spent so much time inside my head that the lines had become blurred and the stories had become conflated with one another.

Names would be changed to protect both the guilty and the innocent, obviously. I would fictionalize enough detail to create a barrier between the real me and my story. And I would give myself a pen name and publish quietly onto the internet, where the expectation was that it would vanish quietly into the vast void of other stories by people who had turned their own fantasies into content and hoped someone, somewhere, might relate.

At least they had done it. At least they finished something and put it out into the world. But I wasn't quite there yet. I didn't just need the pen name to publish. I needed a pen name to even take the next step and start really writing, but before I could even get that far, there was one final blockage to clear.

* * *

I watched from the ether as Styles stood over my lifeless body, debating what to do with me.

"I can't just... leave you here," he said, pacing in the sand. "You deserve... something."

It was cute that he was still talking to me. Sweet, really. I mean, it had been both therapeutic and a bit of a peep show to watch him grieve me like he had, and it was satisfying that he was now deeply concerned with my posthumous dignity. Soon my body was going to cease being a reminder of our companionship, and become an unbearable blob of human detritus that would need... disposal.

His first idea was to bury me, despite not having a shovel. He found a place near the tree line, some distance from our shelter but still within eyeshot, and tried to dig a grave using a jagged scrap of airplane fuselage that had washed ashore. He hacked at the ground almost violently. Ten minutes in, he had dug a shallow, ragged hole and had a bleeding gash on his shin.

"Shit," he muttered, inspecting the wound. "Now I'm going to die of tetanus."

'You're right, this is all about you', I thought. Did his despair bring me a glimmer of joy? Yes. Did it also make me wistful for the time we'd spent together? Okay, fine, you got me.

After the failed burial attempt, he stood for a long time looking at my body. "I can't burn you," he said aloud. "That just feels wrong."

I kind of liked the idea of him cremating me though, and tried to nudge him in that direction with my ghostly powers.

"Although... I could keep your ashes in a hollowed-out coconut. That might be kind of nice. You'd still be with me, sort of."

It worked! And I was truly moved by the sentiment of him wanting to keep me around like that.

"Nah. Bad idea," he wavered. "What if the smell of your flesh on the fire makes me hungry?"

Oh. Wow. I did not see that coming. Seriously. Sometimes my brain goes places I never expected, and this was one of those times. It was almost like Styles had taken over and was controlling my daydream. Determined to not become a BBQ meal at my own funeral, I wrested control back, pushing him to make another decision.

He fashioned a makeshift stretcher out of palm fronds and rope, moved my stiff corpse onto it, and dragged me up the lookout cliff where the ocean churned and foamed below. I hovered along beside him on the journey.

"We had some nice times at this spot," he said solemnly, setting my body down. "Best view on the island."

My ghostly heart swelled. 'You know me so well', I thought.

He stood at the edge, breathing audibly, wiping sweat from his brow. "I'm sorry," he said. "You deserved better than this."

Maybe I did, maybe I didn't. But who was I to argue, I was dead. Apology accepted.

And then, with a deep exhale, he shoved my corporeal shell over the cliff. It cartwheeled in the air, and I watched him wince as my body very nearly clipped the edge of a jutting rock. I considered making it get hung up there, like having my clothes catch on the protruding point, leaving me to dangle over the rough water. It would be a sight that was sure to dangle in his mind's eye for eternity. But I let that idea go, and instead, watched him watch me crash into the waves and disappear beneath the surf.

It was a pretty efficient burial, all things considered.

Afterward, Styles sat on the cliff in silence. He stayed for a long time, until almost dark, when he finally returned to our camp. He skipped the fire that night. As he went to sleep, I watched him hug our washed-up backpack to his chest like he was holding onto me. My eyes burned with tears. I could put myself right back there... but I didn't.

As the next days wore on, I watched him talk out loud, sometimes narrating his actions, sometimes asking questions I couldn't answer. He played solitaire with seashells. He sang to himself, badly.

Then, a few days after my burial at sea, another plane appeared in the sky during daylight. It passed overhead, low enough that there was no doubt they spotted him. Styles jumped up, waving his arms, screaming. I waved my ghostly arms and screamed too, even though no one could see or hear me. I was ready for him, for both of us, to be free of this saga.

He gathered the hairbrush, the towel, the multi-tool and a few other items, and packed them into the backpack. He was going to be returning to all the necessities and comforts of home, and didn't need any of those things. But I guessed it was just baggage he wasn't ready to let go of yet.

A helicopter came later that day to pick him up. "If you could have held on for a few more days, you'd be getting off this island with me," he said out loud as he waited for the helicopter to land.

"We could have been rescued together. It could have been our survival story. Our miraculous return from the dead. I'm so sorry, Cara."

As he boarded the helicopter, the pilot asked him if there was anyone else. That was the last thing I heard before the helicopter door closed with my apparition on the other side of it. I could have gone inside with him, but that wasn't how this was supposed to go. I had to let him go without me. But I did wonder how he would answer the pilot's question. Would he say that there was someone else, and she almost made it? Or would he say, "No, it's just me". Would he keep me a secret, a ghost of the island, folded neatly between the chapters of his own survival memoir?

Either way, I hoped he wouldn't mention the part where he almost considered eating me.

Chapter 39

Choosing a pen name probably should not have been as hard as it was. In theory, it sounds like a simple task. In reality, for me anyway, crafting the perfect pen name was like trying to find that perfect bag. It had to be aesthetically pleasing, but also do a lot of heavy lifting. It couldn't be too similar to my real name, but it still had to feel like me. Or at least, a version of me that didn't suck.

After rejecting approximately eleventy-billion options that sounded like TV news reporters or serial killers, I settled on Zinnia Sherwood. I could explain how I landed on it, but does it matter? As much as I labored over it, it wasn't really about the name itself. It was about what it would mean to me. Zinnia Sherwood was my extension, the version of me I could hand the power to. She was the one who would, who *could*, hit the "publish" button.

She would be the version of me who was brave enough to take the blame for what I was putting out into the world. She would take the criticism. It would be my biggest mask to date, ironically, so that I could be the most authentic version of myself yet. And while I was excited to step into her shoes, there was a part of me that mourned that if it somehow all went right instead of wrong, she would get all the credit.

* * *

"Show, don't tell," they say. But the process of me turning my hot garbage maladaptive daydream in journal form into a novel manuscript wasn't exactly a feast for the eyes. No *training for the big fight* montage that I can describe. I could pretend that in between bursts of writing I was running up and down some stairs in the city and waxing on and off in an exotic location to motivating pop-rock music, but it wasn't anything like that.

That doesn't mean it wasn't emotional torture. But like, in a good way, sort of. Moments of anguish punctuated by bursts of zen-like flow. An endless cycle between narcissistic surges of "I am an actual fucking genius" and self-nullifying waves of "This is literally the worst piece of shit ever written." After spending an embarrassing amount of time on writer's forum threads, I am of the understanding that this is not unique.

The journal ended up serving as an outline, allowing me to pull what I wanted from it, and reshape the contents into a narrative, fueled by daydreams both productive and maladaptive. A voice emerged through fragments of my internal monologue. It became a story. *This story.* And when I felt like giving up, like *what's the point?* I kept going. I finished it, and then I finished it again, and again, until it was *finished*, finished. It took for-fucking-ever.

* * *

I uploaded the book, *this book,* to the online self-publishing platform. It felt bigger and more nauseating than anything I had ever done before. Even bigger than moving to LA to chase an unoriginal stereotype of a dream. Whatever the reaction was going to be, whether it was love, hate, or the cold silence of nothing, I needed to push the button.

So I did it. After all of that, with a click, I was one of those people who *did the thing*. I reasoned with myself that whatever happened next didn't matter. I had put something out into the world that was mine, to be judged or not, whatever, by an unknown audience of people who could say whatever they wanted about Zinnia Sherwood without hurting Cara Becker's feelings. Right?

I closed my laptop, pretending to be unaffected by the cliffhanger of it all. I found myself leaning into hoping for *nothing*. Because *nothing* meant I hadn't done any damage. I could just walk away from it and maybe finally be free.

What happened next, shocked me.

* * *

It wasn't nothing. I mean, it also wasn't like I woke up in a four-poster bed in my future mansion with all my literary awards hanging on the walls around me or anything, but it was *not nothing*.

I'd told myself that *doing it* was the point. That the outcome didn't matter. But the first week after publishing the book felt like discovering I had a new secret superpower, except instead of flying or superhuman strength, my superpower was compulsively refreshing browser tabs and huffing analytics.

My novel had... readers. Saying it like that kind of seems like admitting I had herpes (for the record, I did not then, nor do I now, or have ever, had herpes). The feeling was like either going off, or starting, new psych medication. Totally wobbly, extremely floaty, and a little toxic.

Drink some water, I thought to myself. *Touch grass.* I decided I needed to put my phone away and do something non-scrolly or non-refreshy for awhile, so I drove out to my favorite trail for a hike. As I stepped over roots and around boulders I knew well, my thoughts were still so focused on what was happening online that I was ignoring the majesty of nature around me, as you're supposed to do on a hiking trail.

Then, my phone buzzed with a text from Griffin. It was a photo of a book in a shop window. I gasped in surprise and started laughing right there in the middle of the trail. Then came the accompanying text message:

"You're not going to believe this. Just walked past a used bookstore and saw that book in the window. Remember? The children's book we found at the thrift store that time about why everyone has a butt crack?"

Of course I remembered. *Cleft of Love.* Babies' butt cracks are formed by the parents' tears of joy landing in just the right location after they're born. If you have a butt crack, it's because you are loved. It was so ridiculous we almost bought it just because we were sure it must be the only copy to have ever been printed.

That was the text. It was all for me. No request for proof of cat life. Just Griffin sharing something that made him think of me.

My heart swelled and felt like it was going to beat out of my chest. I wanted to tell him about *my* book. How I had taken all the daydreams in my head and turned them into a novel that I'd shared with the world, albeit anonymously. But I couldn't.

I re-read his message a million times. I could picture the bookstore, and him standing there, sunlight glinting on his golden hair, the way his body would shake when he laughed. "I wish I was there," I texted back. I watched the typing dots appear, then vanish.

* * *

The next thing I knew, I was hoofing it back down the trail to my car to head back to town. Hannah would be just finishing work. I needed to connect with another human who I knew wouldn't run screaming in the opposite direction.

I arrived at her place, still in my sweaty hiking clothes, just before she pulled into the driveway herself. She lived on the outskirts of town in one of those converted shipping container tiny homes you hear about, complete with a dreamy herb garden that was the pride of her socials.

She emerged from her car wearing her day job persona, dressed in sleek black pants, a blazer, crisp blouse, and chunky heels, her long silver tendrils tied back away from her face. Only her slouchy homemade patchwork shoulder bag gave any indication of her bohemian leanings.

I ran to her, barely containing myself and threw my sweaty arms around her.

"Han! How was work? All good?"

"Hi babe," she hugged me back, her big hazel eyes smiling through well-earned crinkles. "Wow, you're giving off major manic pixie dream girl energy. What's happening?"

We entered her small but immaculately cozy abode and I mushed myself into the beanbag chair in her living room. Her home was the perfect intersection of Scandinavian hygge meets Eastern mystic, and I always felt at peace there. Her crotchety old cat, Storm, creaked over to the beanbag and found a spot to wedge himself next to me, purring loudly but swiping at my attempt to pet him.

"I mean... nothing, really. Just..."

Hannah's transformation from polished office worker to homey high priestess was complete in sheer seconds. She strolled toward me adorned in a simple tunic, long moonstone pendant and ripped jeans, her hair swinging wild and free down her shoulders.

"Griff texted me! And not about the cats this time!"

"Thank Lilith," she exalted. "What did he say?" she asked, handing me a glass of red wine. I hoped the drink would silence the inner screaming from the sensory overload of my sweaty sports bra sticking to my skin.

"Well, it was just about something he saw. An inside joke, kind of. That's good, right? It means he misses me?"

"Could be." She sat on the floor near me, setting her wine glass on the antique trunk she used as a living room coffee table. "It certainly seems like a good sign."

I was so tempted to ask her to get her cards out, but I felt a little guilty about treating her like my own personal oracle, even if it was something she usually volunteered.

"What else?" she asked. "Feeling productive lately?"

"How do you friggin' know these things. Have your crystals been telling you my secrets again?"

She smiled. "Always. But I want to hear it from you."

I hesitated. "I'm not sure I can, but... you know how it is when it suddenly feels like a light switched on and you get that lightbulb in your brain, and things start to make sense again?"

"Cheers to that." She picked up her glass and held it out for the clink. I did not leave her hanging.

"Give me a sec, I have something for you," she continued, getting up from her position on the floor like a seasoned yogi. I had a feeling I was going to need her to pull me up by my arms later. She calmly walked out of sight into her bedroom, and closed the door until it was open by only a crack.

I tried to pet Storm-kitty again, but he was over my attempts at affection and left me in frustration. To my left, I saw Hannah's tarot cards sitting in a neat pile on a low shelf. I wasn't sure if it was okay to touch them, but I just wanted to flip through them myself, see if they would infuse me with the kind of wisdom that Hannah carried with her.

But because I have all the grace of an excited toddler with icky hands, the deck fell out of my hands onto the floor. I hoped to whichever deity might be watching that this didn't mean I had unwittingly unleashed some type of fresh, otherworldly chaos into Hannah's world... or mine.

She returned to find me trying to clean up my mess. "Leave them," she said, gently. "Let's have a look how they landed."

The cards lay on the floor haphazardly, mostly turned downward so only their decorative backs were visible. But two cards had turned face up.

"The Six of Swords and the Six of Wands. Interesting."

"What do they mean?"

"Well, the Six of Swords is about moving away from something painful toward peace and healing. The Six of Wands is about victory, achievement and receiving recognition."

I wasn't sure what to say. I wanted for both things to be true. I hoped they were. But I was afraid if I opened my mouth to speak, I'd fall apart. And that's when Hannah knelt down next to the beanbag I was never going to get out of by myself.

"I know things have been so shitty, and that it's hard for

you to talk about. I'm here when you're ready. But in the meantime, here." She handed me a small bundle wrapped in burlap and purple embroidery thread.

"What is it? Can I open it?" Hannah nodded. As I unfurled the little package, a tiny trove of objects was revealed. I picked up each one while she explained what it meant.

"The feather is your freedom. The lapis lazuli stone is your voice, it aligns with your throat chakra so you can tell your truth. The acorn is a seed of change. This scrap of red ribbon represents your courage and lifeforce. The bark is for resilience, and to protect your memory so you never forget who you are. And the pressed zinnia flower is your soul's fragile beauty."

I was speechless, and literally about to crumble into a weeping mess.

"I see you, my friend," she said.

That did it.

Chapter 40

The thing about unleashing something you made into the world is that in some way, it ceases to be yours. People are going to get things from it you never intended or anticipated, and you can't control their response to it. But when someone out there *gets it*, the feeling is undeniable. And when that someone *getting it* leads to a whole metric fuckload of other people *getting it*, it's time to maybe start thinking about checking yourself.

I wasn't prepared for just how much the external validation from strangers on the internet was going to fuck with my ego. Watching my book shoot to #12 on the platform's "Humor & Satire" bestseller list was an epic thrill. But the fact that I had also quasi-ironically categorized it as "Self-Help" (What? That's what it literally was. It was my therapy homework after all!), and then it somehow reached #156 in that category made my head spin. I was sure that was a mistake, but the reviews told another story.

Five stars. This book is like therapy, but funnier and cheaper than my actual therapist.

Four stars. I went into this thinking it was a self-help book and ended up getting a hilarious instructional manual about how to win at failing. Best accidental purchase ever.

It felt like I had actually contributed something meaningful to the world, even if that contribution was just making other people feel less alone in their dysfunction.

But not everyone was going to *get it*, and that unlocked a whole other level of mindfuck. The negative reviews were panic-inducing, even if I did repeatedly try to remind myself that receiving them was always going to happen, and that they weren't about *me*. Because they couldn't be, because I was not actually someone named Zinnia Sherwood.

One star. This 100% reads like it was written by someone with ADHD. In a bad way.

Two stars. The author literally wrote her own maladaptive daydream and is shilling it online as fiction.

Oh God, they're onto me, I thought. My heart rate spiked every time I saw comments like that, so I tried to focus on the more satisfying comments about creativity, inspiration, and neurodiversity, and readers sharing their own stories about maladaptive daydreaming and managing impulses and inattention in a world where being different is considered an inconvenience to others.

It was a narrow ledge I was teetering on, between the unhealthy levels of external validation and the fear of being discovered. My daydreams took on a new theme, edging toward the enticing and egomaniacal notion that I had become some kind of elusive superhero. By day, I was Cara Becker, mild-mannered technical writer and hectic life-ruiner. By night, I was masquerading as Zinnia Sherwood, mysterious indie author whose book was climbing the internet charts and maybe even saving lives in the process.

The strangest part wasn't the dual reality. I'd been living multiple lives in my head for years, after all. It was the liberating sensation of having accomplished something that no one in my actual life knew about. No one could diminish it with well-meaning advice about "realistic expectations." No one could be shocked or dismayed or disapproving of what I had written, or ask "Is this character based on me?" At most, Hannah's mystical intuition might have been attuned to *something*, but even she didn't know the whole story.

But there was also something super lonely about it. It took everything I had to quash the urge to spill the beans to Griffin or Hannah, or even, shock-horror, my parents, only to remember that Zinnia Sherwood's victory had to remain my secret.

Mostly it made me even more lonely for Griffin. All of the online validation in the world couldn't fill up the empty hole in my chest where my heart used to be. It was becoming increasingly unbearable that he wasn't present to witness this version of me who was actually making my dreams come true on my own.

What was even the point of this if I couldn't share it with him?

* * *

The rush of the book's success combined with the daily struggle to manage wild swings between euphoria and despair meant that I was becoming increasingly anxious about when it would all come crashing down. It was inevitable. About a month after publishing, the initial burst of activity had already started to slow down to something more low key. If I had learned anything about life up to this point, it was that a crushing reversal of fortune was most assuredly coming my way.

How to Prepare for and Survive the Inevitable Crash from the Heights of Unexpected Success

Prerequisites: An extended period of manic productivity, inevitably followed by a breathtaking face-plant into oblivion.

1. Recognize the warning signs. Are you operating on 54% dopamine high and 46% impending psychological breakdown? Are you getting a max three hours of sleep a night? Are you getting up to reorganize your spice rack by *vibe*, AGAIN? Are you responding to messages telepathically instead of for real? You might be in the Downward Spiral Anticipation Zone.
2. Hoard your earnings in a separate account for tax purposes, and also just in case someone official swoops in to claim the rest of it on behalf of the haters who say you owe them damages for the time they'll never get back after reading your book. This is known as the Imposter Tax.
3. Create a *crash kit*. Order a subscription meal service, make sure you have at least a month's supply of pajamas, and acquire a Vitamin D sun lamp. Begin using the crash kit immediately, because you're basically already there.

4. Write yourself a note explaining that your value as a person is not defined by this or whatever happens next. Hide it in the pocket of the sweatpants of despair so you find it at the right time.
5. Accept that the crash is not a punishment for succeeding or an invitation to self-sabotage. It's just your brain returning to its regularly scheduled programming.
6. Remember that while the crash might be unavoidable, the work you created during the high is permanent. The book exists whether you're riding the wave or drowning in self-doubt.

Safety warning: May result in the realization that internet success only makes you feel like you're driving the proverbial sporty convertible along the coast, until you swerve around a death-defying turn to find you're riding a rusty bike down a steep hill in a snowstorm.

* * *

As anticipated, the comedown wasn't particularly fun. It had the all-too-familiar effect of sucking me back into a vortex of inattention. I found myself scanning all the tabs in my brain looking for a satisfying place to land, but there was nothing in my mental catalog that would scratch the itch.

So I went for a jog, hoping to rekindle some of the energy I had been running on, only to find my body moving on autopilot while I grasped for a familiar thread in my mind.

* * *

Griffin was in the backyard of the LA rental at sunset, his perfect butt parked in one of the patio chairs, nursing a beer while the fire pit hissed and popped. The other chairs sat empty around the flames, their lonely shadows stretching across the lawn.

The back gate clicked, and Styles knocked on it quickly before pushing the door open.

Griffin turned, and for a second, he stared blankly at what might have been an apparition. If only he'd known that I, an actual ghost, was floating around watching this unfold with, I have to admit, a fair amount of erotic jealousy.

"Holy shit," he said, jumping to his feet, dropping his beer bottle onto the ground.

"Hey," said Styles, stepping into the yard, looking smaller than Griffin remembered. He was thinner, and seemed weathered and weary, like a man who had seen some shit. The cargo shorts he was wearing revealed a scar on his shin from that time when he tried to dig me a grave.

Griffin gawked at him, still half in disbelief. "I saw you on the news, when you were rescued. The only survivor of the plane crash. Dude, we thought you were dead. You and Cara both. There were funerals."

"I know," Styles said quietly. "It's weird, being home and alive when everyone else has moved on. Willow's happy I'm back, but..." He gave a half-smile that didn't stick. "It's an adjustment for her."

They stood there for a moment, the fire popping between them.

"There's something I didn't tell the media," Styles said finally. "I probably should have, but..." he trailed off. "I wasn't alone on that island. Cara survived with me," he hesitated. "Until shortly before I was rescued."

Griffin threw his hands to the back of his head where they lingered briefly before traveling to his face and covering his mouth, agape with shock.

"Fuck, are you serious?!" His eyes flicked to the canvas backpack slung over Styles' shoulder. "Wait, is that...?"

Styles shifted the backpack from his shoulder and held it out. "Yeah. This is the backpack that washed ashore. The things in it helped keep us alive." Griffin exhaled and his hands dropped to his sides before he crossed them around his chest in a self-embrace. His eyes were wet. I wanted to hug him so much.

Styles continued. "These are the last things she used and touched. You should have them. And you should know, this backpack was a life saver, but without Cara, there is no way I'd be standing here today. She kept me hoping. I'd even say she saved my life. And I'm so sorry I couldn't save hers."

'Damn right', I would have said, if they could have heard me. But my ghost form didn't have that kind of power.

Griffin took the backpack from Styles and studied it for a moment before hugging it like it was me. Which was sweet, but also, ew, that thing needed a wash, badly.

The handshake that followed was solid, but quick, and loaded with an unspoken forgiveness.

"So, if she didn't die in the crash and she was alive with you all that time, how did she...?" Griffin asked.

Styles opened his mouth, and then froze. "Uhhh..."

Chapter 41

Griffin walked into the house, *our house*, like it was just a regular day, no big deal. Meanwhile, my mid-crash wallowing had been interrupted by a minor nervous breakdown with my eyeballs glued to my phone and my heart in tachycardia.

Five minutes earlier, I'd been scrolling through my socials... I mean *Zinnia Sherwood's* socials, when one of the feeds served me a video of a popular bookish influencer sobbing into the camera. The caption read, "This book turned my life upside down in the BEST WAY possible." She was holding a print copy of my book. And apparently, 2.4 million other people had already watched her ugly cry about it.

By the time I clicked her hashtag, there were dozens of other reaction videos. One with a girl reading a passage out loud and throwing the book across the room. Another with a guy pacing and yelling, "NO, because this is *me*." Someone else made a fan fiction thirst edit shipping alternative character pairings... and groupings. I'll let your imagination run wild with that one.

Notifications were lighting up my phone so quickly I couldn't keep up. I received a DM that said, "Hey, I run a channel with 400K subs. Can you come on and talk about your book and maladaptive daydreaming?" There were other

DMs from vloggers, influencers, and a book reviewer tagging me in a "Top 5 Indie Reads of the Year" reel.

I was about to tap on the reel, when a text message from River appeared and I tapped on it instead. Unfortunately, I panicked and swiped the wrong way, accidentally deleting his message. Fuck. *What could River want?* I wondered, uncertain whether I had the guts to text him back to find out.

Then I received an email from someone whose name rang a bell. It was Mona Willinger, with the subject line: "Let's talk series development." I remembered her as one of the executives Styles and I had met at the *Sixty-Six* pitch meeting.

My mind was doing the math meme thing trying to suss out if this was legit or not, when the front door opened and there was Griffin just... standing there, in the doorway, just like I had wished for. Had I manifested him? It was like the multiverse had collapsed on itself and erased the time, distance, and events that had separated us.

"Hi," he said.

"Hi," I replied, in shock.

Daisy and Clover, who were both curled up on the couch next to me, jumped up and made the trilling sounds they always made whenever Griffin would walk in the door. They bolted to him, and he sat down on the floor to pet them both while they cooed and mewed all over him. He held a paper bag out in my direction. "Pad Thai, with extra peanuts..."

"...for the crunch," we both said, in unison.

My brain was trying to process two unexpected realities:

1. Griffin was actually home, like for real.
2. My book was going viral on the internet.

I had to pick one to react to, or I was going to irreversibly short circuit and possibly disintegrate into a pile of dust.

"Hi," I said again, finally leaping off the couch toward him, regretting that I was wearing my sweatpants of self-loathing and my greasy hair updo.

"Hi," he repeated, and we stared at each other in near disbelief at being in each other's presence again. I felt all of the emotions in the universe (yes, all of them) well up inside me. I resisted a sudden intense urge to push him over onto the floor and assault his deliciously freckled face with wet sloppy kisses, opting to play it cool instead, as if I wasn't absolutely fucking losing my mind with, like I said, *all the emotions.*

"Um, are you... home now?" I asked, stupidly, unable to believe my own eyes. My phone dinged.

"If that's okay," he said, sort of tentatively, which made my heart skip a beat. "I mean, if you're not too busy with... whatever."

I glanced down at my phone, which was still open on Mona Willinger's message, and locked my screen. "Nothing that can't wait."

The food play was genius on Griffin's part. I'd seen enough mafia movies to know that meals are a unifying, humanizing force, sometimes even between mortal enemies. Whatever drama we're all going through, we all got to eat. So, we sat at the kitchen table, *our* kitchen table, and divided the Pad Thai across two bowls that I pulled out of the cupboard, like this was just any normal takeout dinner we might have had together on any normal evening.

My phone dinged again. I turned it screen-down on the table.

After validating the restaurant choice and agreeing that the

Pad Thai was on point, we finally started talking.

"How have you been?" Griffin asked.

Another *ding*. I shifted in my seat and spun some noodles onto my fork.

"I've been..." I paused, trying to find the words. I couldn't say I was *good*, but I also couldn't say I was *bad*. "Weird. I've been writing again."

"That's great," he said warmly, with a disarming smile on his lips and in his eyes. I almost told him everything right there. Almost explained about the book going viral and the message from Mona and the fact that I had accidentally become a moderately successful author by disguising my maladaptive daydream as fiction under a secret identity.

Another *ding*. I pushed my phone across the table, as if I wouldn't be able to hear it from a foot away.

"How about you?" I asked quickly.

"Lonely," he said without hesitation. "I mean, work was good. Apparently one of my more A-list clients spread the word about me fixing his chronic back problem, and..."

Ding.

"...I kept thinking about how I wanted to tell you about it, you know? Like, I'd have these amazing days and then come home to an empty house and remember that the person I most wanted to share things with was three thousand miles away."

I nodded, but the dinging of my phone was pulling at my attention. What if it was one of the big online book community influencers? Or Mona following up? What if something major was happening?

Ding. Ding. My leg was bouncing so hard and fast I was afraid it might come unhinged from my body.

"Geez, you're popular tonight."

"Yeah..." I laughed and finally switched my phone to silent.

"Anyway. I need to apologize..." he started.

My phone buzzed.

"Griff, no..."

"I was jealous," Griffin said.

Buzz.

"I mean, not just about... what happened... with..."

Buzz. Buzz.

"...but about you changing, and me not knowing where I fit anymore."

I couldn't believe what I was hearing. After what I had done to him, I couldn't bear to listen to him take the responsibility. I reached for my water glass, which seemed to get a ripple in it each time my phone buzzed, but that might have just been my hand shaking. "Griff, you really don't have to..."

"Let me finish," he said gently.

Buzz.

"I forgive you. At least, I'm getting there."

The shock of him saying those words almost made me black out. I took a swig of my Jurassic Park water.

Buzz.

He leaned in. "I thought a lot about it, and I'm ready to try again."

My chest felt tight, but not entirely from emotion. I wanted to be fully present for this, give him my whole attention. But part of me was still focused on my phone, on the notifications piling up, and me not knowing what *the buzz* was all about.

"I want that, too," I said, forcing myself to look at him instead of the face-down buzzing rectangle between us. "And this isn't a *but*, but... I'm different now. I'm not sure how to explain it yet."

He nodded slowly. "I know. Me too. And I know we can't go back to how we were before but... maybe we can figure it out as we go."

Another *buzz.*

I smiled, though my heart was pounding for two entirely different reasons. Griffin was home. My book was blowing up. They were both the best thing that ever happened to me. And clumsy as I was, I had no idea how to hold both in my hands at the same time without dropping one.

"Look at you go," Griffin said, peeking under the table at my bouncing leg which I promptly stopped bouncing in response. "I should have called first, I know how you hate surprises."

"It's okay. I'm glad you're here."

"I didn't mean to stress you out."

"It's good, I'm good," I reassured him, anxiously.

"Maybe we could..."

"Fuck, yes," I blurted.

Griffin stood from the table, took my hand and pulled me to his chest. I had to mentally check myself for a moment to make sure I wasn't hallucinating. That this wasn't just another daydream that felt too real, inevitably leading to me waking up from a catatonic state to find that none of this was really happening and that my mind had become fractured beyond repair.

Then he kissed me, and it was the best kiss I had ever tasted, because in no fantasy scenario would I ever have imagined our reunion kiss tasting like the remnants of Pad Thai.

Chapter 42

Buzz.

I had ignored my phone since Griffin's return home the previous evening. If there was one thing I was certain of, it was that I was not going to fuck up our reunion by giving in to the compulsion to let myself become distracted by anything other than him. So the fact that my new secret identity was about to become the internet's favorite viral mystery was something that I was yet unaware of.

It hadn't exactly been a restful night, but at least it was for all the right reasons, if you get where I'm coming from. That morning, Griffin had awakened *ready to go* and was pressing himself against me as we spooned in bed. I turned around to face him, running my fingers through his soft hair, which had a little more gray in it than it had before I'd left LA.

"I could get used to this," I cooed at him. "You should be a stay-at-home cat dad."

"You don't want me to go back to work?"

"Not today." I went in for a kiss, breathing in the scent of him, when my phone, of course, buzzed again.

"Seriously, Car, what's up with all the notifications? Your phone hasn't stopped since I got home."

I hadn't had the opportunity to rehearse any responses to

this situation, and my mind was blank as to what to tell Griffin that wouldn't be a lie. And I was done with lying. Mostly.

"I better see what it's all about."

Sighing loudly, Griffin released me from his embrace, and I picked up my phone.

"WHO IS ZINNIA SHERWOOD?" screamed the headline from BlurbBlab, a popular literary news site that featured indie books and authors. The article's subtitle read, "What we know about the elusive and mysterious indie author who's making internet waves."

I slid out of bed dizzy with anxiety-induced vertigo. I could hear Griffin's voice echoing "Cara? Is everything okay?" from the back rooms of my mind, but a fierce headache was beginning to rage inside my cranium, rendering me unable to respond. Instead, I stumbled my way out of the bedroom to the kitchen. I was going to need to chase some painkillers with a pot of coffee to process what I had just seen.

The article was an exploration of Zinnia Sherwood's "enigmatic persona," complete with amateur literary analysis and speculation about her "deliberately elusive media strategy." The author had apparently done some investigative work, noting that Zinnia Sherwood had very little social media presence, no author photos, and apart from a brief and awkward AMA, not much interaction with her readers.

"Sherwood's novel has become a word-of-mouth phenomenon," the article continued, "but the author herself remains stubbornly invisible. Industry insiders are beginning to wonder if this mysterious persona is actually a brilliant marketing strategy."

I nearly choked on my coffee at what I was reading, because it was clear that I was 100% being misunderstood, and because my book didn't have any right being anywhere near the a sentence containing the words "marketing strategy", unless the fear of being misunderstood sells books, in which case, *go me*! But also, *fuck my life*.

The article had been published four hours ago and already had 691 comments. I scrolled through them with horrified fascination, unable to look away from the trainwreck.

BookLoofah99: *I bet she's actually a celebrity writing under a pseudonym*

ShiftyMcNifty: *This is obviously a publicity stunt for someone established*

MrCheezWheelz: *Wasn't there a snaggletoothed page 3 girl named Zinnia Sherwood in the early 2000s?*

I don't know how long I had been sitting there doomscrolling and clicking down the rabbit hole of the latest mess I had created. Enough time for Griffin to go to the gym, come back, take a shower, and engage in a video game marathon, all while I fixated on reading every last word on the subject of my apparently controversial secret identity.

The story had been picked up by various entertainment sites and something called the "Anonymous Authors Appreciation Society," which I hadn't known existed but apparently had strong opinions about my alleged identity. There was even a video with 1.3 million views where some jerk explained why my "mystery author brand" wasn't genius, but deeply problematic.

A banner notification appeared over top of the tabloid mess

on my screen.

"Babe. Your energy is absolutely unhinged today. I just checked your birth chart and saw that Uranus and Jupiter are transiting your Midheaven. I legit just googled you to see if you were arrested for flashing a weatherman giving a live report or something."

Hannah's otherworldly abilities were sometimes terrifying. Imagine having a friend who seems to receive intel about you directly from the cosmos. Is there a constellation up there called "The Rat" or "The Mole" or something?

"You know I can't resist a weatherman," I texted her back.

"LOL. So what's up?"

"Nothing, yet. You know I can't start fucking shit up until I've had breakfast."

"It's 3:30."

"And your point is?"

"Cara. The cards practically jumped out of my hands when I thought of you today. The Ace of Wands, The Wheel of Fortune, and The Moon. This is some seriously weird energy."

"Your cards need to mind their own business."

"My cards ARE minding their business. That's literally how tarot works. What did you put out into The Universe?"

I set my phone down without responding, partly because I wasn't ready to confess my literary crimes and partly because Hannah's accuracy rate was approximately ninety-seven percent and I wasn't emotionally prepared for whatever cosmic insights she might have about my situation.

The most alarming part was that the internet detectives were starting to voice more specific theories about my identity. One commenter was convinced I was a Hollywood insider writing a roman à clef about the entertainment industry.

Another theory involved me being a well-known male author experimenting with a female perspective. The most popular theory was that I was definitely a bored suburban mom using fiction to process her midlife crisis (maybe a little too close for comfort, that one). Hypotheses abounded.

Dragonteats404: *The ADHD descriptions are too clinical, I bet they're a therapist or psychiatrist.*

SharniReads: *The technical writing background seems too true to be fictional. Does the author actually write user manuals for sex toys? Somebody somewhere knows who this is.*

BradInfinitumm: *I'd put money on this being someone famous. The 'no-marketing-strategy' marketing strategy is too sophisticated for a nobody.*

My butt was sore from the hours it had been planted on the hard kitchen chair, so eventually I relocated and spent the next several hours on the couch next to Griffin as he played video games and cuddled the cats, pretending not to be in a state of low-level panic. To him, it looked like I was just having a low key hyperfocus trip, meanwhile, I was high-key incessantly refreshing news sites and social media feeds like I was monitoring the progress of a natural disaster heading directly toward my house. Niagara Falls isn't exactly hurricane country, but the spiraling I was doing could have spawned one from the river. I was jittery and nauseous.

"I think I'm going to go for a walk," I said calmly, while Griffin leaned over and gave me a kiss between shooting monsters on the TV.

* * *

My life as I knew it was over. Everyone knew, and it was exactly as I'd feared.

The internet lost interest in Maladaptive and the Zinnia Sherwood mystery the moment I was outed. Turns out the not knowing, the guessing game, had been the most interesting thing about it. To find out I was just... Cara Becker, a regular person from not-Hollywood with inconsistent hygiene practices and a habit of walking out into traffic while daydreaming, was enough to make the internet's collective attention span drop me like a hot potato that had gone cold and moldy.

I'd already had the inevitable crying-into-the-phone conversation with my mother, who was obviously disgusted not only at the appalling lasciviousness that had sprung from my brain into the novel, but the fact that I had chosen to publish it for others to see. My authorship of the sex toy manuals was at least uncredited, and therefore far more acceptable. Her tone implied she was still weighing whether to call a priest.

Even Hannah, my dearest friend and biggest supporter, was disappointed that I couldn't at least tell her about my book. She had known all along that something big was happening, and the fact that I had kept it to myself was too much to bear, and she needed some space to think about how to process the betrayal. She mentioned something about the Hanged Man card. That sounded bad.

But the worst was when Griffin approached me with an exasperation that said he was done, like really, really fucking done. He didn't say a word. Just walked up to me with the most delicious bed head I've ever seen on him, holding his phone out for me to read. It was Zinnia Sherwood's AMA thread:

BooksAndBanter · 27 days ago: *"You seem kind of extra. What's your to-go coffee order?"*

ZinniaSherwood · 27 days ago: *"Pretty basic, actually. Just a large plain black coffee, with 7 ice cubes in it, in a double cup. I used to go to this little place called Magic Roast when I was living out there. Miss that place."*

BaristaBitch420 · 4 hr. ago: *"Wait... I work at Magic Roast. Only one customer ever ordered that exact thing, routinely. We had iced coffee on the menu, but she said that was too cold and it gave her brainfreeze. She used to come in with that podcaster guy, with the pretentious nickname. The name she gave me for her cup was Cara."*

I must have paled, because Griffin seemed satisfied that I had fully taken in the comments. "You published a book about everything that happened in LA framed as a bizarre fantasy... and just... didn't tell me?"

"Loosely inspired by..." I started to say. "Most of it isn't even..."

"Am I in it?"

"Not you, specifically..."

"What the fuck, Cara?!"

"It was just supposed to be therapeutic. I didn't think it would get any attention."

"What hurts the most about this is that you're still keeping secrets from me. After everything. How are we supposed to make this work if you can't just tell me the truth?"

He was right, and I had no good answer for that. I watched as he stormed up the stairs to our bedroom and heard the sound of the bedroom door slamming. It flashed me back to that fateful moment, when it was Griffin who had been hiding something, and Styles who slammed a door and peeled out of our rental house driveway.

Styles. He must know, too. Oh God.

* * *

Just as I was about to step daydream-blind into oncoming traffic, my phone buzzed in my pocket as if it was slapping me in the face and yelling "Snap out of it!" I checked the notification. Seeing a message from Styles Chilton via the contact form on Zinnia Sherwood's author page was yet another shock to the system. I stood still in the middle of the sidewalk to open the message. The subject line read "Guest Invitation". Beneath it, the first line got right to the point.

"Dear Ms. Sherwood, would you be interested in appearing as a guest on my podcast, *Making It*?"

Chapter 43

My eyeballs tripped and fell over the first line of Styles' message to the point where I thought I had a concussion. I blinked the dizzy stars away, breathed deeply, and started over.

Dear Ms. Sherwood,

Would you be interested in appearing as a guest on my podcast, Making It? My name is Styles Chilton. I host Making It: Conversations about the Spark, a long-form interview podcast focused on the inspiration behind creativity, the who behind the what, unconventional paths to success, and the impact of art on public consciousness (and vice versa). My video channel currently reaches just over 4.7 million subscribers, with an additional 3 million monthly listeners across other platforms.

I've been following your meteoric rise from nowhere to everywhere. A debut self-published novel going mainstream viral without a traditional press push or even an author bio or photo to hang it on. A very limited online footprint and a horde of readers trying to reverse-engineer the person behind the book.

The buzz about your novel is too tantalizing to ignore. A mysterious, neurodivergent author who seems to be hitting several different audiences at once? That alone was enough to get my attention. And your deliberately evasive promotional approach is bolder than it seems at first glance. Frankly, it's rare, and fascinating.

I'm sure you've noticed there is a lot of wild speculation going on about your identity and your intentions. The world wants to know who Zinnia Sherwood is and so do I. Let me be the person to help you safely reveal yourself on your own terms. Not that you need my help with exposure, but I can help you stay in control of your narrative and reach new audiences.

I've just gotten my hands on a print copy of Maladaptive and will be reading it in full over the next few days in preparation. From what I've seen so far, this is exactly the kind of story that resonates deeply with my audience. I'd love to talk with you about the book, the process behind it, and what it's like to watch something so personal take on a life of its own.

The interview can be recorded remotely or in-studio in Los Angeles. If this is something you'd consider, I'd be happy to work around your schedule and help with logistical concerns.

Warmly,

Styles Chilton

* * *

I read the email a quadrillion times. Of course Styles would reach out to Zinnia Sherwood, an intrepid creator going viral on the internet. It was exactly his niche. It was kind of stupid how much sense it made and that I didn't see it coming.

He was certainly persuasive, to the point where, for a few insane minutes, I actually considered doing it. That bit about controlling my narrative safely and on my own terms was the balm that my fear of being misunderstood was itching for. Would I be nuts to turn down the chance to address the speculation about the book and my anonymity being some kind of publicity stunt? Should I lean into my new identity and come out visibly to set the record straight and embrace a public persona?

There was another angle to it, of course. I mean, imagine me booking the interview, showing up to Styles' studio and the look on his face when I, Cara Becker, the former friend and co-creator he jilted, walked in to claim my victory.

* * *

Styles, wearing his signature charismatic smile that permeated up into his sparkling eyes, came out of his studio into the office to greet his most anticipated guest of the season, Zinnia Sherwood. Upon seeing his guest, furrowed confusion swooped in to wipe the welcoming grin off his bedimpled cheeks.

"Cara? What the... what are you doing here?"

"Hi Styles, thanks for inviting me."

"What do you mean? Listen, I'm prepping to record a podcast episode, my guest should be here any minute..."

"Ta da!" I said, extending my arms and doing a performative curtsy.

Styles spun around on the spot as if to check to make sure he was in the right place, and then shook his head to reset the scene, but I remained exactly where I stood.

"You're... Zinnia Sherwood?"

"In the flesh. So... are we doing this?"

He stared at me with an undefined expression, his bluish gray eyes wide with surprise, or maybe even horror. Then he pivoted and regained his composure, extending his hand to shake mine as if we were meeting for the first time.

"Let's do it," he said, and led me into the studio where we sat at a table in a comfy room that could have doubled as a small, kitschy museum of all the arts. He handed me a pair of headphones. When the light turned red, he opened with his standard greeting.

"Hello everyone, and welcome to another episode of Making It. I'm Styles Chilton. This is the show where we talk about the spark behind the creative compulsion, and today's conversation is a special one. My guest today is an indie author whose debut novel has been impossible to ignore. We're going to talk about the path that led her here, and what it means to make something that takes on a life of its own. Zinnia Sherwood, welcome to the podcast, we're honored to have you."

"Thanks." I was abrupt, but cheerful. It seemed to throw him off a little, which was amusing.

"Since you're familiar with the show, you know I love a good origin story..."

"Oh, how do you know that?"

I didn't know it was possible to stumble while seated, but he actually did. In a discombobulated spasm, the King of Debonairville dropped the pen he always held during his interviews and very nearly did a face plant on the desk between us while his chair tried to roll away from under his butt. He laughed it off, which magically had the effect of overwriting my clapback.

"Woops, uh, so the big question on everyone's mind over the past several weeks has been 'Who is Zinnia Sherwood?' Should we start there?"

"Zinnia Sherwood is the nom de plume I adopted to allow myself to purge a painful experience from my system through fiction and fantasy, in a way that no one could take away from me."

The words "painful experience" elicited from him a compassionate head tilt and puppy dog-eyed expression. Man, he was good.

"Painful experiences are often the wellspring of truth-telling through creative expression. Still, I'm sorry to hear you went through...

"You haven't even begun to be sorry."

Styles removed his headphones and pushed his chair back as he yelled to the crew, "Cut!"

* * *

Talk about being "too tantalizing to ignore," to use his words. So yeah. I thought about it, as I do.

But knowing what I knew about Styles, once my little revenge fantasy had quenched my craving, I perused the email again to read between the lines. Could I benefit from revealing myself via a popular podcast? Maybe. But it wasn't just about what he could do for me. It would be about what I could do for him.

He did have a weirdly good track record with guests who'd rather die than talk about themselves. If he was the one to get the elusive Zinnia Sherwood in his studio, it could propel him to the next level. I could be his next big viral moment.

But that's not why I declined his invitation.

* * *

Dear Mr. Chilton,

Thank you for your interest, however I must regretfully decline your invitation. My decision to publish quietly was deliberate. I didn't want or expect this kind of reaction and honestly, I prefer to remain anonymous.

Regards,

Zinnia Sherwood

I breathed a sigh of relief. My decision to keep my true identity secret wasn't about denying Styles his next-level boost in revenge, or even about taking advantage of the viral Zinnia Sherwood mystery for passive marketing purposes. It was about preserving my own peace, the peace I had been seeking since coming home from LA. And it was about not having to defend publishing my sexual fantasies against an inquisition from my mother.

But Styles was undeterred.

Dear Ms. Sherwood,

Thank you for your earnest reply. I absolutely respect your wish to maintain your private identity. Public life can be overwhelming, and it isn't for everyone.

However, I've started reading Maladaptive and I'm even more excited about the potential for us to discuss it on my podcast. So far, it's living up to the hype. I'd say there is something almost familiar about the narrator's tone. She's funny, if a little neurotic, but endearingly so. It feels like I'm in the comfortable presence of a dear friend. No wonder your book is doing so well, the relatability scale is off the charts.

In that light, I would like to amend my invitation. I can make arrangements for you to remain anonymous, by obscuring your identity in person in the studio, or over video chat, or through a call-in interview.

There is no expectation that you need to reveal anything you'd rather keep private. The offer stands. Please think about it.

Warmly,

Styles Chilton

Cue the alarm bells ringing and flooding my body with dangerous levels of cortisol. I was flying way too *funnily, neurotically, endearingly, comfortably and relatably* close to the sun. As far as Styles' invitation was concerned, there was nothing more to think about, and I left it at that, without any further reply.

Chapter 44

The knowledge that Styles was reading my book unlocked a whole new level of anxiety inside me, as I spiraled about the inevitable moment when he would put the pieces together and expose my identity to the world, possibly with malice instead of the sensitivity I had just declined.

* * *

Styles was awaiting a reply to his amended invitation that would never come, and in the meantime, he was reading my novel in preparation for an interview he and I would never have.

At first, I had no idea how to picture Styles reading my book. Was he at home? In his studio office? At his favorite coffee shop? For the sake of context, I put him in his office, where we had spent the most time together, and I was merely a fly on the wall, powerless except for my mind's-eye observational abilities.

He lounged comfortably across his office couch, voraciously devouring Zinnia Sherwood's "Maladaptive" with his arm folded behind his head and his socked feet dangling over the armrest on the other side.

Just as so many others were saying, he had fallen for the narrator's affably earnest point of view. But something was starting to unnerve him about it. It wasn't just the author's way with words, the occasional familiar turn of phrase. There was something spookily recognizable about the story itself. And then... there it was. Zinnia Sherwood had turned a sentimental object into a storytelling device that gave it all away. A snow globe.

His face paled. "Oh no."

Styles sat up suddenly as if he had awakened from a dream. No, not a dream, a déjà vu. He put the book down and ran his hands through his impeccably coiffed hair before picking it back up again. Hours passed while he read about a perspective on events that echoed a chapter of his life that he had swept under the rug, for the sake of his career, his marriage, and his sanity.

With each chapter, he contorted himself into a new and different awkward position on the increasingly uncomfortable couch. I was starting to get a little concerned about his circulation, the way he knotted himself up at times.

And then, after straightening himself out on his back with the book in his left hand over his chest, I noticed him move his right hand down to his nether region. He rested it over top his jeans for a moment before pulling the zipper and slipping his hand into the opening of his jeans.

He must have been reading one of the steamier scenes. But as much as the idea of him pleasuring himself to something I wrote hit an arousing nerve inside me, my dominant reaction was that watching him do it in this unsuspecting state where he had no idea I was a fly on his wall was borderline creepy, and I didn't want to perv on him like that. Not even in my mind's eye.

As he began to pull his hand out of his jeans I was about to look away, lest he pull his dick out to go full tilt with it, when he came out empty-handed and pulled his zipper back up. Guess he wasn't feeling that scene, whatever it was, after all. Which honestly left me feeling a little butthurt and wondering which scene it was.

Regardless, through it all, he did not stop reading. By the time he reached the end, his hair was a mess and he was actually sweating.

"Holy shit," he said out loud to himself. "This is Cara."

From my position on the wall in my humble fly form, there was nothing I could do but watch as he tried to process what this could mean. Would I actually do this? What for? To get back at him? Or was there a chance it wasn't me at all, and this was all just a wild coincidence?

His hands began to shake as he flipped through the pages of the book he'd just consumed. This was no fluke. The author (me, it had to be me, he was now 11,098% certain of that) had obfuscated the obvious details of some real events and had woven them into a fictional fantasy story, but he could see right through it. Not only had I too-accurately captured the vibe of our time together, but had also somehow uncovered thoughts and feelings he had shared with no one and had even tried to hide from himself.

Styles moved from the couch to his desk and scribbled a list out onto a lined pad of paper:

1 - Pool. Rescue. Proposition. Stories. Dreams. Taking Chances.

2 - Sixty-Six. Simpatico. Frequency. Wavelength. Connection. Muse.

3 - Attraction. Friend. Pull. Sentimental. Support. Affection. Snow Globe.

4 - Fidelity. Boundaries. Hurt. Run Away. Hide. Lost. Found.

Forgive.

5 - Setback. Losing Hope. Time. Money. Fix It. Keep Going. Resolve.

6 - Retreat. Miscommunication. Intentions. Temptation. Sex. Fun. Real.

7 - Cheat. Self-Loathing. Fear. Denial. Hold On. Push Away. Erase. Gone.

8 - Writing. Broken. Release. Kind. Sympathetic. Rebuild. Heal.

"Oh my God," he muttered, after throwing down his pencil and reading his scrawled notes. I hadn't been unkind, he noted. In fact, I depicted him rather warmly, which made it even worse, because despite my kindness, he still came out looking like an absolute douchebag.

The part where I described him driving off to the hills and going missing was another red flag. But then he thought about that. It had been in the news. Writers use news stories to inspire their fiction all the time. He breathed a sigh of... not relief exactly, but hope. Maybe another writer had used that news story as a basis for their book, and had intuitively guessed the situation correctly.

No, it couldn't be, he shook his head. What were the chances another writer would also compose a cabin retreat scene that captured the vibe and scene with this level of uncanny accuracy? They would have to have been there. He circled his notes about the retreat and drew a bunch of arrows pointing to it.

That chapter was the most concerning. If anyone did connect the dots, there was a horrifying risk that his fans and subscribers *would react negatively to the revelation that he had been unfaithful to Willow, whose loyal and adoring following rivaled his. It could destroy his reputation, his career, his marriage, everything.*

Styles got up from his desk and started pacing his office, occasionally almost tripping over the piles of cords, supplies, books and other office accoutrements that had never found a home off the floor.

It was then that I was stunned to find that he was looking right at me. Staring directly into my eyes with surprise and a dread that I had never seen on his face before. How could he know I was watching him go through this? Had we somehow both tuned into some residual stream from our shared wavelength across the distance between us?

He moved toward me with intent, and I panicked when he raised his hand. Then I caught a glimpse of his reflection in the mirror across the room and saw myself in my fly form on the wall he was facing. I was about to flit away to some other vantage point for safety, when he dropped his hand.

He didn't swat me. Instead, his face was overcome with an emotion I had only briefly witnessed during our time together. I think it was sorrow. Remorse, maybe. He walked back over to his desk where his list of notes sat, and circled the line about the retreat aftermath, which encompassed how he'd denied me access to our web series project, and the manuscript that had inspired it.

From the look of him, he could barely swallow the knot that had formed in his throat. "Cara," he said out loud, collapsing onto the couch. "I wasn't going to make it without you."

As a humble fly on the wall, I was surprised to hear him address me directly. "Maybe I just kept it as a way to hold on to you... hold onto us, the only way that I could."

The idea that he might have kept it as a souvenir of our time together was almost enough to make me forgive him. Almost.

Styles stood up from the couch, a brand new emotion flashing all over his face. I'd never seen him scared like this before. He went back to his desk and stood over his list, adding a new note.

9 - Book. Revenge. Paranoia. Insanity. Hidden Messages. Conspiracy.

I did my best to interpret his scribbles. Was my book meant to be some kind of revenge? Or was he just being paranoid? Was he losing his mind? Seeing connections that could be interpreted as anything, like horoscopes or one of those conspiracy theorists who found hidden messages in cereal box designs?

He needed to check his theory with someone who'd been there. Someone else who might remember the details. It was time to call River.

* * *

"Hey, River. Weird question," Styles said, trying to sound casual while his heart rate suggested he was on the edge of a nervous breakdown. "Have you heard about this book 'Maladaptive'? By Zinnia Sherwood?"

"Oh yeah," River said with a tone of recognition. "Naomi's reading it, she's pretty obsessed with it."

"Have you read it?"

"Not yet, but Naomi has read some of it out loud to me. Why?"

Styles took a breath. "Does any of it seem familiar to you?

River was quiet for a moment. "I mean, it's a pretty classic redemption arc trope. A scared dreamer leaves their comfort zone, finds a new community, discovers new things about themselves, makes it big, falls from grace, then changes as a person."

"River." Styles' voice dropped to a serious tone. "I think Zinnia Sherwood is Cara, and I think she wrote about everything that happened between us to get revenge on me for canceling our project."

River laughed the laugh of a man who didn't necessarily find what his friend had said funny, but who was wondering if his friend was losing his grip on reality. "Cara? Styles, come on. She could be a little haphazard, but vindictive? No way, she'd never do a thing like that."

"I'm serious. It's not exactly the same, but some things are eerily similar, like the snow globe I gave her..."

"You gave her a snow globe?"

"That's not the point. The point is, you're in it too, River. There's a character who's obviously based on you."

"Styles, you're being paranoid. You're seeing things that aren't there because you want them to be there. It's a fictional novel about someone pursuing their dreams. There are probably millions of people who could recognize themselves in it."

"But..."

"Look," River interrupted, his tone sounding slightly annoyed. "Let's say you're right. Let's say Cara wrote a novel and some of the characters and events are loosely based on her experiences here. So what?"

"So what? River, this could ruin my entire life."

"No offense, dude, but that would be your own doing."

Styles went silent, presumably lost in thought.

"Dude," River continued, his voice gentler now. "If Cara did write this book, and if it is about her time here, then good for her. She turned a bunch of complicated bullshit that ended

in heartbreak for her into a redemption story. And if you're recognizing yourself in it, maybe that's because you screwed her over pretty hard."

Styles reacted like he'd been punched in the stomach. "I didn't mean to..."

"But you did, man. She was living her dream, and then when things got messy, you bailed. You imprisoned her dream inside your own little bubble, never to be realized. If she wrote about that, she had every right to. You practically served it to her."

Styles was speechless. Was River right? Was he the villain in this?

After River hung up, Styles sat back down on the couch in his studio office, staring at the cover of Zinnia Sherwood's book and trying to figure out if River had just given him the perspective he needed or completely dismantled his sense of reality.

And in that moment, all his ambition about being the one to unmask Zinnia Sherwood and reap the praise and rewards for it turned into dread. If he was right about her being me, and he was more sure than ever that he was, he didn't need to unmask her anymore. And if anyone else somehow managed to connect the dots between Zinnia Sherwood and Cara Becker, and then between Cara Becker and Styles Chilton, then it wasn't just my secret on the line. It was his, too.

"Fuck it," he said to himself. "If this is going to blow up and cost me everything, then I'm going to do it on my own terms."

* * *

To be honest, I wasn't super surprised at the text message that yanked me out of my fly-on-the-wall imagining of Styles' reaction to the book and his realization of who actually wrote it. When my phone buzzed, I knew exactly what I would find waiting for me.

"Cara, it's me, Styles. Can we talk?"

Chapter 45

I did not reply to Styles' text message. Or the one he sent after that. Or the phone call from him after that. For days, I ignored his attempts to get a hold of me. I didn't need to answer to know what it was about.

As I sat on the toilet in the pub restroom, I scrolled through my text and call records and deleted every instance of his name and number. Once all traces of him had been removed, my eyes fixed on some recent unanswered messages from River, and the one from Mona Willinger. With every minute that passed, it felt more and more impossible to bring myself to respond to either of them.

Then I checked my feed one more time for any new articles about my book or developments in the Zinnia Sherwood case. A new wrench had been thrown into the situation. In lieu of having the intrepid Zinnia Sherwood on his podcast to expound on her creative journey, Styles had launched his own exploration, bringing in experts to discuss the book, its author, and the frenzy surrounding them. He was getting a fair bit of praise for it in the media.

But I couldn't go down that rabbit hole. I put my phone away, finished up and went back to the table at the pub where Griffin sat waiting for me.

"Sorry about that, long line in the ladies' room," I fibbed.

We were on a date at our favorite pub. I had made the decision that whenever Griffin and I were together, anything related to my book and alter ego's new viral fame could only be attended to in my solitary moments. It was excruciating at times, but it was necessary. As agonizing as it felt, I could live with whatever injuries my ego might endure at the hacking hands of internet sleuths. I couldn't live without my heart.

He took my hand and kissed it as I sat back down. "Are you sure you don't have a UTI or something? You've been going to the bathroom a lot."

"Just hydrated, I guess," I said, and then took a swig of beer from my pint glass. Trying to keep Griffin from meeting Zinnia Sherwood meant doubling down on my double life, and to be honest, I was pretty fucking bad at it. Griffin's continuing hiatus from work meant that he was always around.

I know it sounds like I'm complaining, but I'm really not. It was exactly what I wanted. We were making up for lost time, and I relished his company. But my alter ego's crisis was screaming for my attention and constantly threatened to come crashing in and ruin everything.

Which resulted in some unfortunately secretive tactics, like stealing moments away to manage the crisis whenever I could. I tried like hell to be discreet. As far as Griffin was concerned, I had left my "hold on, I have to take this call" lifestyle behind in LA. There were no "hold on, I have to take this call" kinds of crises in my job at Uncle Keith's warehouse. I had absolutely zero "hold on, I have to take this call" credibility or excuses.

But my attempts at discretion were starting to look suspicious. I had already taken an inordinate number of bathroom breaks on this date to check messages and feeds. And honestly, there wasn't really much I could do about anything that was happening in Zinnia Sherwood's realm. All I could do was watch it unfold and try to be ready for it to explode into my physical proximity, while hoping it would all just go away.

So when the banner notification of another text message from Styles appeared on my phone, it looked like something it wasn't. I flipped my phone over instinctively (not suspicious at all) but Griffin had already seen the banner.

Griffin's eyebrow twisted with aggressive irritation. "What does he want?"

"Don't know, don't care," I said, stuffing a wad of French fries in my mouth and trying to look nonchalant. I wasn't sure he was buying it.

"Can't seem to get rid of that guy. I finally leave LA, and now suddenly he's everywhere I look."

"Oh yeah? Like how?" I asked, still playing dumb while my stomach twisted itself in knots at the notion that Griffin might have thought that Styles and I were still involved with each other.

"Oh, come on. You know what I mean."

You know that feeling when someone accuses you of something you didn't do? From the outside, the reaction looks a lot like guilt. I was searching for a way to respond that wasn't a version of "it's not what it looks like" when Griffin continued.

"His podcast is going viral. He's doing a thing about that book everyone is talking about. With the anonymous author."

"Ohhh. Right. I did see something about that." I breathed a sigh of relief, sort of.

"On that subject..." he said, reaching into his backpack.

Oh God Oh God Oh God Oh God Oh God Oh God Oh God Oh God

Oh God Oh God Oh God...

Griffin pulled out a copy of *Maladaptive* and handed it to me. I had a watermarked proof copy hidden in my filing cabinet, but had not seen a *real* one in person, let alone held it in my hands. It was in pristine condition, with no spinal crackage or evidence of pages being turned.

"I got this for you a little while ago."

"Have you read it?"

"Nah, not really my thing. But it seemed like something you'd like."

Don't cry don't cry don't cry don't cry don't cry don't cry don't cry don't cry don't cry don't cry...

"Thank you," I managed to squeak out, just barely.

* * *

My workspace in the warehouse office was as uninspiring as any unadorned, fluorescently lit, windowless nine-to-five hellscape, but it did afford me the privacy I needed to stay on top of the Styles situation.

"Diving Deep into Zinnia Sherwood's *Maladaptive*" was the title of his new podcast mini-series, and very quickly, it had become his most popular and acclaimed content since the River Deane interview that had put him on the map. But what had started, seemingly innocently enough, as an exploration of the intersection between anonymous creativity and mainstream success, had started to look like an obsession.

The media praise dimmed, and then turned into concern, and eventually disdain. While this had no negative effect on his engagement or subscription numbers, the roster of expert guests started dropping out, leaving Styles to dig his heels in, continuing his investigation on his own. In his attempt to tidy up what he saw as a loose end, he pulled at the offending thread, unaware that he was unraveling publicly to a growing audience.

* * *

"Welcome back to *Making It*, as we continue our deep dive on Zinnia Sherwood's *Maladaptive.* I'm Styles Chilton. Last time, we explored the concept of the unreliable narrator, and whether the central protagonist of this story falls into that category."

I listened with panicked curiosity. Styles' voice was as engaging as always, tinged with a slightly edged, over-the-top excitement.

"With that in mind, a fascinating aspect of the story is how the author captures the intimacy of creative collaboration. The way the narrator talks about her dynamic with her creative partner doesn't feel imagined, it feels authentically lived. You really get a sense of the mutual respect between them. You have to wonder if the author has drawn him from real life experience.

"We also know that artists have the freedom of creative license. So there is this duality between how much of the story could be informed by real life, and how much of it is edited, twisted or embellished to add drama. Of course, a collaborative relationship without tension would be one-dimensional in a story such as this, so while we expect that whoever inspired this character certainly had his or her flaws, the author has a duty to the reader to inflict damage to create drama and conflict."

As infuriating as it was watching Styles try to cast doubt on the reliability of the storytelling and rewrite the narrative into something he could live with, I couldn't look away.

His audience couldn't either, with active discussions in the comments from amateur detectives who were still trying to crack the case. Styles engaged in these discussions indirectly, often asking questions during his podcast that viewers and listeners would respond to in the comments. Now that he was flying the podcast solo without guests to speak to directly, he was relying a lot more on this tactic for discourse.

"In the last episode, I asked if we could ever really identify the line between reality and fantasy in a story such as this, and some of you had a lot to say about that. I loved the response from JoeBlowBolero who said, quite insightfully, '... the successful blurring of that line is where art and truth live.' Joe, I couldn't agree more. But I know some of you disagree with that. So, my follow-up question is, if *Maladaptive*'s narrator is unreliable because her overactive imagination is a central part of her character and the story, then what exactly is the truth?"

I had to admit the diabolical genius of what Styles was doing. He was subtly trying to nudge the internet sleuths away from the objective of exposing Zinnia Sherwood's identity, the result of which would implicate him as the bad guy in the book and in real life, to establishing that any details that might have been inspired by real events should not be trusted.

Unfortunately for him, his fixation on the character he had privately identified as himself was looking increasingly unhinged, and people were starting to notice.

"I want to talk about the moment when the narrator describes her creative partner blocking access to their project, claiming ownership of it, after their transgression. At first glance, it looks like we're seeing his real character exposed. Villainous, opportunistic, maybe even pre-meditated. But when you look deeper, it's messier than that. The emotional impact goes beyond the protagonist's own perspective. There are things she couldn't know. Like maybe he just couldn't let it go. Not because he wanted control, but because giving it back would mean admitting the partnership was over."

He paused to let it land, then continued.

"I think a lot of us can relate to that. When a common goal or interest between friends becomes a stand-in for something more, losing it can lead to acts of desperation. Outwardly you're cutting ties, but inwardly, maybe you're just... holding on to whatever you can."

In one sense, Styles' tactic had worked, just not in the way he had intended. The internet's response was swift and merciless, turning from *Who is Zinnia Sherwood?* to *Why is Styles Chilton so obsessed with her*? The podcast's comment section lit up with speculation about his motives.

BigBoots2024: *I know this is a deep dive but this seems beyond, even for Styles. What's his stake in this?*

OddiohGoohGooh: *The way Styles talked about that character holding on to the project, he sounds defensive. Does he think the book is about him?*

ThePurpleListicle: *I have always respected his work but something feels off about this, are we all watching Styles Chilton having a break with reality on his podcast?*

* * *

I was inclined to agree with the public sentiment that Styles was losing it. But what made this situation even more unfortunate was that his public breakdown was linked to the most successful content of his career. His "deep dive" was pulling massive numbers, with listeners fascinated by his increasingly over-the-top exploration of a fictional story that he was seemingly trying to decipher like it held the secrets of the universe within it.

But he couldn't ride the wave of that success forever. As the tide turned, the backlash began with critics calling out the tone of his analysis, which had started to drift from piqued curiosity to something with stickier implications. The headlines were brutal.

Styles Chilton's Unhealthy Fixation on Indie Author Mystery Raises Questions About Boundaries – **BlurbBlab Book News**

Literary Analysis Turned Parasocial Obsession: A Podcast Host's Troubling Behavior – ***Mediality Magazine***

The Agony of Limerence: A Public Figure's Pursuit of an Anonymous Author Sheds Light on the Condition – **PsyCulture Weekly**

While internet sleuths' speculation about Zinnia Sherwood's identity was still considered harmless fun, Styles' deepening fixation hit differently. Instead of joining the conversation, he was unwittingly inserting himself into it. His strategy to control how the Zinnia Sherwood mystery unfolded was now working against him.

His podcast sponsors pulled out, claiming "brand safety concerns" and "misalignment with values." The video platform issued a "violation of terms of agreement" warning and demonetized his Zinnia Sherwood deep dive series. The comments sections of his social media filled with people calling him everything from "creepy" and "inappropriate" to "the reason some creators stay anonymous." He was being canceled.

Honestly, it was awful. I felt terrible for him, and it added to the list of reasons I was regretting publishing my book. I might have daydreamed about his suffering and my own vindication at times, but I never wanted any of this. And with his life imploding in public view, I couldn't help but think about what that meant for him at home.

* * *

Willow had poured everything into moving forward. It was a self-preservation thing too, because she wasn't innocent either. But she couldn't ignore this. After learning about the fallout from the Zinnia Sherwood podcast series, she placed her phone face down on the breakfast table and confronted him in an alarmed state.

"What the hell is going on with you?" She didn't want to ask, but she had to.

Styles looked like a pale, disheveled, and far more anxious version of himself, amped and jittery, like he was mainlining pure adrenaline.

He looked up from his coffee and deflected her question. "It's just a podcast series. I've had episodes go viral before."

"It's more than that and you know it. Look at you, you're coming apart," she said, leaning toward him and gesturing

exasperatedly. For some reason, she was nude. Why? I don't know, I just kind of assumed she walked around their house naked all the time. If I looked like her, I would, too.

"Everyone can see it and people are talking," she continued. "Your name is trending for all the wrong reasons. This obsession with Zinnia Sherwood is not cool, or edgy, or even subtle. It's like you're the relentless suitor in a romcom movie. I don't know if you've been paying attention, but that trope is dead in this day and age."

That seemed to hit him hard. His throat tightened. "It's Cara."

Willow stared at him. "What?"

"Zinnia Sherwood is Cara, I'm sure of it. And this book, even if a lot of it is fiction, is really about everything that happened when she was here in LA."

And there it was, the thing they weren't supposed to say out loud. Willow fell back in her chair, as if the force of his revelation physically repelled her and her magnificent tits. "We agreed," she said, her voice cracking with disbelief. "We agreed we weren't going to talk about that. We said we were moving on."

"You asked, and I'm telling you the answer."

Willow's face reddened as she silently fumed, crossing her arms over her chest to hug herself while he continued.

"And if I'm right, then... then it's all out there, in the book. And if anyone figures it out, I'm cooked."

"Seems to me you're already cooked," Willow said, her eyes glassy. "You could've just let it go, but no. You had to fuck around and find out."

"I admit it didn't exactly go like I thought it would, but... I can come back from it, I think."

Willow stood and walked away from the breakfast table, her perfect butt cheeks glowing in the morning sunlight. She turned back around to face him in all her exquisite glory. How on Earth could Styles be obsessed with anyone but her?

"You can come back from it. Great. And what about us?" she asked.

Styles looked surprised. "This is just something I need to deal with. It's not anything to do with us."

Willow shook her head and walked towards him. She put her hands on the table and leaned in close to him, her face inches from his. If you're imagining what her boobs were doing as she held that position, I can't say I blame you. It would have looked like she was going in for a kiss, if she hadn't looked so stern and sad.

"You don't get to torch our whole life because you're scared of the consequences of something you did. I forgave you, Quinn. You said it was over between you two, and I was cool with that. But it's not really over, is it."

As he looked into Willow's glistening eyes, he was about to deflect again. Remind her that she wasn't the only one who had been forgiven. But he knew that if he pulled that thread, the damage would be beyond repair. Instead, he broke his gaze from hers and silently stared down at his coffee mug.

His silence was the answer Willow had suspected. She stood up. "Well, I don't know if we can come back from this," she said, her voice shaking, her anger giving way to grief. "Because maybe 'it's over now' was just another lie we told ourselves. And maybe you're not done telling lies."

There was no door to slam, but Styles felt Willow's exit like a cold blow to his system. The warm morning light had followed her out of the room, leaving him alone in the shadows.

* * *

The sound of an email notification pulled me back to reality to find that I was crying. Not for myself, but for Styles and Willow. After wiping the tears away, I checked my email, but it wasn't work-related.

Cara,

I know you're Zinnia Sherwood. I read your book, and I can see all the places where you blurred the lines between fact and fiction. I recognize every word. I lived it with you. Even the parts on the island. Everyone thinks I'm crazy, but I'd know your voice anywhere.

And I've probably just destroyed my career because I can't let it go. Maybe you've heard. Maybe you're laughing, or crying, or scared.

Well, I'm scared too. I need to talk to you. If this was revenge, then congrats. You won. But I need to know if what happened between us was real, or if it was all just research for your novel.

If you won't reply to me, then I'm coming to you.

Quinn

Chapter 46

"Remember that journaling exercise you gave me?" I asked Paige, immediately regretting the question. She looked up from her notes a little bit surprised that I'd bring up a therapy homework assignment. I wasn't historically great at handing those in.

"Yeah?" she asked, raising her eyebrows.

"Well... I did it."

She perked up. "That's great, Cara. I'm really glad to hear that. How did it go?"

"It... kind of got away from me."

"Got away from you how?"

Why did I bring this up? I thought. But I knew the answer. The secrecy, the stress of the double life I was living, the lies I didn't want to keep telling, and the discomfort of knowing that the book's existence was negatively impacting at least one human being, and possibly others, was becoming more than I could carry. I had to come clean to someone who wouldn't have a conniption.

"I sort of... kept going. Like there was all of this momentum, where it stopped just being a journaling exercise and turned into a story. Like it kind of generated something new, in a way."

Paige tilted her head, imploring me to keep talking. I stared at the corner of the rug while I tried to spit out the words.

"I wrote a book." Saying it out loud felt dirty, like I had just admitted to a felony.

She leaned forward with a surprised smile on her face. "You wrote a book?"

"Yeah. And then I published it." Not just a felony, a fucking crime spree.

The silence that followed was indeterminable. Was it the bad kind? The good kind? Probably the shocked kind. Definitely the "Who are you and what have you done with Cara?" kind. Probably, but you never know.

"I'm sorry, you published a book?"

"Self-published."

"Wow," Paige said, taking off her glasses and polishing the lenses with the hem of her sweater before putting them back on. It made me aware that my own glasses needed a wipe as well, but I didn't want to copy her, so I forced myself to endure the torture for the rest of our session.

"That's a hell of a follow-through on your homework. What made you decide to do that?"

"I don't know," I said, my heart racing. "I didn't think anyone would read it. That wasn't the point. I just needed to get it out of me. Like, after LA, after everything that happened, it wasn't enough to just purge it from my system. I needed it to... be a *thing*."

"That's incredibly brave."

"I used a pen name, though. So, not that brave."

"Plenty of writers use pen names," she said matter-of-factly.

She paused, and I sat there with my heart beating out of my

chest, afraid that my confession was going to unleash some new catastrophe into the world.

"I'm not sure it was the best idea," I admitted. My eyes flicked toward the window as if the FBI's secret Literary Crimes Division would be arriving any second. Paige rested her chin on her fist in a ponderous position, which was my cue to keep going.

"It sort of... blew up," I said. "I mean it *really* blew up. There are people trying to figure out who actually wrote it. It's like a whole internet thing. A meme, even. It's gotten a little intense."

Paige nearly fell off her chin and out of her chair with surprise and a dawning recognition. "Wait, are you saying *Maladaptive* is yours? That you're..."

"I knew you wouldn't believe me."

"I do believe you," she said, shaking her head like she was trying to clear it. "I'm just... a little awestruck. And starstruck."

I laughed. "As if."

"Cara, I'm so proud of you!" she beamed, putting her hand to her chest.

"You don't think it's stupid?" I felt like a baby as soon as I said it, but it also felt pretty good to just drop the mask for a minute and lean into my big feelings.

Paige looked confused. "Why would I think that?"

"I don't know. Using my chronic daydreaming problem as a source of creative inspiration feels like cheating."

"Cara," she said, "where do you think art comes from?"

I froze. The gears were turning in my brain like I was doing complex math. But some days I wasn't even sure I could trust myself to put two and two together.

"But what if everyone finds out it's me? Then they'll know the kinds of things I think about." I stared at my lap, my heart racing again like I was running away from a hungry bear hot on my heels.

Paige didn't miss a beat. "Then they'll know you're an artist."

I can't even tell you how much I wanted to accept what she had just said, to embrace it and hold it up like some kind of award that I could put on my mantle at home. But for reasons I can't explain, an undefined emotion welled up inside me and tears started to fill my eyes. I choked it back, because God forbid my therapist see me cry. Then I simply ignored her praise, deflecting it like Wonder Woman deflecting bullets with her wrist guards.

"No one else knows." But that wasn't exactly true. "I mean, I haven't told anyone else," I corrected myself. "Not even Griffin."

She nudged me with her trademark look that said "Why do you think that is?"

"I'm just so happy he's home, and we're working things out, and I'm so afraid of making another mess."

"Telling me was good practice," she said. "You nailed the dress rehearsal. I think you're ready."

* * *

I wasn't super into video games, but since Griffin had come home, we'd gotten into a habit of playing a co-op game in the evenings. It was a pleasant distraction from doomscrolling the internet and the inside of my own brain. I wasn't very good at it, but Griffin handled the heavy lifting, like completing quests and engaging in combat, while I mostly wandered around collecting shiny objects and accidentally jumping off cliffs.

"Why are you carrying that watermelon?" he asked, curiously, as my tiny character ran in the wrong direction for the quadrillionth time.

"Because it's sparkly and I'm manifesting abundance," I said, as if this were a perfectly logical contribution to our quest.

"You sound like Hannah," he laughed, tossing me a healing potion and taking down two ogres with enviable panache.

"At least one of us does," I snarked back, quick to follow up with an air-smooch. He air-smooched me back, not taking his eyes from the screen. I swooned, slightly. Not just at his ogre-slaying mastery, but at *this*. It felt like we were in sync again, even if he was playing the game semi-seriously, he didn't mind if I was there mostly for the vibes.

And those vibes were exactly why I kept putting off telling him about the book. The lie was dismantling my soul, but I just didn't want to do anything to break the blissful rebuilding of trust that we were working on.

So, when another dreaded email came in, it felt like a devastating crack in a foundation that wasn't yet completely set. I glanced at my phone, sitting face up on the couch next to me.

New Message: *Styles Chilton*

Subject: *I'm here*

My mood immediately went from tranquil to feeling like I was actively being chased by something with sharp teeth and a taste for liars. My video game character dropped her watermelon and got stuck trying to walk through a wall.

He wouldn't just show up here, would he? I grabbed my phone, got up and ran to the front door to peek through the window. Dusky shadows were setting in and I couldn't see much. I opened the front door and stepped outside, looking up and down the street. I couldn't see anyone.

My phone buzzed again to remind me that I hadn't opened Styles' email. My thumb hovered over the message in my inbox with the intent to swipe it straight into the trash can unopened. Instead, against my better judgment, I tapped it.

Cara,

Now that I have your attention, I hope I didn't scare you too badly. Despite the fact that the world now thinks I'm some kind of stalker, I wouldn't just surprise you at your house. But I am hoping that having come 95% of the way, that you'll meet me the other 5%.

I'm staying at the Thundering Falls Motel. Getting a room in a decent hotel away from the tourist district was unexpectedly difficult. There's a sex toy convention this week, apparently occupying all the hotels in the city, did you know that? Guess that's not your world anymore.

Anyway, they couldn't check me in until later this afternoon, and the motel has no bar to hang out in. So, to kill time, I spent the day wandering around. I thought it would be cool to see where you came from, walk some of the same streets you've walked. Clifton Hill is a weird head trip, but the Falls are breathtaking. And humbling. Standing in their presence, you really realize how small and insignificant you are.

I have to say, I was underprepared for how cold it is up here. Literally, but also figuratively. Nobody knows me here. Crowds of people flocking the sights, and yet not a single person recognized me or asked me for a selfie. Honestly, it was kind of refreshing for a change, to be able to walk around in public without worrying about what everyone is saying about me. But also kind of depressing.

Have you ever gone to that wax museum? I went in there to warm up. Wasn't expecting much but they have a "Celebrity Hall of Fame." Guess who I found? None other than our good friend River. I chatted him up, but he wasn't very talkative, kind of just stared right through me. To be fair, he didn't look well.

A lady there did recognize me, though. Well, kind of. She asked me for a selfie, but then it turned out she thought I was somebody else. An actor. I mentioned how I get mistaken for Cillian Murphy a lot, but she seemed confused by that. River saw the whole debacle. When I asked him if he thought I'd officially hit rock bottom, you know what he said? Nothing. Not a word of support. Can you believe that? The nerve of him.

Anyway, I'm back at the motel now. Room 425. I'm here 'til the day after tomorrow. If you can get away, please come by. It's important. And then I promise I won't bother you again. We don't have to hang out here, but you know where to find me.

Quinn

* * *

"Everything okay?" Griffin asked as I came back inside the house.

"Yeah, fine," I said, even though it felt like an object the size of a watermelon was lodged in my throat and I was trying to swallow it whole. I returned to the couch and picked up my video game controller.

"If something is bothering you, you know you can tell me

about it, right?"

"Yeah, I know," I said, which I wanted to be true, but wasn't. Because while I could theoretically tell Griffin about Styles' coming to town, I wasn't sure I was emotionally equipped for the conversation that would follow. But there was a conversation I *had* prepared for.

"I wrote a book."

"I know. *Sixty-Six.* The one you were turning into a web series." Griffin continued playing the game.

"Another book."

Griffin looked at me, a loving grin spreading across his face. "You wrote another book? Cara, that's awesome!"

"It's this one." I pointed to the print copy of *Maladaptive* he had gifted me at the pub the other night, now sitting on the coffee table. He chuckled softly, like I had told him a cute joke. When I didn't laugh along with him, he paused the game.

"Wait, are you serious?" I nodded, reluctantly. A wave of that undefined emotion started to move through me. I was certain he didn't believe me.

"Holy shit." He picked up the book and examined it, the front cover, the back cover, and then flipped through the pages. "Cara, this is... you're so awesome!"

The mixture of surprise and admiration in his voice was so genuine that I felt like I might cry with relief but also something else. Joy? He put the controller down and hugged me. Tears spilled out of my eyes all over his shirt.

"You can't tell anyone," I said quickly, because the last thing my anxiety needed was Griffin accidentally blowing my cover. "I mean it. This has to stay between us. Promise me."

"But why?"

"Because... I'm not ready to deal with people who won't

understand it."

Griffin nodded almost solemnly, in a way that said he understood at least that.

"I'll try but... all I want to do right now is shout from the rooftops that I'm married to the coolest chick in the friggin' world."

"Stop it," I laughed, pretend-slapping his arm. Then he pulled back to look at me, and I could see the exact moment when he fully processed my request.

"I won't tell anyone. This is our secret. Nobody else gets to know unless you decide to tell them."

His promise felt like a magical bubble that enclosed us inside a dimension with only enough room for the two of us and the things we only shared with each other, protected by the feeling of being truly known and celebrated by the person who mattered most.

"Can I read it? What's it about?" he asked, lovingly flipping through the pages.

Chapter 47

Despite the fact that I lived nowhere near the tourist entertainment district and was likely safe from a potential run-in, knowing Styles was afoot and at large in my city, I decided to stay home the next day, just in case. Which meant finding ways to keep myself from going stir crazy.

Griffin had a meeting with the clinic manager to talk about starting work again, meaning I would be on my own and limited to solo activities, adding difficulty to the challenge. The only way I was going to survive my day of Styles avoidance was by treating it like a game.

Even though he said he wouldn't just show up at my house, I wondered if there might be an unsaid "yet" buried underneath that sentiment. Surely, he wouldn't just go home unsatisfied after coming all the way across the continent to get whatever he was seeking? At some point, he was going to realize I wasn't coming, and then what?

Whatever. I don't have to answer the door, I decided. It would be one of the rules of the game.

I'll be honest though. There was absolutely a part of me that wanted to see Styles. Of course I did. But something in me needed to prove that I could wrestle that impulse down to the ground and force it into submission. Letting myself daydream all day would certainly have satisfied that impulse to some degree, but I couldn't let myself get sucked in and lose the whole day to it. But I could build a daydream-based dopamine reward system into my game. I might be easily distracted, but I can win if you let me do it my way.

So, without further ado, behold! My structured strategy for surviving a self-imposed sequestration. Welcome to...

Distraction in Action: Impulse Domination Edition

LEVEL 1: The Cleansening

Objective: Pick one room to clean and organize like HGTV is on their way over to arrest me for domestic housekeeping atrocities.

The kitchen was always my biggest weakness. The surfaces might have looked clean and shiny, but they were only a veneer to the horrors that lurked inside the drawers and cupboards.

Cupboards where somehow the one thing I needed was always in the back, requiring the removal of everything else to find it. Something sticky on the bottom shelf that I totally intended to clean but forgot about every time I closed the door.

A fridge door full of nearly empty condiment bottles that still had that one unattainable glop of whatever still in them. A massive, nearly-full container of kimchi from eight years ago. That jar of gherkin pickles that no one had ever bought but was somehow there anyway.

Shelves of random dishes that had been relegated to the

upper levels in case they were needed someday.

The utensil drawer with the organizer that had too many utensils in it including that one fork that liked to stick up and stop the drawer from opening.

I made them all my bitch. By the time I was done, I felt like one of those grinning women in a commercial for a drug that you should absolutely ask your doctor about. Find out if Getting Off Your Ass and Getting Rid of the Random Jar of Gherkins is right for you.

Points: 500 awarded for effort and amount of time spent productively.

Reward: One daydream snippet with a timer set to 15 minutes.

* * *

It was cold out with a bitter wind blowing right through my jacket to my bones. I ran from my car to the motel lobby with my hood up, trying to block the wind, but also to avoid being seen, because for all I knew, this meetup was an elaborate staged coup with reporters and paparazzi, designed to reveal Zinnia Sherwood's true identity and give Styles the last word.

Thundering Falls Motel, Room 425.

Inhale, exhale. I knocked on the door with a plan firmly in place in my mind. I'd go in, leave my coat on, keep my distance, and remain standing. Give him the floor to tell me whatever he wanted to tell me, let him ask his questions, answer them honestly, then GTFO. No drama, just clear the air, and get out, and let that be the end of it.

Styles opened the door, looking literally the best I've ever seen him. Like the poster boy for pure sex and adrenaline and raging desire. He must have thought the same about me because we didn't even say a word. We just tore each other's clothes off on our way over to the bed like they do in movies you try to avoid watching with your parents.

And the positions. My God. I wasn't even sure some of them were physically possible with Earth's current gravity levels, but the laws of physics must have suspended themselves for us whilst in the throes of passion. I didn't know my body could do... that. Or that. Or that.

After having achieved Olympic levels of pornographic performance with full points awarded for noises and bodily fluids, we fell asleep in each other's arms.

When I awoke an undetermined amount of time later, a sudden snowstorm had rendered the world outside invisible with weather advisories warning against unnecessary travel. A text message from Griffin told me it was better if I just stayed at Hannah's, where I had told him I was going, and to go home in the morning.

Oh my God, what the hell was wrong with me.

* * *

My time was up. The next challenge awaited.

LEVEL 2: The Cattening

Objective: Actively play with the cats using any of the seven million toys scattered around the house.

Could I get two bored, lazy cats who barely tweaked an ear at the sound of a bird outside to actually play for a full twenty minutes without dying of boredom myself waiting for them to engage?

The answer is no, but not for lack of trying. I wiggled the hell out of the feather on a stick. I ran back and forth across the living room repeatedly, dragging the long ribbon with a knot in the end of it. I rolled balls and threw plushies and booped their little kitty nosies with catnip mousies.

The result: Daisy blinked at me with silent cattitude that spoke volumes about her agency as an adorable domesticated killing machine. Clover gave me a half-hearted swat and then flopped dramatically onto his side like a Victorian child fainting from ennui, and began licking his paw.

Hey, at least I burned some calories.

Points: 100 awarded for effort and not taking their rejection personally.

Reward: One daydream snippet with a timer set to 5 minutes.

* * *

Thundering Falls Motel, Room 425.

Inhale, exhale. I knocked. Styles opened the door, looking like an egotistical, narcissistic douchebag art thief holding a glass of wine.

He might have been about to offer me a glass, but I wouldn't know, because before he could say anything, I grabbed that glass of wine and threw it in his stupid, egotistical, narcissistic douchebag art thief face.

"That's for Sixty-Six," I said, relishing the way the wine soaked his too-perfect hair and stained his designer clothes, and then I

whirled around and walked out.

As I exited the lobby, the motel exploded in spectacular fashion behind me like a Robert Rodriguez film while I walked away in slow motion, glowering intensely, my hair blowing dramatically in the breeze, and a rogue droplet of red wine running down my forehead.

* * *

Ding ding ding! Back to the game.

LEVEL 3: The Snackening

Objective: Build an award-winning snack plate that not only meets all the criteria for girl dinner, but transcends it.

After burning a fuck-ton of calories whipping my kitchen into shape and putting on a clown show for my cats, this next challenge was practically a reward in itself.

The snack: A well-balanced assortment consisting of one meatball, four baby carrots, a hunk of leftover brie, a handful of popcorn, eight grapes, and three dark chocolate almonds.

Was it pretty? Sort of, in an expressionist art kind of way. But something was missing. Gherkins. Gherkins would have tied the whole plate together.

Digging in, I felt like one of those stock photo ladies laughing alone with their salad, which is to say, they're only laughing on the outside, because on the inside, they're sobbing about the lack of French fries.

Points: 200 awarded for technical execution, 100 for overall enjoyment, but 100 removed for the lack of foresight that led to me throwing out the gherkins in Level 1.

Reward: One daydream snippet with a timer set to 10 minutes.

* * *

Thundering Falls Motel, Room 425.

Inhale, exhale. I knocked. Styles opened the door, looking like the saddest puppy dog I'd ever seen in my life. He backed away from me slowly with his proverbial tail between his legs as I entered the room, which smelled like... I don't know, if shame had a smell, that would be it. But it permeated through my whole being, like it was pulling my own shame out of me and into the room where we could both just sit there and wallow in it.

He didn't hug me, or even say hello. We just sat at the edge of the bed in heavy, soul-wracking silence for what felt like an eternity. It was like our silence was doing the talking for us. After a while, the weird shame smell went away and was replaced with something fresher and sweeter. Oddly, it smelled like cucumber. I don't know where that came from, but the mood lifted, and suddenly we were both free of the heaviness we shared when I arrived.

* * *

And.... time. On with the next challenge...

LEVEL 4: The Artening

Objective: Revive one abandoned hobby for a sustained period of time. If it doesn't stick, try another one. I had plenty to choose from.

I'd been thinking about this one for a while. The wax letter sealing kit that I actually bought myself strictly for the tactile enjoyment of smashing melted wax with a stamp. I used it once to write Hannah one letter with the calligraphy set I also bought for the same purpose, wax sealed it and put it in the mail, only for it to get lost. She never got to break that seal, and it kind of put me off the whole thing.

But the feeling of smashing that wax... I'd thought about it a lot after that. I mean, like, a lot. Almost daily. It was time to get satisfaction.

I dug out both kits, and wrote myself a series of lists (grocery, to-do, a list of words I like) in fancy calligraphy on heavy stationery paper, folded them, and then I wax-sealed the fuck out of those lists, reveling in the glorious sensation of the wax smash.

And then, when I was done and the seals were cool and hard, I cracked those babies open. I don't smoke, but I almost went out to buy a pack because fuck yeah, that felt good.

Points: 500 awarded for using up two whole hobby kits and slaying the experience. A delayed, but solid return on investment. 400 points removed for getting wax on my favorite jeans.

Reward: One daydream snippet with a timer set to 5 minutes.

* * *

Thundering Falls Motel, Room 425.

Inhale, exhale. I knocked. Styles opened the door, looking like he had never been happier in his life to see me, grinning like an ecstatic fool, like the fact that I had shown up at his request had made his entire year.

That smile very nearly disarmed me, but there was something about it that wasn't quite right. It kind of freaked me out. And suddenly, it was all I could do to not slap that stupid, gorgeous, freaky dimpled grin off his face, but before I could grab the glass of wine in his hand and throw it at him, he threw it at me.

"That's for your fucking novel, Zinnia," he jeered, before closing the door and leaving me bleeding a light and fruity merlot on the other side of it.

Touché.

* * *

Time. The next level of the game awaited.

LEVEL 5: The Workening

Objective: Open and reply to unanswered messages without checking in on my fake, meaningless, addictive internet life.

I mean, I couldn't read and reply to *all* of them, that would take forever. But there were two in particular on my mind.

The first bit of business was to read River's messages. I'd been avoiding him mainly out of shame for how I left things with him. I couldn't possibly imagine what he would want from me. There were too many to start from the beginning, so I started with his most recent message from two weeks ago.

Cara,

The Riptide EP is set to drop the 30th of this month. Ace Road Records is putting it out. I assume that since you didn't get back to me about the track listing, the cover art, how you want to be credited, or any promotional involvement, that you're waiving your input on those decisions.

I'll have the record company send your royalties to the address I have for you, unless you want to set up something else. If you don't want to talk to me, you can get in touch with them directly.

Unless I hear otherwise, I'll assume you're not contesting the release. I hope you'll understand that I couldn't just let these songs get lost in my vault. They need to come out, so even though they're half finished and a bit rough, I'm putting them out there. Maybe one day I'll revisit them for a fully realized album. Maybe when that day comes, you'll join me. But until then, let this EP serve as proof that you can catch lightning in a bottle.

With gratitude,

River

To say that I was in shock and a little freaked out was an understatement. I checked the date. It was the 30th. Too late to give River the answers he was seeking from me. Possibly too late to explain my silence in a way that he would understand or care. But it wasn't too late to reply, and tell him with the few words that I could muster, how grateful I was to be a part of it.

With my reply to River sent, I decided that I didn't ever want to be too late again. There was one more task I needed to complete for this challenge.

I had put off responding to Mona Willinger from the streaming platform. At this point, I figured she had probably lost interest or forgotten about her message to me about adapting my book into a series. Still, I needed to get into the habit of replying to people, even if I was late, and even if it was only to say thanks for their interest and decline their offer. After the green light for *Sixty-Six* turned red, I wasn't sure I could endure another carpet pull of that nature.

When I opened my laptop, I was still waffling, but leaning heavily toward declining. Then, for reasons I still don't understand, I typed, "Thank you for reaching out. Apologies for my late reply. If you're still interested in adapting my book, would you mind setting up a meeting with me to talk through what you envision and what the next steps would be? I'd like to find out more." I hit send, and closed my laptop.

Task completed with successful avoidance of creeping on my analytics, social media feeds, book reviews, and Zinnia Sherwood memes.

Points: 1000 awarded for doing the things while successfully avoiding doing the other things. 500 of those points in suspension for *what the fuck did I just do, Mona Willinger?*

Reward: One daydream snippet with a timer set to 30 minutes.

* * *

Thundering Falls Motel, Room 425.

Inhale, exhale. I knocked. Styles opened the door, looking like himself. Tired, and little worn down around the edges, but still him. The same charismatic disposition, the same bright, curious eyes scanning me for a sign. Of what, I'm not sure. Forgiveness? Closure? Or maybe he was still hoping for a chance to rewrite the ending.

I stepped inside. The room was beige to the point of being annoying. The bed was unmade behind him, and the desk was littered with empty takeout coffee cups.

He gestured to a chair. I took it, keeping my coat on. I was not going to be staying long.

"Congratulations on the book," he said, sounding more restrained than I remembered him being. "I knew it was you from page one."

"Thanks." My throat tightened around the word like it didn't quite want to let it out. I sat on my hands to stop from jittering.

And then he laughed, warmly. "I'm really impressed with how you told your story. If I were interviewing you right now, I'd want to know everything about your daydream world. The mechanics of it, the recurring themes, the emotional arcs..." He was trying to keep it light, but something in his eyes betrayed him.

"Well," I said, "you're not interviewing me... are you?" I looked around, half joking, half paranoid, scanning the room for recording gear, in case my initial suspicion had been right.

"No," he admitted with a chuckle, leaning back in his chair. "But I did want to ask you something. I just want to know... did you write this book to get back at me? Or was this always your plan? Like... was I just an unwitting part of some bigger scheme to write about the whole 'trying to make it in LA' experience?"

That hit me weird. While I'd been wondering if he had used me, I hadn't considered that he might be wondering if I had used him.

"None of this was planned, and I wasn't trying to get revenge. I never meant for it to get so much attention. The pen name was supposed to be a shield, not a sword. I'm sorry it caused

you so much anguish. For the record, I don't think you deserved to be dragged like that." *I took a breath.* *"I left LA feeling so... unfinished. All I wanted to do was to finish something and put it out into the world."*

He nodded slowly.

"What about you?" *I turned the question back to him. Why should he get all his answers? What about the answers I needed? "Were you just looking for someone to exploit?"*

"No no no no no," he insisted, his eyes wide with alarm. "You just... inspired me."

"So, you didn't mean to hurt me, and I didn't mean to hurt you. I guess that means we're even." He looked right into my eyes, but didn't say a word in response. I got up and went toward the door, with a lump in my throat, wondering if this would be the last time I'd ever see him.

He didn't run after me, but just as I was about to open the door, his voice held me in place like a tractor beam. "I think I loved you."

I didn't turn around. "I think I loved you, too," I said. And that was it. There was nothing more to say. There was no hug, no kiss, and no goodbye. He just let me go.

* * *

Ding, ding, ding! With that out of the way, I had unlocked the final challenge in my game.

Chapter 48

THE FINAL CHALLENGE

LEVEL 6: The Romancining

Objective: Plan a sexy at-home date night as the ultimate prize for successfully beating all the previous levels.

I approached this with a "What would Griffin like?" mindset, which led to me moving all the living room furniture to one side of the room and setting up the big inflatable mattress on the floor in front of the TV.

I dug out an old DVD porno movie and queued it up to play on the big screen. I found a *Lovemaking Grooves* playlist online and checked to make sure it didn't contain any River Deane songs on it.

And the final touch... an arrangement of all of the personal pleasure devices I had written instructions for over the years, to use, or not, whatever, while engaged in full body exploration like we used to do when our bodies were new to each other.

Reward: Mutual orgasms.

Caveat: I needed Griffin to be horny when he got home.

* * *

Griffin texted me that he was on his way home. I was a little behind in getting myself ready, and I was getting flustered, trying to find something in my drawer resembling lingerie, and failing. Determined to sexify myself in some way, I broke into the Halloween costume box to see if maybe I had that old sexy nurse costume kicking around from the days when we used to actually go to Halloween parties, but all I found were random residual costume scraps.

The goal of sexifying myself was starting to feel like a lost cause, and the mess I had made of the bedroom trying to achieve it was rattling me. That was when Griffin texted me again, from the car.

"Turn on the radio."

"Are you texting and driving?" I texted him back.

"Red light. Just do it."

There was really only one station that we ever listened to. I switched off the *Lovemaking Grooves* playlist, and turned on the radio to that station, as instructed. I don't know if I can adequately describe the surreal feeling of hearing my own voice coming from the speaker, blended with River Deane's, on a song we had written together. He hadn't changed anything about it. It sounded exactly the way it did the last time I'd heard it. It felt like a trillion years ago.

When the song ended, I listened as the DJ wrapped it up.

"That was the new single, *Riptide,* from River Deane's new studio EP, featuring unknown vocalist Cara Becker, who shares songwriting credit on the album. It's a surprise departure from his established country sound, and it's ripping up the charts as a crossover hit. Word is, the album never got finished as planned, but River released it anyway, saying he wanted the songs to speak for themselves. With a psychedelic melody that slips into discord, haunting harmony vocals, and a rhythm that stumbles in and out of time, what *Riptide* says to me is that this is the shake-up that the music scene has been waiting for."

The sound of the front door opening and Griffin calling my name yanked me out of my stunned state.

"Cara?" he called up the stairs.

My outfit wasn't exactly sexy-time-ready, but I was out of time and a little dazed. I started down the stairs as carefully as possible in my three-inch heels that I never wore because I was afraid I'd break my ankle. When Griffin saw me, he practically doubled over laughing that whole body laugh that I love so much.

"Why are you wearing a bikini and fishnets with a clown wig? And are those... vampire teeth?"

The teeth fell out as I opened my mouth to speak. "Admit it, this is what you've always wanted."

"Well... you're not wrong."

I met him at the bottom of the stairs, standing one step up from the main floor to line my face up with his.

"Did you hear it?" he asked. The radio was still on, so I was pretty sure he already knew the answer.

"I can barely believe it," I admitted.

"You sounded like an angel. What are you going to tell people?"

"That Cara Becker is a pretty common name?" I laughed, but I was dead serious. "What's that?" I asked, noticing that

Griffin had something in his hand.

"Someone left you a package." He held up a manila envelope with my first name written on it in block letters, and a small box. "They were sitting on the front step in front of the door."

"What the..." I said, taking the items from him. I opened the box first. Inside it was the snow globe that Styles had given me when we started working together, with the Hollywood hills inside. I'd deliberately left it behind in the LA rental house, and evidently so had Griffin.

"He was here?!" Griffin exclaimed incredulously, almost furiously, spinning around to open the front door in case Styles might still be lurking.

"I don't see anyone," he said turning back around and closing the door behind him, a look of relief on his flushed face.

Big black sinister butterflies fluttered in my stomach as I opened the envelope, terrified that it might contain some new life-shattering information. Inside was a folder containing my original *Sixty-Six* manuscript and the remnants of my original work for the web series that I hadn't been able to retrieve. Character notes, plot outlines, script drafts, all the creative work I'd unwittingly signed away to Styles. And the contract I'd signed, torn into a few ragged pieces.

On top of the folder was a letter written on Thundering Falls Motel stationery.

Cara,

I'm returning your work. It was always yours anyway. I should have given this back to you instead of keeping it like some kind of pathetic souvenir of what might have been.

I went by your LA house. Don't ask me why. It's still empty, but I found your snow globe. I get why you left it, but I hope you'll let me give it to you again, if not to inspire your continued creativity, then as a symbol to remind you that you made it. All on your own.

I hope your book brings you everything you've ever dreamed of. You earned it.

Quinn

It probably looked to Griffin like I was re-reading the short letter over and over again, but I was stuck in a looping fast-forward flashback of everything that had happened since we first went to LA. It kept playing on repeat in my mind like a spoiler-filled movie trailer.

"You okay?" Griffin asked.

"Yeah," I said, my eyes watering as I hugged the envelope against my chest. "Actually, I'm really okay."

I handed him the snow globe. "Where should we put this?"

He looked at it skeptically, then shook it and watched the fake snow swirl around the tiny Hollywood sign. "The trash?" he asked, but he was smiling, so I was pretty sure he was joking.

"Let's keep it," I said. "It's part of our story."

Griffin walked carefully through the love nest I had set up in the living room over to the fireplace and set the snow globe on the mantle, where it sort of disappeared among the clutter of the other trinkets that piled up there before it.

"Now, let's dry those eyes, you sexy sad clown."

* * *

If you've never engaged in sexy-time shenanigans with your

favorite person while wearing a clown wig on a blow-up mattress in your living room with an array of sex toys and lubes while watching porn, I have to say, I highly recommend it. 10/10, would absolutely do it again. But a little piece of advice. If you have cats, lock them up first. I mean, that's just good sexy-time advice in general. Those little shits want to be involved in everything.

Which is why I suppose it was my own fault when the countdown to O-town was rudely interrupted by the sound of a heavy, breakable object hitting the floor next to the inflatable mattress where Griffin and I were getting our lovemaking grooves on.

Clover, looking innocent as hell, perched on the fireplace mantle where the snow globe should have been, licking his paws contentedly like he had just beat his own final boss. The snow globe didn't shatter, but it cracked a little. The glittering snow swirled around inside, threatening to burst through the hairline fracture in the glass.

"Clover, you little shit," I said from my cowgirl position on Griffin's hips without breaking my riding rhythm, the wig askew on my head with my regular-colored hair sticking out from under it.

"Forget it," Griffin said, his breath accelerating. "I'm almost there."

Then suddenly, the floor rippled beneath us. Just the subtlest wobble, like the kind you feel when you think of someone you've got it bad for and your knees turn to jelly and give out just a little bit.

"Whoa..." I blurted, surprised.

"That felt like..." Griffin stopped short of saying the word, because *as fucking if.*

"Here?"

That was when the radio DJ announced a breaking news alert. A freak blizzard had hit the Los Angeles metropolitan area. Something about a polar vortex.

"Don't stop," said Griffin, orgasmic bliss breaking across his gorgeous, freckled face.

"Weird," I squeaked, reaching my climax while glittery water leaked onto the floor from the snow globe's broken dome.

About the Author

Zinnia Sherwood writes stories for the daydreamers who like their sugar with a lashing of strong coffee, have a penchant for relatable messy humans, and harbor a compulsion for watching a wish fulfilled go tantalizingly, catastrophically wrong... with a sprinkle of magical realism and a happy(ish) ending (phew)! ***Maladaptive*** is her debut novel.

What did you think?
Zinnia would be grateful if you'd take a moment to leave a review.

www.ingramcontent.com/pod-product-compliance
Lightning Source LLC
LaVergne TN
LVHW050915080826
845145LV00001B/99

* 9 7 8 0 9 9 4 0 4 0 7 2 5 *